MICHELLE VERNAL LOVES a happy ending. She lives with her husband and their two boys in the beautiful and resilient city of Christchurch, New Zealand. She's partial to a glass of wine, loves a cheese scone, and has recently taken up yoga—a sight to behold indeed. As well as Staying at Eleni's, Michelle's written seven novels and a series, The Guesthouse on the Green — the books are all written with humour and warmth and she hopes you enjoy reading them. If you enjoy Staying at Eleni's then taking the time to say so by leaving a review would be wonderful. A book review is the best present you can give an author. If you'd like to hear about Michelle's new releases, you can subscribe to her Newsletter here:

http://tiny.cc/0r27az

To say thank you, you'll receive an exclusive O'Mara women character profile to introduce you to the Guesthouse on the Green series.

https://www.michellevernalbooks.com/

https://www.facebook.com/michellevernalnovelist/

https://www.bookbub.com/authors/michelle-vernal

Staying at Eleni's

By

Michelle Vernal

Staying at Eleni's formerly known as Being Shirley is a work of fiction. The characters and events portrayed in this book are fictitious with the exception of the artist Yanni and the movie Shirley Valentine and the author acknowledges their copyrighted and trademarked status.

Staying at Eleni's

By: Michelle Vernal

PROLOGUE

TO: KASSIA BIKAKIS

From: Annie Rivers

Subject: Hello!

Hi, Kas

Sorry I have been so slack in replying to your last email. I know you always worry when you don't hear from me since the earthquakes but there have been no big aftershocks for a while—touch wood. I don't have any decent excuses for not writing sooner either, only that it is coming up to that time of the year again and well, you know what I get like. It's hard to believe it's been twenty years. Twenty whole years! Gone just like that. It feels like yesterday sometimes and then other times it seems like a lifetime ago. You know, when I look around me these days, I realise that Roz wouldn't even recognise Christchurch anymore. I think it's true that saying, time really doesn't stand still for anyone.

Speaking of which, I can't believe you are going to be a big proper grown-up of thirty-nine on Saturday either. I hope you get thoroughly spoiled by your lovely boys. Thanks by the way for letting me know your parcel arrived okay—hope you like it.

Carl and I will do our usual to mark the day. The plan is to meet up at the Botanic Gardens like always and then we'll head back to his place to open the bottle(s) of bubbles and watch the concert. It goes without saying that we'll raise a happy birthday glass to you too.

Mum says to tell you hi. She always asks what you're all up to and likes to be kept in the know. To be honest with you, Kas, she has been driving me nuts since she joined Weight Watchers last month. Do you know the phrase born-again Christian? I suppose not what with you all being Greek Orthodox but it means that someone is really zealous—sorry, I forget English is your second language. Um, how about enthusiastic or in Mum's case fanatical—about something?

Does that make sense? She's not only a reformed smoker she is now a born-again dieter too.

Last Saturday, I popped round with a couple of chocolate éclairs, Dad's favourites. I picked them up from the local bakery and they had fresh whipped cream oozing out the sides. Just yummy but then Mum totally spoiled the moment by telling us how many calories were in each one. She waited until I had a big gob full of choux pastry, chocolate icing, and cream to pass comment too! I'm putting money on it that this wannabe slim Jim phase of hers won't last, though, because they've been looking at cruise brochures again but this time I think they'll actually pack their bags and go. Come August they could be sailing around the Pacific Islands for a week.

Dad's sold a couple of houses in the last month with insurances being paid out finally and people resettling after the earthquakes, so they are in the money. There's no way anyone, not even my mother, could diet on a cruise. It would be an impossibility with all that food laid out just ready and waiting for you to eat all day every day. I heard the average weight gain on a seven-day jaunt round the Pacific is 3.5kg, so there is hope I will get my cuddly, caramel slice-loving mummy back. Fingers crossed, Kas! I'm pleased they are going to get away for a bit, though. It will do them both good to feel a bit of sunshine on their faces and to forget about insurance wrangling for a while. It seems like they have been going head to head over their payout forever. I mean, if the land under your house was dodgy, would you want to stay?

Oh, now here's a complete change of subject but while I think of it, I saw my dream dress on the way into work yesterday. It was on display in the window of Modern Bride—which should actually be called Take out a Mortgage Bride—but oh, Kas, it is so utterly and completely fabulous. Um... so how can I describe it? Well, it's ivory. Remember I had my colours done and was told with my red hair and green eyes I was a Warm Spring and as such should never go for white, always ivory? The style is fitted because I'd look like a well-risen Pavlova in a full skirt so there's another box ticked. The neckline is a sweetheart shape and it's very low cut but hey if you've got it, flaunt it! Sadly, though, big boobs I may have—big bank account I don't.

I really want to try it on, which I know seems stupid considering Tony and I have progressed no further with setting an actual date for the wedding than we had this time last year but hey, maybe the time has come for me to take the proverbial bull by the horns or boy by the balls so to speak and move things along.

You know, though, I sometimes think that the more people go on at us about tying the knot, the more we both dig our heels in and shy away from actually doing anything about it. So anyway, I'm thinking that seeing the dress was a bit of an omen and that it's time for us to progress things because we are in kind of a rut. He has his indoor cricket, rugby, and boys' nights and I have my book club, Pilates, and girls' lunches—oh and I've got Carl of course, too. The thing is Tony and I don't seem to do much together other than blob out in front of the tele these days. Me thinks the time has come in our relationship where we need to find a hobby we can both share—one that doesn't involve bats of any kind. Did I ever tell you that story about the time we entered the doubles table tennis comp at our local pub? I must have but if not, the crux of that story is that Tony's so bloody competitive I nearly thwacked him over the head with my bat. Anyway, enough about that.

Not much has changed on the work front either. I still think it was completely selfish of Mel to go and have a baby, clock ticking or no clock ticking. How could she leave me with Attila the Hun? I know Mama almost drives you demented sometimes but I am telling you your mother-in-law can't hold a candle to what I have to deal with on a daily basis. Think pit bull with PMT and you're halfway there. Still it's up to me to get off my backside and do something about it, I suppose. The problem is I'd need a bit of oomph for that and I don't seem to be able to conjure much of that up where work is concerned at the moment.

Enough about me and life in Christchurch—what about you? How is life in gorgeous Crete? Has your perm settled down? Crazy, isn't it? You spending all that money getting your hair curled and here's me with a headful of the things I'd love to get rid of! Swap you. It sounds like you are run off your feet managing Eleni's, which is a good thing, I guess. Yes, you are in for an interesting time when Alexandros gets home but don't you go letting that brother-in-law of yours get away with too much. The guesthouse is his livelihood, too, and now that you have it humming along nicely, he needs to pull his weight this time round and not treat it like his personal dating agency. You tell him from me that I said he is to leave the English girls alone! Maybe you should suggest Mama finds him a nice Greek girl and that way she will be too busy matchmaking to continue spoiling Mateo and Nikolos rotten. To be fair, though, Kas, I do think it is every yaya's prerogative to spoil their grandchildren.

I hope your lovely Spiros is knocking that bestseller out and that Nikolos's tooth comes through soon so you can all get some sleep. Don't go worrying about Mateo, either; he is only three and from what my friends who have boys say, it is perfectly normal for him to be fascinated with his winky. It doesn't mean he will grow up to be a flasher.

Be sure to give my love to Mama, and Kas, please tell her she has to stop sending me the baklava. It's not just because I definitely don't need fattening up—Customs keeps intercepting it. Tell her she is singlehandedly keeping those sniffer dogs in full-time work.

Right, my friend, it's nearly eleven pm and I have to get to bed now or I will never cope with Attila at work tomorrow. It is time for me to love you and leave you and to say night-night. Hear from you soon and have the best ever birthday!

Lots of love and kisses to you and all the Bikakis family.

Annie

xox

Kassia Bikakis was replying to reservation requests on the computer in the office that also served as a reception room at Eleni's Hotel when the message from her New Zealand friend bounced in. She stopped what she was doing, scrolled through, and read it eagerly. She leaned back in her chair after she had finished. She frowned as one particularly confusing phrase in the many her friend peppered her emails with jumped out at her. What on earth did a well-risen Pavlova look like? she wondered as she clicked on Reply.

PART ONE

Chapter One

"YOU KNOW, ROZ WASN'T just a druggie—she was my sister, too, and a pretty darn good one before she got into all that crap." Annie Rivers pursed her lips indignantly as she tucked the red curls, making a bid for freedom from her topknot, behind her ears. "I really hate the way that when anybody mentions her name, the word *drugs* is always whispered in the same sentence." She kicked at the autumn leaves that swirled around her feet with the toe of her boots, and admired the shininess of the new red leather. It had been a magnetic force on a par with the Bermuda Triangle called Nicole who had dragged her into the shop after she'd spied them in its window at the mall last night.

So much for just popping out to do the groceries. It was all Nic's fault, she decided deftly as she shifted the blame for her purchase onto her friend. She had been minding her own business, nose pressed to the window of the shoe shop, when Nicole had happened upon her. All the girls in their circle knew she was a bad influence when it came to spending, drinking, and well, pretty much everything, which was also why she was loads of fun. True to form, it hadn't taken her long to prise Annie's nose off the window, herd her inside the shop, and persuade her to try the boots on.

She should have been on a sales commission, her talents were wasted as a receptionist, Annie decided as she thought back to how she had held the correct size out to her like it was Cinderella's glass slipper before she helped her slide her tootsies inside them. So it was, that after a quick trot round the shop, she had been convinced that she would never survive the approaching winter without this pair of magic boots to see her through it. Just like that and without further ado, she had been parted from her credit card. She'd linked arms with Nicole and swung the carry bag joyously as she left the shop; she had gone on to shout her friend a couple of drinks at the bar across the road. It had been gone eight o'clock before she finally got round to doing what she had come to the mall to do in the first place. There was nothing like a wine or two under one's belt to make for a quick grocery shop and she had come home having not picked up half of what had been on her list and a new pair of boots to... uh, boot.

Tony complained at how long she had been and had rifled through the bags in search of his deodorant. He'd wanted a quick spray before he headed out the door to indoor cricket and had gone mad when he had instead fished out the incriminating Visa receipt. He couldn't see the allure of the boots' lovely leather redness and he didn't believe in magic. Okay, yes, Annie conceded now with a wiggle of her toes, they had cost a bomb but they were so worth it—Roz would have loved them, too. A frown settled on her forehead at the thought of Roz and she turned towards the eternally youthful yet soon to be officially middle-aged man seated next to her. "You and I both know that there was so much more to her than just her addiction but nobody ever remembers any of the good stuff. It's like when a prostitute is murdered and the media latches on to her occupation. That's what people wind up remembering her as—a prostitute who got murdered. Not a person who was someone's sister or daughter or mother, but for what they did. I really hate that."

Carl nodded his agreement as he ran his fingers through artfully dishevelled locks. Annie looked on enviously. What she wouldn't give for hair like that, so fine, so silky, so sandy-coloured instead of her own mad, red curls that absolutely refused to do what she told them to do. Across the river, the remaining leaves on the trees that overhung the icy, shallow waters had turned the same burnt rust as her hair. A dressing gown, slipper-clad patient from the hospital behind her sat there and puffed furiously on a ciggy. She had an entourage of what Annie's nana would have called ne'er-do-wells gathered round the park bench she sat on. Behind the group was the Riverside entry of Christchurch Public Hospital.

Annie looked up at the cloudless blue sky. A glorious day like today must be therapeutic, even if the cigarettes weren't. Who was she to judge, though? There were far worse addictions to have, as she had found out thanks to Roz. For all she knew, smoking might be the only pleasure left in the poor woman's life. She pulled her eyes away and focused on Carl instead. She didn't want to dwell on other peoples' tragedies, not today. "I used to idolise her, you know? All I wanted to be when I grew up was her. I wanted my freckles to bugger off and I wanted a straight nose instead of an upturned pug nose and a perfect rosebud mouth like hers. But most of all I wanted her hair." Annie sighed. "Remember her glorious, straight, strawberry blonde hair that flicked over her shoulders and just stayed there?" She gave her own hair a disparaging pat. "Instead, I got Great-Grandmother Maggie's ginger mop." She raised her eyes heavenward as though the long since passed Maggie could hear her. "Thanks a lot, Mags."

"Annie Rivers, you do not have a pug nose! Your nose is cute. Women shell out good money for perky noses like yours. Haven't you ever seen *Bewitched*? As for your hair, well, it's high time you changed the tune, sweetheart." He gave one of her escaped curls a tug. "Those gorgeous red curls are what make you, you. They set you apart from the madding crowd."

Annie pulled a face.

"Okay, I get that being called the Ginger Minger might have had a detrimental effect on your self-esteem but put it into perspective because you haven't been at school for quite some time now. Time to move on, sweetheart."

"Roz punched a boy who was teasing me once. She took him by surprise and he landed flat on his backside in front of all his mates who thought it was hilarious. It was great having an older sister." Annie smiled at the long-ago memory. "He never did it again. In fact, he'd turn and walk in the opposite direction when he saw me coming."

"I remember." Carl placed his hand gently on Annie's arm. "She used to stand up for me, too. The skinny, awkward boy with the plummy English accent who didn't fit in no matter how hard he tried. She might have been your big sister but she was my best friend." His blue eyes misted over. "I had my first slow dance with her, you know."

Annie did know but she let him continue uninterrupted because their meeting at Roz's favourite hangout, the Botanic Gardens, and the conversations that played out each year, were all part of this, their annual ritual on Roz's birthday.

"It was our 1984 high school disco. We're talking way before your time, sweetie." He waved his hand to emphasise his point. "*Careless Whisper* by George Michael was playing. Had Georgie Boy come out by then?"

Annie shrugged.

Carl frowned, or at least he would have if the Botox in his forehead had allowed him to do so. "No, I don't think he had because from what I remember, Roz still really fancied him. Anyway, I'm getting off track but that song still brings a tear to my eye, especially when it gets to the bit with the sax."

Annie smiled at his heartfelt sigh as he hummed a few bars of the song. Then he remembered she sat next to him waiting to hear the rest of a story she knew inside and out anyway, so he carried on in plummy tones long since muted by his years in the land of fush and chups.

"She looked so gorgeous in her off-the-shoulder T-shirt and stonewashed jeans that came all the way up to here." He made a cutting motion just under his chest to demonstrate how high in the waist her jeans had been.

Annie grimaced. The eighties had a lot to answer for. And he wasn't finished yet.

"Her fluorescent orange socks were luminous in the dark and she had a matching side bow in her hair." He kissed his fingers. "Roz was perfection, pure perfection, and we cleared the gym floor with our smooth moves under the strobe lights." His smile was wistful. "Annie, my darling, that's when I knew it was love."

It was a story she had heard time and time again but she still managed a rueful smile as she elbowed him gently in the ribs. "Love, you reckon? Who with, Carl? Roz or George Michael?"

He flashed an impish grin, which caused his cheeks to dimple and made him look so much younger than his nearly forty years. "George, of course. It was always going to be George, and Roz got that even when I didn't." He shrugged. "She understood me when it wasn't cool to be gay, not like it is now. The term fag hag might have been fashionable when *Will and Grace* was a hit TV show but it's bordering on retro these days and it hadn't even been invented when Roz and I hung out together." His hand fluttered to his chest. "I mean, homosexuality was still officially illegal until 1986 in this country, for God's sake! But you know, when I was with her, who I fancied was irrelevant. She made sure I fitted in and I basked in her popularity. I'll always love her for that."

Annie shook her head and the curls she had just tucked behind her ears sprang free once more. "It seems so unreal now when you can switch on the TV and see gay couples kissing and that it's legal for same sex couples to marry here but less than thirty years ago it was against the law to be homosexual."

"I know it's a crazy world we live in, Annie, my sweet."

"Have you and David patched things up yet?" A mental picture of the butch and buff but rather temperamental David sprang to mind and Annie once more lamented the fact he was gay. It was such a tragic waste for womankind.

Carl flapped his hand dismissively. "Nope. I've changed the locks. I don't want him back. Honestly, the man is so self-absorbed. It's all me, me, me with him. He spends all his time down at the gym gazing in the mirror and pumping iron or whatever it is he does down there. All the while, totally oblivious of my needs and the fact that I am on a fast track to a midlife crisis. I mean, forty, Annie! My God, I am going to be forty in two months. That's ten years off half a century and look at me. Look at my life—what have I done with it?" He hung his head, a forlorn study of the latest fall *GQ* men's fashion trends.

Carl was prone to histrionics and his life—from the outside looking in, at any rate—Annie thought, wasn't too bad. He had gotten off scot-free in the quakes by being out of town on a fashion shoot when the big one of twenty-second February back in 2011 had hit. When he arrived home, he might have found his city gone and its people grieving but his townhouse, with all the latest mod-cons, in the posh suburb of Fendalton was largely unscathed, as was David. There had been no port-a-loos set up on the street for him to share with his neighbours.

His career as a freelance photographer was a lucrative one and the name Carl Everton could more often than not be spotted in the byline of the likes of *Fashion Quarterly*. He was forever tripping off to the islands for photo shoots or, when he wasn't working, to Melbourne and Sydney for long, lazy, four-star, foodie weekends. Until recently, he'd had his rather gorgeous de facto boyfriend accompanying him too. Annie reached over and rested her hand on his arm and as she did so, her diamond solitaire caught the sun. Its prisms of blue light didn't fill her with the same sense of joie de vivre today that it had two years earlier when she had picked it out with Tony. She took a deep breath and tried to muster up the enthusiasm for the pep talk she knew was now required of her.

"Listen, Mr Everton..." She prodded him in the chest. "You have a great life. As for you and David, you'll patch things up. You always do, and what's that saying? You're only as old as the person you're feeling?"

Carl nodded.

"Well, David's only thirty-five, so there you go—you are nowhere near middle age."

"Humph, that's easy for you to say. You're still a babe in the woods and besides, I'm not sure I see myself with David for the long haul anyway. Not unless he starts putting me first for a change."

"Thirty-one does not make me a baby and I've heard that before too."

"It does when you're an old man like me who is getting far too long in the tooth to play the kind of emotional on-again, off-again relationship games David seems to enjoy. Living with him is like being on a perpetual roller coaster."

"At least—"

"Don't say it." Carl held a hand up to silence her and looked abashed. "I know you're right and I do count my blessings every day, so just don't say it, okay?"

Annie nodded and left the words 'at least you get a chance at being forty' hang on the crisp afternoon air like the halo of cigarette smoke that hovered over the little group gathered across the river.

They sat in silence for a moment, each lost in their own thoughts, until Carl broke it when he decided it was time for a change of subject. "So, how is my main man Testosterone Tones doing these days?" He patted his pocket to reassure himself his trusty appendage, the latest, fresh-off-the-shelf iPhone was still there. "I saw on Facebook he had a ruggers win last weekend." His upper lip curled in distaste. "I must say, I was impressed by the pic he posted of his teammate—Jason, was it? Did you know he can balance a jug of beer on his belly? I thought to myself, look out *New Zealand's Got Talent*, here he comes."

Annie cringed at the thought of the latest round of boozy shots Tony had uploaded on the social networking site. *Beer, beer, and more beer!* was the after-match motto, win or no win. He was a bit of a living, breathing Southern Man cliché at times and lately he seemed to be getting worse. Or maybe she was just getting less tolerant, because it was that side of him that had first attracted her to him.

After what had happened to Roz, she'd had to grow up fast as she found herself catapulted from her role as the baby of the family to the strong one on whom her parents leaned. She'd wanted to find someone who would look after *her* for a change. By the time she met Tony, she'd had a succession of boyfriends who definitely were not keepers. The latest in the long line had been a namby-pamby life skills coach who hadn't made the grade. She should have known better because, instead of being on a date, she'd felt like she was the star of a self-help episode of *Oprah* with his need to analyse everything she said and did. Then, along came Tony—breath of fresh air, rugged, gorgeous Tony. Annie closed her eyes against the strong rays of afternoon sunlight that danced through the trees as she remembered.

The dance floor had been dark but not dark enough that she couldn't lock eyes with him as he jostled his teammates on the sidelines of the crowded floor.

She'd leaned over to scream in her girlfriend Jo-Jo's ear, "Hey, see that big guy over there—the touch rugby player with the dark hair?"

Jo-Jo did a twirl to send her long, dark hair flying like a whip and screamed back over the top of the music, "Yeah, he's not bad—quite nice, actually."

"I know. Keep your eyes and hands off because he keeps looking over at me." Modesty went out the window after a few drinks when Annie and her pals all started to fancy themselves as New Zealand's Next Top Model.

Unbeknown to her, though, Tony was at that precise moment shouting in his mate's ear, "Whoa, would you look at the set of hooters on Ginger Spice bouncing around over there."

Cyndi Lauper's *Girl's Just Want to Have Fun*—every party girl's anthem—blared out, and Annie put on a real tummy sucked in, boobs out show for that one and bopped around the pile of handbags tossed into the middle of the gaggle of girls, who all screeched along to the song. She knew with that confident certainty a woman in a little black dress has at twenty-five that when the song finished, the handsome stranger would come over and say hi. She was right.

For her part, she'd admired his solid build as she followed him onto the dance floor a few wines later for a slow groove. She'd gazed into a pair of beautiful dark blue eyes and her last conscious thought before she homed in for a good old snog was *such a waste, eyelashes like that on a man*.

For his part, Tony was attracted to Annie's tangle of red curls—he'd always had a thing for Nicole Kidman and this much shorter, curvier version had a nose that was cute and upturned and her eyes were the exact colour of a green marble he'd once played with as a kid. Of course, it went without saying that the clincher was her all-important, must-have set of assets: a 36C cup size.

When Annie removed her beer goggles, she discovered Tony really did have lovely eyes. His hair was black as night and cropped short. He had the muscle-bound physique of a man who played sports and the broadest shoulders she had ever had the opportunity to lean on. He was just what she'd been looking for and with a contented sigh, she'd snuggled into him for the long haul.

Six years and a mounting house deposit later, Tony still liked to keep his hair short but these days he had loads of squiggly little grey ones beginning to sprout. He thought that these made him look distinguished but Annie thought they made him look like what he was: a thirty-five-year-old man who seemed of late to have developed a penchant for acting like a twenty-five-year-old. And when she was feeling particularly premenstrual or if they'd had a fight like the one they'd had over her new boots, she would think unkind thoughts and liken him to a freak of nature with pubic hair growing from his head!

She had a horrible feeling, too, that he was a prime candidate for excess ear and nostril hair in later life. His father, Doug, happened to be the living proof of this. She shook the spectre of Tony and his hairy father away and turned her attention back to Carl, who would rather die than allow a stray grey make an appearance.

"*Tony* is fine, thank you." There was no love lost between the pair of polar opposites. It didn't help that Tony flirted with homophobia. Whenever Carl was around, all his macho tendencies went into overdrive and he wound up acting like a complete Neanderthal. Carl didn't exactly help matters, either, by camping things up as much as he could and revelling in Tony's discomfiture.

Annie shivered and rubbed her arms to ward off the cold. She wished she had brought a jacket with her instead of her flimsy cardigan. It was that time of year when you really needed to cart at least three changes of clothing around to cope with the variants in temperature throughout the day. No wonder Cantabrians were renowned for their conversational abilities when it came to the weather. It was like the Crowded House song *Four Seasons in One Day*.

"He's got his brothers over to play with the Ford this afternoon." Tony claimed his newly acquired gleaming white beast of a motor vehicle, which had featured heavily as a rebuttal in the new boots argument, was a necessity. It was a tool of his trade as a plumber, he reckoned. Annie would have liked to argue that a brand-new Toyota Rav4 was a necessity for her role as a secretary, so why couldn't she go get one but had kept quiet. In her opinion, a second-hand van would have done the job of carting his gear from job to job just as effectively as the Ford and as far as she was concerned, it was a prime example of big cars being extensions of—

"Ugh, no, not the Brat Pack." Carl derailed that train of thought as he muttered his nickname for the three Goodall boys.

Craig, the youngest of the Goodall brothers at twenty-three, was currently doing a Bachelor of Commerce or was that Bachelor of Bonking? Annie wasn't sure because the lines were blurred as to what he actually went to Canterbury University for. It seemed to her that the only slightly commercial thing he did was constantly cadge cash off family members. Stephen, the middle brother, was a roofer by trade, who, despite it being

2014, still sported a mullet. He had a penchant for hard-living, pool-cue-wielding women—a bit like his mother really, the bleached blonde family matriarch. Ngaire, clad in her skimpy tops and too tight jeans, sprang to mind.

"And how is Mumsy-in-law?" Carl asked, as though reading her mind.

Annie poked her tongue out at him. "She is not my mother-in-law yet and do you really want to know?"

"*I do* actually." This was said tongue-in-cheek as it was these two little words Ngaire Goodall hankered to hear between her oldest son and his fiancée. She was desperate for her big day.

Annie filled him in on how she'd seen Ngaire last Sunday after Tony, bless him, had invited the entire Goodall clan over for an impromptu BBQ. She'd been standing at the kitchen sink with a mountain of carrots to peel alongside a cabbage to chop for a coleslaw when Ngaire, under the pretence of helping, had swayed inside. She had plonked her big leather-clad bum down at the kitchen table, staple G&T in hand. As she watched her don that petulant look so unbecoming on a woman pushing sixty, Annie knew what was coming next.

"When are you and Tony going to set the date?"

There was a blissful silence while she took a swig of her drink but then, not having gone into the anaphylactic shock Annie silently wished upon her, she'd swallowed and carried on. "What are you waiting for? You're not getting any younger and once you pass thirty, it's all downhill from there." She shook her head. "There's nothing worse in my opinion than a bride who is mutton dressed as lamb."

This coming from the long in the tooth, leather-clad apparition seated in front of her! Annie remained stoically silent as she carried on with her peeling.

"By the time I was your age, Doug and I had been married for ten years and I'd produced three strapping boys who were already at school! Not that you'd have known I'd been pregnant once, let alone three times because my figure just bounced back. It does when you have your babies young, you know."

Blah-blah-blah. It was a speech Annie had suffered through many times before but on that particular afternoon, her hand had twitched uncontrollably. It had taken all her willpower not to shove the Majestic Red she was halfway through peeling somewhere where the sun don't shine!

"I tell you, Carl, Ngaire will never know just how close she came to spending the rest of her days walking round with a carrot up her arse!"

Carl threw his head back and laughed. "She does have a penchant for dressing like a geriatric call girl but she may well have a point. You've been engaged forever and I've got a lovely little three-piece suit, just dying for an outing, hanging in my wardrobe."

It was the million dollar question really, Annie mused and something she and Tony didn't seem to be in any particular hurry to answer. But as she had mentioned to Kas in her email, maybe it was time they talked about it. "Well, I did see a rather gorgeous dress the other day in the window of Modern Bride."

Carl clapped his hands, his face instantly animated as though someone had flicked a switch. "Right, sweetie, I want you to find out when they do a late night and we'll make a proper date of it. Deal?"

"Deal." Annie shivered again and she realised they had begun the gradual slide towards winter. She glanced at her wristwatch. "Hey, it's nearly four o'clock. We should probably make a move because when that sun drops, it will be freezing."

"You're right." Carl got to his feet and flicked his scarf over his shoulder before he linked his arm through Annie's. "Are you on popcorn duty or am I?"

Chapter Two

"CAN I TEMPT YOU WITH more popcorn, my sweet?" The bowl of salty, buttered popcorn was waved under Annie's nose.

"Shush, this is my favourite bit." Her eyes didn't move from the screen as she grabbed the bowl off Carl, scooped up a handful of the fluffy white snacks, and shovelled them in her mouth. She chomped furiously before she washed her mouthful down with a swig of bubbles. On Carl's ginormous flat-screen television, an elegant blonde woman clad in black and white stood alongside a curvaceous black woman and had launched effortlessly into *Aria*, or the *Flower Duet* as the famous opera song was otherwise known. So electric was the concert's atmosphere that it almost jumped from the screen into the living room. "Look, I've got goosebumps." She rolled the sleeve of her cardigan up to prove her point. "I'd love to sing along with them. They make it look so easy but I'd never be able to hit those high notes."

"Please don't attempt it. Personally, I always think of the old British Airlines ad when I hear this song." Carl sniffed, piqued at being shushed. It didn't last long, though. "Ooh, look, there he is—Conan the Barbarian drummer!"

A man with either a bad perm or just unfortunate natural curls, who was clad in a tightly fitted singlet, banged his bongos, or were they kettle drums? Annie was never sure but Carl didn't care either way as he watched, mesmerised by the man's biceps. His attentions were fickle, though, because when the star of the show himself appeared—a vision in head-to-toe white—Conan was forgotten.

"Look, look there he is!"

Annie wished he would stop poking her in the ribs; she wasn't blind.

"Oh my God, he's so gorgeous. That soulful lost in the music look of his is just to die for. And the way he wiggles those hips and tosses his hair back!

OOOH!" He gave a faux shudder. "It makes me melt every single time. I can see why Roz loved this concert. I never get sick of it."

"That's because we only watch it once a year. I always think he looks like he's about to have sex or a really, good p—"

"Don't you dare blaspheme the Yanni!" Carl ordered and cut her off with a flap of his hand.

Annie couldn't help herself. New Age just didn't do it for her, no matter how good the man was at playing with his synthesiser. All that long hair and droopy moustache—ugh, no thanks. As for the white silky trouser and shirt ensemble, well, it was all a bit too much in her book but hey, each to their own. There was no disputing the fact that he was phenomenally successful and her sister had adored him and the way he filled out the rear of those white pants too. She'd adored all things Greek, for that matter. *Ah, Roz.* Annie sighed and blinked back the familiar hotness that pricked at her eyes.

The date of the concert was September the twenty-fifth, 1993 and its setting was the truly spectacular Acropolis in Athens. It never failed to amaze Annie when the camera panned to where the world-famous outline of the Parthenon was perched on top of the hill overlooking the Herodes Atticus Theatre. The ancient buildings lit up against the backdrop of a night-time Athens sky were quite simply breathtaking.

Oh yes, Greece was definitely on her bucket list, too. She'd always figured that she would go there with Tony one day. How romantic would a Greek island-hopping honeymoon be? They could finish up at Eleni's, and she could finally get to meet Kas and the rest of the Bikakis family in the flesh. It would be a dream come true. She sighed. It wasn't on the cards, not with the state of their finances. There was the drudgery of saving for a house that seemed further and further away each time house prices increased, the Ford monster truck repayments, and okay, if she were really honest, the boots. They had been an unnecessary splurge, especially now that she had seen *the dress,* as she had come to think of it. If they ever did get round to setting a date, she'd be lucky to get a Registry Office service followed by a couple of nights caravanning in the nearby town of Ashburton for her honeymoon, let alone the dress of her dreams.

Greece had been on Roz's bucket list, too. That gorgeous Georges Meis print of the island of Santorini had hung on her bedroom wall for as long as

Annie could remember when she was growing up. These days, the volcanic cliffside tumble of white buildings, so starkly vibrant against an infinity of blue, adorned her and Tony's bedroom wall. The inevitable thoughts of how differently things might have played out if Roz had spent her money on a trip to Greece instead of blowing it all on drugs crept into Annie's thoughts. She swiped at her nose with the back of her hand as she remembered:

The day it became clear to her that her adored big sister was a drug addict, she had been about to saw into an ice cream cake. Her innovative mother had made the cake by turning a tub of vanilla ice cream upside down and piping a big number eleven in pink cream on the top. She had then piped the same pink cream around the edges and voila! Annie had her birthday cake. It hadn't been the fancy multi-flavoured cake she'd picked out from the Wendy's ice cream cake display but as her mother had explained to her, the choice was hers to make. The homemade cake and ice skating or the expensive cake and no skating.

The chance to show off her moves to her friends on the ice rink had won out. So it was, her gang, including Sarah Jenkins whom every eleven-year-old girl in her class wanted to emulate, had clustered around her, each awaiting their slice. It was a coup for Sarah to have accepted the party invitation and Annie had high hopes it would put an end to the taunts about her hair that the popular tween liked to make at any given opportunity. It was silently understood that with her own fashionable haircut and up-to-the-minute outfit, Sarah would get the first piece of cake, and indeed she would have if Hurricane Roz hadn't burst into the kitchen at that very moment.

She looked different, Annie registered straight away, but then she hadn't seen her for a couple of months either. It wasn't anything obvious, like she'd cut her hair, although her normally gleaming mane was dull and in need of washing. She looked skinny and her clothes hung off her but the biggest difference was more subtle than that. It had taken her a moment to pinpoint what it was that had changed in her sister but then it had dawned on her. The light that had always glowed brightly within Roz, that special something that made people gravitate towards her, want to be with her. That special something—that if she were honest, she had always been a teeny bit envious of—had dimmed.

As she looked at her in the harsh afternoon light that flooded into the kitchen that day, Annie was ashamed to admit that although she was pleased her older, by nine years, sister hadn't forgotten her birthday after all, she didn't feel the pride at standing alongside her she normally did. In fact, she felt a surge of embarrassment as Roz lunged at her with her present and talked as though someone had pushed a fast-forward button on her ghetto blaster. In her manic delivery, she was totally oblivious of the group of young girls who stood back, goggle-eyed as she insisted Annie stop what she was doing and open her gift.

In the hopes that her sister would calm down if she did what was demanded, Annie put the knife down and forgot the cake for a moment to rip off the gift wrap. As the Barbie doll hidden beneath was revealed, her insides had shrivelled. She hadn't played with dolls in years. She was turning eleven, for goodness' sake, and at that moment, she'd felt the small bridge that had sprung up between her and Roz over the last year widen into a chasm too wide to breach. As she stared at the doll in disbelief, she tried to ignore Sarah and the other girls' giggling. How could Roz have done this to her?

"It's a lovely gift, Rosalind, but I think it's time to go. Come on now, let Annie get back to her friends and her cake before it melts." Peter Rivers sensed his youngest daughter's discomfort and had stepped forward to take his eldest child firmly by the arm.

Roz had shrugged him off in a jerky motion. "Get off me!" She tried to focus on her sister. "Do you like it, Annie? Do you? I picked it out especially because I remember you were always playing with my old Barbie. Remember you used to call her Barba?" Her eyes were wide, unblinking, and her pupils were huge, almost covering the dull blue rings of her irises. Every limb of her body seemed to take on a life of its own as she twitched and jerked in agitation. The scene that ensued of her father hauling Roz from the room, followed by the shouted discussion on the front lawn, was indelibly printed on Annie's brain when she thought back on her childhood. All her friends, including Sarah, had overheard the heated exchange and she had hated her sister that day. She hated her in that self-contained way that a child can—not just for ruining her party and making her look a fool in front of her friends, but for making her mum cry and for making her dad so angry on her birthday. Most of all, she hated her sister who had once been so beautiful, who had always in the past been there for her, and whose potential had been unlimited, for what she had done to herself.

Roz's dreams, once upon a time, had been to visit the city of Athens and wander the Acropolis, to sail around the Greek islands on a yacht, and to have a holiday romance conducted under a hot Mediterranean sun. All of this she had declared passionately on numerous occasions to her enraptured little sister before the drugs had come along and sucked every ounce of ambition from her. She had been fascinated with Greece and all things Greek, including the musician who presently tossed his hair back on the screen in front of them: Yanni.

Carl had bought the video for Roz's birthday not long before she died and Annie could remember hearing the strains of it coming from her sister's room. Something in his music had spoken to her and made her feel like if she held out her hand, she could catch her dreams, she'd told her wide-eyed sister, who had yet to move past the Mickey Mouse Club.

Annie blinked the memories away and took a tissue from the box Carl had had the foresight to put on the coffee table. She wiped her eyes before she gave her nose a good blow and then concentrated her attentions on the video Carl had converted to disc. Yet another sign of just how much time had passed: nearly twenty years. She and Carl watched the concert every year on Roz's birthday. It had been Carl's idea, this ritualistic viewing of *Yanni: Live at the Acropolis*. He'd found the video among Roz's sparse collection of things when her parents had asked him whether there was anything of hers he might like to keep. He'd snatched it up and held it tight to him as though it were Roz herself; the following year when his best friend should have turned twenty, he invited Annie round to his place to watch it.

Despite her parents' apathy where she was concerned back then, even they might have raised an eyebrow or protested about their young daughter going to watch a video at a twenty-year-old man's house. Of course, where Carl was concerned, there was no need for concern and besides, Annie was sure her parents were secretly relieved at not having to share their grief with her on such a poignant date. So it was that while her parents would troop off to the cemetery, her and Carl's annual tradition had been born.

That first year, and for a good few years after it, the drink of choice for Annie had been lemonade and not the bubbles she was partial to having with her popcorn these days. In a funny way, the soothing ritual of allowing the music to wash over them year after year really did help. As she had matured, the age gap between her and Carl had become irrelevant, just like it would have between her and Roz, had she lived. It was an age gap that hadn't been intentional on her parents' part—nature had just played it that way. Through Carl, though, she had not only found a brother, she had also gained a very good friend. When she was with him, she didn't have to pretend. In a way, he provided her with what Roz had for him and that was the ability to just be herself. Because he got her. He understood.

She stole a glance at him. A single tear tracked a path down his smooth cheek. His alabaster skin was the result of regular facials, as well as a facial hair phobia. She reached over and brushed the tear away, not needing to say a word. That was the thing with true friends; they didn't always need to clutter their friendship with words. She pulled her gaze from his familiar profile and rifled through the last grotty bits of un-popped popcorn before she licked the salt from her fingers. As she reached for her glass, she saw it was in need of topping up. That's when she remembered her promise.

"Come on, let's have a toast to Kas. It's her birthday as well today, remember, and I promised her we would."

Carl poured the remains of the bottle into their flutes. "Of course."

Annie accepted her drink and raised her glass towards his. "To Kas. Many happy returns."

"Hear, hear."

Their glasses clinked and the bubbles tickled her nose as she took a sip.

"So come on then, spill the beans. Just how are the lovely Kassia and the rest of the Bikakis clan getting on these days? You haven't given me an update in ages." Carl put his glass down on the table before he swivelled round to face her.

"They're good. It really was the best thing they ever did, leaving Athens."

"They didn't have much of a choice in the matter though, did they?"

"No, that's true." Annie sipped her drink. Kas, who was an Athenian girl born and bred, had sent her an email that confided her doubts about moving to the small coastal resort of Elounda on the island of Crete. That wasn't the only thing bothering her about the move, though. She had explained that as much as she loved her mother-in-law, there was no escaping the fact that she was bossy and opinionated. In her eyes, her two sons—Kas's husband Spiros and his younger brother Alexandros, who had swanned off to Rio de Janeiro in Brazil to do God knows what—could do no wrong. So how would the two women manage to live under the same roof?

It wasn't a situation Kas had foreseen arising when she and Spiros enjoyed their comfortable married life together in Athens. But then the talk of austerity measures had begun. It wasn't long until Spiros had lost his long-held job as a journalist, along with some four thousand other media employees. Kas, at home with Mateo, was pregnant with Nikolos at the time and things had looked bleak for the couple until Mama Bikakis stepped in. She had been running her namesake, Eleni's Hotel singlehandedly since her husband Abram had died and she was tired, she had told them.

Unlike some of the other islands, Crete, with its geographical location, had a tourist trade all year round. It quieted down in winter but the weather was still mild enough to carry it through the cooler months. That she was exhausted and in need of help Mama had announced in her usual dramatic hand-wringing style. Yes, she had stated, she was now an old lady and it was time for her oldest son to come home and reclaim his roots. Eleni's was his birthright and a mother needed her son close by in her old age. The wily old Greek woman had it all worked out. Spiros could write the novel he had been fostering in his mind for as long as any of them could remember, maintain the grounds, and take guests out on fishing excursions and for day trips to a nearby island. While Kas—with Alexandros away—could pick up where he'd left off and help with the day-to-day running of Eleni's, as well as take over the managerial side of the guesthouse. This in turn would free Mama up to spend more time with her longed-for grandchildren. To the old lady's mind, it was the perfect solution and a foregone conclusion that they come to her, and so they had packed up their life and moved to Crete.

Annie traced a finger round the top of her glass. "Well, the latest is that Alexandros has had enough of swanning around Brazil. He's on his way home and Kas is not looking forward to being outnumbered."

"Yes, all that testosterone could be a real leaving-the-toilet-seat-up conundrum." Carl took a sip of his drink and wrinkled his nose. "I think I prefer the Fraiche to the Sauvignon—what about you?"

"Nope, I like the Sav. The Fraiche tastes like baby shampoo to me."

"Hmm, not a comparison I would have made but each to their own. So the golden boy's coming home, eh? He must have run out of funds or a female sponsor. That will throw a spanner in the works, won't it?"

"I hope not, for Kas's sake. Anyway, Eleni's sounds like it is busy enough to sustain the pair of them these days because from what she tells me, they're already fully booked for most of the summer. Of course, Mama is in raptures about the prodigal son's return. Her two boys and her grandchildren all home to roost! Kas says she keeps clapping her hands and exclaiming that it is all just too wonderful."

Carl smiled at the mental picture of the ecstatic Greek mama. "Where does Kassia fit into that equation, though?"

"Oh, don't worry about her. She can hold her ground where Mama is concerned. Besides, if Alexandros is true to form, he will be too busy wooing the guests to do any actual work." Annie placed her empty glass down and hauled herself off the couch. The concert had ended and as she stretched, she realised she felt drained as she always did after their Yanni session. With a glance at the now empty bottle on the coffee table, she realised she felt a bit light-headed too.

"I don't think I should drive. I'll phone Tony and see if he can pick me up, shall I? Oh, hang on, I think he said something about heading around to watch the rugby at his mate Dean's place tonight. I'll call a taxi. What company do you use?"

"Why don't you just stay here tonight? The spare room's yours, sweetie, you know that. And to be honest, with David gone, I could do with a spot of company tonight." He pulled his puppy dog face.

The thought of not having to move from the couch was appealing and Carl's expression was rather pathetic. "Okay, but only if you agree to an Indian takeaway."

"Annie Rivers, think of all those calories. Ugh, all that cream, all those spices—you'll never fit into *the* dress! Why don't you act your age for a change, girl, and come out with me for a night on the tiles. I know this great little tapas bar..."

Chapter Three

TO: KASSIA BIKAKIS

From: Annie Rivers

Subject: Why I am never drinking again.

Hi Kas,

It sounds like you had a wonderful birthday. Being surrounded by your family and friends is exactly what a birthday should be all about. It was a horrid precursor to a winter's day here when I opened the pics you attached and I was so jealous of you all sitting outdoors under that gorgeous blue sky with the olive trees in the background. It looked like a picture you would see in a travel brochure, you lucky thing. Who was the dark-haired girl next to Alexandros? Don't tell me he has a girlfriend already? He's only been home five minutes. I wish I could have been there and raised a glass with you all. Though of course I wouldn't have been drinking that Retsina you are all so fond of sitting in the sunshine and knocking back because I am a teetotaller these days. As of last Sunday that is, thanks to Carl and those bloody Long Island Iced Teas he's so partial to.

April 28th started off innocently enough with Carl and I meeting at the Botanic Gardens to talk about all the same old Roz stuff that we talk about every year on her birthday. We went back to his place in the late afternoon because it gets cold earlier and earlier at the moment to watch the Yanni concert. It made us both cry like it always does, though Carl did get his knickers in a knot at one point, accusing me of blaspheming Yanni. I didn't mean to. I just pass remarked that sometimes he looked like he could do with a really good bowel motion. No offence, Kas, because I know the man is a cultural icon over your way but hey after all these years of watching that concert and his various facial expressions, I feel I am entitled to comment. Anyway, you know Carl: he got over it pretty quick and when the concert finished, I suggested we drink a toast to your birthday too as promised in my last email. So, in a way, Kas, now that I think about it, it is actually your fault too because it was downhill from there on in.

I wanted to get Indian for dinner but Carl insisted we go out for tapas, which was actually just another word for cocktails because I don't remember seeing food until three a.m.-ish when I picked up a mince pie at the petrol station on my way home. It was pretty gross too, full of gelatine. I'm getting off track though, sorry—anyway, we wound up at some dark little bar that Carl insisted was the latest 'in' place to be seen at. From what I could see, what 'in' meant was that the clientele all looked like they'd sneaked out on a school night. Carl was in form, keeping the drinks coming, which I think was an excuse to keep chatting to the cute bartender. Either way, I'd no sooner finished slurping my way through one concoction and then Carl would be there at the ready with another. He was on a mission to get slaughtered because he is on a break from David at the moment and he never does well when he is on his own. It's alright for him, though; he didn't make a holy show of himself.

Oh, Kas, I cringe every time I think about it. I wish us Kiwis were sensible with our alcohol consumption like you Greeks are. Sure, you might like to toss a plate or two over your shoulders when you have had a couple of Ouzos but we, my friend, are a nation of binge drinkers. You would think I'd know better at my age than to drink like that on Roz's birthday or anybody's birthday for that matter. Apparently not, though, because I vaguely remember Carl being off on the dance floor while I leaned all over some poor guy in an effort to keep myself upright. I told the lucky chap all about my dream wedding dress, which is just what every single man out on the pull wants to hear about. That wasn't the worst of it, though. I spotted a girl with a sheet of blonde hair dancing by Carl and there was just something about the way she moved that reminded me of Roz and it all came alcohol induced, flooding back. That poor, poor man had me dribbling and crying on his shoulder.

Annie shuddered as she recalled how she had bent the stranger's ear and leaned away from the screen for a moment. She shut her eyes at the myriad memories that had assailed her.

If Roz had dabbled in drugs as a young teenager, then the family was unaware of it. Carl maintained it had never been part of their social scene at school but that all changed when she started work. At eighteen, she'd begun work for an advertising firm as their Girl Friday and it was at one of their industry parties that she first encountered and fell in love with methamphetamine. At least that was what her parents had managed to piece together from her friends. It was ironic that Annie, too, had wound up working in an advertising company but nobody could accuse Manning Stockyard, the firm she worked for, of being anything other than staid. They didn't even do Friday night drinks—mind you, the thought of winding her week down over a casual glass of wine in the company of her boss Adelia Hunnington, or Attila the Hun as she not so fondly liked to call her, was an unappealing one.

With a nine-year-age gap between them, Roz's life outside of home was a side to her sister that Annie hadn't been privy to until the day of her eleventh birthday party. After everybody had left and Roz was long gone with her latest boyfriend in a squeal of burning rubber, her parents had no choice but to sit her down and explain as plainly as possible what was wrong with her sister. They'd calmly told her they were trying to help her but she had to want to help herself too. The shouted conversations that had ensued every time Roz had visited over the last year, conversations that were cut short were Annie to walk into the room, suddenly made sense. It was only later, though, after *it* happened, that she really understood the implications of her sister's addiction. Her affair with the substance was all-encompassing but then Roz had never been the type of girl to do anything by halves.

Annie rubbed her eyes. She knew she was smudging her mascara but she didn't care because her mind refused to curb the memories of what they had gone through as a family.

The pressure of what was happening to their eldest daughter had nearly torn her parents' marriage apart as Roz played them off one against the other. Her addiction had driven not only her friends away and lost her her job, but it had the flow-on effect of tainting their own social lives. They became known as the parents of "that girl, you know—the one on drugs." For her part, Annie stopped having her friends home, preferring to visit their houses for fear of one of her sister's impromptu quest for cash, out-of-control visits. There was no doubt more, much more that Roz had been driven to do when she had found herself out of a job and still hungering for the meth but she had slowly cut herself off from everybody who knew and loved her. This had spared Annie and her parents from knowing that side of her life further.

Instead, they chose to cling to the daughter and sister beneath the horror of her dependency. She was the person they wanted to hold onto, the girl they had once known who had had a life to lead and a dream to chase after. That was the girl they hoped would come back to them.

Their dreams, along with Roz's, had ended the day she'd stayed up all night partying and had driven her car into a tree on her way home to the latest flat she had been dossing down in.

For Annie and her parents, though, that wasn't the end. Oh no, she shivered and wished she'd been bothered to light the fire as she thought back, it was just the beginning. Her mum started smoking again and seemed to be in a perpetual fog of non interest after that knock at the door had come cutting herself off from Annie emotionally. As for her father, a big man with an argumentative nature, well, he seemed to simply give up, if the slump in his shoulders and disinterest in what was happening around him was anything to go by. Annie didn't just lose a sister that day but for a long, long time afterwards she lost her parents, too. They were a physical presence but they weren't engaged in the day-to-day minutiae of their youngest daughter's life when she'd needed them most. Both of them were seemingly oblivious of the changes that a young girl goes through because neither had the energy left after the day-to-day, going through the motions of simply living for that. Annie understood that—she really did—but it didn't make it any easier to take.

At first, her grief was too painful too touch and so the eleven-year-old she had been was unable to talk about it; she bottled it up and hid it away from her friends. She didn't want to share it because how could any of them possibly understand what she was going through? Not when they got to go home each night to their own safe, happy little houses where nothing bad happened. Suddenly the normal teenage interests they'd once shared seemed trite and she found herself having to bite her tongue when they'd whittle on about the latest boy band or who was wearing what to whoever's party. What did it matter? She no longer cared and she soon found that people's sympathy only stretched so far for so long.

She could recall just sitting in her sister's old bedroom; she stared at that print of Santorini and felt like the world was closing in on her. It was only the knowledge reinforced by that print that it was a big wide world with lots to see that stopped it from doing so. More than anything as she lay curled up on Roz's bed, she wanted to wake up and get back to a normal life but this void she had found herself thrown into was the new norm and it was up to her to find a way to move through it. The time eventually came for her to sink or swim and somehow she managed to swim.

The first thing she had done the day she decided to tentatively try to dog paddle was to contact her sister's old pen pal. She didn't know as she penned that first letter that she herself would form a lasting bond with the girl on the other side of the world. Of course, when Roz and Kassia had been in touch, email didn't exist and there had been a wodge of handwritten letters still in Roz's desk. Their lives at opposite ends of the earth had been brought together via a school pen pal program, with a shared birthday their initial common denominator. The two girls' exchanges had been an innocent recounting of teenage angst and they'd written back and forth regularly throughout high school and beyond. Until, Kassia relayed later, one day her friend who was getting into a new social scene through her job had just stopped writing and she had never known why. She hadn't known about the drugs, she didn't know about any of that but through reading their letters, Annie had been provided with an insight into her sister's life before. That was the way she thought of her now—the Roz before drugs and the Roz after.

The year of the firsts passed with all the usual anticipated emotional upheaval around each and every significant date. Then the second year passed, a muted version of the first and then the third until one day Annie realised that her mother laughed occasionally and no longer smoked like a train. Her father, too, stood a bit straighter and began to state his opinion a tad more forcefully. As for herself, well, she found herself unwittingly beginning to look forward and not backwards. And so life went on, because although Roz would always be there in their thoughts and forever in their hearts, time, as they say, is a great healer. It allowed them not to get over her death—that would never happen—but rather to learn to live with it.

Annie blinked the memories away and the screen came back into focus. The time in the bottom corner of the screen blinked midnight. *Crumbs, it was getting late.* Jazz stretched languidly on her lap, as though sensing his time for snuggling was nearly up. She'd better start winding her letter up if she was going to be fit for work in the morning.

You can picture it, can't you, and I don't need to tell you it wasn't pretty. Even less so the next morning when I woke up with a stonking headache. So now you know why I am never drinking again. It's gotten late here, Kas, and I have work in the morning, so it's time I went off to bed. Na-night.

Lots of love and kisses to you and all the Bikakis family

Annie

xox

She clicked Send and waited a moment before going through the motions of closing down her laptop. Her hand stretched over to switch the lamp off on the desktop but hovered there for a moment as her eyes alighted on the photo framed beneath it. In front of their boutique Cretan hotel, Eleni's stood, its' namesake the short, rotund Mama Bikakis. She had insisted on wearing widow black since her husband dropped dead some ten years earlier. With her cheeks puffed out proudly, she was flanked on either side by her handsome sons. On her left was Kas's husband Spiros and on her right his younger brother Alexandros. The latter was a somewhat clichéd, tall, dark, and handsome with straight white teeth set against the deep olive of his skin. Hence his rip snorting success with the female tourists who came to stay at their family-run accommodation. Spiros was slightly shorter than his brother and although his hooded black eyes gave him a serious look, the smile that twitched at the corners of his mouth belied his good humour. At his side was Kassia.

Annie smiled involuntarily as she always did when she saw her dear friend. Her two sons had rounded her figure out in the last few years but her face was still that of the girl she had first started writing to nearly twenty years ago. Thick, long black hair she insisted on getting her hairdresser to curl framed a strong face. Almond-shaped brown eyes behind which a wicked sense of humour to match that of her husband's lurked to soften her features. She wasn't pretty as such but she was arresting in her own unique way and her looks would stand the test of time far better than mere prettiness would.

Nikolos, the baby, was perched on his mother's hip and Mateo stood in front of his parents, who each had a restraining hand resting on his little shoulder. Both boys had an unruly shock of black hair and an impish grin to match their Bambi eyes. They looked every inch as cheeky as the tales their mother relayed in her letters.

Annie sighed and blew the family a kiss before she flicked the light off. She'd dearly love to give those two little boys a hug from their honorary New Zealand aunty but a visit to Greece wasn't on the cards. Not with saving for a house, and the never-ending bills that went hand in hand with the cost of living. Who knew? There might be a wedding to organise too, one day, one day very soon if she had her way.

"We'll get there, Jazz," Annie murmured and scratched behind the old tomcat's ear. He'd curled up on her lap as she typed her email. At the sound of his beloved's voice, he sighed contentedly, opened one beady yellow eye and fixed it on her. "Well, actually, you won't but don't fret. I'd never leave you for longer than a couple of weeks and Best Cats is rated a five-star in the world of catteries, so you'd be well looked after."

Jasper narrowed his eye, not liking the sound of the word cattery before he stretched and left one paw dangling lazily in mid-air. Annie looked down at his tattered gingery fur. He'd never win any cat beauty pageants, that was for sure, but he'd needed a home and she had needed the unconditional affection he provided.

When he'd disappeared for three whole weeks after the second big earthquake they'd had back in February 2011, she had been beside herself. It was enough that the city she had grown up in had been destroyed in a fateful few minutes but people had actually died too. So, trying to make sense out of something that made no sense at all, she had pounded the pavements, night after night. She called Jasper's name and pictured him quivering in a corner of some stranger's garage or worse, crushed by the bricks of a falling chimney. She'd all but given up hope when she got up one morning to find him sitting at the back door, looking none the worse for his extended walkabout. Although she had been over the moon to see him, scooping him up and smothering him with kisses, Tony had been nonplussed to see his nemesis staring smugly at him from his vantage point in his fiancée's arms once more. "Look who is home!" Annie had exclaimed excitedly. She decided to take his return as a sign that maybe things would be okay after all. "Say hello to Daddy, Jazz."

Jasper had hissed.

"Oh, don't be a nasty boy." She'd known full well the pair's relationship would always be strained, thanks to their dodgy start. Shortly after she had moved in with Tony, Jasper had made his feelings at having to share his mistress's affection very clear by piddling in Tony's work boots.

She smiled at the memory of the expression on Tony's face as he had stuffed his foot inside the sodden boot. Annie got to her feet and tucked Jazz under her arm. "Come on, you. It's time to go out."

Tony drew the line at sharing a bed with Jasper.

As she opened the front door a crack, she saw the night was misty with the onset of cooler weather. Jasper mewled his protest at leaving the warmth of the house behind. But then something caught his eye and he jumped out of her arms and ran out the door with a speed belying his years and disappeared into the inkiness. She hoped she wouldn't be presented with a dead mouse or worse, a rat, on the doorstep in the morning. She shuddered at the thought as she turned and padded up the hall to the bathroom.

Annie picked her wide toothed comb up from where it nestled next to Tony's razor in the vanity drawer and tugged it through her hair. She sighed. Her hair frizzed out around her face, like Little Orphan Annie, her namesake, but if she didn't stick to her nightly ritual, she'd wake up to a headful of ginger dreads in the morning.

When she was satisfied there were no knots left, she moved on to Step Two. She pulled a facial wipe from the near empty packet and took off her make-up. As she peered into the mirror, her newly naked green eyes grew wide as she spied something she didn't like the look of. She leaned in even closer to the mirror and frowned. What on earth was that angry red monstrosity on her chin? Homing in on it, Annie gave it a squeeze for good measure. Ouch! Yes, it was definitely a spot. Surely at thirty-one years of age, she should be past getting corkers like that? Apparently not, if that monster glaring back at her was anything to go by. Nope, there was nothing else for it: she'd have to nuke the bugger. She smeared toothpaste over the raised lump. She was sure she had read somewhere that toothpaste dried pimples out. It must be all that menthol, she decided, as she cursed Attila. It was all her bloody fault: stress played havoc with your skin, everybody knew that. With one last sigh, she brushed her teeth.

She smelled like a tube of Colgate as she tiptoed out of the bathroom and pushed open the darkened bedroom door. Tony was asleep, so thankfully she wouldn't have to launch into an explanation as to why she smelled so minty fresh. She slid in next to him and warmed herself against his slumbering bulk for a moment before she closed her eyes and willed herself to sleep.

Tomorrow was going to be manic at work. There was the much anticipated signing-off of an account Manning Stockyard had been wooing for months and her boss, Attila, did not work well under pressure, which in turn meant she was going to need all the sleep she could get. Annie cleared her mind of all thoughts of work and drifted into one of those vivid half sleeping, half waking dreams where she told Attila she had a face on her that could curdle milk. When a loud oink of a snore erupted from Tony, she jolted back into wakefulness. Her leg twitched under the covers as she contemplated kicking him but she resisted the urge. She knew from past experience that a good boot would only make him more restless. Instead, she counted sheep.

Chapter Four

ANNIE CAUGHT A GLIMPSE of her hair in the reflection off the big glass doors of the Albrecht Building where she worked in Victoria Street, and immediately wished that she hadn't. Her mass of curls had, in the twenty minutes it had taken her to get to work, escaped Houdini-style from the bun she had secured them into. Instead of the efficient PA to up-and-coming advertising guru and extremely horrible boss, Adelia Hunnington, she had portrayed upon leaving the house that morning, she now looked like a madwoman. The toothpaste on the spot had not been a good idea, either, as she now had an angry red pimple on her chin that was also surrounded by flaky skin. Suffice to say, it was not shaping up to be a good hair or face day, which from prior experience Annie knew did not bode well for her general working day. *Bloody Tony and his snoring!* She sent him a mean telepathic message.

His grunting like a stuck pig had been the root cause of her tossing and turning most of the night and she needed her sleep. Not just for beauty purposes, either, although the fact she'd aged ten years in the last six months was down to Attila and her workaholic tendencies. She'd had her working through half her lunch break most days and always managed to pop out and waved some urgent document that had to go out that night just as Annie put her coat on to go home. She sighed at the injustice of it all and she had finally drifted off into a deep sleep just as Tony got up at his usual ungodly time of six o'clock, which meant she'd ignored her alarm for a good twenty-five minutes when it had shrilled an hour later.

She glanced at the stairwell and momentarily contemplated taking the stairs two at a time to the fourth floor offices where she had spent the last few years of her life in full-time employment. It would be good exercise and her skirt did feel on the snug side today but oh sod it, she decided and headed for the lift instead. She wasn't that keen on the stairs since the earthquakes; actually, she wasn't that keen on the lifts either. It was a bit of a problem really. Half a second later, she wished she had opted for the stairs, though, as a familiar nasal voice sounded behind her.

"Morning, Annie. You're looking lovely as always."

He could only see her rear view, so Annie could only assume that Pervy Justin from the accounting firm on the floor above hers was in fact referring to her bottom. She ignored him and stepped into the lift. He wasn't deterred by her silence.

"It's going to be a cold day out there if that frost this morning was anything to go by. Brrr." He shivered for effect and rubbed the tops of his arms. "You probably should have put a warmer top on." He felt his way around until he hit the number five button. His eyes never once strayed from the thin fabric of her blouse.

Annie sighed and pulled her jacket closed. She really should lodge a complaint with someone about him but that would take energy and lately all her energy reserves had been zapped. It was the same every year: the emotional build-up followed by the exhausted aftermath of Roz's birthday. It wasn't as though she was consciously thinking about her sister during this time. She was just there—a constant on the periphery of her mind. She took a step back from Justin so she was pressed up against the railing and silently willed the numbers to hurry up.

Tammy on reception didn't look up from her iPhone as Annie called out a cheery good morning to her. The greeting was not given because she meant it—Tammy was an uppity little madam whose main focus in life was the electronic gadget currently in her hand. No, it was given automatically, done out of habit. The receptionist mumbled the same token pleasantry back, not bothering to peek out from behind her waves of brown hair as Annie breezed past the screen behind her into the typing pool area.

Once upon a time, it had been a nice place to work with its floor-to-ceiling windows that showcased a smattering of Christchurch's high-rise buildings and the Avon River. Nowadays, the only constant in the outlook was the river. Slowly the buildings were pulled down around them and at present, the vista resembled what she imagined a post-war zone would look like. It was hard to visualise the bright, new modern city the powers that be assured them all would rise up from the rubble. She had nothing to complain about, though, she reminded herself as she did every morning, because she was one of the lucky ones and life really does go on. That was a lesson she had learned years ago.

She pulled her eyes away from the window, slung her bag down on the ground and barely had time to drape her jacket across the back of her chair when the door opposite her desk was flung open. Attila made a beeline for her secretary. She was resplendent in head-to-toe taupe. "Annie," she barked, "I want this contract re-typed and on my desk in an hour. The Crunch n Go people are due in at eleven for signing off and I'll need to proof it before you run a final copy off." She smoothed her chignon but needn't have bothered because no hair on her perfectly coiffed head would dare make a bid for freedom. As she dumped the stack of papers she'd been carrying down on Annie's desk, they sent a waft of cold air up but she was oblivious of the sudden chill as she fixed her PA with her steely-eyed stare. "Understood?"

"Consider it done, Adelia." Annie resisted the temptation to stand, click her heels together and salute, and hoped that the expression she had forced her face into wearing was a sweet smile and not the constipated grimace it felt like. She glanced down at the papers; she knew it would be heads down, bums up for her if she was to get it done in time. *Oh yes, it was definitely going to be one of those days.* She flipped the birdie at her boss's retreating back.

"Did you hear that?" She sat down heavily and turned to Sue, who sat at the desk next to hers. "No good morning, Annie, how are you today, Annie? Or even better, you look nice today, Annie. Followed up with a polite request to type this load of old codswallop up by ten o'clock."

Sue blinked at her from behind the thick lenses of her glasses. She reminded Annie of a near-sighted frog. She sighed for the second time that morning. *Why did she bother?* Sue had the personality of cold porridge. Annie settled herself down for the morning; her fingers flew over the keyboard. She only came up for air to answer her phone.

"Hello, Manning Stockyard. You're speaking with Annie Rivers. How may I help?"

"Hi-ya babes, it's me. Have you got a sec?"

The "me" on the phone was Carl and his singsong voice down the line made her smile. It was funny, she'd muse from time to time, how the two people she counted on as her very best friends in the whole world were Kas and Carl and they had both been her sister's friends first. "Not really. I have to get the contract from hell typed up and on Attila's desk in half an hour, and I am only a quarter of the way through it."

"Multitask while I talk then, sweetie. You girls are supposed to be good at that."

Annie laughed and cradled the phone in the crook of her shoulder. She glanced at the contract and carried on tip-tapping. "Okay then, for you, I will attempt to multitask. Now what's up?"

"Not a lot. It's far too cold where I am for that kind of carry-on."

Annie didn't bat at an eye at the double entendre; they were par for the conversational course where Carl was concerned. "Where are you?"

"I am freezing my butt off on New Brighton Pier, that's where. I tell you, Annie, that easterly is a bitch and quite frankly so is Cassie."

Carl did not feel that his job as freelance fashion photographer should extend itself to model therapy and he had no time for the temperamental moods of some of the girls sent his way.

"She's probably just hungry, Carl. Offer to go get her some food. A Big Mac and fries should do it."

Carl laughed. "Does that work for Attila?"

"No but then she's not a stick insect, just a complete cow."

"Touché, sweetie. Anyway enough of all that. I am ringing to see if you have thought any further about going to try the dress on?"

"Of course! I've made an appointment for seven o'clock Thursday week. Are you keen to come with me?"

"Do you need to ask? Listen, I have a bit on between now and then, which means I will be incommunicado so why don't we go for an early catch-up dinner beforehand. Nothing that will make you bloat, mind, so your beloved Indian is out, sweetie. How about Thai? If you stay away from the Beef Massaman Curry you should be fine."

"The Lemongrass Diner's supposed to be good and it's just down the road from Modern Bride. Shall I book it for say, five thirty—or is that too early for you?"

"No, five thirty will be perfect."

"I can't wait! The dress is a one-off design original according to the lady I spoke to, by Julianne someone or other."

"Not Julianne Tigre?"

"That's her."

"Better start saving, sweetie—*Cassie, I said I wanted windswept and moody, not cold and constipated*—give me patience! Listen, I gotta go, hun-bun. See you Thursday week. Be good." He blew her a kiss down the phone and then the line went dead.

Annie's mood was much improved as she hung up. She glanced at her screen and saw she had typed in *a Big Mac and fries should do it*. She quickly backspaced over the text that she didn't think would go down too well with the health conscious Crunch n Go CEO, and she got back to work.

At one minute to ten, she pushed her chair back and clasped her hands together, flexed her fingers. It felt good and she wondered how much money she'd get if she were to hit the company with an RSI suit. Or, even better, a personal liability suit on Attila. Annie gathered up the contract, marched over to her boss's office and rapped on the door.

"Entah."

She rolled her eyes. *Who did the woman think she was, the Queen of England?* "I have the Crunch n Go contract ready." Annie opened the door. As she stood in front of Attila's desk, she couldn't help but feel like she was back at school being raked over the coals by the headmistress for having her skirt too short or some such misdemeanour. Attila's glasses were perched at the end of her nose as she looked over the top of them to check her watch pointedly. Satisfied Annie had completed her task in the specified time frame, she took the proffered papers. "Don't disappear on me. I'm probably going to need you to make some more changes to this but in the meantime I'd like a coffee."

"Sure." Annie's teeth were gritted as she mentally added, *a please would be nice*.

"A proper coffee, not that weasel piss you usually make."

She turned on her heel before she could say something she'd regret. Annie marched out of the office and closed the door forcibly behind her the way she used to as a teenager so her mother was never sure whether it could be classed as a slam or not. She stomped past the other secretaries and pushed open the cafeteria door, relieved to find the room empty because she wasn't in the mood to make conversation.

I hate my job. She flicked the switch on the kettle before she bent down to fish Attila's special mug out of the cupboard. Actually, that wasn't true; she didn't hate her job. What she hated was working for that cow. *Oooh, someone had bought choccie biscuits.* The unopened packet next to the mugs distracted her. She grabbed it as her inner voice told her sternly, "You really shouldn't, Annie Rivers. Your skirt was feeling tight this morning, remember." To which she silently replied, "Get stuffed." Annie ripped open the packet. She instinctively knew that one wouldn't cut the mustard, not with the morning she was having. It was definitely a three biscuit day. *Oh, make it four.* She glanced over her shoulder to make sure no one was headed her way. Round it up; she'd always preferred even numbers. Satisfied the coast was clear, she bit into one and relished the sweetness for a moment as the chocolate melted on her tongue. She felt better already; it was true chocolate really did possess stress relief properties.

Attila was simply not human and that was all there was to it, she decided as she munched away. Before her arrival six months ago, when the mild-mannered and good-humoured Mel Humphries had left to go on a year's maternity leave, Annie had enjoyed her job. She and Mel had often lunched together or partaken of a Friday night tipple after they'd put in a hard week until Mel had gone and gotten pregnant. Yes, she used to arrive at work each morning with a spring in her step—okay, that was an exaggeration, but she had been happy enough.

There were worse firms around than Manning Stockyard, that was for sure, but these last few months she had been feeling... Annie paused with her teaspoon hovered in mid-air. *What had she been feeling?* She couldn't put a label on the unsettled sensation at the bottom of her stomach. It wasn't down to the four biscuits she had just snaffled either because it had happened before. Lately, it seemed to flare up more and more. She shook her head and decided not to delve too deeply into that one. Besides, she always got a bit antsy around this time of year. The fug that descended in the week leading up to Roz's birthday didn't just disappear; it hovered over her for days afterward. Telling herself that she knew better than to try to analyse this new feeling, she turned her attention instead to stirring the acrid brew you could stand a spoon up in. She was positive that it wasn't blood that flowed through her boss's veins but rather Nescafe.

While Attila was busy overdosing on caffeine and scouring the contract's fine print for typos, Annie decided she needed to distract herself. She wasn't in the mood to type or ring crusty old Mr Milner to change his appointment time; she'd do it later. No, she needed something non-work related, something positive to focus on. Remembering how she had mentioned to Kas that she and Tony needed to find a pastime they could share outside of the bedroom, she clicked online and ignored the pile of filing that laid forlornly at the bottom of her in-box. *I've got more important things to do than put that pile of old guff away.* She gave it a derisive glance before she turned her attention back to the computer screen. Her fingers hovered over the keys for a moment as she decided what she should Google before keying in *Top Sports for Couples.* She scrolled past the smattering of smutty ideas that popped up as a result of her search; she homed in on the site titled "The Top Five Sports for the couple who wants to stay together to play together" and clicked on it.

A loved up, attractive-looking couple that, as she peered closer at the screen she decided could pass for brother and sister, appeared on her screen. She noted they were both wielding golf clubs and looking pretty darn happy about it too. Golf—now that was something she hadn't thought about trying before. Would she have to wear a cap and plaid trousers like the lady in the picture? Deciding the sight of her in said outfit wouldn't do much for their relationship, she moved on. Next up was tennis; they'd been there and done that and nearly come to blows despite the cute white skirt. Table-tennis didn't get a mention and besides, that hadn't ended well either. Bowls got short shrift as being boring but skiing gave her pause for thought.

Annie chewed on her thumbnail and read the blurb eagerly about chasing each other down the slopes and following it up with hot toddies and goodness knows what else in front of a roaring fire. It did sound pretty tempting! But then her face fell as she remembered there was no snow on the slopes of the nearby Southern Alps at the moment. *That puts the kibosh on that one.* She crossed her fingers for number five. As she clicked on the arrow to the side of the picture, yet another laughing, deeply in love couple appeared but this time they bobbed about at sea in a kayak. Perfect!

Annie had not known until that moment that kayaking was something she'd always wanted to try but try it she would. Feeling more energised than she had in days, she picked up the phone to ring Tony.

ANNIE CHEWED HER SANDWICH as she sat hunched over down by the banks of the Avon and wished she had brought her jacket to work because Pervy Justin was right: it was a bit on the brisk side today. She mulled over the conversation she had with Tony before she left the office for lunch. He hadn't been impressed to hear her voice because he'd had his free hand down a toilet when she rang. In a thoroughly pissed-off voice, he informed her that his mother had drummed it into him and his brothers when they were growing up that the golden rule was always none for a wee and two for a poo. So why was it then that some kids felt the need to use a whole bloody roll, he'd demanded as though she held the answer to this great mystery of life. She hadn't thought that telling him *it was just one of the many perils of the world of plumbing* would be deemed a helpful answer and instead she'd tried to move the conversation along and around to what she was in fact ringing him for. "Tony, let's go kayaking this weekend."

Her blurted announcement had been met by silence except for a background sloshing noise and she hadn't gotten a chance to hear his thoughts on her proposal because at that moment Attila had flew towards her and waved the contract she had edited that morning like a whirling dervish. "Annie, what's this?"

"I've got to go. Talk to you tonight." She'd hung up just as the paper hit her desk. Highlighted in yellow was the sentence "*no but she's not a stick insect, just a complete cow.*"

It hadn't been the finest moment in her working career, Annie mused. She took another bite of her sandwich and eyeballed a duck as it waddled past her. She had a deep mistrust of ducks ever since one had nicked off with her Friday lunch treat, a souvlaki. She still cringed as she thought about the show she'd put on for her fellow alfresco riverside diners as she chased the greedy thing. She hadn't a chance of catching it, though, because it had made a break for the water and dragged her double chicken with extra chili along behind it. Snaffling the rest of her sarnie before any ducks could launch an attack, she pulled her mobile out of her pocket and contemplated ringing Tony again. No, on second thoughts, perhaps their impending kayaking expedition was a conversation best covered face to face. She popped her phone back in her bag. She swiped the crumbs off her lap before she got to her feet, slung her handbag over her shoulder and dragged her feet back to work.

Chapter Five

CARL NUDGED HER LEG with his knee under the table. "You didn't answer me." They were sitting opposite each other by the window inside the Lemongrass Diner. The popular Thai restaurant wasn't difficult to find, with its oversized gold Buddha perched on the roof outside that grinned away at the passing trade. Annie had arrived with ten minutes to spare; Carl hadn't been far behind her. At this hour of the day, there were only a handful of other patrons dotted about its dimly lit interior. The walls, she noticed as she glanced around, were decorated with a smattering of posters. There was one of elephants being ridden by local village men through the jungle, another of the Grand Palace, and a disturbing poster of tribal women with strange gold bangles wrapped around their necks that elongated them. *It did not look a very comfortable way of carrying on*, Annie thought and rubbed her own neck as their twin bowls of aromatic Pad Thai had arrived in record-breaking time.

She had been lost in thought about her and Tony's kayak outing that she had finally managed to talk him round to this coming Sunday as she savoured the pungent rice dish. Outside, the streetlights had come on and office workers, huddled into their coats, strode past in a hurry to get home. "Sorry, I was miles away. What did you say?"

"I asked if you've told Tones what we're up to tonight." At the expression on her face, Carl answered for her, "I can take that as a no then."

"I didn't see the point. I mean, I don't even know if I'll like the dress until I actually try it on."

"If you say so." Carl speared a piece of chicken with his fork. "Mmm, this is delish."

"It is. You will never guess what Tony and I are doing tomorrow?" She scooped up a forkful of fluffy, savoury rice.

Carl raised a questioning eyebrow. "Do I want to know?"

She put her fork down, leaned over the table and thumped him playfully. "Don't be rude. We're going kayaking."

Carl snorted. "Pardon?"

"Don't look so surprised! I can be outdoorsy from time to time, you know."

"The last time you did anything remotely outdoorsy was that team building bush walk your firm organised and"—he giggled—"when you dropped your drawers to go for a behind the bush wee, a bee stung you on your bum and it swelled up like a dinner plate. Ha-ha!" The giggle turned into a guffaw; the demure Thai waitress who was taking an order at the next table glanced over in alarm. Carl wasn't in the least perturbed as he carried on. "You said Tony kept calling you his girlfriend with three cheeks for days after!"

Annie wriggled on her seat at the uncomfortable memory he had just conjured. It was not her most dignified moment, having to present her swollen left cheek to her doctor for inspection, who desperately tried to keep a straight face as she relayed her tale of woe. "It wasn't funny—it was horrific and trust you to bring it up. What if I'd been allergic and gone into anaphylactic shock? Carl, stop laughing!" Once she was satisfied he had his breathing under control again, she said, "No, I've decided Tony and I need to find something we can do together and I've always wanted to try kayaking so—"

"I don't remember you ever having expressed a desire to kayak before."

She hadn't but Annie wasn't about to admit it. "Well, I have always wanted to and now finally I will get the chance."

Carl wasn't convinced and he raised a sceptical eyebrow. "Yes, well, I'll wait by the phone with bated breath to hear how it goes. Sorry, that was really snarky!" He patted her hand apologetically. "It's this business with David; it's upset my natural balance. So come on then, tell me more about this kayaking trip of yours."

Annie filled him in on how she'd managed to persuade Tony—only after threatening to show up down at the clubrooms after his next game in her leopard skin Onesie and matching slippers—that they should head out to Pegasus Town. There was a man-made lake at the subdivision there where they could hire a kayak for an hour or two's bonding as they bobbed about together on the water. Given her reluctance to wear anything else at home during the cooler months than the Onesie, Tony was easily convinced that she would indeed carry out her threat and so had acquiesced fairly quickly on the kayak front.

She ignored Carl's raucous laughter as she finished her explanation. She glanced at her watch, surprised to see it was already six fifteen. "Hey, we better eat up. I was hoping to get some dessert in."

"No dessert for you, young lady." Carl waggled his fork at her. "Not when you have a Julianne Tigre waiting for you to try on."

FIFTEEN MINUTES AFTER they'd gone Dutch on their dinner bill, Carl's dulcet tones rang out from the behind the shop-side counter of Modern Bride. "Have you died in there, sweetness? Because I am at risk of passing away of old age if you're much longer."

"No, I'm not ready yet. Hold your horses! It's not that easy getting into one of these things, you know."

"Does Madam require assistance?" That from haughty Amanda, who hovered like an annoying wasp by the next size up in the rack of dresses from which Annie had lovingly plucked her Julianne Tigre from.

"No, thank you, I am fine. I won't be a sec—*and you lot can shove your harps where the sun don't shine, too*," she hissed at the cherubs that gazed out at her from the wallpaper in a fitting room that was size wise on a par with her master bedroom. Its over-the-top Regency theme was at odds with the shop's namesake Modern Bride. She frowned as she prepared to suck in one last time, because nobody loved a quitter.

At last she wrested the zipper into place and exhaled slowly, relieved there was no sudden ripping sound. She paused in front of the mirror for a glimpse before she opened the door and did the big reveal. She blinked. *Oh my God—was it really her?* Unable to believe her own eyes, she blinked again as she registered the reflection that gazed back at her. *Yes, yes, alright so the dress was on the snug side*, she thought as she ran her hands down all that lovely soft satinyness. But all brides lost weight before their wedding due to the stress of organising it. Everybody knew that—it was a fact. Or at least she was fairly sure it was a fact. Aside from not being able to breathe, though, she and the dress—the combination of them both together—well, it was everything she had ever dreamed of.

This really was her princess moment but it wasn't a surprise. She'd known the moment she'd laid her eyes upon the swathe of ivory fabric on display in the shop window that it would be. She twirled slowly and became aware of an impatient foot that tapped outside the fitting room. With one last glimpse in the mirror over her shoulder, she called out, "Okay, I am ready, so shut your eyes!"

"She's ready—thank God for that!" Carl glanced over at Haughty Amanda, whose lips pursed as she raised her eyes heavenward and sent up a silent prayer that madam hadn't split the delicate seams of the satin.

Annie opened the door and glided out onto the shop floor. "Okay, you can open them now." Fully aware that Carl was peeping anyway, she smiled tremulously at him. "Well, what do you think?"

Carl clasped his hands steeple-like in front of his mouth as his eyes swept from her head to her toes but gave nothing away as she slowly twirled around.

Annie shifted awkwardly; her hands dropped back down to her sides. "Come on then, what do you think—do you like it?" She was surprised at how much it mattered to her that he approve.

Carl blinked rapidly.

"Don't cry."

He fanned his hand in front of his face in an effort to compose himself. "I can't help it. Oh, it's, Annie, it's—oh, you just look so—"

"What? What do I look? Spit it out!" Annie nearly shrieked, desperate for the verdict.

"Beautiful, exquisite, perfect—oh, I'd need a thesaurus to put all the adjectives to describe how you look into words—"

"It does rather become Madam, I must agree, although perhaps it is a little tight across the hips?" Haughty Amanda homed in to give the bodice a little tug where the fabric had wrinkled ever so slightly thanks to the snug fit. Annie was having none of it as she shied away from the older woman's hands.

"It's fine, truly. It fits me just fine." *Or it will once I drop the choccie biscuits at morning teatime*, she self-affirmed.

"Oh, I thought of some more: stunning, gorgeous, ethereal—" Carl continued to wax lyrical, "but—"

Annie lapped up all the adjectives until she froze. "But what?"

"It's just that—"

"It is not too tight like I told Haught—I mean Amanda here. It is NOT TOO TIGHT."

Carl held a hand up, well versed in his day-to-day dealings with models at calming a woman's potential histrionics. "No, no, sweets, of course it's not. It fits you like a glove. That's not it at all."

Annie placed a hand on her hip and looked at him searchingly. "Well, what is it then?"

"I don't know how to say this—"

Carl was not usually one to be lost for words or to beat around the bush. Her skin went goosy as she wondered what it was he struggled to tell her.

"Would you just say it please—whatever it is, I can take it, I promise." Annie lied.

"You're sure?"

"Of course I am sure. Good friends can be completely honest with each other." She lied again.

"I'm glad because you know how much I love you but I can't let you spend this kind of money on a dress, let alone go to the altar in good conscience, if I don't say my piece."

Haughty Amanda and Annie's breath was bated.

"Annie, my sweet, the dress is perfection—you are perfection—but the man you are planning on marrying is not right for you. I've gone along with things and humoured you where Tony is concerned but seeing you now in that dress, well, I am sorry, sweetie, it's a keeper—the fiancé is not." He swiped his brow, oblivious of the hurt that flashed across Annie's face as he added in a jokey tone, "There, I said it. That wasn't so bad, Carl, now was it." He registered the shock on her face as he looked at her and took a step towards her. Annie held her hands up as though to ward him off. "I'm sorry, sweetheart. I know I should have said something before but I got swept up in this—the trying on of the dress thing. I can't help it, though; I just love a bride." He attempted a feeble smile. "Besides, it can't be that much of a shock—you know how I feel about Tony."

That was true. He had never hidden his feelings about him from her nor had Tony made any secret of his dislike for Carl either for that matter. The feeling was mutual; there was no love lost between either of them. Still, she shook her head. "But I don't get it. You were asking me when we were going to set the date not long ago and telling me you had a suit that needed an airing and well, everything. I was going to get you to be my best man." She sniffed.

"Really, me? Your best man?" Carl looked like he would like to retract his earlier statement.

"Yes really."

He shifted on the balls of his feet and shoved the image of himself looking suave next to the blushing bride aside. "Oh, sweetie, I would dearly love to be your best man but not if I feel you are making a mistake. Besides which, you and I both know Tony would walk before he'd stand near me at the altar." He ran his fingers through his fringe. "Despite these enlightened times we now live in, liberal minded Tony is not and you know what else? Now that I am being honest, I suppose I never thought that the two of you would ever get round to making it formal. I thought you'd be one of those couples who'd stay engaged until one day you'd both wake up and well—break up. Seeing you here now in that gorgeous creation," he gestured at the dress, "well, it's brought it home to me that you are serious and I needed to tell you how I feel."

"I wish you hadn't."

"Oh, come on, darling, surely you don't see yourself spending the rest of your days with Macho Man?"

"Of course I do, otherwise I wouldn't have gotten engaged to him." Her bottom lip trembled. "And he is not macho—he is just a man's man, that's all."

Carl's expression grew petulant. "Well, I owe it to Roz not to let you make a monumental mistake." This was stated with a sanctimonious flourish that said he had made his point.

Roz's name was the red rag to the bull. "Don't you bring her into this! It's not as though she made sterling life choices, is it? And nobody made you my guardian either, thank you very much." Annie's face heated up, along with her temper, as her voice rose and the seams of the dress strained. "Besides, look at the state of your relationship—you're hardly in a position to be advising me on marriage!"

As soon as the words were out of her mouth, Annie regretted them. Hurt flickered over Carl's face. "Oh! I'm sorry, Carl. That wasn't called for."

Carl, however, was a world-class sulker and as his bottom lip jutted out, it seemed they'd reached a silent impasse.

Haughty Amanda's head stopped swinging back and forth as though she watched a particularly feisty game of tennis and her attention settled on Annie.

"Ahem, might I offer Madam some help getting out of the dress?" She was petrified this lull in bickering was the calm before the storm. A catfight while Madam was wearing a one-off, Julianne Tigre design she did not need, thank you very much!

"No thank you, I'll manage." Annie nearly tripped over the hem as she turned. Amanda gasped but Annie ignored her and flounced back into the dressing room. She locked the door and huffed over the fact that while she had apologised, she certainly wasn't going to grovel. Carl could just get over himself. She gave the cherubs a two-fingered salute before she unzipped.

When she came back out dressed in her civvies, Carl had gone.

Chapter Six

TO: KASSIA BIKAKIS

From: Annie Rivers

Subject: Why I am never drinking again and this time I mean it.

Hi Kas,

Okay, so I will start at the beginning. I made an appointment (it is a very posh place) to try the dress on at Modern Bride for last Thursday night and Carl and I arranged to meet up first for an early Thai dinner. I wanted him to come with me because I know that I can always count on him to be honest, except this time I got a bit more honesty than I bargained for, though I don't know why it came as such a shock. Remember that time I got my hair cut to shoulder length and he marched me back down to the salon and told the stylist to give me my money back because no woman should have to pay for the privilege of looking like a red-headed sheep who had encountered a stoned shearer? Sometimes it amazes me that we are still friends but then I know I can always count on him to never let me head out the door with my skirt tucked into my knickers or any other such fashion faux pas. Anyway, we had a nice meal—have you ever tried pad Thai? It is yummy and according to Carl doesn't have the bloating properties of an Indian curry. Do you even have Thai restaurants in Crete? After we had eaten, we headed to Modern Bride, which was only a couple of doors down from the restaurant, for my big moment.

Oh, Kas, it was perfect. Every gorgeous ivory inch of it was exactly what I dreamed my wedding dress would be. It was made for me, and Carl agreed, although the woman who owns the shop, Amanda (I have nicknamed her Haughty Amanda), kept insisting it was a bit tight around my middle—it wasn't. Anyway, back to Carl; what he doesn't agree with, he told me in no uncertain terms, is my choice of fiancé. He doesn't think we are right for each other and apparently has always assumed that eventually our relationship would run its course. He's been humouring me over the whole idea of getting married but the sight of me in an actual wedding dress made it clear to him that the time had come to say his piece where Tony is concerned. He didn't hold back and to cut a long story short, we had a fight.

Annie yawned and flexed her fingers as she tried to ignore the niggling kernel of guilt that she had yet to even tell Tony about the dress's existence. She'd made the excuse that she was working late the night she'd tried it on, not wanting to tell him what she was really up to. That was down to timing, though, she assured herself, because he hadn't been in the best of moods the night before thanks to a non-paying client. Interrupting his rant to inform him she was going for a wedding dress fitting the following evening and not just any old wedding dress either—oh no, this was a one-off Julianne Tigre no less—well, it hadn't seemed like the best of timing. Haughty Amanda hadn't mentioned the cost over the phone; she'd been too busy gushing at the simplistic beauty of the design—which reading between the lines meant the gown was hideously expensive—but well, she'd cross that bridge with Tony when she came to it. They could always pilfer a bit from the savings account because the way house prices had gone lately, buying their own home was a bit of a pipe dream anyway.

She decided not to dwell on the fact that they hadn't *actually* talked about the wedding since they had gotten slaughtered last New Year's Eve. They'd both been far too seedy in the light of day to think about guest lists, venues, menus, cars, flowers and the rest, so they hadn't pursued the conversation. Most terrifying of all, though, was the thought that were she to confess what she was really up to, Tony would insist she invite his mother along for the big try on instead of Carl and there was no way that was happening. Cripes, her Julianne Tigre dream dress would remain just that—a dream—and she'd wind up a ginger version of Pammy Anderson in her Tommy Lee days, kitted out in white thigh-high boots, leather mini skirt, and boob tube with matching veil!

She blinked, and willed the nightmare vision of Ngaire's mother of the groom, or whatever her official title would be, ensemble away and carried on typing.

We didn't talk all day Friday and I had a horrible day at work, thinking about what he had said, even though it is not true. Seeing as I had already apologised for the nasty remark I had made to Carl about him and David breaking up, I figured it was his turn to apologise to me. He caved at ten on Saturday morning and we agreed that where my fiancé is concerned, we will agree to disagree. We also decided that as we were both at a loose end Saturday night—him because he is single and me because Tony was going over to his brother's to watch the rugby—that we would go out for dinner to that Thai restaurant again. Like I said, the food was really good but unfortunately it wasn't just the food that was good; it was also the wine and by the time we left the restaurant, we both had our dancing shoes on. I tell you what, Kas, we cut some mean moves at one club to 'Summer Nights'—you know, that song from Grease? I was Olivia, of course, and Carl was John. We even got a standing ovation for our efforts! Cringe—why, oh why, do I do it? I blame Carl—he is a horrific influence on me.

Anyway, come Sunday morning, I had a sore head the likes of which I am sure Olivia Newton-John is far too wholesome to have ever suffered from and I was in trouble with Tony. I'd arranged, as part of my campaign to find a shared interest for us, to go kayaking together on Sunday at a nearby lake but as I was suffering from severe shrinkage of the brain, I was hoping to postpone our outing and just head to Burger King instead. There was no way Tony was going to let me off the hook, though, not even for a Whopper burger. Mostly because I'd made such a fuss about going in the first place. Oh, Kas, it was awful. I was green—lime green—and Tony kept barking at me to paddle when all I wanted to do was throw up over the side of the stupid excuse for a boat, curl up and have a little snooze. Honestly, when we got back to shore, I had sore arms, a churning tummy, pounding head, wet bum, and one pissed-off other half. So much for my little theory that doing an activity together would make us feel closer as a couple. Next week, he can bloody well bugger off to Speedway like he normally does with his brothers and leave me in peace.

Don't worry, though; we made it up on Monday night. That's the only bonus of falling out, I reckon—the make up sex, which, by the way, was pretty average. Therein lies phase two of my little plan to find things that Tony and I can do together. A shared hobby obviously isn't for us, so I am going to vamp things up in the bedroom department with a visit to a certain saucy shop (sex shop) on my lunch break tomorrow. Variety is the spice of life, so they say! Do you have shops like that in Crete and more to the point, have you ever been in one? I haven't but, oh well, there is a first time for everything.

Speaking of lunch breaks, they are the only bright spot in my workday week at the moment. Attila is still awful. Not much else to say on the subject, really.

Anyway, I am beginning to ramble, which means I need some sleep. I am sorry this email has been all me, me, me but you know you and your gorgeous family are always in my thoughts. Has Alexandros's little friend—the one in the birthday pic you said was on holiday from Ireland—gone home yet? Gosh, he is a fast worker, that one; shame he isn't quite so fast when it comes to actual work. Give the boys a kiss from their Kiwi aunty and tell Spiros I hope his writer's block has passed but, if not, I looked it up and read that a change of scene is a good way to cure it—tell him to go for a long walk or try writing in a different room. Bye for now.

Lots of Love, Annie

PS: Please don't let Mama see this letter. I don't want her knowing I have sex before marriage! Or that I frequent sex shops, either, which I don't—tomorrow is definitely a one-off!

Annie shut the laptop down and yawned before she scooped up a protesting Jasper. She popped him out the door and she tried not to feel guilty about the cold night air she sent him out into. "It's your own fault you have to go out, Jazz. You know that if you were a bit nicer to Tony, your life would be a lot easier." The cat turned a baleful yellow eye on her as he swivelled his body back around in the direction of the door. "No, don't even think about it! Off you go. Go and play with your friends—catch some mice together or something. It'll be fun. I'll see you in the morning." She shut the door before he could attempt his usual dash back into the warmth of the inner sanctum because the last time she had relented, the naughty tomcat had shot straight off to the bedroom and jumped on the slumbering Tony's head nearly giving him a heart attack.

Not much chance of a repeat performance of Monday night's rumpy-pumpy then. Annie glanced at her snoring fiancé as she pulled the bed cover back a few moments later and slipped in beside him. She snuggled down and closed her eyes but her mind was still on the Bikakis family. That's what happens when you sat up late typing emails, Annie thought as an image of Kassia flashed before her.

They had never met in the flesh, never talked on the telephone or Skyped each other. Kas always maintained that with the dodgy Internet at Eleni's, Skyping would be like trying to communicate with Mars and that when they did finally meet she wanted it to be face to face, not via a computer screen. Instead, they preferred to exchange photos and written words. Somehow there had never been the need to talk to each other over the phone because everything they needed to say they'd already said in their emails. Both women had agreed it was easier to open up and be honest when you wrote things down rather than trying to say them out loud. It was thanks to their letters that Annie felt they knew each other's lives inside and out, and while there might have been nine years between them, it had somehow never mattered.

A snore from Tony made her jump. Annie thumped her pillow and rolled over as she remembered how she had reached out with that first snail mail letter to Kas as a volatile eleven-year-old, her sister's death still raw. Kas, who had been shocked to hear what had happened to her pen pal, had written back straight away and it had been the beginning of a new friendship based around an old one.

Annie had grown up reading about Kas and her long-held romantic quest to find Mr Right, whom she eventually met in the form of Spiros Bikakis. She was thirty-four when they married, well and truly on the shelf by Greek standards, but she'd always maintained good things take time. She'd said the same thing when she'd finally gotten pregnant with Mateo, too. Annie smiled in the dark as she thought of how in the last email Kas had written that Mateo refused to use the toilet because he didn't like the flush but was quite happy to piddle in the geranium pot. This wouldn't have been a big issue if it weren't for its location on the veranda outside the hotel's breakfast room. Apparently he was happiest when he had an audience. On the bright side, she had written the geranium was thriving and added that it could have been worse, much worse.

A random thought intruded then; she really would have to talk to Tony about setting a date for their big day. She was glad she hadn't told Carl that she was yet to get around to discussing this, or anything else for that matter, with Tony. He didn't need any more ammunition. She might have made light of their falling out in her message to Kas but his words had gotten under her skin and unsettled her. Despite his apology, he hadn't taken back what he'd said but merely said, "I'm sorry, sweetie. I can give it out no problem; I just find it hard to take."

To clear her mind, Annie counted sheep. *One sheep, two sheep, three sheep—hmm, perhaps the right moment to bring the subject up would be after she'd injected a little va-va-voom into their bedroom—four sheep, five sheep...*

That night when she eventually dropped off to sleep, she dreamed unsettling dreams of sheep frolicking, not in paddocks but sex shops.

Chapter Seven

THE FLASHING NEON PINK sign for the Spice of Life was not as inconspicuous as Annie would have liked. Situated a ten-minute fast-paced trot from work at the edge of a busy mismatch of businesses that included a plus size fashion shop, café, hairdresser's, and Chinese takeaway, it, despite having a name that sounded like a Moroccan souk, still managed to scream to the innocent passer-by that inside was an Aladdin's cave of all things naughty but nice.

She wished she had worn a cap so she could pull it down low before executing a commando-style sweep of the street from left to right to ensure no familiar faces lurked nearby. Satisfied she didn't recognise any of the pedestrians pushing past her, she decided that the coast was clear and opened the door. She took a deep breath and reinforced to herself the message she had sent to Kas the night before: there's always a first time for everything.

It took a moment for her eyes to adjust to the dim lighting as she stepped in, but it took her a good minute longer to stop gawping at what she had initially thought was a model rocket ship on the centrepiece display. God, she was naïve, she realised, as it dawned on her that the pink monstrosity was most certainly not something invented by NASA. Her eyes flitted from one mind-boggling item to another and she shook her head in disbelief. What a sheltered life she had led. She frowned and leaned in for a nosy at what couldn't possibly be a bag of marbles—or could it? *What on earth were you supposed to do with those?*

"Good morning, madam. We have a great special on the orgasm balls this week if you're interested."

Annie's head spun exorcist fashion in the direction of the shop counter, where a woman of indiscriminate age with jet black hair and piercings in every visible orifice smirked over at her. She knew her discomfiture was coming off her in waves and that the woman didn't need to be an ace poker player to be able to read what her body language currently screamed: FIRST TIMER, FIRST TIMER! She flushed and quickly did a scan of the shop. There were only two other people perusing its wares. A nondescript woman in office attire rifled through a rack of leather bondagde gear. Who would have guessed? Annie thought as she spied a chap in a raincoat ogling a DVD. She glimpsed the cover, which featured a girl with a Kardashian proportioned bottom—yes, well, you didn't need to be Einstein to figure out he was a regular. Neither customer looked in the least bit perturbed by what they had just overheard the shop girl call out to her.

"The orgasm balls are fantastic for doing your Kegel exercises, you know. They come highly recommended, especially when you've had children." The woman looked pointedly at Annie's midriff.

Annie forgot to be perturbed at the assumption she'd had a baby in her haste to ask, "My *what* exercises?"

"YOUR WHAT EXERCISES?" Carl screeched, his arm linked through Annie's as they wandered down the street for an after-work drink that evening. The street lights had just come on and a pervasive onset of winter gloom settled in for the evening. Nothing could dampen Annie's spirits, though, not even her excruciating visit to a sex shop.

"Kegel exercises. Not having had children, *obviously,*" she patted her middle and Carl smirked, "I had never heard of them either but apparently they're akin to good old pelvic floor exercises, which I have heard of. And I shall do mine minus the marbles, thank you very much—special offer or no special offer!"

"So did you buy anything on this *CSI* mission of yours?"

Annie tapped the side of her nose. "That would be telling."

"Please don't tell me you bought a nurse's outfit." Carl turned and stared hard at her. "Oh my God, you did! *I know how to make you feel better, Mr Goodall.*" He put on a high-pitched falsetto.

A couple of passers-by turned to look at them curiously and Annie hit him lightly on the arm. "Shush and no, it's not a nurse's outfit." She hoped

Carl would leave it at that but she wasn't surprised when he stopped walking and hissed, "If you don't tell me, I shall buy you a stethoscope and call you Nurse Rivers everywhere we go. Try explaining that one, *Nurse Rivers*."

"Oh, alright, but promise me you won't laugh."

"I promise."

Annie knew he had his fingers crossed behind his back and she sighed. There was nothing else for it, because Carl was like a dog with a bone when he thought he was missing out on vital gossip. "It's a bunny outfit."

His eyes grew wide and then he let rip with an ungentlemanly snort before he curled his hands up in front of him like paws and did a little bunny hop. "Er, what's up, Doc?" He twitched his nose.

"Carl! You promised."

He showed her his hand and his crossed fingers. "I had them crossed."

"I knew it and that's exactly why I didn't want to tell you. Besides, it's not a bunny *rabbit* costume, you idiot—it's a Playboy Bunny outfit."

"Oh, thank God! For a moment, I was worried our Tones had some sort of carrot fetish but nevertheless I was right, insomuch as you will have a little pompom tail and ears." This time he just waggled his bottom. He put on his falsetto once more. "Would you like a drink, Mr Hefner?" His hand flew to his chest. "Oh my God, I just got a mental picture of Tony with a big cigar in a silk dressing gown."

Annie shot him a look. "Stop fixating on it just because you've shut up shop."

"That was a low blow."

"Yes, well, you asked for it. Anyway, let's move things along. Guess what happened when I left the shop?"

Carl forgot he was mortally offended as he turned all ears once more.

"I got busted by Pervy Justin who works in the accounts firm in my building."

"No! Oh, sweetheart, you didn't!"

"Yes, of all the people, and why do things like that always happen to me? Honestly, he just about walked into a lamppost in his excitement when he saw where I'd been."

"What did he say?"

"He raised an eyebrow and gave me that horrid slimy grin of his and asked if I'd been shopping. Honestly, Carl, he was bad enough before but now he's going to think I am some sort of nympho or deviant."

"Well, you are the only girl I know planning on dressing up as a bunny for her partner."

"Not helping!"

Carl grinned. "My advice?"

"Please."

"Play on it. Have a bit of fun with him, that's what I would do."

"You're terrible, Carl." Annie mimicked *Muriel's Wedding,* one of their top ten movies of all time, as they stood, arms linked, at the lights as they waited to cross the road. As the green man appeared, she filed away his advice nonetheless.

"So, have you put a deposit down on the dress?" Carl hedged as they crossed the road and the pub came into sight.

"No," she replied curtly. As she pushed open the door of the heaving Irish bar a few minutes later, she was glad of the loud music that assailed her ears. It was a welcome distraction; she didn't want to think about the fact the shine had dimmed a little where the dress was concerned because Carl had said things that really couldn't be unsaid.

"I WANT THIS LETTER on my desk in ten minutes, Annie. ANNIE!"

Annie blinked and came back to earth. Attila stood over her looking as if she suffered from a terrible bout of piles. Perhaps she was, Annie thought randomly; shingles could be bought on by stress—perhaps piles could be too. "Uh, I'm sorry, Adelia. I didn't catch that?"

There was a dramatic eye roll before the older woman repeated her request and banged a stack of papers she obviously wanted editing down on her desk. Ready to flounce off, she hovered on one heel with her eyes snakelike slits. "You know, your head is all over the place at the moment and you've been making some pretty silly mistakes of late."

For a moment, Annie thought she was going to be asked what the matter was, followed by a nice dose of afternoon tea and sympathy, but she should have known better.

"But, and I want to make myself very clear on this, whatever it is that is going on in your private life is nothing whatsoever to do with your working life. As a professional, I expect you to leave your problems at the door between the hours of nine am and five thirty pm, to focus on the job at hand! Do I make myself clear?"

Attila never made herself anything but clear. *Was this some sort of formal warning, though?* Annie nodded meekly. Either way, her boss's underlying message was very clear: shape up or ship out. She wouldn't cry, she determined as she blinked rapidly and flicked the birdy at her retreating back before she opened the letters folder on the computer. Trying to focus her attention on finding the one she needed to edit, she refused to glance over at gormless Sue, who she just knew was gawping at the drama of it all. In her current state, if she were to make eye contact with Toad of Toad Hall sitting across from her, she would likely swing for her and then she'd be in for far worse than a verbal warning.

What stung the most, though, was that she knew Attila was right. She *was* all over the place. What Carl had said about her and Tony being unsuited played over in her mind like a broken record despite her attempts to put his words aside. Evenings like the one she'd spent at home with Tony last night didn't help matters either. It had left her with that unsettled feeling in the pit of her stomach again, and not just because of the Indian takeaway they'd shared.

She'd come home after her glass of wine with Carl at O'Shea's Bar, pumped with grand plans for the bunny outfit. The wine had smoothed away the edges of inhibition but then Tony had texted her to say he'd had an emergency call-out and would be late. They'd agreed to get takeaway; he'd pick up Indian on his way home he told her. That's when she had stashed the bunny outfit in her drawers beneath a pile of jumpers. Indian was not conducive to romance and she wondered, not for the first time, how Tony could stomach a beef korma after some of the jobs he had to do. She'd never know, but he maintained it was his favourite. For some unspoken reason, they always got two containers of it instead of one of her favourite, mango chicken.

Was that what married life to Tony would be like? she'd wondered later as she chewed apathetically on her naan bread. They' watched a minor rugby game when she'd really rather watch a movie over on another channel. *Would it be one big compromise?* Although, the more she thought about it, their relationship wasn't based on compromise so much as capitulation on her part. She didn't think of herself as a weak person, so why did she let him get away with it? *Was she that frightened of being on her own?* Not wanting to deal with that question, she pushed it aside. In an attempt to clear her congested mind, she heaped another spoonful of the brown curry on top of her rice and wondered why this was all suddenly news to her anyway. She'd been living with Tony for the past six years, after all.

She blinked and the computer screen came back into focus. Annie turned her eyes away from the onscreen letter to flick them over the hard copy she held in her hand. As she looked at the myriad angry red squiggles, she wondered why it was the woman couldn't just use email like everyone else. She had a thing about keeping a paper trail and obviously no conscience when it came to the Amazonian rainforest. She'd obviously never read *The Lorax* as a kid either, she thought, with a sigh that came all the way from the bottom of her red boots as she got on with the job at hand.

She tapped on Attila's door half an hour later and placed the amended letter in the woman's outstretched hand. She didn't bother looking up from whatever it was she was so intently poring over and Annie was glad no further instructions were barked at her. She tiptoed out of the room, flopped back down into her chair and glanced over at her empty in-tray. Empty, except for the same stack of filing that she was so adept at ignoring. *Why change the habit of a lifetime then?* She flipped into her contacts, her mind made up to finish the email she had started to Kas before lunch.

I have this horrible sick feeling sitting in the pit of my stomach and it won't go away. The chocolate biscuits at morning teatime didn't help and my lunchtime Pilates class usually calms me down but all of that arm flapping in the Pilates 100's just peed me off today and I wanted to hit the teacher. I got a right telling-off from Attila when I got back to the office, too, which didn't help either. I know that I need to bite the bullet and talk to Tony about setting a date for our wedding—will you come by the way? I would absolutely love it if you could. But I am frightened of what he will say and then there are times like last night when I wonder if I even want to get married or if it is just something I think should come next. I guess all couples have moments like these before they take the plunge. Isn't it called pre-wedding jitters? Did you suffer from nerves before you married Spiros? I don't remember you mentioning it if you did. Though technically, the reason I am feeling like this can't be down to pre-wedding nerves because we haven't got further than the engagement ring.

So, Kas, I am in a state of misery at the moment and I am sorry my message is one of such doom and gloom. Some words of wisdom from my older and much wiser dear friend ASAP would be appreciated.

Lots of Love Annie

xox

The reply came through half an hour later as she half-heartedly tidied her desk drawer and counted down the last hour until home time. It was short and sweet, as befitted the ridiculously early hour her friend rose in Crete to help with Eleni's guests' breakfasts, but it was written in true Kassia style, straight to the point. Annie skimmed over the text, eager to read what she had written. A moment later, she leaned back in her chair, disappointed. Kas had told her that she needed to follow her heart and that despite Carl being unable to help himself at times, it was not for either of them to tell her what she should do. According to Kas, she needed to stop being frightened of change like Roz had been.

Follow her heart? That was easier said than done, thank you very much, Annie thought disgruntledly as she picked up the pile of papers in her in-tray and shuffled them around to look busy. She felt a pang, as she did every now and then, at the reference to Roz. Perhaps if she was still here and hadn't bloody well left her when she did, she'd know what she should do. That's what big sisters were supposed to be for, after all. The uneasy stirrings deep down in her stomach started up once more and Annie, determined to ignore them, got to her feet. She wandered over to the filing cabinets with a handful of old letters and half-heartedly attempted to locate the files from whence they'd come. As she did so, an idea took shape for the evening ahead and her mood buoyed.

Yes, she thought, narrowly missing trapping her fingers in the cabinet as she pushed it shut with renewed gusto and returned to her desk to grab another sheaf of papers; *tonight would be the night.* It was time she was proactive and took action! Moved things along. All this dillydallying would not do. It was confusing her when there was no need to be confused at all.

Tony was a man, after all. A man of simple needs who was not likely to come around to her way of thinking without her using her feminine wiles of persuasion. It had to be tonight because tomorrow Bear Grylls' *Man vs. Wild* was on the tele and Tony never missed an episode. His reckoning was that you never knew when some bit of information gleaned might stand them in good stead. Given that their idea of being in the wild was their annual summer camping holiday in Nelson, not the Northern Territory of Australia, Annie didn't think it likely they'd ever have to bite the head off a snake and drink its blood just to survive. Tonight, however, he might be doing a spot of wrestling with a woman in a bunny suit and she with a python. Well, python might be a stretch of the imagination, but either way it was time the bunny suit was unearthed from its woolly confines for an outing. A secretive smile played on her face as she flicked through the stack of 'T' files.

Chapter Eight

ANNIE'S EYES WERE WIDE open. Things hadn't exactly gone to plan, she thought as she lay in bed and listened to Tony's rhythmic breathing. Despite the humiliation the evening had wrought, she could still muster up irritation at the way he could always sleep no matter what had transpired prior to bedtime—be it a barney or a bonk. And it certainly hadn't been a bonk. She'd been doing such a good job of shaking her little bobtail around, too.

Oh, it wasn't bloody well fair! She rolled over again, this time onto her back. The curtains weren't shut properly and car lights snuck in through the crack between them. As she gazed up at the ceiling with its speckle of dancing lights, she was reminded of a 1970s disco, except the debauched goings-on at Studio 54 were a far cry from what was currently going on in her bedroom. As Tony emitted a tiny snore, she threw back the duvet cover in frustration. It was no good; her mind raced. She'd be better off making herself a drink and reading a book than just lying here getting more and more agitated by the fact she couldn't sleep. She shrugged into her dressing gown and slippers, and padded through to the kitchen to pop the kettle on.

The living room was still warm but she grabbed the throw rug off the side of the couch anyway and snuggled under it before she opened her book with her mug of tea at her side. She'd been enjoying the story so far. It was a bit of a bodice-ripper but tonight as the words swam in front of her eyes, she really couldn't care less what happened when Ava got home to find her philandering husband Gregory in bed with her best friend. She could write her own novel after what had happened to her tonight, although it would be far from a bodice-ripper. A sudden thud made her drop her book. She realised the source of the noise had come from outside, so she got up and pulled open the curtain, fairly certain she knew what was behind it.

Sure enough, an angry ginger face was squished up against the frosty window; one beady yellow eye glared back at her. She had to smile. Bloody Jazz didn't miss a beat. Oh well, it was his lucky night; he could come in for a bit because she was in need of a bit of a snuggle-up just as much as he was.

She scooped him up as he mewled his utter joy at being let back in. "Quiet down, you, if you want to stay in," she whispered and carried him back through into the lounge. She rearranged the blanket over herself, and she patted her lap. It was all the invitation he needed and he joyfully leaped onto his rightful place in the world before he began his kneading ritual. Having clawed his mistress satisfactorily, he stood up, turned around twice and flopped back down again, finally happy. Annie leaned down and kissed the top of his head. "You're a funny old thing, Jazz. I love you, you know that?"

He purred by way of reply.

"And I know you love me, too, but I am beginning to wonder if Daddy does."

Scratching behind the nonplussed cat's ears, her face grew hot at the memory of what had transpired earlier in the evening. It was a memory she knew had just gone straight to the number one spot on her top ten most embarrassing moments ever. "So Jazz," she whispered, "coming in at number ten is the time I tripped over on the steps on my way up to the stage to collect that stupid certificate in the fifth form." God, that had been excruciating at an age when maintaining one's cool was oh-so-important. "Number nine was the day I dived into the pool at swim sports and lost my top." The question still remained as to why she had opted to wear a bikini to school swim sports. In hindsight, Annie thought her sixteen-year-old self had been trying to impress Christopher Jenkins. Well, she had certainly managed to do that; in fact, she had been very popular with most of the lads at school for quite some time after that incident.

She stroked the purring cat's knobbly back and then to his chagrin paused as she cast her mind back to those agonising teenage years when everything was so new and raw. "Um, number eight would have to be when Mum dropped me off at my first ever party with Tessa Roche and then sat outside the house and honked until one of the boys came in and announced in front of everybody that my mum was still parked outside and that she wanted to see me. All she wanted was to tell me that Dad would pick me up at eleven pm sharp, but Jazz, it wasn't a good look. Still I can't blame her, really; she had more reason than most to be strict." The memory of that agonising eleventh birthday party Roz had crashed raised its head and she squashed it. It was far too horrible to be embarrassing and she swiftly moved her list along.

"At seven, we have choking on a cigarette down the back of the school field." She'd been desperately trying to impress the circle of so-called cool kids. "I am glad I didn't persevere with getting the hang of that, Jazz, and anyway, I should have known better. Let me see, oh yeah, next would have to be that awful haircut just before the sixth form prom." Annie's hand inadvertently flew up to check her hair was still there, the way it always did when she conjured up that haircut. She had thought her world was ending when she arrived home from the hairdressers the day before the dance with what amounted to a red afro. "I said a trim, Jazz, not a butcher, and I tell you what—if it was something we did in this country, I would have sued." She shook the memory away and decided to leave the teenage years in the past where they belonged.

"I think number five would be the time Tony and I went camping by Lake Brunner, and during the night I got bitten on the eye by a mosquito. I could hardly see out of it the next day and all our fellow campers spoke really slowly to me all day." She remembered how Tony had thought it was hysterical until one of the campers had squared up to him and pass remarked about it taking a weak man to hit a woman. After that, he'd refused to be seen with her unless she wore her sunglasses. "Number four is the day I asked a client when her baby was due and she told me she'd had him three months ago." The look on the woman's face still made Annie squirm; she'd felt terrible for days after and had learned a hard lesson.

"At number three, we have the time I got the roll of loo paper stuck to my shoe and trailed it right across the office and into a client meeting." Still, at least Mel had found it funny, even if the client hadn't. Annie smiled at the memory; had Attila been there, she would have spontaneously combusted. "Number two, of course, is swanning around the Rugby club on prize-giving night with my dress tucked into my knickers." She had not felt like a winner that night and her face still flamed at the memory despite three years having passed. These days she hardly ever frequented the clubrooms. It wasn't just due to the catcalls of "Hey, Annie, nice knickers!" she could pretty much guarantee getting from Tony's teammates. It was more that she felt disconnected from that whole scene. It was Tony's thing, not hers.

"And taking the prize at number one, Jazz, we have being busted by none other than Ngaire while wearing a Playboy Bunny outfit."

Jazz let out a tiny blissful sigh as Annie stroked him again. She'd had such grand plans, too, as she'd stood at the filing cabinet at work that afternoon and envisaged how the evening would play out.

She would dress up in her little outfit and surprise Tony when he arrived home from work. Keeping in character, she would offer him a drink and then run him a shower—if he'd been unblocking loos again, she didn't particularly want to canoodle until after he'd had a chance to clean up. Also, knowing Tony, she always got further with him on a full stomach so while he showered, she would rustle up his favourite meal. Steak, egg, and chips. She'd even cook the chips in the deep fryer the way he liked them instead of the lower fat version of oven baked chips she normally served up. Then, when he was totally relaxed with a proper drink in hand, and not a can of beer, as befitted the occasion, she'd bring up the subject of their wedding and when it was likely to happen. Later, of course, well, if he played his cards right...

Things had gotten off to a great start, too, with the gods being on her side for once as she drove home from work and struck every green light going on the way. It had meant she arrived home ten minutes earlier than normal. Plenty of time to make herself beautiful, she had thought as she unlocked the front door and headed straight for the bedroom with a spring in her step. She pulled the bunny outfit from its hiding place; she'd laid it out on the bed and scanned the room as though searching for hidden video cameras. Satisfied she would not one day find herself on *America's Funniest Home Videos* courtesy of Carl sending in footage, her gaze resettled on the tiny garment splayed out on the bed.

As she gave it the once-over, she frowned, suddenly unsure as to how she would squeeze into the bloody thing. It looked awfully small laid out as it was, almost Kylie-like in its proportions—and Miss Minogue she was definitely not. She hadn't wanted to try it on in the shop because she'd been in far too much of a hurry to get out of there. Now she regretted her haste.

She stripped off and gritted her teeth, reminding herself that if she set her mind to something, she could do it. Look at her Julianne Tigre dress—she'd managed to get into that, hadn't she?

Wriggling her goosy flesh into the satiny all-in-one strapless, corset-topped leotard, she also wished she had a heat pump in the bedroom. The one out in the hall was not sharing the love. With a deep breath in, she managed to wrest the side zipper into place without too much difficulty and exhaled. "Did it!" With her bow tie clipped into place, she turned her attention to the mirror and gave herself the once-over. "Right—first things first. You need to slap on some fake tan, my girl." She had some of that instant stuff in the bathroom, which was fortunate—otherwise Tony might think he had come home to an albino rabbit!

Swivelling around for the rear view, she looked over her shoulder at the little white pompom tail and giggled. Annie stuck her bottom out and gave it a waggle. Okay, so Hugh probably wouldn't give her a job unless she dropped a few pounds but all in all, she didn't look too bad—faintly ridiculous but not too bad. Now, though, it was time for the final touch and she opened her sweater drawer to produce the headband with its bobbing bunny ears. She placed it on her head and asked in her best breathy Marilyn Monroe voice, "Can I get you a drink, sir?" She wondered randomly whether Mr Hefner had ever had a red-headed bunny at the mansion before. Surely in these enlightened times they weren't all blondes? She fluffed her hair out, and cursed its stubborn curliness for the trillionth time.

Hoping she could keep in character and keep a straight face, she leaned into the mirror to make sure her cleavage was up to standard. It passed muster and rifling through her make-up bag, Annie vowed to pick up mascara next time she was at the supermarket because her current one was getting manky. She swept the wand over her lashes before fishing out her red lippy and, smacking her lips together when she finished applying it, she took a step back to admire her handiwork. Oh, she'd have to do; Tony would be home any minute. She heard his wagon pull up the driveway and took a deep breath.

"Surprise!" Like one of those girls popping out of a birthday cake, she had popped—not hopped—out of the bedroom and into the hallway as soon as she heard his key in the lock. Tony, having just that minute stepped in the door, was not expecting his very own Playboy Bunny to appear and his eyes were out on stalks as he dropped his work bag in shock. Annie spotted Ngaire bringing up the rear. As she peered around Tony's broad frame to see what had rendered him immobile, her face registered shock at the sight of her son's fiancée clad in next to nothing with bunny rabbit ears on top of her head at five forty-five on a Tuesday evening.

"What the fuck are you wearing?"

In a reflexive action, Ngaire slapped her son around the ear. "Don't swear."

Annie shut her mouth, turned, and raced back into the bedroom. She heard Tony say, "Was that a rabbit tail on her butt?"

Annie had leaned against the bedroom door, her hands pressed to her hot cheeks. "Oh my God, that did not just happen." Tony murmured to his mother in the hallway. She cursed and glanced down at her attire. It had been a stupid, stupid idea! What did she think she was doing? She wrestled her way free of the costume, and kicked it across the room before she slid into the safe fleecy confines of her onesie. She flopped down on the end of the bed to wait until the coast was clear. As she caught sight of herself in the mirror, she swore softly. She still had the damn rabbit ears on.

Tony had opened the door cautiously as, simultaneously, Annie heard a car start up outside the house. "I suppose your mother is off home to spread the word about what she saw tonight?" Not giving Tony a chance to answer, she got up and pushed past him. "And don't you say a word. I don't want to talk about it."

She'd still served up the steak for dinner—that wasn't going to go to waste. To be fair to Tony, he hadn't made a fuss about the long, curly red hair that had found its way into his egg white either, but he had snickered every now and then between mouthfuls. Annie refused to see the funny side of Ngaire catching her out. How was she to know she'd pick that evening to call in to pick up her stupid jacket? It had been sitting here for weeks, so why tonight of all nights? Because it was her rotten luck, that was why, and although she knew she would laugh about it one day, for the moment she needed to wallow in her humiliation. In the meantime, she knew how to wipe the smirk off Tony's face. Oh yes indeed; the time had come for her to broach the subject of marriage.

She'd begun with, "I think we are procrastinating, Tony." She'd leaned earnestly across the table towards him. "I mean, as your mother is always telling me, I am not getting any younger and well, I suppose I just don't know what we are waiting for anymore." Annie held her hand up before he could interrupt. "I know you say we should have our own home first but a wedding doesn't have to cost the earth. We could keep things simple and do it in a Registry Office with a low-key reception afterwards." She didn't add, *so long as she got to wear her beautiful Julianne Tigre dress, she didn't really care how she got that gold band on her finger*.

Tony had drained his beer and belched before he stated his case and Annie had tuned him out. There had been no need to listen; he'd said exactly what she had known he would say.

Now, snuggled under the blanket, she scratched behind Jasper's ear. "His excuse is that his mum would kill him if we got married in a Registry Office, Jazz. I reminded him that it is actually my day, not hers, but that didn't go down well. He lives in terror of that woman. Mind you, I do too, and... oh crap! I just remembered we have to go to dinner there tomorrow night." She sighed deeply. Jasper opened one weary eye at the stuffing escaping his cushion. "Oh well, I suppose I will have to face her sometime. Better to get it over and done with sooner rather than later." Annie pushed the picture of the bleached blonde harridan away. "Tony reckons we will be in our own home by the end of the year, if we tighten our belts a bit but do you know what I think?" Jasper didn't reply; he had overexerted himself by opening that one eye. "I think all that will happen then is, we will have a mortgage to pay and rates and insurances and all that stuff that goes with owning a house and Tony will have the perfect excuse to keep on stalling where a wedding is concerned." Annie sighed. "Do you know what else I realised tonight? We have never discussed kids. I mean, I am officially over thirty and I know that people are having their families later in life so I suppose I just assumed we would get married and then start a family. But we have never even talked about it apart from when we have been joking around about Ngaire wanting to hear the pitter-patter of tiny feet. I mean, after six years together, we have never got further in planning our future together than buying a flipping house! What does that say about us as a couple?"

Jasper just stretched and closed his eyes.

Chapter Nine

ANNIE WAS WOKEN BY the sound of the shower running and she stretched languidly for a moment, having forgotten about the events of the night before. She happily floated in that lovely warm abyss between sleep and wakefulness where the running water from the shower wasn't Tony going about his morning ablutions but rather the rushing flow of a waterfall on a tropical island. Then the water had gone off and a moment later Tony had banged back into the bedroom and issued a reminder to her that they were due at Ngaire and Doug's for six o'clock sharp that evening. He'd added that he'd meet her there as he had a big job on and it was way over the other side of town, before he slunk out the door, not giving her a chance to protest.

Wide awake now, Annie lay there for a moment and cursed because, despite her decision that facing the music was the best course of action last night, in the cold light of morning she really did not want to. If she had her way, they'd stay home so she could pursue the wedding conversation with Tony. She needed to chip away at his defences bit by bit, not head over to the Goodalls' place for scintillating chatter about car parts (Doug) or how shocking the amount the hairdresser charged these days was (Ngaire) followed by a meal of meat and three veg.

God help the woman, she would not be responsible for her actions if Ngaire mentioned what had occurred last night or brought up the subject of weddings, Annie vowed as she sat up and rubbed at her eyes. They felt scratchy like sandpaper but then, it had been after two am by the time she'd popped Jazz back out and crawled into bed next to the snoring Tony. He'd gone to bed with his nose well out of joint because she had refused to dress up in the bunny suit for a second time. She caught sight of herself in the dressing table mirror now and recoiled. *God, she looked a fright!* Her hair was all over the place, thanks to a night spent tossing and turning, and she had the pallor of an albino rabbit. *Enough of the rabbit references, Annie!* She then pondered whether she should call in sick. It wouldn't really be a lie because from where she sat, she certainly looked sick but then she realised that with Attila on the warpath, she'd probably demand she produce a doctor's certificate. *Nope, better not give her any more ammunition.* She tossed the duvet aside and padded towards the bathroom. A hot shower and a hot coffee in that order, followed by lashings of make-up, was the prescription needed.

By the time Annie stepped into the lift of the Albrecht building, she felt much improved. A glimpse at her reflection in the glass doors had confirmed she had re-joined the human race, even if she was still a bit pasty despite the promises of her new BB cream. She went even pastier as she spied who was sprinting for the lift. Pervy Justin forced the doors open with his shoulders and stepped into the little box with a smirk. "Phew, made it. You're looking well this morning, Annie."

If my boobs could talk, they'd tell you to piss off. Annie remembered what Carl had said; she smiled to herself and stood a little taller. "Good morning, Justin. Actually, I'm not feeling that great." She rolled her shoulder for effect. "I think I might have dislocated my shoulder using the whip last night."

As the lift door slid open at her floor, she snuck a sideways glance at Justin's gobsmacked face and felt marginally better. She'd have to phone Carl later and thank him for his advice.

"HOW WAS YOUR DAY AT work then, Annie?"

Annie forgot where she was momentarily as she opened her mouth, ready to tell Ngaire how she had a mouth ulcer on its way thanks to being on edge all the time where her boss was concerned. Today, for instance, Attila had called her in to her office and hauled her over the coals for not proofing an email before it went out. She really didn't think the fact she had accidentally left the letter *p* off a word was going to be a deal-breaker, despite it being a tad unfortunate that the word she'd made the boo-boo on was *pass*. Most people would see the funny side of it but not Attila, sitting there in all her immaculate glory, her hair back in its sleek chignon and black pinstriped suit under which she wore a crisp white blouse upon which a coffee stain would never dare deposit itself. She peered over the top of her glasses, lips pursed to reveals the lines of a smoker in a past life; it was obvious she had been born without a sense of humour or any human emotions, for that matter.

Annie had been oh-so close to telling the woman to shove her job, only in not such polite terms but then she'd realised as she stood there with steam pouring out of each ear that that would be letting her win. So, instead she'd taken a deep breath and remembered the look on Pervy Justin's face earlier that morning in an attempt to restore her good humour, before she muttered an apology. As Attila waved her out of the room, she'd closed the door behind her and mouthed the word "Bitch." *Why did she allow the woman to get away with making her feel so inept?* There was just something about all that immaculateness that made Annie, clad in her own business skirt and blouse with its tiny brown stain that refused to come out in the wash—not even with Napisan—feel like a scruffy little girl. It didn't help that her hair refused to stay put in the low pony she'd tied it back into that morning. Oh well, might as well behave like a child and go and raid the biscuit tin, she'd decided as she pulled the band out of her hair.

Annie realised Ngaire was more engrossed in a chip in her burgundy nail polish as she slouched over the kitchen side of the breakfast bar and studied her jewel-encrusted nails than in a long-winded reply, so she swallowed all of this back and shrugged. "Oh work's work. It was fine, thanks." Last night's debacle hovered between them. It was the elephant, or rather rabbit, in the room but Annie was not going to bring it up and so far Ngaire had not felt the need to either. She noticed that the usual skunk streak down her future mother-in-law's part wasn't visible. "Your hair looks nice, by the way. Have you had it done today?" Not that she was interested in hearing about how it was daylight robbery the way Gina charged like a wounded bull just to do her roots, but at least it would keep her off the subject of bunny outfits and weddings. Annie shifted on the hard bar stool and wished she were home, sprawled out on her own comfy couch instead, as Ngaire's tirade against her hairdresser began.

"If it wasn't for my regrowth, that woman wouldn't be swanning off to the Gold Coast tomorrow for the third time this year." With a pat to her new coif, she stood and stalked over to the oven. She bent low to prod at the lump of meat plonked in the middle of the roasting dish. Annie wished she had averted her eyes. *Why did Ngaire insist on wearing skirts that short and, if she had to, then why-oh-why couldn't she at least wear big knickers like every other woman her age?*

"Um, can I do anything to help?" Annie hopped off the stool to take her mind off what she had just seen.

"This isn't far off." She straightened up as she closed the oven door. "So you can test the spuds and if they're nearly done, put the peas and carrots on for me."

Annie dutifully took her place in front of the hob as Ngaire called out from the depths of the pantry, "But make sure you cook the vegetables properly. Last time we ate at your house, I nearly cracked a molar on that broccoli of yours."

As Annie poked her tongue out at her back, she heard the grumbly roar of Tony's Ford coming too fast up the driveway. She knew that within seconds, Doug would extract himself from his La-Z-Boy recliner in the lounge, flick the TV off, and head outside to check that all was well with his son's vehicle before they'd both head in, talking engines, sniffing the air appreciatively and looking to be fed.

It was going to be a long night. Annie stabbed the potatoes. A movement in the garden caught her eye. She wiped the steam off the window above the kitchen sink and spied Tony's youngest brother, Craig. What on earth was he doing crouched down on all fours like that? she wondered as he bunny-hopped across the grass.

TO: KASSIA BIKAKIS

From: Annie Rivers

Subject: The Bunny Incident

Hi Kas:

I told you in my last email that I was going to be visiting a certain kind of shop in the not so distant future and I did. Like I said, there is a first time for everything and there is also a last. Never again. The whole experience was rather surreal and a little disturbing. I never realised what a sheltered existence I have led until I saw what I thought was a display model rocket ship—I'll say no more other than the mind boggles as to what tickles people's fancy—it really does. I didn't leave empty-handed, though, and despite the shop girl's best efforts, I managed to keep things relatively tame but risqué enough for me, thank you very much, by purchasing a Playboy Bunny costume. Carl twisted my arm and found out what I'd bought and you can imagine the Bugs Bunny impression that followed, can't you? He thought the whole thing was hilarious and unfortunately for me, so did Tony and his family. My plan to razz things up between me and Tony kind of backfired when I jumped out at him in my costume. I was hoping to surprise him as he walked through the door from work, you know like one of those girls popping out of a cake? The thing was I surprised him and his mother, who happened to be with him.

Honestly, Kas, I was mortified but despite this, I followed through with my plan to pin Tony down to talk about our future wedding plans. I got the expected financial projection spiel so I have progressed no further. I did, however, glean satisfaction from withholding services last night by way of payback.

We had dinner at the Goodalls' tonight (I went under extreme duress) and I knew bloody Ngaire wouldn't be able to keep Bunny-gate to herself because I caught his younger brother doing a rabbit impersonation out in the garden for mine and everybody else's benefit. I hope you are not laughing, even if it is kind of funny. Do you know what else, though? I think Tony told his mother not to mention weddings because it's the first time in ages she hasn't brought it up at the first opportunity. Either that or she's finally given up on the idea. I have to say, Kas, that the thought of even Ngaire having given up the ghost where my big day is concerned makes me feel a little sad.

The late-night news was on the television and Jazz, who was curled up over on the couch, gave a contented mewl. Annie glanced over at him fondly. She couldn't help but wonder what was happening to her and Tony. They'd driven home from dinner in separate cars and to her it had seemed almost symbolic. Silly, she knew, when it was due to the fact they had arrived in their own vehicles but still it felt like the chasm that had opened up between them of late grew a little wider each day. When had they begun this slow drift with no particular destination in sight?

The anniversary of Roz's birthday had been and gone but she still felt out of kilter, as if the world had tipped on its axis slightly. Roz continued to lurk at the periphery of her mind instead of being tucked neatly back in the compartment of her brain where she was normally kept. She knew the way she was pushing the wedding idea when she was feeling so uncertain about—well, about everything really—was crazy. *Perhaps she was ill?* Annie frowned. Maybe this was what bipolar was like, up one minute, down the next. Maybe she should go to the doctor and tell her how she was feeling. The thought made her shudder; she had an aversion to the idea of medication. Or maybe it was more straightforward than a mental health problem. *What if Carl had been right in what he said to her that night at Modern Bride?* She couldn't help but wonder whether on some subconscious level she was pushing the wedding as a distraction to facing up to the fact that things weren't what they should be between her and Tony. That, and the fact that Kas had been right in what she had written in her last email about the idea of change absolutely terrifying her.

Annie pushed all these confusing thoughts aside and decided she'd sign off and, sending Kas and the rest of the Bikakis family her love, she pushed Send before she turned the laptop off. She saw there had been a derailed train somewhere or other and she switched the television off. The news was all doom and gloom anyway, and the mood she was in, she really couldn't handle watching other people's misery paraded out for all to see. She tucked the disgruntled tomcat under one arm before she headed towards the front door. The air outside signified a frost in the morning and she felt guilty as she sent him out into it. Still, she thought as she deposited him on the ground, he had a fur coat of sorts, even if it was a bit tatty. She shut the door before she could soften and change her mind.

Tony was still in the bathroom, she realised as she pushed open their bedroom door. They were finishing the day the way they'd started it. She pulled her flannelette pyjamas out from under her pillow. The water stopped. It was followed by the sound of him humming as he dried himself off. He was obviously in a good mood then, unlike herself. She had just fastened the top button of her PJ top when he appeared in the doorway with nothing but a towel wrapped around him. It wasn't his well-defined chest with its smattering of dark hair that she noticed as he stood there for a moment, but rather the clouds of steam that billowed down the hallway behind him. I wish he'd use the bloody extractor fan, ran through her mind as she pulled the covers of the bed back and clambered in. *It was no wonder they always got mould on the bathroom ceiling and it was a sod of a job to clean it off.*

She snuggled down, glad she'd had the foresight to put the electric blanket on. But then she caught the look of invitation in Tony's eyes as he dropped the towel and sauntered around to his side of the bed. She groaned inwardly. It was a look Annie knew all too well. He pushed himself up against her and she wriggled as close to the edge as she could go without actually toppling out of bed. Most nights she'd be in like Flynn, as eager as a beaver, or whatever those sayings were but not tonight. She just didn't feel like it. Too much swirled around her brain to make way for any pheromones or whatever a girl needed for a rev up. "Sorry, Tony, it's been a big day and I'm really tired." She was tempted to throw in the age-old excuse of *I've got a bit of a headache* too but decided that was probably overkill.

Apparently it wouldn't have been because Tony was not going to be put off that easily. He suggested with a waggle of his thick black eyebrows that she didn't have to expend much energy if she didn't want to and added that she could always lie back and think of England; he wouldn't mind.

"Oh, go tie a knot in it!" She gave him a half-hearted smile before she rolled over to kiss him a chaste goodnight. He homed in for the kill but she meant it. She really wasn't in the mood and so she pushed him off, said goodnight and moved back to the edge of the bed as she tucked the duvet around her to ward off the chilly night air.

Tony muttered something about her still being annoyed over Craig's antics and that she needed to lighten up a bit because it was only a joke. He was probably right, she thought reluctantly. She freed her hand from the duvet so she could reach over and flick off the bedside light. Just look at Ngaire's outfits—she looked as if she'd be far more at home serving up beers in some seedy bar for hardened bikers than living in suburban St Albans on the best of days. Her bunny outfit really wasn't that big a deal and so what if she had been caught out? Move on, Annie, she'd told herself, because if it had been anybody else on the receiving end of Craig's little joke, she would have found it as funny as the rest of the Goodall clan had. For some reason, though, it had stung and as she'd stood at the window with the pot full of potatoes threatening to boil over, she had tried very hard not to cry. She would not give Craig the satisfaction of knowing he had gotten to her. He had, though, and she didn't know why but it seemed to crystallise that things weren't going right between her and Tony, no matter how hard she tried to fix things. Lying in the dark, with her eyes wide open, she waited until he rolled away from her with a huffy sigh. One hot salty tear slid down her cheek.

Chapter Ten

"WHAT'S THAT?" TONY muttered. It took Annie a moment to realise someone had tapped on their front door.

"It's someone at the door, I think," she mumbled, still half asleep.

Tony grunted that was fairly obvious before he rolled out of bed to pull on a T-shirt and some pants. He drew the door behind him as he went to investigate and left Annie to slowly come to. She glanced over at the red digits of the clock on the bedside table; it was only ten past six. God, it had taken her forever to get off to sleep and when she had, she'd slept fitfully. Roz had starred in most of her dreams, which she hadn't done for a long time. She was the before Roz, beautiful and vibrant, and it was as though she was trying to tell her something. It was still a shock even now to wake up and realise it wasn't real and that her sister hadn't been with her for a long time. She wiped the sleep away from her eyes, and wondered who on earth would pop over at this time of the morning. As the realisation hit that it was far too early for a social call, her mind jolted into alert wakefulness.

What had happened? Something must have happened. As she swung her legs over the side of the bed, she flashed back to the earthquakes. There can't have been another big jolt; she would have woken up. Surely she hadn't gotten that complacent about them that they didn't even penetrate her sleep these days? She shrugged into her dressing gown and made her way down the hall. She could see Tony's outline silhouetted in the open front door. An icy shiver ran through her. Something was wrong; she could tell by the rigidity of his stance.

At her approach, he swung round and told her, in the brusque tone he usually saved for the boys under him at work, to go and sit in the lounge.

"What's going on?" Annie wrapped her arms tightly around herself as though trying to fend off the inevitable bad news she knew she was about to hear. Nobody knocked on the door before seven am with good news. The jumble of panicked thoughts swam through her head. If it wasn't an earthquake, then had something happened to her mum or dad or both of them? Had one of Tony's brothers been in a car accident? "Is everything okay?" Her voice quavered as she ignored Tony's instructions and pushed past him to see who stood in the doorway, fully expecting to see a police officer.

Her mind registered Campbell Bennett instead, a middle-aged family man who lived on the corner of their street. She hadn't seen him since they'd shovelled that horrid post-quake liquefaction off the pavement together after the last round of shakes. Now, though, she stared at him uncomprehendingly because instead of the tracksuit ensemble he had been wearing then, he was in a suit, obviously on his way to work. But what was he doing on their doorstep at this time of morning and why, instead of a shovel, was he holding something small and stiff wrapped in a towel? As the realisation of what it was he cradled dawned, Annie's knees buckled.

"I LOVED HIM, YOU KNOW, Carl? He was more than just a cat—he was my baby." Annie sniffed loudly and huddled further into the depths of her dressing gown, unable to summon the energy or the inclination to get dressed that morning. "I'm going to miss him so much."

"I know, sweetie. I'll miss him too. Jasper was a character right up there in the realms of Grumpy Cat." He sat next to her on the couch and draped his arm round her shoulder; he pulled her close and stroked the top of her head. "What was that story you told me about him getting his head stuck in a can of cat food that time?" Carl was very much a believer in the Irish wake theory whereby when somebody died you sat round and shared stories about their life. He was pleased to see it was working when Annie raised a watery smile at the memory.

"Oh yeah, I'd forgotten all about that. He could be such a little pig!" She had a sip on the cup of sugary coffee Carl had made her before she cleared her throat. "I'd given him his dinner but he wasn't happy with the new portion control regime the vet suggested I put him on, so he managed to nudge the empty tin of food out of the recycling bin. He got his head wedged inside it, trying to lick the bottom of it out. Honestly, Carl, you should have seen him wandering around the house smacking into things with this tin can stuck over his head. If I'd had a camera handy, I would have filmed it and sent it in to *Funniest Home Videos*. He looked like a tomcat version of Ned Kelly."

Carl laughed at the image conjured. "Remember your birthday dinner party?"

"When he licked the cream off my birthday Pavlova?" The cream-filled meringue dessert was Annie's favourite.

"Yes, I went to fetch it from the spare room where I'd hidden it away as a surprise and found bloody Jasper sitting on the bed with his face covered in cream looking like—"

Annie actually laughed now. "Don't say it—the cat that got the cream. I'd forgotten about that and you weren't laughing at the time—you were highly pissed, as I remember. He was naughty at times! You know, I remember this one time we were having a barbecue with Tony's family and we were all sitting out in the garden having a drink when this ginger streak ran past, dragging a meat tray behind him. Ngaire went berserk because it was the fillet steak she'd bought specially for 'her boys'. He had expensive tastes, that cat," she lamented, still laughing at the memories and then sobered once more as the realisation that he'd never taste fillet steak again dawned fresh. "Oh, Carl, how could someone hit him and then just leave him there on the side of the road like that?" She swiped angrily at her eyes, which had welled up again. "It's Tony's bloody fault. If he hadn't made me put him out at night..."

Carl reached for the box of tissues he'd had the good sense to bring round with him, along with a big box of chocolates. He'd omitted including alcohol in his care package, given his friend's current state and not wanting to be responsible for a maudlin wine drinking session. They would bypass that part of his Irish wake theory. He handed her a wad of tissues and waited until she had given her nose a good blow before he replied. "You know, people do some strange things when they get a fright, sweetheart. Who knows—perhaps they thought they'd hit a possum or something?"

"Possums aren't ginger." Annie wasn't going to be that easily appeased because whoever had done this to her Jazz was nothing short of a psychopath, in her opinion. She balled the soggy tissues and shoved them in her dressing gown pocket.

"Yes but it was dark when it happened and at least that nice neighbour of yours had the decency to bring the old boy home for you. You can't blame Tony either. It's not his fault some idiot ran into him. It's just a sad, sad accident, that's all."

Annie didn't reply. She wasn't ready to let go of her festering anger yet. She needed someone to aim and shoot it at, and right at the moment Tony was her target.

"Besides, he's done a lovely job of burying him for you, I'll give him that."

"Why are you suddenly his cheerleader?" Annie spluttered, fighting off angry tears. She didn't want Tony to be kind; she wanted him to be horrid and selfish so she could stay mad. It was true what Carl said, though; he had been thoughtful after Campbell had left. She'd been a mess when she'd realised what had happened and he had put a supporting arm around her, shepherded her into the lounge and settled her on the couch. He'd fetched a blanket out of the hall cupboard and draped it over her before he kneeled down to light the fire. When that was roaring, he'd gone through to the kitchen and made her a cup of tea; he even stirred an extra teaspoon of sugar into it before he phoned her work and left a message to say that she'd had a bereavement in the family and wouldn't be coming in that day. He'd had the sense not to mention it was her cat that had passed away because Annie didn't think that would wash well with Attila. She'd be the type of person who'd pull the wings off a butterfly for fun, so she'd hardly relate to the grief her employee felt over losing a pet.

Tony himself hadn't gone off to work first thing either, which was unheard of. Instead, he had waited until the garden centre down the road opened. At nine am on the dot, he'd hooned off down there and come back with a cherry tree sapling, along with a little plaque that now dangled off one of the sapling's spindly bare branches, beneath which Jasper was buried. It read: *You left paw prints on my heart.*

Next to the verse was a picture of a dog. It was all they had, Tony had told her with an apologetic shrug as he'd disappeared off into the garage in search of a spade. And yes, she knew the thought was there, so she'd said nothing as they'd stood out there on the dewy morning grass while he'd dug the hole.

She'd said nothing too when he placed Jasper, along with his favourite mouse toy, into the gaping earth and filled it in. At the sign of the first frost, the sapling would die too. Just like poor Jazz had.

Next to her now, Carl tightened his grip around her shoulder. "I'm not Tones' biggest fan. I'm the first to hold my hand up to that but I am fair and I like to give credit where credit is due. What he did this morning for Jasper and for you was sweet, really sweet." He frowned, or at least Annie guessed he frowned, as he pushed his long swishy fringe out of his eyes. "Perhaps I have underestimated him."

Annie didn't answer; her bottom lip trembled mutinously.

"Right then." Carl gave her shoulder one last squeeze and got to his feet. "I really hate to leave you like this, sweetie, but you do have chocolate, and I have one beanpole with attitude waiting for me to shoot her at Sumner Beach. So how about before I go, I run you a lovely warm bath with lots of bubbles for you to have a good old wallow in?"

"I'm not a hippo," Annie mumbled.

Carl ignored her. "Then when you get out, I want you to get dressed, put some make-up on because that always makes you feel better, and then as part of your grief therapy, I prescribe eating the whole box of chocolates while watching the trashiest daytime soap you can find. Plus, I am dying to know what happens when Olive finds out that Honey has slept with Ryder on *Under the Big Sky*, okay?"

His tone brooked no argument as he marched off in the direction of the bathroom.

ANNIE DID HAVE THE bath Carl ran for her and it was soothing to immerse herself in the soft, sweet smelling bubbles but it didn't change anything. Afterwards, once she'd towelled off, she had a cursory glance in the mirror. Her hair framed her face in a halo of red frizz and accentuated the fact she looked a red and white blotchy mess, with her nose swollen from being blown constantly. She didn't care. She felt like crap so it was only right she should look like crap and she had no intention of putting on make-up as Carl had suggested, even though he was probably right. As for eating chocolates, the very thought of tucking into the ginormous box sitting on her coffee table turned her stomach. And she really couldn't face *Under the Big Sky* or *The Bold and The Beautiful* or any other daytime TV offerings. Carl would just have to forever wonder what Olive did when she found out about Ryder's infidelity because, quite frankly, she did not give a damn.

Instead, she shrugged into her dressing gown and took herself off to the bedroom, where she flopped down on the bed and cuddled her pillow to her chest. A rose bush branch scraped against the window as outside the wind got up, the steady drizzle that had set in for the day befitting of her current grey mood. She felt alone, lonely, and as she closed her eyes for a moment, Annie tried to imagine the imprint of Jazz curled up in the crook of her legs the way he'd always done. He always seemed to sense when she wasn't well or was just in need of company. Cats knew when you were out of sorts. She was sure she had read somewhere about a cat that lived in a hospital and always went to lie on the beds of the people who needed him most. Jazz wasn't that selfless; he would never have curled up with Tony but he'd always been there for her.

The warmth of his body as he purred contentedly, happy at their daytime rendezvous, almost felt real to her now and she tried to hold onto the sensation. It slipped from her grasp because he wasn't there and would never be again. Annie opened her eyes and for a moment she stared unseeingly at the wall until, like a camera being tweaked, the print of Santorini came into focus.

She let its scene wash over her. It never failed to make her wonder at the beauty of the place; even now, feeling the way she did, the island's tumble of white buildings gave her pause. She pulled herself up into a sitting position, knees to her chest and arms wrapped around them. It had just dawned on her that she finally saw what Roz had seen when she looked at it. Not some mass-produced print that had probably hung on hundreds of bathroom walls when the blue and white Greek look was last all the go, but rather the dream of anything being possible. Surely the world couldn't be anything but your oyster once you had set your eyes upon such a vista?

The volcanic rock that was home to Santorini had held a special kind of allure that had entranced Roz. It was at the thought of her sister that another wave of sadness broke over Annie. All the things she could have been, should have been, and what she might have done with her life had she chosen a different path swirled in front of her mingling with the anger that always lay beneath the surface—her gorgeous big sister. She gripped her knees tighter; she knew she had to push these thoughts aside or they would wash her away like a shanty hut in a tsunami. She chewed her bottom lip, and forced herself to look straight ahead at the dressing table mirror, almost not recognising the girl who peered back at her from under the tangled hair.

"You only get one shot at it, this life business," she whispered to the wan reflection. She knew this better than most. So what was she doing with hers? She had a job she no longer enjoyed thanks to the complete cow she worked for. Her relationship seemed to be on a fast track to absolutely nowhere. And to top it all off, her beloved cat had just died. That book that had been all the rage a few years ago sprang to mind—what was it called? She frowned. *Eat, Pray, Love*—that was the one. She hadn't read it but she had seen the movie and as she stared into the mirror at a person she did not want to be, she realised that just like Julia Roberts in the movie, she too had just hurtled to a stop in front of the 'what's next' crossroads of life.

In all honesty, she knew she shouldn't be so shell-shocked. This intersection had been heading towards her, like the train she'd seen derailed on the news last night, for a long time now. Somehow she'd managed to ignore it and keep things on the tracks. Mostly by burying her head in the sand and distracting herself with this farcical idea of getting married. Now, though, with Jazz's passing, everything had finally imploded. She'd hit the wall and it was time she faced up to what it was she was going to do next.

"Do I want to go to Italy and eat pizza like Julia did?" she asked her reflection. She thought that didn't sound too bad because she was rather partial to a margherita. Then again, she didn't fancy having to buy the inevitable big-sized jeans that would come with all that pizza snaffling. What about Bali then? She could find someone new to have a torrid fling with. Definitely a better option for her figure but she really wasn't in the mood to expend all that energy and the way she was feeling had nothing to do with needing to find a new man. She needed to find herself. God, she hated that phrase; it was so self-indulgent but it was also true. So would a meditative retreat in India do the trick then? Annie shuddered. She'd probably get the trots the entire time she was there and from what she'd read about the country's sanitation in parts, well, that wouldn't be much fun. Besides which, she thought with a rueful glance at her hair, she'd have a permanent ginger afro, what with the country's hot and humid conditions.

She did want more than the square she found herself boxed into at the moment, though. Of that much she was certain. Her green eyes moved back to the print. She stared at it for so long that she felt almost hypnotised by the clarity of those white buildings and the seemingly endless blue. It was at that precise moment that Annie felt an all-encompassing urge to watch a movie. Not just any movie; it was one she hadn't seen in a long, long time. It had been one of Roz's favourites.

She got up and re-knotted her dressing gown around her waist before she padded through to the living room. The fire had almost gone out so she crouched down to toss a dry bit of kindling on to it and waited for it to reignite. Once she had it blazing, she opened the TV cabinet and scanned the rows of DVDs. No, she thought fingering the box set of *Rocky*. She didn't want to watch those. She'd bought it for Tony; he was a fan and she always knew when he'd been bingeing on the old Stallone boxing classics because he would engage in a lot of air punching with a bandana tied round his head afterwards. *Ah, there it was.* She spotted it next to *Dirty Dancing* and felt a frisson of sadness that Patrick was no longer with them either as she pulled out *Shirley Valentine*.

The movie had been before her time but she could recall Roz watching it and their mother had loved it. Of course, back then it had been on video and now she was glad she'd had the foresight to buy the DVD version in a sentimental moment at the shops. It was the story of the middle-aged Shirley, a repressed housewife who leaves her husband for an impromptu holiday to the Greek islands and then decides to stay. The way Shirley falls in love with both a different life on the island and with herself again, had gone over the young Annie's head. She was surprised Roz, at the age she had been, had enjoyed the film as much as she had but then the scenery was spectacular and the actress, Pauline Collins, played her part wonderfully. She blew the dust off the cover and then slid the disc into the machine. She settled herself under the blanket on the couch and pushed play.

Once it had finished, Annie sat in the darkening room and thought about the underlying story and how brave Shirley had been. She had thrown caution to the wind and found happiness—and not thanks to a man, either. Oh, sure there was the scene with Tom Conti on the boat where he woos her with his bad English but that had more to do with Shirley experiencing life first-hand again than her wanting a romance.

Outside, the familiar jingle of Mr Whippy's ice cream truck sounded. It was awfully cold for ice cream, she thought but then raised a rueful smile. *When as a child had she ever thought it was too cold for ice cream?* If the van was parked out on the street now, it must mean it was after three o'clock and the children were home from school. It was funny how certain sounds could instantly transport you back in time. She remembered how her dad had headed to the front gate many years ago, intent upon getting her a treat that hot summer's afternoon only to find that the van had moved on. He had been almost manic in his need to find Mr Whippy, as though by doing so he would somehow fix things. All but shouting at Annie to get in the car, they'd driven off in search of the white ice cream truck. They never did find it. The bells always sounded somewhere in the distance. It had been like one of those dreams where you fell but never quite got to the bottom. In the end, he had taken her to the corner dairy and she had been allowed to choose an expensive ice cream—any sort she wanted. That had been a treat indeed. As she raised a smile at the memory, Annie noticed a warm sensation tickle the tips of her toes, as though she had just waved them in front of a fire. She pulled her sock-clad feet out from under the blanket and stared at them, bewildered.

They definitely felt warm. She wriggled them and the perception of heat slowly spread farther up her foot, past her ankle and moved up into her calves. Her thighs, splayed on the couch, felt the warmth next and then it continued to progress steadily into her stomach and filled it like a hot air balloon. Up, up it seeped into her chest, her neck. A flush crept over her face and as the heat reached the top of her head, her scalp tingled. It was as though she'd been standing outside in the snow before coming inside and plunging herself straight into a hot bath. The strange warmth brought with it a sense of calm. Annie's breath slowed as she sat immobilised on the couch.

"Is that you, Roz?" She didn't know why she asked because she already knew the answer and she didn't expect a reply. She got none either, apart from the hiss of spitting wood in the fireplace. The warmth intensified, though, to the point that had she been in her late forties, she would be fairly certain she was experiencing her first hot flush. Once more, Annie was filled with an overpowering urge and so, following what her mind screamed at her to do, she hauled herself off the couch and found herself back in her bedroom. Her eyes fixed once more on the print of Santorini as understanding dawned as to why Roz had come to her now, after all this time, when she had needed her so often in the past. She was finally doing what a big sister should do. She was steering her in the right direction, to show her the right path to take. Annie knew exactly what she had to do.

"Okay, I'll do it," she said to the empty room. "For me and for you and for Shirley bloody Valentine, I'll do it."

Chapter Eleven

THE AFTERNOON OF HER epiphany, as Annie had come to think of what she was convinced had been a visit from Roz, she had thrown on her clothes, snatched up her car keys and headed straight down to her local travel agent, oblivious of the fact she had mismatched shoes on.

As she sat down in the window seat of Flights R Us, she looked out to the busy street to see a wild woman staring back at her from the reflection in the glass. Car lights sluiced their way forward as they crawled along through the puddles on the road outside. It really was a miserable day. She turned back; the pasty, stick-thin couple booking a holiday to Samoa were still deep in conversation with the only agent at her desk. It must be afternoon teatime. She couldn't blame the couple for wanting to escape to sunnier climes; she just wished they would get a bloody move on. Eyeing them, she wondered whether with Air Samoa's new weight policies they might actually garner some cash back on their tickets. Either way, they didn't look like they'd be vacating their seats in the next few minutes so, with a sigh, she dug her phone out of her bag. She was bursting with the need to confide her crazy plan to Carl.

He sounded a long way away as he answered and informed her that the weather was diabolical and that he had pulled the pin on the shoot. Why the powers that be would organise a bikini shoot at the beach in Canterbury at this time of the year was beyond him, he muttered. "Honestly, sweets, Sabine looks like an underfed turkey with all those goosebumps, which is not a good look when you are trying to sell swimwear and not cranberry sauce." She heard his car door slam. "Phew, that's better. Hang on a sec—just let me put the heater on."

After a load of background rustling, he came back on the line. "Right—all sorted. I'm all yours. Now then, have you rung to tell me you are ensconced on the couch in front of the tele with a half-eaten box of chocolates on your lap like I prescribed?"

"Um, no, not exactly. Actually, Carl, I'm at the travel agent's."

As she relayed her plans, his voice shrieked down the phone, "Okay, stop right there!"

Even Mr and Mrs We'd Like to go to Samoa Please turned round to see what the squawking was about. She held the phone away from her ear and shot them an apologetic grin. She listened while he ordered her to leave the shop and head across the road to Coffee Culture immediately.

"Give me fifteen minutes, Annie, and don't you dare do anything until I get there!"

Fully expecting him to try to talk her out of what she planned, she'd nevertheless done as he had bidden. She slung her bag across her shoulder and told the perplexed travel agent she'd be back shortly. She ducked her head down to brave the weather and made her way the short distance across the road to where the coffee shop stood out like a lighthouse beacon on a stormy day.

Annie ordered her drink, picked up a magazine to read while she waited, and slid into a booth seat. She didn't want to think about all the things Carl was going to come up with in order to talk her out of what she was determined to do. No, she decided, she would deal with it when he arrived. She flipped open the magazine to lose herself in the latest celebrity misdeeds instead.

"Right, now, my sweet, what on earth is going on and what is all this poppycock about you going to Greece?"

Annie looked up, startled, from the article about Miranda Kerr's post-baby bikini body—honestly, the woman would make you sick—as Carl placed his order marker down on the table with a bang. She watched warily as he shrugged out of his coat, flopped down opposite her and ran his fingers through his fringe in that oh-so familiar mannerism of his. It swished back artfully and she wondered why his hair never misbehaved in wet weather. She didn't wonder for long because it was straight down to business as he stared hard across the table at her, one brow arched as he waited for an explanation as to why he would never find out what had happened today on *Under the Big Sky*.

Unable to meet his gaze, Annie fiddled with a sugar sachet as she explained, as best she could, what had transpired that afternoon. She knew she sounded deranged.

"Honestly, Carl, it was so strange. This warmth—I've never felt anything like it before. Roz was there with me, I'm sure of it. It was like the fogginess around everything I have been doing lately cleared because all of a sudden I knew exactly what it is I am supposed to do next and it doesn't involve splurging on a designer wedding dress." She noticed Carl's sceptical look and looked away quickly. She couldn't blame him; she did sound potty. "Oh, I know what this must sound like but that's the only way I can describe what happened." She shrugged and, with a sip of her coffee, waited to hear what he would have to say. Plenty, she was sure.

To her bemusement, he slowly stirred his latte, deep in thought. He picked up the chocolate-coated coffee bean on the side of the saucer, popped it into his mouth and chewed for a moment. "First off, let me just say thank goodness you have seen the light regarding getting married."

Annie pulled a face at him but he was too busy trying to make sense of what she had just told him to register it.

"Next, I want to get this straight in my mind. So there you are, sitting on your bed, grief stricken after losing your beloved cat, when suddenly you get this overwhelming urge to watch *Shirley Valentine*. A great movie, I'll concede. Pauline Collins is superb and the end bit where she gets her table moved to the water's edge so she can enjoy her wine while the sun sets should make movie history."

Annie nodded her agreement. It was both an empowering and poignant moment in the film and she'd read somewhere that the beach on the island of Mykonos where the scene was filmed was now referred to as the Shirley Valentine beach. Carl bought her back from Mykonos to Coffee Culture as he carried on intoning.

"After which, you receive a celestial visit from Roz, who guides you back to your room, whereupon you find yourself gazing at the print of Santorini, and filled with a conviction that you need to go to Greece?"

"Yes, Your Honour, that's what happened."

"Right so, on that basis, you get yourself dressed—and what is with the blue sneaker and the white Skecher, by the way? You then drove down to

Flight's R Us, where you planned on booking yourself a one-way ticket to Athens without consulting your best friend, fiancé, or family. Have I got that right?"

Annie looked up from where she stared at her mismatched shoes in bewilderment. *She really had been running on autopilot.* Then, feeling as if she had just taken the witness stand, she returned his gaze steadily. She was determined to make herself heard loud and clear. "Like I said, I know it sounds mad but yes, that is what happened and yes, that is what I am going to do as soon as we have finished our coffees. You know I love you but please don't waste your breath trying to talk me out of going because I have made up my mind."

"Alright then." Carl sat back in his seat. "What about Tony? I take it you haven't had time to talk to him yet?"

Annie wriggled in her seat uncomfortably at the mention of Tony. "I'll tell him what I'm doing as soon as he gets in from work tonight and then I'll head over to Mum and Dad's for the night to let him digest it."

Carl shook his head. "Don't be silly. Come and stay at mine because I can guarantee your folks will need time to digest this crazy plan of yours, too. And it is crazy, you know that, Annie, because it was only a week or so ago that you were squeezing yourself into a wedding dress."

"I didn't have to squeeze, thank you very much, and what was it you said to me that night about Tony?"

"Since when did you actually listen to what I say?" Carl shot back.

Annie poked her tongue out at him. "As hard as it is for me to say this, I think you may have been right. The kayaking, the bunny outfit—they were all sticking plasters I was applying to try to cover up that we weren't all that happy." She rearranged the sachets of sweetener before she added, "As for suddenly wanting to set a date, I think I might have been using the idea of getting married as a way of distracting myself from what was really wrong."

"Yes, well, I suppose I can see how a nice big diamond ring and a Julianne Tigre wedding dress might provide you with a happy distraction in the short term." His eyes rested on Annie's hand, where her ring sparkled defiantly. "You'll have to give that back, you know."

"I know and it's fine—it will all be fine." At that moment, as she watched the young waitress scurry past, balancing empty cups and saucers, Annie wasn't sure who she was trying to convince—herself or Carl.

"Honestly, sweetheart, I can't quite believe that you've just told me that you are leaving Tony and well..." He gave a shoulder-padded shrug. "Everything, really—your friends, your family, your job—to flee to Greece. Why?"

Annie reached across the table and rested her hand on top of Carl's. "I told you why and it's been coming for a while now. I've been ignoring my unhappiness because to change things would be hard. I didn't have the energy for hard and I was scared."

"What and now suddenly you're not and you're fizzing like you have overdosed on a can of V?"

"Yeah, kind of, except you know I don't do energy drinks. Tony and I have been drifting in different directions for a while now and with all the crap at work—well, it's been weighing me down. Now that I have made the decision to do something about it all, it's like this ginormous weight has suddenly lifted and I feel all sort of bubbly—almost buoyant." Annie gave him a little half-smile.

"Are you sure that's not just wind? And we'd all feel light and free if we decided to cast off our responsibilities and just bugger off but, my lovely girl, sadly, real life comes with a duty to others."

"That's not fair because I'm not being selfish, Carl." She caught his raised brow. "No, I'm not! If I stayed with Tony for the sake of it being the easier path to take, then that would be selfish. I'm giving him a way out because he doesn't want to marry me either."

"I'm not suggesting you stay with Tony. Break it off by all means but why the midnight flit? I hope it's not down to what's happened to Jasper because you know I read somewhere that you shouldn't do anything rash when you're in the grieving process."

"This is something I would have come round to doing eventually, anyway. Jazz's death probably just brought it all to the fore a bit sooner, that's all. It's something I have to do." She softened her tone. "Can you understand?"

"No."

Annie drained her coffee. It was nearly cold and this time Carl twiddled with the little packets of sugar before he muttered, "Well, go easy on the poor sod, alright? Because he won't see this coming."

"Of course I will. Anyway, I don't think my leaving is what's really going to upset him. Nope, once he gets over the initial shock, it will be the handing over of my half of our house deposit he'll really struggle with."

A flicker of amusement crossed Carl's face. "Ah, so that's what's going to fund this mad jaunt of yours?"

"Yes and it's not a mad jaunt; it is an adventure. An exciting and long overdue adventure of throwing caution to the wind. Think of it, Carl! I'm going to sit on the stone steps of the Herodes Atticus Theatre and listen to *Aria* on my iPod and I am going to wander the ruins of the Acropolis. I'm going to watch the sunset in Santorini. I'm going to—"

"What about your job?" Carl interrupted her reverie.

Annie crashed back down to earth. "Huh? What about it? It's not as though I'm resigning from my dream job, so no, that will be one bridge I'll enjoy crossing. I can't wait to see the look on Attila's face when I tell her to stick her job where the sun don't shine."

Carl pursed his lips as he fished around for objections. "Okay then, Kassia. What do you think she will make of you coming to Greece out of the blue like this? It's one thing being friends with someone via letters and email for all these years but to land on her doorstep?"

Annie's stomach did a flip-flop. She was scared as to how this trip was going to pan out but she bit her lip and injected bravado into her voice. "I hope she will be as excited at the thought of finally meeting face to face as I am and if things don't work out the way I am sure they will, well then I'll move on. I'll pick up casual work and island hop." *Island hop—yes, that's what she would do.* Annie liked the phrase and she rolled it around silently in her head a couple of times for good measure before she picked up her teaspoon and scraped the froth from the sides of her cup. Satisfied she'd gotten as much of it as she could, she put the cup back in its saucer and slid along the booth seat before she got to her feet. She gave her footwear another doleful glance before she turned her attention back to Carl. "I'd really like you to support me on this because I'm going to need you."

Carl stood and looked at her for a moment before he picked up his coat and shrugged back into it. "Yes, you are going to need me, and I'm glad because I'm going to come too."

"What?" If she'd been holding something, Annie would have dropped it as her hand shot out to grab the table for support.

A pleased with himself smile played at the corner of Carl's mouth. "See? You're not the only one who can drop bombshells. And do you really think I'd let you trot off and have the trip of a lifetime without me?"

Chapter Twelve

ANNIE'S HEAD HAD BEEN buzzing by the time she got home from the travel agent's. Her plans had acted as a temporary salve to her grief over losing Jazz but as she waited for Tony to come home, her eyes had strayed outside. Through the veil of misty rain, she could see the cherry blossom wavering on the wind. It looked so fragile and forlorn as it braved the elements, that her eyes had welled up again. It had been a sweet and thoughtful gesture on Tony's part and look how she was about to repay it. By the time the front door banged shut and signalled his arrival home, she had no fingernails left and her stomach was in knots.

You are doing the right thing, Annie reaffirmed silently. She closed her eyes for a moment and tensed as he came up behind where she sat at the kitchen table nursing a glass of wine. He planted his customary kiss on the top of her head before he grabbed a beer out of the fridge. Annie stared at his broad, familiar back. The easy option would have been to write a note for him to digest at his own pace while she camped out at Carl's but it would also have been cowardly. She couldn't do that to him, no matter how tempting. She was hopeless at confrontation but she didn't have a choice; she'd just have to brazen it out.

Her hands had been clasped in her lap, her nails dug into her palms when Tony sat down opposite her. He'd looked at her quizzically for a moment as he pulled the tab on his beer and she'd launched straight into what she had rehearsed since she had booked the tickets, before she lost her nerve. The words tripped off her tongue in a nervous jumble and all the while, Tony had sat with his beer untouched as he stared at her uncomprehendingly and tried to make sense out of what she said.

As she slipped the ring off her finger and slid it across the table to him, he finally seemed to get it. She was leaving—it was over—and then the disbelief turned into anger as he accused her of having someone else on the go. He'd looked like a stranger as he demanded to know how long it had been going on and why in the hell she was going to Greece, of all places.

Her tears hadn't garnered sympathy as she tried to explain, without going into what had triggered her decision, that she wasn't doing this trip for anybody but herself and Roz. Tony had stared at her uncomprehendingly before he lowered his head and muttered under his breath that she was bloody mad. As for Carl going with her—he just shook his head slowly from side to side as he tried to make sense of what she had told him.

At least he couldn't accuse her and Carl of doing the dirty on him, Annie thought as she tried to lay things out as plainly as possible for him. "I have to do this. You know that things haven't been right with us for a while now." She leaned towards him and willed him to understand. The look in his eyes told her he knew she was right; he just wasn't ready to accept it.

They had stagnated, not that he would ever admit that he had no intention of them ever actually getting married. And even if he had, she knew now that it wasn't what she wanted anymore. Oh sure, they could have continued as they were and just drifted along for a few more years but in the grand scale of a lifetime together, they weren't right for each other and it would not work. She knew, too, that all this would dawn on him soon enough, as would the fact that she had given him an easy out from the big white wedding where his mother was concerned. He could lay the blame for Ngaire not having her moment as mother of the groom squarely at Annie's feet, which, not wanting to lose his halo, she knew he would do without batting an eyelid.

She hadn't liked to mention the deposit money they'd been saving—not so early in the piece because it felt mercenary—but half of it was hers, and she had no choice. The tickets she had booked that afternoon had to be paid for in full before the week was out or she'd lose the special offer and that would be that, she wouldn't be going. This revelation had set Tony off again and he played the part of the wronged man to the hilt as he ranted that he'd be forty by the time he got the money together for a house.

As she tuned him out, an idea that was such a glaringly obvious solution to the house scenario came to her. She interrupted him with the tentative suggestion that perhaps he could pool his resources with his brothers and buy a house. As she shuddered at the thought of a Goodall bachelor pad unleashed on an unsuspecting city, she caught the glint in Tony's eyes and knew that the idea had registered. It would be filed away to be brought out again and dusted off when the disbelief—and it was disbelief, not distress—of their breakup had worn off.

Yes, Annie decided, he wouldn't act on it for a while but the seed had been planted. She'd bet money that before the year was out, the Goodall brothers would make a trip to see the bank manager together. She could see it now—the boys would take their washing round to Ngaire and come back with a week's worth of meat and three veg frozen dinners. They'd all be in heaven.

Tony, never one for big discussions or dragging things out, had drained his can, scraped his chair back in that way she hated, and stood. Without a backwards glance, he headed towards the door. He told her that he was going out for a while and that when he got back, it would be best if she was gone.

The finality of the front door shutting, followed a moment later by the roar of his Ford's engine, sank in. Annie's eyes burned. So that was that—the end of six years together, all done and dusted. She threw back her wine not liking the bitter taste it left in her mouth. She forced herself to get up and headed through to the bedroom. She needed to keep moving or she would crash. Annie pulled things out at random to take with her. As she grabbed a jumper, she spied the bunny outfit hiding beneath it and couldn't hold back the tide any longer. She picked the costume up, rabbit ears and all, and sat down heavily on the edge of the bed.

She didn't know how long she sat there, shared moments with Tony—good and bad—flashing before her, but the sound of her mobile announcing a text jolted her from her torpor. She swiped at her cheeks with the backs of her hands and rifled through her bag for her phone. The message was from Carl, wanting to know whether she was okay. It spurred her into action. She couldn't sit there all night because it wouldn't be fair on Tony if she was still here when he came back, so she got to her feet. First things first, she thought and, still clutching the bunny outfit, she headed outside to dump it in the rubbish bin.

She came back in the house and texted Carl back to tell him she would take him up on his offer of accommodation and be round shortly. She thought that they would be living in each other's pockets soon enough anyway, so she supposed they might as well get used to it. Besides, there was no way she could face the Spanish Inquisition her parents would subject her to, were she to show up there tonight with her bag in hand. She chucked one last pair of knickers onto the bed before she grabbed a bag to stuff everything into from the bottom of the wardrobe. *Oh hell, she still had them to face yet.*

As she made her way through to the bathroom, she swept her toothbrush and moisturiser into her toilet bag; her shampoo and conditioner could stay put. Carl used a pricier brand than she did—she'd use his.

Satisfied she had packed life's bare necessities, Annie zipped the holdall up and glanced around the bedroom at all the things she'd accumulated over the years. They were just things—they didn't really matter. Tony could keep all the sundry household items that make a home function because she didn't plan to cart a toaster, kettle, or a microwave—even if she had paid for half of them—with her on her travels. Once she'd told Attila what she could do with her job tomorrow, she'd be a free agent until she got on the plane and it seemed kinder to come back to pack up the bits of herself that would remind Tony of her when he was at work. Besides, she had no desire to run into Ngaire when she took it upon herself to come round and comfort her son. As it was, she knew she wouldn't get away scot-free; she was sure to get a mouthful down the phone between now and when she left.

The thought of Ngaire no longer being a part of her life perked her up. She allowed her eyes to sweep over the room and pushed the sadness that came with this unexpected ending to one side as her eyes settled on what had set the wheels of change in motion in the first place. Unhooking the Santorini print carefully from where it had lived for the past six years, she tucked it under her arm. With her bag over her shoulder, she walked out the front door.

Chapter Thirteen

CARL HAD INSISTED SHE ring her parents as soon as she'd arrived on his doorstep that evening. She'd been looking a sorry state with her bag at her feet and the print tucked under her arm when he opened the door, but at least her shoes had been a matching pair.

"Good grief, girl, your eyes look like two wee-wee holes in the snow. Cold tea will fix that. I'll sort a pair of old bags out for you while you give Mum and Dad a call. You don't want them hearing what you've been up to second-hand— that wouldn't be fair." He ushered her inside before he picked up her holdall and slung it over his shoulder. "Here, give me that." He took the print from her and held it out in front of him for a moment. "Cheesy but at the same time magnificent. Hard to imagine we'll be looking at a view like that in a couple of weeks."

"I know. I can't quite believe we are both going. I don't think any of this will feel real until we are actually on the plane cruising down the runway."

"Well, it has all been rather sudden but I have to say, now that we are all booked, I for one can't wait. I'll put these in your room. Go on through—you know where the phone is."

Annie wasn't sure that letting her parents know her plans over the telephone was the right thing to do but as she heard her mother's voice, she was glad she hadn't gone round there to tell them in person. She could not have faced their fully justified astonishment and she knew they were going to need a night to mull over everything she'd just told them to get their heads around her abrupt change of direction. Tomorrow they could sit down and talk through her plans properly.

"Where's all this coming from, Annie?" her mother had asked bewilderedly as Annie had shifted from foot to foot in Carl's living room, willing the conversation to end.

She knew, though, that once they got over their initial shock, they would realise that had they had a choice in the matter, Tony was not who they would have picked out of a line-up for their future son-in-law. They would probably be left with a feeling of relief the pair had gone their separate ways. It was the news of the trip that had thrown them the most. The fact she wouldn't be a few blocks away when they wanted to see her which was something they did more and more of late having need of a post-quake stress, sounding board.

"I understand you're upset that your cat died, dear, I really do, but breaking it off with your fiancé and flying to Greece is rather an extreme reaction, don't you think?"

Annie could picture her mother's puzzled, tired green eyes—mirrors of her own in years to come—looking over at her father, who would look back at her equally baffled. Their need for her to be readily available to them was at times hard to take because when she had needed them most they had been too absorbed in their own private loss to let her in. She had kept how isolated she had felt when Roz died from everyone. It had felt disloyal to share her feelings of having been let down by her parents with anyone, including Carl and Kas, because she knew it wasn't their fault. Grief didn't come with a text book and they had done what they had to do to survive it.

"Oh, Mum," she'd sighed. "It's not just Jasper—it's everything. Truly, it's not as out of the blue as it seems and I promise I'll explain it all properly to you, just not tonight. It's been such a huge day."

"Roz always wanted to go to Greece." There were traces of sadness in her mother's tone as she changed tack. "She had a real thing about the place."

"I know," Annie answered simply. She did not want to open old wounds by telling them that it was Roz who was the main instigator of her upcoming trip. "She'd approve of what Carl and I are doing, Mum."

"And you've bought your tickets, you say?" Her voice had taken on the distracted tone of someone lost in memories.

"Yes, we leave a week tomorrow. It's a direct flight, apart from a couple of hours in Singapore and Heathrow. Then it's straight through to Athens."

"All that way." Her mother sighed as she tried to get her head around the distance. "Well, at least Carl's going with you—that's something, I suppose—and if it doesn't go well, you can always come home. Your room is always here for you. You know that, don't you, Annie?"

"Thanks, Mum." Annie didn't like to correct her assumption that she had purchased a return ticket.

"And you'll be with Kassia."

"Yes, we'll be with Kas."

"So you two girls will finally get to meet after all these years of writing to each other."

"Yes." She didn't tell her mother Kas was still in the dark as to her and Carl's impending arrival.

Annie rang off after receiving a summons for the pair of them to come to dinner the next night. As she placed the phone back on its charger, she gratefully accepted the large glass of wine Carl proffered. She needed it.

"Sit back and put your feet up," he ordered. When she had kicked her shoes off and stretched out, he scurried back into the kitchen and reappeared with two teabags in a saucer. "I've had these chilling in the fridge. Close your eyes."

She did so and had to admit as Carl placed the cool bags on her swollen lids that they felt wonderful. He sat down on the other end of the couch and lifted her legs up so her feet rested on his lap. She raised her glass tentatively and tried to find her mouth. It wasn't that easy with a pair of teabags blocking her vision but like a homing pigeon, the glass found her lips and she took a sip. The wine was cold and crisp and she savoured the sharp bite of the Sauvignon grapes for a moment. She could always rely on Carl to buy a good wine. Mind you, he wasn't price driven like she was, she mused as she felt a surge of gratitude to her friend. "Thank you, Carl."

He gave her sock-clad foot a squeeze. "You might not feel like it right at this moment but you and me, sweetheart—we are going to have a blast."

"I hope so," Annie murmured.

"Well, I know so. Are you hungry?"

"Not really. You go ahead and have your dinner. I'll be fine."

"No, I'm not hungry either, and this is going down rather nicely on its own at the moment." He raised his glass to inspect its contents. "I'll fix us something later if we feel like it."

The something to eat didn't eventuate as Carl kept their glasses full while he flicked through his newly purchased guide book. After they'd booked their tickets that afternoon, he'd insisted they find the nearest bookshop. Hotfooting it into the nearby mall like a child heading for his presents under the tree on Christmas morning, he'd spied what he was looking for and homed in on the bookshop's travel section. Snatching up the Lonely Planet's latest edition of the Greek Islands off the shelf, he'd hugged it to his chest as though someone was about to try to take it off him. Then, as he banged the book down on the counter a moment later, he had announced in an overly loud voice that he was going to the Greek islands in a couple of weeks. The disinterested young girl serving smiled at him politely as she zapped his card, bagged the book and looked beyond him to the next customer.

"I don't know, Annie—you can't get good staff these days," Carl huffed as they left the shop. "She could have had a companion sale there without even trying. I gave her the opener by telling her about the trip so she should have had the nous to offer me one of those leather passport holders. They were on the rack by the travel section. Selling is not rocket science," he muttered as he stalked back through the heaving mall. Annie didn't care; she just wanted to get back to her car and away from the bemused stares her mismatched shoes were garnering.

Now, lying on the couch, she felt her eyes well up again beneath the teabags. The realisation that her life as she'd known it for the last six years was over, snowballed with having lost Jazz. It was a double whammy and she was glad she was here now with Carl. Despite his idiosyncrasies, he was an amazing friend to have, especially when she was ill or down or just not having a very good day. He could always make her smile and she really would be lost without him, she thought as she tried to blink. It was impossible, so she removed the bags and plopped them in the saucer on the side table. She batted her damp lashes a couple of times. As her vision cleared, she saw that Carl sat on the floor. His back leaned up against the couch and his fringe had flopped into his eyes as he pored over the book. Feeling a rush of affection, Annie leaned over to plant a kiss on the top of his head. He looked up at her in surprise and grinned. "What was that for?"

"For being you." Annie picked up her glass and held it aloft. "A toast."

"Oh, goodie, I like toasts." Carl picked up his glass and swivelled round to face her.

"To you, Carl Everton, for being the most amazing friend a girl could have."

"I'll drink to that—to me!" he giggled as he stretched over and clinked her glass.

As she took a sip of her drink, Annie spotted the framed picture of David and Carl's grinning faces on the mantel. It was a selfie by the looks of it and she felt a stab of guilt at how happy they looked. She had been so caught up in what was going on with her that she hadn't spared a thought for how Carl must have been feeling of late. She knew, despite the way he made light of the breakup, it had to have knocked him. She placed her hand on his shoulder. "Are you doing okay?"

"What do you mean?"

"Well, I know it can't have been easy for you breaking up with David, and I have been so caught up in my own drama that I haven't really been there for you."

Annie watched as Carl's eyes wandered over to the frame on the mantel. "Don't be silly, sweetie. I love a good drama, you know that, and I wouldn't have missed yours for the world. I am fine. David is history. He can sweat it out at the gym while I..."Carl flicked through to the photo pages of his book, "...sun myself here."

Annie squinted and focused on the picture Carl's finger pointed to. An azure inlet curved like an arm around a tiny whitewashed fishing village. Excitement pushed past the heavy, flat feeling the day had wrought. She was doing the right thing; she knew she was. All the horribleness of this moment right now, it would fade into the background once she plonked her bum down on a deckchair on a pebbly beach in the sun. "It's going to be good, isn't it, Carl?"

"Of course it is, babe. Of course it is."

BY THE TIME SHE OPENED the laptop and sat down to write to Kassia, she had polished off the best part of a bottle of wine and eaten two pieces of peanut butter toast. Carl had taken himself off to bed. With her vision ever so slightly impaired, she decided the best course of action was to take a feather out of her friend's cap and keep her message short and straight to the point.

To: Kassia Bikakis

From: Annie Rivers

Subject: Hello!

Hi Kas,

So much has happened in the last couple of days since you told me to follow my heart. My lovely cat Jazz was run over, after which I decided to leave Tony and head to Greece. Are you still breathing? I hope so because on the 16th of June, Carl and I will arrive in Athens. We haven't had a chance to make any plans other than a spot of island-hopping down to Crete and the only definite on our itinerary to your part of the world is that we will visit Santorini (remember Roz's print that I told you about?). It's all happened so fast and I will explain everything to you properly when we meet. WHEN WE MEET! Can you believe it? It hasn't sunk in properly that I am actually going to meet you after all these years. Please don't panic, though; we know this is incredibly short notice and don't expect you to put us up, especially with it being peak season and you no doubt being fully booked but if you could keep an ear out for any work or accommodation around your way that would be wonderful.

Lots of love and kisses to you and all the Bikakis family.

Annie and Carl

xox

THE REPLY SAT THERE blinking out at Annie from the laptop the next morning as, huddled in her dressing gown, she sipped tentatively at a glass of fizzy orange vitamin B. She'd slept soundly, too soundly thanks to all the wine, and now she needed a serious dose of motivation, which she hoped the vitamin drink would provide her with quick smart. Her eyes flitted over the message and she beamed at the effusiveness of Kas's reply when Carl mooched through. He was wrapped in his black kimono-style silk gown and his nose twitched as he sniffed the air in the hope that she had put a pot of coffee on. Annie tapped the screen. "See, oh ye of little faith?"

He leaned over her shoulder to read the message as Annie said, "I told you she'd be excited. She can't wait for us to come and we are more than welcome to stay with them. We're family." She downed what was left in her glass, wiped the bubbles away from under her nose and made to shut the laptop down, catching sight of the time displayed in the corner of the screen as she did so.

"Oh crap!" She jumped out of her seat, as though someone had put a whoopee cushion on it, and pointed in the direction of the front door. "I'm going to be late if I don't get myself out that door in the next fifteen minutes."

Carl's hand flew to his head. "Do you mind not shouting? I'm feeling a bit delicate this morning and besides, what's the big deal? It's not as though you're going to be there much longer anyway. Who cares if you are late?" He headed through to the kitchen with a swish of silk. "What are they going to do? Sack you?" She heard a cupboard door open as she stamped down the hall to the bathroom. "Annie! Where did you put those god awful vitamin B thingies that always turn your pee yellow? They certainly put a rocket up you."

She didn't hear him; she was too busy stripping off and willing the shower to warm up.

WHEW! MADE IT AND WITH two minutes to spare. Annie pushed open the door and stepped forward, placing one sensibly heeled foot inside the foyer of the Albrecht building. With the other foot following suit, she strode over to the lift and realised this was the last time her work shoes would trot this familiar path. In a week's time, her footwear of choice for the foreseeable future would be flip-flops. As she pushed the Up button, an involuntary smile twitched at the corner of her mouth. This was one part of the build-up to D-Day—as she and Carl were now referring to their departure date—that she was actually going to relish. Telling Attila that she would no longer be her lackey and that she could shove her job would be very satisfying. "Oh yes, very satisfying indeed." She didn't realise she'd said the words aloud until she caught sight of Pervy Justin's startled face behind her in the reflection of the lift's doors. The lift pinged its arrival and as the doors slid open, she stepped inside, expecting him to follow. As she turned, she saw that he still stood outside and looked antsy. "Are you coming?" She held the door open with one hand for him.

"Um, actually, no. I might take the stairs. It's, uh, it's a good way to keep fit."

"I know much more fun ways of keeping fit," she said, with what she hoped was a leer, and felt a stab of pleasure at the look of terror that flashed across his weasel-like features before he darted off towards the smoke stop door and the safety of the stairwell. As the lift doors slid shut, Annie burst out laughing. *There was something to be said for being thought of as a sexual deviant. It served him jolly well right.* She punched the button that would take her to the fourth floor victoriously.

As she sailed past Tammy with a genuinely cheery good morning, Annie didn't pause to see whether the receptionist would look up from her iPhone. Today she didn't give a toss whether she acknowledged her greeting or not, and it felt good. Heading towards her desk, she noticed that Sue's head was down and she typed in earnest. For once, the woman being consistently early despite there being no monetary benefit in it for her didn't annoy her. Annie sang out a bright and breezy hello and draped her coat on the back of her chair. Then, after she'd shoved her handbag under her desk, she looked up to see that Sue had paused with her fingers hovering in mid-air over the keyboard to gawp over at her. Annie gave her a little wave. Sue blinked twice at her before she resumed her typing, more furiously than before. Annie smiled as she sat and switched her computer on before she turned her attention to clearing her in-tray.

She had decided the best course of action was to bide her time until Attila provided her with the perfect moment to sock the news to her. With a glimpse at her diary, she saw that she was going to be in a meeting for the best part of the morning. *Good, that would give her plenty of time to tidy up her work station.*

She had just deleted the last of her personal emails and clipped a piece of correspondence, that had lurked at the bottom of her filing tray for at least six months, into its client file when the boardroom door opened. Attila, as immaculate as ever, and a self-satisfied looking silver-haired client walked out of the meeting room, their noses nearly touching the ceiling as, not sparing a glance at the minions who sat behind their computer screens, they strode through the office into the reception area. Annie peered over the top of her computer to watch as Attila held out her hand to the silver-top. He nodded curtly and gave her hand a brief shake before he moved off to wait for the lift. Attila turned around to reveal a face like thunder and, looking like a schoolteacher about to bust a group of teenagers smoking down the back of the field, she marched back into the office.

Oh goodie, thought Annie, no longer intimidated by her. *The meeting hadn't gone well and her boss was obviously in foul humour.* That would make what she was about to do just that little bit more enjoyable!

"Annie! My office right now," Attila barked, without so much as a glance over in her direction as she slammed her office door behind her.

Sue glanced over at her with wide eyes and Annie grinned across at her. "Don't worry about me, Sue. I'm going to enjoy every moment of what's about to happen next but I'd take cover if I was you."

Not bothering to knock and wait to be summoned, she marched into the flashy office. Her head was held high and her back was straight as she stood in front of the desk she had quivered in front of far too many times over these last six months. Attila's coiffed head was bent as she breathed fire over the stack of paperwork she shuffled through.

"I'd ask you to knock next time," she stated, her head still down. "Franklin's Meat. So, their marketing executive has just informed me they are not happy with our last performance review, which means I am not happy."

"Yes, I can see that."

Attila looked up at that, unsure whether she detected sarcasm in her secretary's tone of voice and not liking the fact that she certainly didn't detect fear.

Annie just smiled saccharinely back at her with her hands clasped patiently in front of her black work skirt and bided her time. She planned to donate her skirt, along with her numerous work blouses, to the Salvation Army once today was over.

The older woman's flinty eyes narrowed and Annie was fascinated by how much she reminded her of a snake that was about to strike. "Which also means I need this re-drafted ASAP." She all but threw the sheaf of papers at Annie.

"Oh sorry, I can't. It's nearly lunchtime."

"Pardon me?"

"I'm going to lunch in five minutes. I have plans." It was true—she was meeting her girlfriend Charlotte, who worked nearby, for a bon voyage luncheon. "And there's not really much incentive for me to work through my lunch break, is there? Seeing as I don't actually get paid for it. It never seems to suit you, either, for me to take time off in lieu for all the extra hours I have worked since you took over from Mel, and from my calculations, I have two full days owing at least."

Attila swallowed and licked her lips, not quite fathoming what she was being told.

"So you might want to go and speak nicely to Sue to see if she'll stay behind and do it for you."

Attila pushed her chair back, stood, and then gathered herself together. But despite her superior height, Annie didn't find herself shaking in her black pumps this time. She was enjoying the gobsmacked look on her boss's face far too much for that.

"Do you value your job, Annie? Because let me tell you—"

Annie held her hand up and interrupted, "Um, no, actually, Adelia, I think I have let you tell me quite often enough. It's my turn now and I want you to know that you have made my working life a complete misery these last six months. You are a bully of the worst kind who deserves to find herself in front of the Employment Tribunal. That's why I hope the letter I have just written and sent through to them explaining your appalling treatment of me serves such a purpose. Unfortunately, I won't be around to see things through because I am going away. You'll find my letter of resignation on my desk." Annie turned on her heel and stalked out of the office. She tossed back over her shoulder, "Oh, and don't worry about a reference. I won't need one, thanks."

With a grin plastered from ear to ear, she gave a victory salute to Sue, who stared open-mouthed at her. Annie was sure she glimpsed a flicker of admiration in the woman's eyes but it was hard to tell from behind those milk bottle glasses of hers. She scooped up her coat from the back of the chair and slid into it as she felt a set of boa constrictor eyes bore into her. Attila had moved from behind her desk and stood in the doorway of her office, arms folded across her chest. Annie watched her for a moment, fascinated by the way her face had mottled in pockets of puce. Even from where she stood, Annie could hear her breath coming in short bursts as she stamped her Hush Puppy-clad foot, Rumpelstiltskin style. Corns weren't responsible for her ill temper then, she thought with a desultory glance at her former boss's sensible footwear. With her handbag over her shoulder, she walked out.

PART TWO

Chapter Fourteen

"RIGHT, THAT'S IT. I'VE had enough. I'd like to get off now!"

"Carl, we are somewhere over the Atlantic Ocean. You can't just get off when you feel like it. For goodness' sake, you're in an aeroplane, not on a bloody bicycle. Now, do your seatbelt back up—can't you see the sign's on?" Annie pointed at the overhead symbol, her patience wearing thin with her disgruntled travel companion. At her sharp tone, Carl pouted. He looked like a little boy who had just been chastened by his mother, she thought as she watched him do as he'd been told. The poor lady seated on the aisle side of him looked pained, so she leaned across him and tapped her lightly on the forearm and mouthed, "I'm sorry. He doesn't travel well." The passenger was from Singapore and was tiny, which was to her advantage with Carl thrashing around in the seat next to her like a river monster hooked on a rod. She gave Annie a weary but polite smile in return. The Singaporean people were so polite, Annie thought as she watched the woman close her eyes in an attempt to get some sleep. *Chance would be a fine thing!* She turned her attention back to Carl.

"Come on, just try to relax; that's what you have to do on a long flight. Why don't you watch a movie or something if you can't sleep?"

"I couldn't possibly concentrate. Honestly, a cage-reared chicken has more room than I do, which is why I never buy anything other than free range eggs because, Annie, it is inhumane! So you tell me how in the hell I am supposed to relax?" He bordered on hysteria as he crossed his arms and demanded to know how much further London was.

Annie wished she had an elephant-sized tranquilliser gun to hand because she would, in her present state of mind, have no qualms about firing it. Given a choice, she would rather travel with a toddler than with Carl because she was sure a belligerent child would be easier to deal with than the fidgety six-foot male seated next to her. She wondered idly whether there were any doctors on board who might be able to sedate him, or even better an African game park-keeper.

"Look, at least we've broken the back of the flight; it's only around another three hours until we touch down in Heathrow. So, come on, just try to make the best of it and read your book or something if you can't sleep."

"MY GOD—THREE HOURS!"

"Shush!" Annie's finger flew to her lips. "People are trying to sleep." She glanced around but couldn't see much apart from the darkened tops of strangers' heads. The cabin's lights were off except for the smattering of reading lights that illuminated the dimness. Down the aisles, arms and legs stuck out at uncomfortable angles and clogged the narrow walkway. The last time she had done a toilet trip, she'd nearly fallen over one man's outstretched leg. He was oblivious, slouched as low as he could go in his seat with an eye mask on and a trail of drool escaping from his open mouth. It wasn't a good look. As she'd picked her way down towards the toilet, she'd decided that this whole flying business was an undignified affair. The air hovered over her, heavy and stale, as she opened the toilet door and tried to banish all thoughts as to how many others had visited the throne room before her. Needs must, Annie; this is no time to be precious. Besides, one prima donna on the plane is more than enough, she told herself as she locked the door behind her.

"Bully for them. They've probably all popped pills to knock themselves out, which is what I would have done, except I have no wish to feel like I've been hit by a bus when I finally get off this excuse for a flying tin can." He paused to draw breath. "My ankles are beginning to swell, too, which means I am at risk of deep vein thrombosis, I'll have you know." When Annie didn't elicit concern as to the state of his ankles, he carried on. "I knew I should have bought some of those compression tight thingies. I would have, too, if they weren't so darned hideous." He shuddered.

Annie decided the best course of action to follow with Carl and his current fit of hysterics was to ignore him. She'd heard it said that acting as though they weren't there was the most effective course of action when children were in the throes of a tantrum, so that was what she'd do. She pushed her earplug back in as far as it would go and shifted her neck pillow in an effort to get comfortable; she hoped for maybe an hour or two's sleep before they landed at Heathrow. So far she had managed about a half hour's oblivion shortly after they'd taken off from Singapore but then Carl had elbowed her and whispered excitedly, "Are you awake, Annie? Dinner's on its way and you don't want to miss out." As it turned out, she could quite happily have forgone the meal.

"Ow!" She sat up in sudden fright and rubbed at her calf, which Carl, trying to cross his legs for the umpteenth time, had just booted. Sleep was going to be nigh on impossible. She shot him a dirty look, crossed her own arms across her chest and slunk down in her seat. To be fair, his knees did graze the seat in front of him and he did have one of those horrid people who'd pushed their seat right back as far as it would go before the plane was even up in the air sitting in front of him.

"That's it, you know. I am never—read my lips, Annie," Carl enunciated each word to be sure she'd get his message despite her earplugs, "never flying to the other side of the world direct again. It is like a slow, torturous death being squished in here."

Oh yes, he was in full-blown dramatic mode now and Annie realised there would be no stopping him as he held his hand up and waggled his fingers at the flight attendant. She was doing her rounds, trying to push a few wayward limbs out of the aisle, when Carl managed to catch her eye.

"Excuse me! Yes yoo-hoo, hello, over here." Satisfied she was headed his way, he turned his attention briefly back to Annie. He pushed his fringe out of his eyes as he muttered, "I knew I should have tried to pass this flight off as an expense or something and gone business class but I didn't want to leave you sitting on your own. I have learned a valuable lesson, though. It doesn't always pay to play the Good Samaritan, no matter what the Bible says."

Annie bit back the retort that she would love at this present moment in time to be sitting on her own.

"Did you see the legroom those bastards have in there?" He waved his hand in the direction of business class. "It's evil the way that when you board the plane you march past lovely spacious business class before going through the iron curtain to the bowels of cattle class. God, I don't know, the things I do for you, sweetie."

"Yes, sir, is everything alright?" The well-groomed flight attendant interrupted his spiel as she leaned over the dark head of the woman who sat next to Carl and smiled down at him.

How on earth did she manage to look so pristine after all these hours up in the air? Annie's hand automatically reached up to smooth down her own mop, which was currently tangled beyond redemption, thanks to all her fidgeting about.

"No, actually, it's not alright. Not at all and I'm afraid I am just not coping very well with my current circumstances. So I wondered if there was any chance of being upgraded because as you can see, my knees are just about touching my nose, which means my legs are cramping up." Carl paused in his grousing to draw breath. "And I don't want to be responsible for the plane having to perform an emergency landing due to my poor circulation. I'm worried about deep vein thrombosis—look." He tried to lift his leg in an attempt to show her his puffy ankles but all he succeeded in doing was drawing an angry look from the passenger seated in front of him whose seat he'd kicked.

The flight attendant, who, in Annie's opinion, looked far too young to have to deal with difficult passengers like Carl, blinked her heavily mascaraed eyes blankly at him for a moment. Then realising what he was on about, she apologised and told him that the flight was full so 'Sir' would have to stay seated where he was but could she perhaps demonstrate a series of ankle and wrist twirling exercises to get his circulation moving again? Carl was not impressed and he did a finger twirling exercise of his own at the attendant's retreating back.

"Fat lot of help she was, over-made-up excuse for a waitress."

"Carl! Don't be nasty! She's just doing her job and if you ask me, she was very patient with you. Besides, you can't expect her to pop anybody who complains they're uncomfortable into first class for a glass of champagne and some strawberries. Good grief, she'd have an economy class uprising on her hands if she did."

"I suppose." He slumped in his seat and then sat upright again. "Distract me then—tell me the Ngaire story again."

Annie watched as his expression brightened.

"Oh, I wish I'd been a fly on the wall for that one."

"Only if you promise to keep your feet to yourself for the duration of the flight." Her eyes narrowed. "And don't cross your fingers behind your back."

Carl's smile suggested that she knew him all too well as she insisted he hold both his hands out in front of him while he promised to behave himself. Satisfied he'd keep his word, she drew breath and felt as if she were about to read a bedtime story to a recalcitrant child.

"Well, I saw her black Holden pull up outside your place. Actually, I heard it coming before I saw it. Honestly, what kind of a woman has a boy racer muffler on her car?"

Carl just shook his head. "It's all part of her Ngaireness."

"Hmm, I suppose you're right because I couldn't really see her driving a Mini; it just wouldn't suit her. Anyway, when I heard the car, I contemplated hiding and pretending no one was home. In fact, I got so far as dropping to the floor and lying flat with my arms out like this." She flung her arms out to demonstrate.

"Ow!"

"Sorry."

Carl pursed his lips and rubbed at his nose until he was satisfied it wasn't broken. "You knew, though, didn't you, that if you didn't square up and answer the door, she'd track you down eventually?" At Annie's nod, he continued, "Even if it meant showing up at the airport, Ngaire would make sure she had her say before you left."

"She would, yes."

He nodded sagely. "Yes, wise choice then—better to face the wrath of Khan there and then."

"Exactly. That's why I got off the floor and made myself open the front door. No choice really, not if I didn't want to spend my last few days in Christchurch looking over my shoulder. I did keep my hand on the knob the whole time, though, in case I had to slam it shut in a hurry."

"Tell me what she was wearing again." Carl's hands were clasped in anticipation of being titillated and horrified.

Annie smiled at the memory. "Well, she had really excelled herself this time and I think she must have come straight from line dancing because she had a white Stetson hat on, a white fringed leather jacket, a white leather mini skirt, and fringed, white leather ankle boots."

"Oh my God, she must have looked like some kind of ageing Country and Western angel! I'm thinking Dolly Parton without the knockers or an over-the-hill Taylor Swift! And I can just imagine the wrinkly knees."

Annie laughed. "You have such a way with words, but yes, she was definitely channelling her inner country music chick and her knees just about had facial expressions of their own." Ngaire had the most appalling taste in clothes but in a strange way she would miss being appalled on a regular basis by her wardrobe. She had dined out over the years on Ngaire's choice of outfits. Her smile disappeared, though, as she relayed the mouthful she had been on the receiving end of that afternoon. There had been no pleasantries as like in a scene from that old-time and appropriately named musical, *Annie Get Your Gun*. She'd launched into her, all barrels blazing.

"I'm here to find out just what you think you're playing at, madam, treating my son the way you have?" One ankle boot had pawed at the ground. For a moment, she had reminded Annie of a bull in a ring and she half expected steam to start coming out of her flaring nostrils.

She'd drawn a deep breath, determined not to let her frighten her. "I'm not playing at anything, Ngaire, and I'm sorry that things between me and Tony haven't worked out." She'd paused for a moment to look her straight in her beady, over-made-up eyes. "It's nobody's fault; it's just the way it is. It happens and we both need to make a clean break of things now before we wind up making a big mistake and growing to really dislike each other." She'd given a small shrug, hoping her explanation would suffice. But Ngaire wasn't done—no siree, not by a country mile—and her eyes narrowed even further between their rims of thick blue kohl liner.

"Oh, I know it's not my Tony's fault because he's not the one swanning off to some godforsaken country on the other side of the world, now is he?"

"I'm going to Greece, actually, and it's quite civilised, or at least it was the last time I checked."

"Don't condescend to me, young lady. I know where Greece is. I just don't understand why you are going there."

"It's something I need to do. You wouldn't understand." Annie didn't want to tell her about Roz and the pilgrimage of sorts she was going to make.

The older woman would probably only snort at her plans anyway. Besides, it felt wrong to talk to her about her sister because she had always been quick to mutter on about the past being the past and that was exactly where it should stay.

"Too bloody right I don't understand. You don't just pack up and leave your life behind with no word of warning to anyone. What you are doing is selfish, pure and simple." Spittle flew out of her red lipsticked mouth. Annie took a step backwards and her grip tightened on the door handle.

"I'm sorry you think that, but I have talked to Tony and explained my reasons for going and he understands, even if he doesn't entirely get it right now. He agreed with me, you know—that we weren't really going anywhere and that he wasn't ready to get married. It's just that I'm the one who decided to do something about the rut we were in." Annie didn't like the way Ngaire clenched her fists but she carried on in her attempt to explain her actions. "We'd become a habit and we needed to part ways before we became an unhealthy habit." She was pleased with her summing up; she felt it was rather eloquent.

Ngaire, who must have been digging holes in her palms with those talons of hers, did not.

"Don't you be comparing my son to an unhealthy habit, young lady! He isn't a packet of cigarettes, you know. Tony is a lovely, kind boy with feelings!" She unfurled her right hand and pointed her index finger at her as though she might prod her in the chest but had changed her mind at the last minute. She waggled it at her instead. "Feelings that you've hurt by stomping all over him the way you have."

Annie opened her mouth to protest but Ngaire was determined to say her piece. "But I came here today to tell you, madam, that you needn't think you've broken his heart because there's plenty more fish in the sea. And in my opinion, he's better off without a hardnosed, orange-haired shark like you."

For a moment, Annie had toyed with tossing back that at least she didn't resemble a chocolate-covered raisin like Ngaire did, thanks to the pancake foundation she insisted on trowelling on, but she bit it back. She was bigger than that. "I have shown you the courtesy of hearing you out, Ngaire, even though I don't think that what's going on between Tony and me is actually any of your business, so I'd thank you not to hurl cheap insults."

They eyed each other in a silent stand-off until Ngaire broke it with a sniff. "Anyway, I suppose I should be thanking you really, because you've done us a favour by buggering off. I never liked you much, what with your hoity-toity ways. You always thought you were better than us."

It took all of Annie's willpower to remain calm but she knew from experience that the best way to deal with a rabid ex soon-to-be mother-in-law was to agree with her. "Well, it's probably best all round that I am going then because I don't think there is any going back now you've said your piece. And you know, this might surprise you, but I don't want any ill feeling between Tony and me because we were together too long for that and do you know what else?"

Ngaire opened her mouth to cut her off but Annie was on a roll. "Despite what you think of me, I haven't suddenly stopped caring about Tony and what happens to him, so I'd appreciate it if you didn't stir the pot." Annie was shaking after that little impassioned speech. She had stood up to Ngaire and it had felt good. As she hovered by the door and waited for her to leave, she could almost see the cogs slowly turn in her brain, or at least she would have, had the white Stetson not blocked the view. She was trying to process Annie's sudden cockiness and Annie watched, fascinated by the tiny ribbons of lipstick that snaked out from her pursed lips. To have the last word, Ngaire did prod her in the chest this time.

"Like I said, my girl, there's plenty more fish in the sea for a catch like my Tony, so when you come home with your tail between your legs, having had an allergic reaction to all those olives, don't you even think about sending out a baited line. Got it?"

"Got it, thanks, Ngaire. Goodbye." Annie shut the door on a face she hoped she wouldn't bump into again for a long, long time. She stood in the hallway and exhaled slowly. She couldn't help but feel she had had a lucky escape.

Carl jarred her recall. "I bet she was like a female Clint Eastwood, you know," he squinted and made a pistol with his index and middle fingers aiming it at Annie as he said, "go ahead—make my day."

It was a pretty good comparison, Annie thought as he crossed his legs and gave her yet another good boot in the shin. She bent over and rubbed at where he'd bruised her. Her legs would be black and blue by the time they landed in Athens—not a good bikini body look. She shot him a dirty look before she leaned back into the seat's head rest and thought wearily that this whole nightmare situation would be funny if she wasn't so darn tired. She couldn't help but think, too, that the television networks could make a reality show of this trip titled *The World's Worst Travel Companion*. They'd be guaranteed thirty hours of riveting viewing. She closed her eyes and sent up a silent prayer that this flight would eventually come to an end.

Chapter Fifteen

GOD HAD HEARD HER PRAYER, Annie thought as she forced one sleep-encrusted eye open in order to peek around the unfamiliar room. The walls were painted a shade of buttercup yellow that even in her foggy state demanded cheeriness and, from where she lay in her single bed under a thin blue coverlet, she could see a set of French doors. The thick white paint coating their frames had peeled away in places and gave them a rustic charm that anywhere else might seem shabby. They were framed by an airy set of ineffectual blue drapes that they had left open last night, too tired to bother to draw them closed. Besides, it would have been a pointless exercise, anyway, for all the light they would have blocked out. Now, as daylight streamed in through the doors, Annie could see the tiny wrought-iron balcony that they led out to. She felt a frisson of excitement as the realisation slowly seeped through her half-asleep brain. They were here—they were actually here in Athens!

She stretched languidly and shook off the remnants of what had felt like the never-ending journey before she pulled herself up into a sitting position. Across the small square room on a matching single bed pushed hard up against the wall was the slumbering bulk of Carl. Both his legs protruded out from his identical coverlet, his feet dangling over the end of the bed as he lay face down, star-fished. He had not been impressed upon their late arrival at the guesthouse Annie had booked as a last-minute deal to find that it was also a *budget* guesthouse. Not only did it not have air con but it was, in Carl's opinion, the absolute bottom scraping of the barrel to have to share a bathroom with other guests. Annie had hissed back at him that he wasn't on one of his all-expenses paid photography shoots now and that as they were only in the ancient city for a couple of days, she didn't want to blow *her* budget on luxury accommodation. She fanned herself and wished that the budget had stretched to air-conditioning, though, because the room was already beginning to feel like an oven. It wasn't even ten o'clock yet.

Perhaps if she were to open the doors up and let a bit of fresh air in, it might cool the room a little? She flung her cover aside and tiptoed across the room to unlock the doors. She didn't bother to hook them back as not even a hint of a breeze stirred the hot air that blasted her as she stepped out onto the balcony. Last night on the long bus ride into the city from the airport, the darkened graffiti-scrawled buildings had not taken her breath away.

The vista had improved, however, as they reached the much more grandiose, lit buildings of the historic district. Finding themselves deposited on the side of the road, bags and all, they had tried to flag down a taxi. Mercifully, it hadn't taken long and before they knew it, they were driven at breakneck speed through a tangled maze of streets. Annie had tried not to think about the statistic she had happened upon in her guide book that the Greeks had the highest road fatality statistics in Europe and was relieved when it hadn't taken too many twists and turns before they had ended up here at Achilles House.

Now, as she looked at her surrounds curiously, she could see the guesthouse was tucked away, down the bottom of a narrow one-way street. Across the street were apartments and she watched a woman peg her washing on a line strewn across her balcony. In the distance, she could make out the hectic horn honking noises of a city going about its business. Annie sniffed the air appreciatively and inhaled the scent from the jasmine climbing the wall below her. She leaned over the rail and spied a breakfasting couple seated below in the pebbled courtyard. Cars and motorbikes lined the street, wheels mounted on the pavement in order to park. Hugging herself delightedly, her senses swam with it all and she had to fight back the urge to run downstairs to begin exploring right away. A glimpse down at her T-shirt, which barely covered her knickers, put paid to that idea, though, and as she spied an older gent across the way who had also just noticed the same thing, she quickly ducked back into the room.

Carl still snored as she flopped back on her bed. Lying there for a moment, she watched the ancient ceiling fan rotate laboriously before she cocked an ear. She desperately needed a long, cool shower to rid herself of the stale, sticky reminder of all that travel. Not hearing any signs of life from out in the hall, she decided the coast was clear. She scooped up her toilet bag and tiptoed out the door.

"AH, COFFEE! IT IS INDEED the nectar of the gods," Carl announced, but his words lacked his usual theatrical gusto as the cup and saucer were placed in front of him.

He did look a bit wan. Annie wrinkled her brow with concern as a waft of much-needed caffeine tickled her nostrils. As the smart young waiter removed her own cup and saucer from the tray he expertly balanced on the flat of his palm, she decided to bite the bullet, even if she did feel a bit of a fraud. "Ef-ha-ri-sto." The Greek didn't exactly flow off her tongue as she thanked the waiter.

"Pa-ra-ka-lo." His dark brown eyes twinkled as he gave her a broad smile before he retreated back inside the café to collect his next order.

Ah well, at least her efforts had been appreciated, Annie thought and hoped he had replied something along the lines of *you are welcome* because she'd be none the wiser had he told her she had nice boobs. "How are you feeling?" she asked as Carl took a ginger sip of his brew.

"So, so. Those tablets have helped a bit."

"Are you sure you should be drinking coffee with an upset stomach?"

"It would take more than a bout of the trots to put me off my daily caffeine fix."

Poor Carl had woken with the traveller's runs, which had only served to intensify his distaste for having to share a bathroom. It was the other guests on their floor she felt sorry for. Annie screwed her nose up as she tried to block out the awful sound effects that emanated from the bowels of the bathroom. She hoped her fellow guests didn't think she was responsible for them!

Once he'd showered and dressed, he looked more like his old self. As he checked his hair one last time in the mirror, he'd turned round, arms outstretched, to ask, "Will I do—will Athens love me, sweetheart?"

Annie had to choke back a giggle because in true Carl fashion, he looked as though he'd just stepped out of an advert for the latest in outdoor travel gear.

"You certainly look the part of Metropolitan Man goes global," she managed to reply.

"Good to know, even if I don't feel it." He ran his fingers through his freshly shampooed hair and noticed what Annie wore. He frowned. "Are you going to be alright out and about in that skirt?"

"I have to wear a long skirt because of all the bruises on my legs but what's wrong with it?"

"Nothing. It's pretty, very ethereal. The perfect skirt for floating around ancient Athens in. It's just that I'd hate for you to chafe in that heat. You might be better off in shorts because it can be quite painful, you know."

She didn't want to ask how he was so knowledgeable about such things and so, assuring him her thighs would be fine, thank you very much, they set forth in search of their first stop—a pharmacy. This didn't prove a difficult task as the hard to miss neon green crosses that signified medical help seemed to be on every street corner—unlike public amenities, Annie noticed. She hoped Carl, who swaggered with a cowboy's gait, would be okay.

While he chomped on a Maalox tablet, Annie opened the map they had been given by the Achilles's concierge and pondered the best route to the heart of the old district of Plaka for their first glimpse of the Acropolis.

"My sense of direction is not usually the best but it looks like we carry on up here and then hang a left."

Carl leaned over her shoulder, his breath lemony from the tablet, and traced a finger over the route. "I think you're right. Come on."

The pavements they walked were old and cracked, their kerbs high, and on the road, the traffic was an incessant cacophony of car horns and motorbike engines revving. The smell of exhaust fumes and cigarette smoke mingled on the hot air as they wandered past elderly couples sitting outside their shops on plastic stools, waiting for passing trade to call in. The scene was a curious mix of both the laid-back and a chaotic bustle, unlike anything she had seen before. Annie was determined to soak it all in.

"Look, Carl..." She pointed to a brick church across the road and they paused to admire its quintessential Greek design as its huge brass bell hanging in the tower began to toll. They watched a thin man with impressive facial hair, clad in a long black robe with a black domed style hat perched atop his head, as he hastened up the street. He ducked under one of the church archways and disappeared from view. They grinned at each other in an unspoken delight at the foreign scene they'd just seen unfurl and carried on. Annie willed herself not to look up because there was a precariousness it didn't pay to think about in the way the geranium-filled concrete balconies jutted out over their heads. As they reached the end of the street, the looming old buildings gave way to a fork in the road, which presented them with their first glimpse of the ancient ruins that overlooked the city. Annie nearly walked into an outdoor café table setting. "Oh, I'm sorry." She apologised and reluctantly pulled her eyes away from the Acropolis to the couple clinging on to their table.

"Hey, no problem, honey. It's quite something, isn't it," a broad American accent stated from beneath a cap.

Annie nodded, lost for words, as Carl pulled her away to find a quiet spot, away from the long line of red umbrella-shaded tables, where they could stand and soak up the scene they had come so far to see. Beneath the shade of a tree, they stood in silence with their arms linked and watched the lines of people make the pilgrimage to the Parthenon at the top. They looked like a never-ending stream of worker ants, snaking their way up the hill, Annie decided. She shivered, despite the heat, at the sight that was both surreal but familiar at the same time, having seen it so many times in movies or read about in books. "Think how many changes that building has borne witness to from its perch up there. Thousands of years of changes—the thought of it is giving me goosebumps," Annie whispered. She didn't know why she whispered—it just seemed appropriate.

"It's amazing—absolutely bloody amazing," Carl whispered back. They looked at each other and laughed.

"I really need a coffee." Annie broke their trance as she steered Carl over to an empty table where they could sit and continue to enjoy the view. She was sure the prices would be exorbitant to reflect the throngs of tourists all clustered in little groups around the tables but it would be worth it just to soak up the ambience of it all.

And it was, Annie decided now as she took a much-needed sip of her coffee and enjoyed it despite the temperature. An ice-cold beer could wait until later.

Re-energised after their break and armed with water bottles bought from a street vendor, they made their way over to the Acropolis Museum. As Annie meandered along, unable to move fast due to the heat, she became aware of a slight stinging sensation between her thighs. *Chafing!* she realised with a start. Just as Carl had predicted, and she'd only been out and about for an hour. This was not good. She would not let on to him that he had been right, so she gritted her teeth and tried to ignore her increasing discomfort. They followed along behind the mingling flow of different accents and crossed over a bridge, which took them to the walkway that led up to the museum's entrance. As they came to a halt at the end of the queue, they found themselves standing on thick glass, beneath which were the ongoing excavations of ancient ruins. Annie's excitement built at the sense of history.

Despite the eye candy, it was still a relief to get inside the cool air-conditioned building and, after they bought their tickets, they stood for a moment to get their bearings. The museum shop behind them was doing a lively trade and she made a note to herself to have a look around on their way out.

"Let's go and look over there first." She pointed to several glass cabinets that housed models that depicted how the Acropolis had been built and what it would have looked like in its heyday. It would give them an idea of the scale of work involved in building it. As they strode towards them, she wished she hadn't set forth with such gusto.

"You okay?" Carl asked.

"Fine," she squeaked.

"Because you look like someone just did something unpleasant within your personal space and it wasn't me."

Annie didn't bother to reply, determined to ignore her burning thighs as she found a gap in the horde of people who surrounded the case. She studied the matchbox version of the Acropolis until Carl, who wasn't one to stand around for long, pulled her away with a suggestion they head up to the next level. They stepped on the escalator with the swarm of tourists and glided upwards to step off at the next floor. As they moved out of the way of the escalators, they found themselves staring at a sea of marble. It was an auditorium filled with statues, each individually mounted onto its own plain rectangular podium, which were scattered between the thick concrete pillars—an echo to those of the Acropolis itself. The effect was mesmerising and, rendered silent, they threaded their way through them. Heads were missing on some of the statues and limbs on others; there were even whole torsos dismembered by time.

"Imagine the stories they could tell if they could speak," Annie murmured, caught up in the oozing sense of history.

"Well, that one wouldn't be saying much, sweets—he's got no head."

She ignored him. "I don't think I would like to walk around here on my own at night. It would be a bit eerie with all these broken figures gazing at you."

"Look over there."

Annie followed the direction his finger pointed and found herself staring at an impressive nude. *Adonis perhaps?*

"Typical of you to spot that," she muttered.

"Get your mind out of the gutter, girl. I am talking about the kids over there—watch them."

Two little boys, brothers she surmised, both under ten, were busy pointing at the statue's well-endowed appendage. They giggled and made rude gestures, completely oblivious of their mother who stalked up behind them, her face purple with embarrassment. They watched the show play out with amusement and then decided to explore the second floor.

This level was a rectangular-shaped space, in the middle of which was the same thick glass as the entranceway outside. It let them gaze down at the floors below and made Annie's knees go weak. Suddenly remembering she wore a skirt, she hoped no one had gotten an eyeful as she hurriedly moved off the glass and ventured over to the large windows on the left to admire the stunning backdrop of the Acropolis instead.

"Stay where you are, sweets. I'll take a photo with that in the background."

Annie sat down on the bench seat alongside the window and arranged herself into what she hoped was a flattering pose as a broad Aussie twang offered to take a shot of them together. Carl handed over the camera eagerly and joined her, draping his arm around her bare shoulders.

"Say cheese."

"Cheese!" they chimed, smiles wide.

Carl thanked their fellow traveller and retrieved his camera. He and the middle-aged Aussie, who looked every inch the first-time traveller abroad with his I Love Aussie T-shirt, compared notes briefly on their respective itineraries. His was a coach tour of Europe's hotspots; theirs practically non-existent. They wished each other well and the Australian re-joined his tour group. Annie noticed Carl wince as he clutched at his stomach.

"The toilets are over there." She pointed to the middle of the floor space where the amenities were tucked away. "There isn't a queue if you whizz over now."

"Hold this and wait here. Loitering outside the men's toilet is never a good look." Carl thrust his camera at her and with knees locked together, he scuttled off crablike in the direction of the little boy's room. Annie had to laugh at the sight of him as he elbowed tourists out of the way and he said, "Excusez moi." In his desperation to get to the men's, he had reverted to his schoolboy French as a one-size-fits-all language approach to the European continent.

It was a while before he reappeared but there were worse views to be looking at. Annie was happy to just sit and give her thighs a break while she gazed out at the stunning building on the hill behind her.

So absorbed was she in the vista that she didn't see Carl until he flopped down next to her. She jumped. "Oh, you gave me a fright. Are you okay?" She peered at his sweaty features.

"I'll live, or at least I think I will. Come on, I'd like to have a look at something other than the inside of the men's loos while we're here."

They wandered up a ramp and paused to admire the different sculptures, many of which were busts, the ancients' equivalent of a passport photo, perhaps, Annie thought randomly.

"Have you noticed something?" Carl asked.

"What?"

"That a lot of the sculptures are missing their noses."

"Yeah, you're right actually." She scanned the nearby podiums. "Nearly all of them are."

"I've a theory on that."

"I bet you do."

"It's because the Greeks have big noses."

"Shush." His voice was too loud for Annie's liking and she gave him a light smack on his arm before she glanced around her, hoping she wouldn't see any outraged Greeks glare back at them.

"Well, look, you can see for yourself—it is a historical fact! That's why they've all fallen off because they're too bloody heavy for time to support them."

She had to laugh, especially as her eyes had just landed on a swarthy decidedly Greek-looking man with a truly impressive schnozzle, who was thankfully out of earshot. "You could possibly be right."

As they reached the top of the ramp, they saw that the wall along the back had glass cabinets that housed various artefacts used in the day-to-day life of the ancient civilisation. By the time they had completed the full circuit, Annie felt she was almost on a first-name basis with the Ancient Greeks.

The museum had whetted her appetite and she was keen to mentally place all that she had just seen in its former home up on the hill herself.

"How about we hit the museum shop and then head for the Acropolis?"

"Deal."

So fifteen minutes later, armed with a couple of postcards and a picture book of Athens, Annie pulled her hat from her bag as they exited the building. As she stepped back out into the unrelenting sun, she pulled it down low on her head, flattening her curls in the process. She hoped no breeze would suddenly blow up to whip it off and reveal her hat hair to all and sundry.

"It's past lunchtime, you know," Carl stated unenthusiastically after he glanced at his watch. "Are you hungry? Because there won't be any fine dining to be had top of the hill."

To her surprise, Annie realised she wasn't; it must be the heat. It might be bad for her hair but it might just prove to be good for her figure. "Actually, I'm not."

"That's a first."

"Tell me about it." Annie looked down at her stomach questioningly. "I'm itching to go up there." She pointed to the Acropolis but thought that perhaps she should have said *I'm chafing to go up there.* "What about you—do you feel like eating something?"

"No." He shuddered. "Ugh, the thought of it. Food would go straight through me. No, I'm with you—forward, James."

Chapter Sixteen

ANNIE AND CARL WOUND their way back to where the line of café tables began and crossed the road to the base of the hill. An arid, rock-strewn path led them to the ticket booth, where a handful of tourists waited for their passes.

"Okay, here we go." Annie pocketed her ticket before she linked her arm through Carl's. "Carl?"

"Hmm?" He turned to look at her, eyes hidden behind his Ray-Ban's as they picked their way up the path.

"Do you feel like she's here with us?" Annie couldn't read his expression.

"I was wondering when you'd mention Roz." He paused and pulled her to one side of the path to allow the group behind them to pass. "Do you know, it's weird, but I thought there would be this profound sense of her from the moment we landed in Greece, but so far nothing." He shrugged. "Maybe it's because I've been too preoccupied with needing the loo. What about you?" He took his glasses off and looked at her quizzically from beneath his pork pie hat.

Annie could feel a profound sense of chafing but as for that instinctive knowledge that her sister was with her that she'd felt on that grey day of her Greek epiphany, then no. "I've been too caught up in the magic of actually being here to think too deeply about Roz. I think she'll be with us when we sit down by the theatre ruins, though, whether we feel her or not."

Carl nodded and then Annie pulled his arm. "Come on, let's get moving."

Olive trees dotted the umber soil where no grass grew and rocks littered the hillside; skinks skittered out of their path to hide in cracks invisible to the naked eye. Other sightseers paused to rest from time to time under the sparse shade of an olive tree, a mixture of impractical shoes and bright-red sweaty faces in the afternoon sun. Annie wondered how many feet had trodden the path hers now walked and it made her shiver to imagine women in long white dresses carrying urns of water or men in togas toiling or whatever it was men in togas did back then.

The Herodes Atticus Theatre tumbled over the hill to their right and as they reached it, Annie was assailed with a sense of having been here before. This sense of déja vu undoubtedly stemmed from having watched the Yanni concert time and time again. In a way, it was like when you saw someone famous off the tele and had that feeling you knew them from somewhere or other but couldn't place where, and then when you realised they were a celebrity, you were amazed at how much smaller they were in real life. Now, though, as she gazed down at the stage, she was pleased to find that its scale didn't disappoint because its proportions were perfect. She wished the place were empty, though. If it were, she would clamber over the barriers put in place to prevent any old Joe Bloggs from performing on the well-worn stone flags beneath her to marvel at their own acoustics. If she could be, she would be down there like a shot, arms flung wide as she launched into *Aria*. She and Carl weren't alone, though. A teenage group were crouched about on the dry soil in cliquey clusters and taking notes while a tall man, who looked to be somewhere in his late thirties, strode back and forth. His hands gesticulated passionately as he spoke. Annie frowned; it sounded like Greek but either way she couldn't understand a word of what he said, so she turned her attention to Carl. He had fished out a water bottle from their day pack and was currently guzzling from it.

"Can I have the iPod first? I promise I won't forget that nobody else can hear the music and start singing." As he screwed the lid back on the bottle, she saw that the colour he had only just begun to regain had once more drained from his face. Little beads of perspiration stood out like orbs of sago on his forehead. "Oh no, not again? There will be nothing left of you soon."

His reply was a low moan as he tossed the pack down on the ground by her feet and clutched his belly. "Please tell me you saw a loo on our climb up here."

Annie chewed her bottom lip. The only thing that resembled a latrine she had seen was a round rock with a hole in it that the Greeks might possibly have employed as a toilet back in the times of Apollo or Spartacus or whoever was head honcho back then. She looked round; there wasn't even a decent bush for him to take cover behind. "The only toilets I saw were back down the bottom of the hill, opposite the café where we had coffee this morning."

"Oh my God!" Carl squeaked, "Wait here."

Annie couldn't bear to watch him hobble off, so she found a free boulder on which to perch, well away from the teenagers and the other tourists. She grabbed her own water bottle from the pack and drank long and hard before she replaced the lid. That was better; they didn't need her dehydrated on top of Carl's little problem. She fossicked further into the pack to produce the iPod. With the earplugs in, she sat for a moment and imprinted the mellow gold of the theatre on her brain. She closed her eyes and let the haunting *Flower Duet* wash over her. The enthralled crowds as the two women, blinded by the lights on the stage, sang to the night air felt so very real. Their angelic voices carried, as the Ancient Greeks had known they would when they carefully designed this theatre for the very best acoustics. All the while, Yanni, resplendent in white, with his hair gently blowing on the whispering night breeze, looked on, bathed in the all-encompassing love of his countrymen.

"I'm here, Roz. This is for you." Annie didn't know whether she had uttered the words aloud or not. So swept up in the moment was she that she was unaware of the man's approach until he jolted her rudely forth with a tap on her shoulder.

She swung round, removed a plug from her ear and stared up from under the brim of her hat. She saw the man she had noticed earlier with the teenagers. "Yes?" Her tone was curt at the interruption, unable to fathom why he'd bothered her. This was her moment, her deeply private personal moment, and now she had some strange man hovering over her.

He held out a tissue to her and she looked at him blankly for a moment before she touched her fingers to her cheek. It was wet. "Oh," she said in surprise. She took the proffered tissue and dabbed at her eyes. Hopefully, her waterproof mascara hadn't let her down. All the dreams she'd had of actually being here sitting in front of this theatre had never featured her looking like the world's first ginger panda.

He said something and she shrugged to let him know she didn't understand. "I'm from New Zealand." She enunciated her words slowly and loudly, unaware she sounded as though she were talking to a simpleton instead of somebody who spoke a different language. "I only speak English. Actually that's not true, I can say a few words in Maori like Kia Ora, which means hello." She always babbled when she was caught off-kilter. At the bewildered expression on his face, she bit her lip in order to shut herself up before she demonstrated the fact she could also count to ten in te reo. Somehow she didn't think her very limited Maori language skills would impress him much.

"Ah, so you are from New Zealand? With that wonderful hair, I knew you couldn't be Greek. You're a long way from home then." It was a statement rather than a question and it was said in near perfect English. "Which part of New Zealand do you come from?"

"Christchurch and yes, I am a long way from home."

"Christchurch, yes, I know this place." He nodded his head in understanding. "Your city, it has had a hard time."

"Yes it has but things are getting better slowly." Greece was no stranger to earthquakes either, as her mother had so helpfully pointed out, her brow creased with concern as Annie stowed T-shirts in her backpack. "Have you been there?"

"No but I would like to visit your country very much one day. It looks beautiful." He smiled. "So little people, so many sheep."

"More cows than sheep these days but you should visit it because yes, it is very beautiful." There, she'd done her bit for New Zealand's tourist industry. "Oh, and thanks for this." Annie waved the sodden tissue at the man. She found herself liking the way his eyes crinkled at the corners whenever he smiled—which he seemed to do a lot. He looked kind, too. If he were to be cast in a movie, he would definitely be one of the good guys because there was no way that the dimple on his left cheek would ever lend itself to the role of a baddie. Good looks aside, now that she had her tissue and he could see she was okay, he could move on and leave her to it, thank you very much. She turned her back on him and told herself that rudeness was perfectly acceptable if you knew you'd never see the person again.

"It is no problem but I am curious. I have known the sight of the Acropolis and this," his hand swept over the Herodes Atticus Theatre, "to move people in here." He tapped his chest. "But never quite to tears?" The question hung in the air as he crouched down alongside her and ignored her body language as he raised a dark eyebrow to invite her explanation.

Annie frowned. She was torn between having been brought up to have good manners and telling him to not be so bloody nosy. Rather like a lapsed Catholic, though, when it comes to their faith, her long-ago instilled manners won out. "It's a bit of a long story."

"I am not in a rush. Look..." He pointed over to the group of kids, some of whom had produced packed lunches which they tucked into with relish. Others were in the kind of deep discussions that only adolescents can have where you think they are solving the problems of the world but really they are deciding what to wear to the mall that afternoon. The odd diligent looking one was busy taking notes. They were obviously a good bunch, Annie thought. Mind you, there wasn't much chance of any of them mincing off for a sly cigarette because there was nowhere decent to hide around here unless you were a skink. To emphasise his point, the man she assumed was their teacher sat down on the rock next to hers and crossed his tanned legs with their fine coating of downy black hair. He looked at her expectantly.

Ten out of ten for persistence, Annie thought as she decided he was a tenacious chap who also happened to have a nice smile and kind eyes. *Given that she would never see him again, what was the harm in telling him why she was here? He'd probably think her mad anyway.* With a curious sideways glance at him, it was the kind eyes that decided her. They were the colour of hot chocolate and she was partial to a hot chocolate before bedtime.

"Alright then..." She licked her lips and realised her mouth was dry again. She unscrewed the lid from her water bottle and took a sip before she launched into the reason she had been sitting in front of the Herodes Atticus, listening to her iPod and crying without even registering she was doing so. "My sister died when I was eleven." As she looked over at him to gauge his reaction, she saw sympathy flash across his strong features and she carried on swiftly. "Her name was Roz, and she was a lot older than me. By the time she moved out of home, she had got into drugs in a big way. They took over everything she once was." A chill coursed through her despite the soaring temperature and she rubbed at both her arms for a moment. The fine hairs stood on end. "I don't like to remember that side of her. I like to hold on to the way she was before, because that was who my sister really was and she was gorgeous, you know, before all that ugly stuff."

He nodded and looked at her appraisingly.

"No, I mean she was really gorgeous. She had long reddish-blonde hair, big blue eyes, and I was so jealous of her. I used to think we couldn't possibly have the same parents, not with my mop." She touched her hand to her hair self-consciously before she continued. "She had this way of wrapping people around her finger, too." Annie shrugged, the strap of her singlet slipping off her shoulder as she did so. "The saddest thing is the waste of it all because she could have been anything she wanted if she hadn't gone down the track she chose—and she chose it—nobody made her take the stuff. That's what I have always struggled with really. The fact she did it to herself."

The man took his hat off and ran his fingers through thick black hair a tad too long so that it curled out at the nape of his neck. "I think the problem with the young is that they don't think about their tomorrows. You have a saying, I think?"

"Six-foot tall and bulletproof."

"Something like that, yes. They think that these bad things happen to other people, not to them."

"True." Annie's voice was wistful as she looked at the honey-hued arches below her. "The one thing I remember her really wanting to do, though, was to travel, and for as long as I could remember, she'd had this thing about Greece—the Greek islands. On her bedroom wall there was a gorgeous print of Santorini, and I have this memory of her playing the video of the Yanni concert held here. She'd just stare up at that print with a faraway look on her face. Of course, I didn't know then that she was probably stoned." There was irony in the short laugh she gave.

"Yanni?" The mention of the New Age musician caused those thick dark eyebrows of his to shoot up but he let her carry on with her story.

"Yes, she had a real thing for him. I didn't get it; I mean, he doesn't do it for me." Annie shuddered and then pulled the strap of her top back up where it belonged. The skin under the smattering of freckles on her shoulder was turning pink. She rummaged in her bag for her sunscreen and squeezed a dollop into the palm of her hand. "I can't be doing with a long-haired man in white trousers," she muttered as she rubbed the cream onto her shoulders. "But Roz, well, I think she saw past the trousers." Realising how that sounded, she added, "Not literally, of course."

"No, of course not."

Annie glanced sharply at him, unsure whether he was laughing at her or not, but his face, despite the light dancing in his eyes, was grave so she continued. "She heard something in his music. It was like it penetrated the haze of the drugs and spoke to her. I know that sounds weird and almost spiritual I guess, but then that's what Yanni's all about."

"Yes."

"It wasn't enough to make her stop taking the drugs and follow her dreams, though. In the end, it was a car accident that did it. She drove her car into a tree."

His arm touched her forearm. "I'm sorry."

"It was a long time ago."

"But still it hurts, I think."

"It's being here. It was something I needed to do."

"You came by yourself—that is very brave."

"No, I'm not brave. I came with Carl."

"Carl—he is your boyfriend?"

Annie smiled. "No. He's not long broken up with *his* boyfriend and he is desperate to pay a visit to Mykonos." The island was known as a gay friendly holiday destination.

"Ah, I see."

"He was Roz's best friend, though—mine now and we have been there for each other over the years. It's our thing, you see, to get together every year on her birthday to watch *Yanni: Live at the Acropolis*. Sitting here just before, that's what I was listening to, *Aria*, from that concert."

"I remember that show. I didn't go but it was a big deal at the time and now I know why you were crying."

Annie flushed. "I didn't even realise I was but being here in front of the theatre like this and with that there." She waved vaguely at the Parthenon perched on the hill behind them. "You must think I am a bit bonkers?"

It was his turn to laugh. "I have heard stranger things and I think I understand. You came to fulfil a journey your sister should have gone on in the hope that it will give you a sense of her and a sense of peace." He looked thoughtful for a moment. "I think maybe you have come to say goodbye to her and to find your own metaphorical Yanni, yes?"

Annie's eyes widened. Until now, she had thought that being here would make her feel close to her sister again—a closeness she had craved for so long. But he was right; this was her way of saying goodbye. She looked at him in wonder. "Do you know I hadn't been able to put the reasons for this journey into words but you just did it for me? I've come to say goodbye to Roz and to find my own sense of Yanni." She whispered it again as she sat on that Athenian rock with the sun baking down on her. "I've come to find Yanni."

He smiled. "I have sisters, and I think perhaps it is their influence that has made me more sympathetic to life and things like this, your Yanni quest. I wish you luck finding him." He gave her a glimpse of that lovely smile of his once more. "Metaphorically speaking, of course."

"Of course." Perhaps there was something in what he said about having sisters, Annie thought as she conjured up an image of Tony and his brothers. Sensitivity for others was not a strong point with the Goodall boys and perhaps it was due to the lack of feminine input in their formative years. You could hardly call Ngaire a soft touch.

"It is a magical place, this Acropolis of ours, you know. This is what I tell my students and now I can tell them it has healing properties, too. Perhaps I should have a lesson on how we all need to find our inner Yannis from time to time."

So he was a teacher then. "They might not thank you for it." Annie smiled at him and felt a pleasant jolt of something she hadn't felt for a very long time as he smiled back at her. She looked away, unsettled by her reaction to him, and they sat in silence and gazed off at the magnificent skyline. As far as the eye could see stretched an urban jungle of flat roofs that glinted with tangled aerials and baked under the Mediterranean sky.

"Will you stay only in Athens because you said your friend—he is wanting to go to Mykonos?"

"Yes, he turns forty in a week and a half and he's decided that's where the momentous event will take place. We leave Athens tomorrow but haven't decided which of the Cyclades to head to first."

"Ah well, let me decide for you. You must visit Naxos. It is my island and it will welcome you, I promise. It is the most beautiful of the Cyclades."

Annie had read about Naxos and it did sound rather gorgeous. "Oh, so you are Greek then? I wasn't sure. I thought maybe you were from Spain or Italy or somewhere, travelling with your school group." His nose certainly hadn't given the game away; it was quite an acceptable size with no apparent bumps in the middle of it and his English was superb.

"Yes, I am Greek. I was born on Naxos and my parents still live there. But my sisters and I are all here sprinkled about in Athens. The island offers much but when the tourist season is gone," he clicked his fingers, "there is no work for a history teacher like me." He glanced over at his students, still engaged in their various activities.

"You are on a school trip, then—I got that much right?" Annie stated the obvious.

"Yes, I bring my students here so they can learn their own history first-hand."

"It must be wonderful to grow up with such a strong sense of where you come from. That is something we don't have at home. We are such a new country in that respect."

"Yes, it is wonderful but I think it is easy to take it for granted when you are surrounded by it and you see it day after day. This is why I bring them here because it is important that they understand the stories of this place, as well as the facts. When they understand the significance, then I think it becomes special to them for always."

He has a way with words, Annie thought. "Could you tell me a story—if you've got time, that is?"

He looked at her, bemused for a moment, and then smiled. "Of course—but only if you tell me what your name is?"

"It's Annie. Annie Rivers."

"Well, Annie Rivers from New Zealand with the beautiful, fiery hair, I am Kristofr and it is lovely to meet you." He held out his hand and Annie took it, surprised to find the skin on his hand was rough, like someone who worked with his hands and not his words. For a split second, she thought he was going to raise her hand to his mouth and brush it with his lips but he just gave it a gentle shake before he released it. She felt vaguely disappointed but watched, fascinated, as his expression changed. She realised it was like being privy to an actor preparing to go on stage.

"Herodes Atticus built this theatre in 161BC and commemorated it to his dead wife Aspasia Annia Regilla."

Annie looked at the ruins and imagined someone loving his wife so much that he would dedicate such a piece of architecture to her. The most she'd ever had dedicated to her was the tiny tattoo Tony had gotten of her name on the back of his ankle. Had her name been longer than five letters, he never would have done it and she wondered fleetingly whether he had had it removed yet. She'd heard that the process of getting a tattoo removed was even more painful than getting one in the first place. Given that Tony had demanded morphine during the tattooing process and crutches to hobble about on afterwards, she rather thought it would be more likely that he'd wear socks for the rest of his days.

"Herodes was an orator, an author, and a high priest of the Imperial Cult of Athens. He was also a friend of the Emperor Hadrian."

"I see. So he was a bit of a mover and a shaker then."

Kristofr laughed and Annie felt pleased. "Yes, I like that expression—a mover and a shaker. But..." His voice dropped an octave. "He was also rumoured to be a murderer."

"The plot thickens."

"Some say he was responsible for having his wife killed and that he built the Odeon to assuage his guilt."

Annie could see how Kristofr would be popular with his students; his voice had a melodic quality to it that, along with the visual reality in front of her, brought the intrigue to life. How lucky they were to have a history class like this. It was so different than the stuffy classroom lectures she remembered, where her mind used to drift off and fantasise about dating the lead singer of the latest boy band to hit number one.

"In its day, the theatre had stone walls that were three storeys high and the most expensive roof made from cedar of Lebanon timber."

Annie tried to visualise its grandeur but in a way, the remains were so much more mysterious, hinting at what it had once been like, and added an atmosphere all of their own that perfection would not have.

"It was used for musical performances and could seat five thousand people."

"Wow!"

"All of which was destroyed by human hand in AD267."

Annie gasped. She hadn't known this. "Who was behind it?"

"The Heruli, a Germanic tribe, and so it was left a crumbled pile until the 1950s when it was partially restored. And since then, it has been used to host our annual Athens Festival. That is when it comes alive again with various musical performers like your man Yanni—even Elton John has played here."

"He's not my man, though I think I'd rather see Yanni than Elton; his music seems much more fitting for the setting." Annie wrapped her arms around her knees, which were pulled into her chest. "I'd love to see it all lit up at night. It must be pretty special."

"It is, yes, and who knows, maybe one day you will come back here to see it again."

"Yes, who knows?" Annie reiterated, missing his quizzical gaze.

"So you will visit the Cyclades and then you will go home?"

"No, I have a friend, Kas—Kassia. She is from Athens but her husband was in media work and lost his job when the austerity measures came in."

"Sadly, yes, this is a familiar story."

"But this is one with a happy ending. They have two young sons and they went back to live with her husband's mother in Elounda on Crete. She runs a guesthouse there called Eleni's and it was getting too much for her on her own. I think they have a very nice lifestyle now."

"No stress, the simple life—that is what it is about when you live on the islands. They are fortunate to go back."

"They are. Spiros—that's Kas's husband—is writing a book. He has always wanted to write and Kas helps manage the guesthouse. It is rather idyllic for their children, too, though, I think Kas has a little bit of stress every now and then in the form of her mother-in-law."

Kristofr threw his head back and Annie watched his Adam's apple bob up and down while he laughed. It was a deep rumbly sound and there was something so warm and friendly about it that it made her want to laugh too.

"Ah yes, the Greek mother-in-law. She is an all too real stereotype, sadly."

"Do you have one of your own then?"

"No, not me. I think perhaps I am married to my job but my sister Athena does. Her mother-in-law—she is very, very bossy, especially in the kitchen. Two women under one roof, with one man and only one kitchen—"

He grimaced and it was Annie's turn to laugh. "It is not, how do you say? A recipe for an easy life."

"No, I'd imagine not."

"So you will visit Crete. I have heard Elounda is a wonderful place. It is where the rich and the famous like to holiday."

"And the not-so-rich and definitely not famous but yes, I want to stay there for a while and see if I can pick up some work."

"Perhaps this guesthouse your friend manages will be busy enough that you can work there. That is where you will stay?"

"Yes. I was worried that we might be putting the family out as it was short notice us coming but Kas was insistent we come to Eleni's."

"It is the Greek way; she would be insulted if you didn't. If you don't mind me asking, how do you know this Kassia?"

"She was my sister's pen pal a long time ago and then after Roz died, we struck up a friendship of our own."

"Another Greek connection."

"Yes. I've heard so much about the Bikakis family over the years that in a way I think it will be like going home when we finally get there."

"It will be very special, I think."

"Yes, I think it will be." Annie offered him a small smile.

"When are you due to go home to New Zealand?"

"I'm not. I bought a one-way ticket. Carl heads home in a month's time, though. He's a photographer and has shoots lined up that the money is far too good for him not to go home for. But me," Annie shrugged, "I've not long come out of a long-term relationship and I want to just flit for a while."

"Like a beautiful butterfly."

She blushed, glad for the partial cover her hat afforded her, as she had never been very good at handling compliments. She was spared a reply though, by the sight of Carl as he swaggered up the dusty track towards them. Kristofr followed her gaze. "That is your friend."

"Yes, that's Carl. He's not feeling too well at the moment; he has a bit of a funny tummy."

"Ah, that is not nice."

"No."

A voice floated towards them, a question in its tone. It was one of Kristofr's students, a young man whose frayed jean shorts sat far too low on a set of skinny hips. Kristofr sighed, got to his feet and brushed the dust from his shorts before he nodded at Annie. "I have to go but it was lovely to meet you, Annie, an unexpected bonus, I think." He tipped his hat. "Thank you for telling me your story. I wish you safe travels and I hope you find your Yanni. Who knows, maybe one day we might meet again."

Annie shielded her eyes from the sun as she looked up at him. She felt oddly forlorn at the formality of his goodbye after the intimacy of their conversation. "It was nice to meet you, too, and thanks again for this." She waved the soggy tissue at him as, with one last smile at her, he wandered back to his group.

"Who was that?" Carl's eyes narrowed as he sat gingerly down next to her in the space where a moment earlier Kristofr had been.

"Oh, no one." Annie looked wistfully at Kristofr's white-shirted back as he bent down to study the notes of the student who had called him back. She felt a stab of resentment towards the scraggly-headed youth.

"Well, for someone who is a no one, you have a pretty daft look on your face."

"Oh, don't be silly." She wasn't going there; that wasn't what this journey was about. Besides, it was too soon after Tony to think about anyone else. "How are you feeling? You made it in time, I take it?" Annie diverted Carl from pursuing the topic.

"Only just. It was touch and go." He shook his head and the look of serious consternation on his face made her smile.

"We'll be laughing about this in a few days, you'll see—it'll become one of our travel stories." And when she turned back to look at Kristofr, he and his group of students had gone.

"Pass me the iPod, would you? I want to listen to it." Carl held his hand out for it. "Was it how you thought it would be?"

"Kind of."

"Did you feel her here with you?"

"Not really. It was more like I was finally getting to say a proper goodbye to her."

Chapter Seventeen

"THE FAMILY CAN'T WAIT to meet you both but be prepared—they can be a bit, uh, how you would say... loud?" Kassia took her eyes off the road for a moment to grin over at Annie.

Annie was too swept up in the fact that she actually sat in her old friend's company to pay much attention to what she said. Two whole wonderful weeks had whizzed by since she and Carl had landed in Athens and now here she was in the front passenger seat of Eleni's courtesy van, next to Kas and on their way to Elounda. She was tempted to pinch herself to make sure it was all real. It had been such a long time coming, she thought with a sideways glance at Kas.

Black Jackie O style shades were perched on top of her head, which pulled her dark hair back from her face to reveal a few streaks of grey at her temples. The remains of her last perm blew in a halo-like frizz on the breeze that came in through the open window as they drove away from the city along a wide, open road. Her skin was unlined with the olive hue to it that Annie, with her own pale skin, always envied. Dark eyes were framed by eyelashes that had no need of mascara and eyebrows that had never met a pair of tweezers. She wore lipstick but that was the only make-up she had bothered with, having the aura of a woman who was far too busy to spend her time in front of a mirror. It was her Roman nose that she had always proclaimed to hate, along with her clear-cut jawline, that hinted at the strength of character lurking below the surface, though, Annie decided, her surreptitious study done.

Their ferry had been on time despite the Greek passenger line's notoriety and Kassia waited for them at the terminal as she'd promised. Annie's tummy had fluttered with anticipatory nerves and she hardly noticed the harbour's impressive Venetian fortress as she and Carl made their way towards the waving, larger-than-life vision of their friend. Planes screamed above them, chock-a-block with package holidaymakers, and the mishmash of buildings across the road from the waterfront provided, if not what one could call exactly a pretty, then a bustling backdrop. There would be plenty of time to explore the port city of Heraklion later, though. In the meantime, Annie drank in her friend's appearance as they made their way towards her. She looked exactly as she did in her photos. The camera had not lied. Dressed in a loosely fitted white T-shirt tucked into navy shorts with flat, white sandals, she was a medium build bordering ever so slightly on cuddly.

"Annie! Carl!" Startling white teeth flashed in contrast to her tan skin as her face broke into a welcoming grin. She flung her arms wide. Annie shoved her backpack at Carl and ran into them, throwing her arms around Kassia's neck as she forgot her nerves. Even her smell was familiar, she thought, as she inhaled the lemony essence of her as she hugged her back tightly, even though she knew that was impossible. Carl hung back as the two women, still holding onto each other, leaned back to study the other for a moment. Both grinned inanely as they simultaneously burst into tears.

"These are because I am happy," Kassia stated. "You are beautiful, Annie, even more beautiful than your photos—all that glorious hair! Oh, what I would give for such curls. The money I have paid to try to get such curls—and the colour, it is like fire!" She stroked Annie's hair and watched the sun play on the streaks of gold that ran through it. "I bet the Greek men have been making a fuss of you, yes?"

"I have been unusually popular, actually." It was true; the brilliant red of her hair was a crowd-pleaser and at first Annie had found the stares a tad unnerving. She had been forever patting around her backside to make sure her skirt wasn't caught up in her knickers and upon finding no evidence of that, followed it up with a request for Carl to check that her nose was clean and that there was no food stuck in her teeth. Eventually, Carl had tired of constantly looking at her backside, up her nose and inspecting her teeth, and had told her to enjoy the novelty of being the centre of attention. She'd decided to take his advice and had found that the admiring glances that came her way were beginning to make up for all those years of carrot-top teasing.

Kassia laughed a rich, deep belly laugh. "I can't believe you are here! At long last, you are here. I have dreamed of this moment." She reached out to hug Carl, who had dropped the bags to wrap her in a bear hug, his own eyes suspiciously bright. She linked arms with them both a moment later and led them over to the white van marked with Eleni's contact details. Carl slid the door open and tossed their packs in the back before he clambered in and told Annie to hop in the front so she and Kas could catch up on the drive to Elounda. Given his propensity to car sickness, it was a selfless gesture on his part and Annie flashed him a grateful grin.

As she turned the key in the ignition and headed away from the hustle of Heraklion, Kassia chatted nonstop about the guesthouse and how Alexandros was up to his usual tricks. His Irish friend was long gone but he had moved on to a young English guest whose breasts most definitely were not real. As they wound their way along the open road, hills loomed on either side of them, occasionally giving way to a valley and allowing them a long-distance peek at the villages nestled in them. Annie noted that there was always a church taking centre stage, no matter how small the village.

"Yes, I saw him tiptoeing out of her room first thing this morning and it is lucky for him it was me who caught him and not his mama, or he would have gotten a slap."

Annie laughed; life was never dull where the Bikakis family were concerned.

Kassia pointed out a monastery over to their right with a cluster of curious holidaymakers' cars parked outside its massive stone gates before she inclined her head over to the left. "That's the turnoff to Malia, which is a big resort area. Lots of sunburnt, overweight tourists who like to drink too much and do the karaoke down there." She shuddered before she glanced in the rear-view mirror. "How was your birthday?" She met Carl's eyes. "Did you do lots of drinking and the karaoke?" It was said tongue-in-cheek.

"Kassia, my dear, as the lyrics to a song from our generation went, I partied like it was 1999. I'll say no more."

Annie snorted. "Honestly, Kas, you should have seen him. I think we hit every nightspot in Mykonos. He broke out every dance move known to mankind and he was the biggest flirt ever."

"You're only forty once," Carl protested.

"Thank goodness! I couldn't cope with another hangover like the one I woke up to the morning after, in this lifetime ever again."

Kassia laughed. "I think I have heard that before, yes?"

Annie looked sheepish and then they drifted into a companionable silence until it was broken by a groan from the back seat. Kassia glanced in the rear-view mirror again. A frown of consternation settled between her thick brows.

"Are you alright, Carl? You look a little green."

Carl groaned again. Annie opened her bag and after a quick feel around, produced some tablets and a bottle of water. "He doesn't travel well." She swivelled round in her seat to hand them to him. She decided not to mention the unfortunate incident in the back of the cab on Santorini that had prompted the purchase of the pills in the first place. "Chew on one of these—it will help." So would letting him sit in the front seat but she was reluctant to give up her pew next to Kas. A not so selfless gesture on her part.

Carl nodded meekly, broke the foil pack, popped one of the chalky tablets in his mouth and chewed frantically.

"Oh, I know all about this. Every time Mateo is in the car for longer than half an hour, he is sick. The last time I took him with me into Heraklion, I had to wash him off in the sea before I could do my shopping because he was covered in vomit."

Carl made a guttural sound at the visual and chomped down another tablet for good measure.

"Now I leave him with his yaya; it is much easier and she, of course, loves to have him all to herself."

"I can't wait to meet Mama Bikakis."

Kassia grinned. "Yes, you will love her, and she will love you, especially if you tell her the moussaka she plans to make for dinner is the best you have ever eaten!"

"I can't wait to try it. It's like a lasagne, only with eggplant, isn't it?"

"Yes, it is one of Mama's specialties."

"So far we have eaten an awful lot of souvlaki to make the budget stretch further." The street food was cheap and tasty but she was getting a little over it. And the French fries that were always stuffed in the pita pockets along with the meat and salad weren't doing her figure any good either. Of course, she could always pick them out but somehow it went against her most basic of instincts to chuck a French fry away.

"If you look now, when we get round this corner, you will see Agios Nikolaos. It was once a fishing village but now it is the closest town for us." Kassia had one hand on the steering wheel; the other gesticulated to the panoramic vista that greeted them as they rounded the bend. Annie gasped at the sight of the rolling golden hills and aquamarine waters. A harbour dotted with boats and a pretty town with a river winding its way through it panned out before them. The view was undeniably breathtaking, she thought, determined to ignore the sheer drop on the other side of the road and the banged-up array of cars that hurtled towards them. She was almost, but not quite, used to the take-your-life-in-your-hands feeling every time she was a passenger in a Greek car, thanks to some hairy taxi rides over the course of the last few weeks.

"We are nearly there," Kassia announced as Carl muttered something along the lines of *thank God for that* from the back seat while Annie's excitement grew at shortly meeting the rest of a family she already felt she knew so well.

They drove past a couple of palatial homes that sprawled up the cliffside, built to grant them the best panorama of the bays possible. They were holiday houses, Kassia informed them. Elounda had attracted more than its fair share of celebrities in the last couple of years. It was the boutique, laid-back feel of the place that brought them here. Tourism had made a big jandal-like footprint up the road in Malia and other coastal towns; Elounda, however, due to its tucked away positioning, wore a much smaller flip-flop. Kas was fairly sure, too, that she'd spotted Leonardo DiCaprio whizzing past her on a jet ski earlier in the season.

With the mental picture of Leonardo on a jet ski painted, they wound their way downward and soon the cliffs levelled out and the road narrowed as signs of village life appeared. The main town of Elounda was a little farther on down by the harbour, Kassia divulged, as a smattering of deserted tavernas on the left popped into view. On their right was the requisite green pharmacy cross, along with a smallish supermarket, a stand full of cheap sunglasses outside its open-plan frontage. Annie was too busy staring at a peculiar shop with baskets full of sea sponges and all sorts of fish skeletons rattling in the breeze to brace for the sharp turn ahead and her shoulder hit the window.

"Sorry." Kassia grinned. Unable to make the right angle turn in one go and as her two passengers righted themselves, she executed a swift three-point turn, and narrowly missed the coach that had appeared out of nowhere behind them. With the car pointed in the direction she wanted it to go, they coasted down a steep incline and past a sprawling restaurant whose signage suggested it held nightclub aspirations too. At the bottom was a stretch of narrow road bordered on its rocky edge to the left by the sea.

"Oh, wow, it's beautiful—look, Carl!" Annie wound her window down and pointed out at the gentle lapis water, which was in startling contrast to the burnt umber hills that surrounded it. Faced with a flat stretch of road and armed with the knowledge that they were less than a minute away from their final destination, Carl felt he could afford to muster enthusiasm, so he joined in with her excited exclamations.

"Those are self-catering apartments." Kassia pointed over to the right at the white square three-storey blocks. The upper levels all had small balconies, over which colourful beach towels were draped. Next to the apartments was a taverna strung with fairy lights; vibrant cushions adorned the outdoor seating. Annie tried to visualise it lit up at night with the sound of the sea, as it lapped at the rock wall, just across the road. It would be gorgeous and oh-so romantic. She felt momentarily lost as it hit her that she wouldn't be experiencing any romance in the foreseeable future. This was despite Carl's best efforts at setting her up with anything straight and under sixty on Mykonos. She'd given him a serious talking to the next day, as she rubbed at her temples to ease the throbbing inside her head, over his having left her at the bar with Tom. Carl had hit the dance floor to strut his stuff with some Italian Stallion while she'd had to fend off the fifty-one-year-old divorcee with an appalling toupee and bad breath from the UK.

Nope, she had informed Carl in no uncertain terms, she was single and that's the way it would be staying, thank you very much. She wanted to be by herself. Carl had shaken his head; he hated being by himself. It was taking a while to get used to her new single status, though, and she wondered how Tony was faring. She shook his image away; she refused to dwell on the past, not today of all days. Her gaze strayed to the vacant lot next door to the taverna with its withered blades of grass baking under the sun as they poked wearily up between the rock-strewn soil. *A haven for skinks*. She grimaced.

How some people felt about mice was how Annie felt about the tiny lizards and she had had several close encounters with them since she'd set foot on Greek soil. The lot was overlooked by another low-rise apartment block but this one had an inviting kidney-shaped pool with a few bodies lounging around it out the front. Several people propped up the bar area set up by the pool.

"An English couple manage those apartments. They are lovely people, although they are a bit too fond of the karaoke nights if you ask me. And she—Wendy—cannot sing, although she always insists on doing a number by that woman—you know?"

It was a bit of a vague description and Annie looked at her blankly as Kassia waved her hand impatiently. "You know, that woman with all the curly black hair, lucky woman, who likes to wear the skimpy outfits and has a fondness for the plastic surgery?"

"Cher?" Carl piped up from the back seat and Annie laughed as Kassia nodded.

"Trust you to guess right."

"Yes, Cher, but thank goodness Wendy does not dress up like her. She is a big girl, you know; it would not be a good look."

Annie and Carl both grinned at the mental image Kassia had conjured up of a plump English Cher who couldn't sing to save herself.

An airy bar, kitted out in white and chrome, that was obviously a place to be seen while sipping on a cold beer came into view next. Carl pressed his nose to the window and decided he would plop his bottom down on one of those stools and look out from its open frontage to the sea in the very near future.

Without warning, Kassia swerved the van away from the water onto the other side of the road to park facing the wrong way. Sounding the horn before she switched the engine off, she twisted round in her seat to grin at them both. "Welcome to Eleni's. We are home."

Annie saw a stone, three-storey house. Its yellow paint flaked but, with wrought-iron balconies stuffed full of brilliant red geraniums and the mammoth climbing purple bougainvillea that wound its way up the side of the building, it oozed charm. The blue front door burst open and a short woman, clad head to toe in black, bustled out, wiping her hands on her apron before she called something over her shoulder. She had a tiny tot hanging off her hip and Annie's heart leaped at the sight of little Nikolos.

As she got out of the car, a stocky and rather swarthy looking man rounded the corner of the house. He wielded a hoe and Annie watched as he paused for a moment to wipe his brow with a hanky. She hazarded a guess that he was Kas's Spiros. A mini-me who barely reached his knees trailed along behind him—Mateo!

Mama Bikakis turned back towards the house and called out again. This time an Adonis apparition appeared in the doorway. His face broke into a wide, welcoming grin that, even from this distance, Annie could see showcased a top and bottom set of perfect white teeth. His hair had the casually ruffled look that takes time and effort to achieve. This had to be Alexandros. Next to her, she heard Carl's sharp intake of breath. She elbowed him swiftly and hissed out of the corner of her mouth, "Forget it."

All of a sudden, it seemed to Annie that the pebbled courtyard in front of the house was filled to overflowing and she, suddenly shy, hung back on the pavement for a moment longer, Carl glued to her side.

Kassia was having none of it, though, and gave them both a gentle shove in the back as she herded them forward.

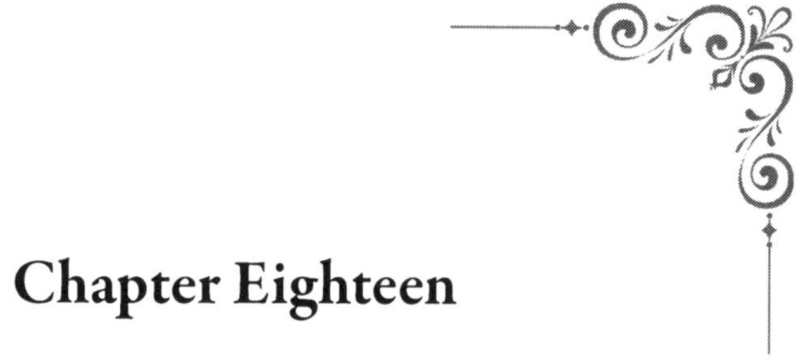

Chapter Eighteen

"*Yassas*! Let me look at you both," Mama Bikakis, in all her rotund glory with wisps of grey hair that escaped from a loose bun, cried. She handed Nikolos over to his mother's outstretched arms and stepped forward, her broad smile revealing a gold tooth. She clapped a hand on either side of her face, planted a kiss on both of Annie's cheeks and held her firmly so she could study her for a moment. Her unmade-up coffee bean eyes danced as she exclaimed, "*Omorfi kopela*! You are beautiful—all that hair, it is beautiful!" She released Annie's slightly startled face and repeated the performance with Carl, who stood alongside her. "Oh, so handsome! This boy, he is so handsome." Carl preened and felt instantly at ease while Annie took a moment to study the woman she had never, like the whole family, seen in the flesh before but already felt she knew so well thanks to Kassia's emails. It was like watching a photograph come to life, she mused as her eyes swept over Mama: her plain black frock, and sensible flat shoes, which shod feet that did a sterling job of supporting an impressive set of cankles.

Little Nikolos buried his face in his mother's bosom before he peered out at her shyly to reveal a set of limpid eyes so dark they appeared to be black. Annie gave him a smile and resisted the urge to grab his chubby cheek. As though sensing she was a possible cheek squeezer, he instantly buried his head once more. *Oh well, he'd warm up once all the fuss had died down*. Annie turned her attention to Mateo. The little boy stood to one side of his father on a set of sturdy tanned legs, which poked out of grubby yellow shorts. He clutched his own hammer, albeit a small one. Ah, Daddy's helper, she thought as she crouched down to his level to say hello. He stared at her with open curiosity and Annie was just about to give him a kiss on his cheek when he lunged forward, grabbed a handful of her hair and gave it a good tug.

"Ow!"

"Mateo!" his father admonished but Annie looked up at Spiros with a smile.

"It's fine. He took me by surprise, that's all. I think he's just checking to make sure it's real, aren't you, Mateo?"

There was laughter as the little boy released the handful of hair and treated her to a cheeky grin that Annie reckoned had probably saved him from a good telling-off many a time. Yes, he definitely had the self-assured stance of an older brother, she decided as she stood back up. Carl, who was busy getting his back slapped and his hand shaken, was beginning to look a little overwhelmed by the effusiveness of their welcome. She smiled at the relief on his features as Kassia shushed her family and began the formal introductions.

Spiros, on closer inspection, was every bit as lovely as Annie had known he would be. His twinkling eyes gave away the fact that his stern features were not a true indicator of the personality that lurked beneath that hooded brow of his. As for Alexandros, he was tall and lean with the chiselled features of an old-time matinee idol. His bearing was laid-back and languid, like that of a big cat, and Annie could see his appeal with the ladies. She caught him eyeing her hair appraisingly but was pleased that he managed to refrain from snatching at it like his nephew had just done. He had an aura of manliness and it wasn't just her all that testosterone was affecting. Carl flushed, too, when he stepped forward to shake his hand. Although the grin he bestowed on them was self-assured, it held the same hint of naughtiness that she had detected in Mateo's. Oh yes, she thought, as she hoped he hadn't noticed her clammy palm, this was a man who was well aware of the impact he had on people.

As for Mama Bikakis, with her pudding face and those dark eyes that sparkled with the zest of a life well lived, she was a living, breathing caricature of a Greek mama. She stood now with her hands forming a steeple at her mouth; eyes sparkling with tears as she gazed at her newly arrived guests. Annie watched on, fascinated as the waterworks dried up as abruptly as they had started and her chubby arm shot up to give Alexandros a light thwack about the back of his head. She barked something at him in Greek which, judging by the way he laughed and then wandered down to the van to retrieve their bags, had been instructions to do just that.

"I could have got those, Mrs Bikakis," Carl said.

She frowned at him. "No, no, not Mrs Bikakis—you are family. You call me Mama like they all do." She waved her hand expansively over the group.

Annie and Carl weren't going to argue and they both chimed in, "Yes, Mama."

She smiled, pleased, before she clapped her hands. "Now you must be hungry after your journey and the food on those ferries—bah." She stuck her tongue out. "It is overpriced and tasteless. A disgrace!"

Annie thought back to the dried-out cheese roll she had eaten and had to agree with her.

"But first I will show you Eleni's, yes?" Annie nodded enthusiastically and Carl replied, "Yes, please," as they followed the older woman's lead.

They stepped in through the open doorway and two things instantly assailed them: a delicious smell hovered on the air and the welcome drop in temperature as the cooler air settled over them. The air-conditioning was a welcome respite. "Something smells wonderful." Annie inhaled appreciatively.

Mama beamed. "Moussaka."

"I've heard wonderful things about your moussaka, Mama. I can't wait to try it." Carl instantly became her golden boy.

They stood in a hallway with rooms leading off to either side. The walls were painted a crisp white, which made it seem wider than it really was. At the end of the hall was a staircase that led to the first and second floors, where Annie supposed the guests' rooms would be. So far Eleni's was pretty much what she had pictured it to be. She followed behind Carl as Mama led them into the first room that veered off on their left. "This was my Abram's bedroom when he was a boy but now it is our reception room."

It wasn't a large room but it was ample for the old wooden desk that dominated the space with the window behind it that let in the light. An open laptop rested on it alongside a stack of unopened mail and a charging telephone. Kas probably hadn't had a chance to go through the post yet with driving to Heraklion to pick us up, Annie thought. Her eyes strayed to a beautiful beach scene photo on the wall next to her. "Where was that taken, Mama?" She was surprised to find she didn't feel strange in the slightest addressing this warm, old lady so familiarly.

"Spiros took that and I had it framed." She puffed up with pride. "It is our Plaka Beach right here in Elounda."

"It's stunning."

A yellow, floral two-seater couch covered with a blue throw rug was pushed up against the wall opposite the photograph and Mama pointed to it. "For the guests to sit when Kassia checks them in."

Carl and Annie nodded and moved out of the way to let her pass. "Come, come, I will show you the breakfast room."

That's right, Annie remembered as she followed after her; they provided their guests with the option of a cooked breakfast each morning. The room they were led into next was large enough to allow plenty of space to manoeuvre around the eight tables dotted around it. Four double rooms on each floor meant eight tables for breakfast. Annie noticed each table was covered in a pretty blue and white chequered cloth; in the middle was a sugar bowl, a salt and pepper set, and a little vase with a single red plastic poppy placed in it. A wooden butler's chest rested up against the wall closest to the door they'd just come in through and Mama informed them they kept their cutlery and crockery in it. The space had an Old World feel to it, thanks to the height of the ceiling and the well-worn floorboards but at the same time it also felt fresh and modern.

Annie recalled Kassia telling her that when Spiros's father Abram died, Mama had had the guesthouse thoroughly renovated. It was something she had wanted to do for a long time but her plans had always been met with resistance by Abram, who had seen no need to make changes to his boyhood home.

A large picture window dominated the room. It looked straight out to the sea and she stood for a moment and soaked in the scene. "What a lovely way to start the day, sitting in here and looking out at that glorious view," she said, thinking aloud and wondering whether there was a fight each morning to try to nab the table by the window.

Reluctantly, she dragged her eyes away and spied a door in the other wall. She wondered where it led. She didn't have to wonder for long as Mama waddled over, pushed it open, and beckoned at them to follow her lead.

It was the kitchen. A spacious room with French-style doors that flooded the room with golden light and opened up to the garden at the side of the house. The worktops were clear, so Mama was obviously a tidy cook. Annie's eyes flitted to the modern oven, from which the delicious smell emanated. She watched as Mama bustled over to it and opened the door. She prodded at the dish that bubbled away inside with a knife and once she was satisfied all was as it should be, she shut it again. She looked decidedly pinker in the cheeks when she turned around to tell them that she liked to cook her moussaka slowly in order to bring out the flavours. Annie's mouth watered and Carl gazed longingly at the oven.

In the centre of the room was a huge old wooden table that bowed in the middle. A colouring-in book lay open on it and a pile of felt tips, some with their lids still off, were scattered next to it. On the floor under the table, Annie spied a toy truck and a few other banged-up matchbox sized vehicles, which, judging by the dents in the table legs, regularly took part in a Mateo styled smash-up derby. It was this lack of obvious pretentiousness that made the large space homey and welcoming. A rug was laid out on the floor in the corner of the kitchen with a few cushions stacked up on it, along with a jumble of chunky plastic toys. That must be where Nikolos sits and plays, she surmised.

Mama moved them along to show them the large double room that had once been hers and Abram's but was now where Kassia and Spiros slept. The bed was rumpled and the room slightly untidy, which made Annie smile and Mama frown before she herded them on. Mateo and Nikolos were in the room next door to their parents. It was large enough to house a single bed, a cot, and a chest, which was opened to reveal a plethora of toys stuffed inside it. Annie recognised the bright mobile dangling over Nikolos's cot; she'd sent it, along with the iconic New Zealand wooden Buzzy Bee toy that peeked out from under Mateo's bed.

A thoroughly modernised bathroom with both a shower and a bath was next to Mama's room at the end of the hall. A private sign above the door stated that it was for the family's use only. As they poked their heads round the door to Mama's immaculate room, they spied an old sepia photo of a beautiful young woman and handsome man on their wedding day. It was in pride of place on her dressing table and Annie instantly recognised the sparkle in the bride's eyes.

"Your room is around the corner here, Annie." Mama pronounced her name Ahnnee as she led them to a door nestled in the alcove under the stairs.

It was like a secret room, her very own secret room under the stairs, Annie thought as she opened the door and peered inside eagerly. Again, it was painted white and the ceiling sloped with the stairs; she knew she'd have to be careful not to bump her head if she were to sit up in bed too suddenly. The single bed had an old-fashioned bedhead in the bedknobs and broomsticks fashion and was covered in a plain white coverlet, at the end of which was a neatly folded blue throw blanket. To the left of the bed was a set of wooden drawers with a reading lamp placed on it. Annie was touched by the little vase filled with fresh daisies alongside it. Her backpack had been placed at the foot of the bed and there was barely room between it and the wall where the room's only window let in the light. Annie gazed up at the window with its worn calico drapes and instantly imagined herself lying in her little bed at night, looking out at a carpet of stars.

Mama looked worried. "You like it, yes? It is small and simple but I think it will do."

"Mama, I love it—thank you."

The old woman beamed, and patted Annie on her shoulder. "I am pleased. Carl, we have put you in with Alexandros up the stairs. Come and see."

Carl looked flustered. "I don't want to cramp Alexandros's style."

"His style could do with some cramping," the old woman muttered. She panted as she held onto the wooden banister rail and climbed the stairs to the first floor. Listening to her wheeze, Annie realised that despite the circumstances that had bought Kassia and Spiros here, she really did need them. There was no way she would cope with the cleaning of the guest rooms on top of all the other day-to-day chores running Eleni's would entail.

Mama leaned against the banister to rest for a moment when they reached the landing. "All the bedrooms on this floor and upstairs look out to sea." She gesticulated to the rooms, each with a number on their shut doors. "They are all identical to the one you will be in, Carl. We normally rent it out but with Alexandros home—" She shrugged and swayed towards the open door at the end of the landing and pointed out the shared amenities on the way. Annie caught a glimpse inside the large bathroom and her overall impression was one of marble and lots of it.

"Good. Alexandros has made his bed." Mama pushed the door open and gave the room a quick inspection before she turned to Carl. "So this is where you and Alexandros will sleep."

Carl stepped forward with Annie close behind and clapped his hands in delight. Two single beds each with a blue and white embroidered coverlet and plump matching pillows were placed against the wall so that when you lay on your bed, you could see straight out the window, which was draped with floating muslin curtains, to an infinity of blue. Each bed had a dark wood bedside table with a white lamp sitting on it. Annie couldn't make out what was on the cover of the magazine that was splayed open on one of the tables but it did give away which of the beds was Alexandros'. The walls were in keeping with the theme of the rest of the house: white and with a single black-and-white print of a Cretan village scene hung on the wall in between the beds. On the far side of the room was a freestanding wardrobe in the same dark wood, along with a matching chest of drawers upon which a white lacy cloth was home to a staggering array of men's toiletries. Carl and Alexandros would be able to mix and match products, Annie thought with a smirk as she spied Carl's backpack leaning against the engraved doors of the wardrobe. The creaking floorboards had been painted white, too, and were adorned by a swirling patterned blue and white rag rug. The overall effect was utterly Greek and charming in its simplicity. The room, on a hot day, would be a haven.

"It is gorgeous, absolutely gorgeous. No wonder you have a full house, Mama." Carl wandered over to the open window. He'd long ago gotten over his horror of having to share bathrooms—he'd had to—and this would do him nicely, thank you very much.

"Do you want to unpack now or later?"

Carl and Annie looked at each other. They were both itching to go outside and bask in the fact that they were actually here. "Later please."

"Good!" Mama dazzled them with that gold tooth before they plodded back to the stairs. "I have a plan. You two go outside and relax with a cool drink. It is a good one, yes?" She didn't wait to hear whether or not they agreed, and as the trio trooped back downstairs, they got another whiff of the delicious smells that seeped from the kitchen. Mama, as though reading their minds, said, "Dinner will be a while yet, but I will bring something out for you to eat while you talk, yes?"

Annie was beginning to get used to the way this endearingly round little woman answered her own questions for them at the end of each sentence.

Chapter Nineteen

CARL AND ANNIE STEPPED outside and blinked in the sunshine as they did so. Kassia sat at the picnic table in the middle of the cluster of olive trees that provided scant shade, Nikolos dandled on her knee. He was too engrossed in chewing the toy he held between his chubby fists to show them much interest as they wandered over. It was a scorcher. As Annie swept her hair back from her neck, wishing she had put it up, Spiros appeared from around the side of the house and called out for Carl to join him. As she sat down at the table, Annie had to laugh as she watched him disappear with Spiros. Carl and gardening did not go hand in hand but Spiros would no doubt find that out for himself.

"It is hot, yes?" Kassia smiled from across the table. "What are you laughing about?"

"Very hot, and I am laughing at the thought of Carl wielding a hoe or a spade or any gardening implement, for that matter."

"Ah, Spiros will soon make him, how you say, green handed?"

Annie laughed again. "Green fingered."

Kassia nodded. "Yes, that is the expression I was looking for—green fingered."

"It is not one I would have ever thought of applying where Carl is concerned, though." Annie hesitated for a moment. "Kas, can I ask you something?"

"Of course, what is it?"

"We aren't putting you out, I hope?"

"Putting me out?" Kas frowned.

Annie elaborated, "Oh sorry, I forget we have strange ways of saying things in the English language sometimes. We aren't in the way, are we? Carl and I don't want to cause you any bother, um, problems, I mean."

"Stop! Of course you are not."

"Because you know we want to pay the same rate as any of your other guests."

"Pah! Don't be stupid! You are my New Zealand sister and Carl my brother, so say no more about it." Her tone brooked no argument.

Annie smiled at her friend gratefully as Mama toddled over with a tray laden with frosty glasses and a pitcher of iced water. She realised how parched she was.

"I will get some food organised and leave you two girls to catch up. It has been a long time coming, I think." She placed the tray down on the table. "Kassia, will you take a drink to the boys?" Mama reached out and scooped Nikolos, who didn't pause in his chewing, up off his mama's knee. "Come, agoraki mou."

"Of course, thank you, Mama." She glanced at her watch. "I think it is time for Nikolos to have his nap. Would you mind putting him down for me?"

Mama looked affronted as she jiggled the little boy on her ample hip. "No, Kassia, he doesn't need this sleep. I keep telling you this. He is a big boy now—nearly one year old. He will be happy playing in the kitchen with his yaya, so let him be." Not waiting to hear the protest hovering on Kassia's lips, she turned and ambled back from whence she came.

Kassia gave a little grunt of frustration when she was safely out of earshot. "Did you hear that? Nikolos needs his sleep in the afternoon but because he is waking in the night, Mama has decided to do what she did with Spiros and Alexandros at the same age. She thinks keeping him up all day will make him sleep through the night. It isn't, though, and all that happens instead is that by five o'clock, he is crying all the time. It is awful but when I try to tell her this, she points to her sons and tells me to listen to her because she knows best." She mimicked Mama's voice, "Spirosaki mou and Alexandrosaki mou have grown up big and strong, have they not?" She clenched her teeth. "Aagh! It drives me crazy!"

"At least she doesn't have a penchant for line dancing and getting round in skin-tight leathers and Stetson hats like my ex-soon-to-be mother-in-law did."

Kassia raised a smile. "I am sure you exaggerate."

"I'm not—ask Carl if you don't believe me. You're lucky, Kas, because it is obvious that Mama loves you and the children." Annie chewed her lip and chose her words carefully. "She's only doing what she feels is best for them but yes, I can see it must be hard for you too."

Kassia sighed and poured two glasses of water. "Listen to me—you are only here a short time and already I am moaning. I am sorry. It's just that two headstrong women under one roof will always be tough. I do love her, though, and you are right—she does mean well. It's just..."

"Frustrating," Annie finished for her.

"Yes—oh, hello, Adonis." She leaned down, her attention on something under the table. Annie bent down, too, to peer under the table, curious to see who this Adonis was. A plump black and white cat sat there. His head was tilted and he had a daft look of ecstasy on his face as Kassia scratched behind his ear. "Annie, meet Adonis." She laughed as their eyes met under the table.

Annie made some kissing noises and he abandoned Kassia's affections to trot curiously over to her outstretched hand. He sniffed it cautiously, looked at her for a moment, and then sat down at her feet and invited her to stroke him. She obliged. "He's lovely. How old is he?"

"I don't know. He moved in on us a year ago and Mateo fell in love with him so that was it, he stayed. He likes you."

"I like him, too, but who decided on his name?"

"Ah, that would be Mateo. He overheard me telling Spiros that Alexandros likes to think of himself as a modern-day Adonis—you know, the Greek god of Beauty, Desire—all those things. Mateo loves his uncle, so that was that. So now it is my own fault that I feel so silly calling him in for dinner." She laughed.

Annie couldn't help but agree that the title of Adonis was fitting where Alexandros was concerned and her mouth twitched at the thought of Kas standing on the doorstep each evening as she shouted out, "Adonis, here kitty, kitty." It was followed by a little wave of sadness, though. *Poor old Jazz.* She sat up and took the glass her friend proffered.

"You miss your cat Jasper, yes?"

"I do, Kas. He was quite a character."

She gave her a sad little smile and patted her hand. Her nails were bitten to the quick, Annie noticed. She smiled back at her before she gulped her water down greedily. "You know what you were saying about Mama, before Adonis interrupted us?"

"Yes?"

"Well, I met this man, he was a schoolteacher who had brought his class to the Acropolis, and we got chatting. I told him that we were coming to stay with you here and I explained how things are with you and Mama sometimes. You don't mind?" Annie hoped she hadn't spoken out of turn.

Kassia shook her head and looked amused.

"Good. Anyway, he told me that he has a sister who has the same problem as you and that the Greek mother-in-law is a very real stereotype."

With her glass raised halfway to her mouth, Kassia raised an eyebrow and her full lips curved into a smile. "Oh, and do you often get talking to strange men at ancient sites or is this just since you have been in Greece?"

"It wasn't like that," Annie protested before she filled her in on how the conversation had come about in the first place.

"Well, he sounds like a nice man."

"Yes, he was actually."

"So thanks to him, you realised that you have come to Greece to say goodbye to Roz and to find your metaphorical Yanni, yes?"

Annie cringed. "It made perfect sense at the Acropolis but maybe that was just the moment I was in. Sitting here now with you, it sounds rather self-indulgent and don't forget I came to Greece to meet you and the family too."

"I know you did and I am glad you did." Kassia's smile was reassuring. "But tell me, do you feel any different since you have been here in Greece?"

"Do you know what, Kas? I do, I really do. All that wedding business, my job—I've been so muddled for so long, and I didn't know how to go about changing any of it."

"Yes, I was worried but I knew you would find your way."

"And I have, because from the moment Carl and I booked our tickets, my head felt clear for the first time in what felt like forever. I knew I was doing exactly what I should be doing. This is a journey I have to make, for myself and for Roz. I was just bloody lucky that Carl decided to come along too."

They smiled at each other in unspoken understanding and then Kassia poured out two more tumblers of water. "Speaking of Carl, I think I had better take these around to him and Spiros before they collapse. Alexandros promised to take Mateo to the beach this afternoon so I will send him inside to find him. You relax here if you like. I won't be long."

Annie nodded her thanks and sighed happily, glad of a few moments alone to soak up her surrounds properly. It really was a little pocket of paradise, she decided. Her eyes alighted on the three-storied building in front of her with its pebbled courtyard before following the sweep of sparse lawn she sat on that led down to the road. A young couple held hands, beach towels slung over their shoulders, and wandered along the middle of it, the sea an undulating backdrop beside them. She stretched her legs and admired their honeyed hue before she frowned. *Was her light tan due to her freckles having all joined up to blend into one great big one?* She stifled a yawn as she spied Kassia walking briskly back towards her. *If she was sleepy, Carl must be ready to keel over.*

"Spiros has given Carl a spade and he is trying so hard to be masculine, swinging it about like this." She demonstrated before she sat down.

Annie laughed. "Yes, I can just imagine it because when he goes into macho mode, Carl is a sight to behold indeed."

Kassia waved her hand. "Men—leave them to it, I say. Oh, I better help—"

"No, you stay put. I'll give her a hand." Annie got to her feet in order to take the tray Mama, who had reappeared in the doorway, held. This one, Annie noted as she walked towards the old woman, looked to be laden with colourful treats. Spying a carafe of wine, her mouth watered in anticipation of its crisp bite. "Oh, this looks wonderful, thank you, Mama! Look at the size of those olives! Yum!" Mama's ample bosom swelled to enormous proportions at the praise. "You shouldn't have gone to so much trouble, though."

"It is no bother. I want you and Kassia to sit and enjoy each other."

Annie smiled and fell a little bit more in love with the Bikakis family matriarch as she took the tray from her.

Inside the house, a bloodcurdling wail went up. Annie's eyes widened in alarm but Mama didn't seem in the slightest bit perturbed. Kassia heard it too and had gotten to her feet. She strode towards them but Mama waved her back. "It's nothing, Kassia—go sit down. Boys, they fight. Mateo has probably taken a toy from Nikolos, that is all." She shrugged and rolled her eyes at Annie. "It's what they do."

As she lumbered back into the house, Kassia poked her tongue out at her back but did as she had been told and sat down heavily at the picnic table. Annie walked carefully across the spikes of grass with the weighty tray and placed it down on the table.

"She makes me feel like I am not needed in my own home." Kassia helped Annie unload the tray. "But then that's the problem—it was her home first."

"Like I said before, she obviously means well and it must be nice to have the extra pair of hands to help with the boys?" Annie looked over at her friend. Her dark hair had fallen across her face and she couldn't read her expression.

"Yes, sometimes." She speared an olive with a toothpick viciously. "But there are times when I feel left out of things. The boys, they adore her, but I am their mother and it should be me they come to first."

Annie didn't say anything and Kassia carried on. "I know how this sounds but sometimes I think it's not fair. She has had her turn with her boys; now let me have my turn with mine."

This time it was Annie who poured the drinks and pushed a generous glass across the table.

"I am worried that one day I will snap and say something to her that I will regret." Kassia looked up and tucked her hair behind her ears. Annie noticed her lovely olive skin had mottled red patches.

"Have you talked to Spiros about how you are feeling?"

"I have tried but she is his mother and he doesn't want to hear. He is a typical man—all he wants is an easy life."

An image of Tony flashed up in front of Annie's eyes. "Maybe you should try again if it is getting you down as much as this. Like you said, she is *his* mother. It would be better coming from him and she'd probably be more inclined to listen."

Kassia took hold of her glass. Annie winced at the sight of the chewed fingernails at the end of her long, slim fingers wrapped around the stem. "Mama Bikakis is, how you say? A law unto herself."

She looked so down in the mouth that Annie got up and went round to give her shoulders a squeeze. Kassia patted her hand gratefully. "I'm glad you are here. But I am being dramatic. Ignore my silliness. You have not come all these miles to hear me complain."

"Listen." Annie sat back down. "You're my friend, and friends are there for each other so if you want to moan, you go ahead and moan! You've put up with me and my moans for years."

Kassia smiled at her friend's earnest face and held her glass up. "Okay, so I will raise my glass to friends and moaning."

"To good friends and moaning." Annie raised hers.

"To best friends and moaning!" Both women chorused and clinked their glasses before they took a sip of the wine.

"What's this?" Annie smacked her lips together.

"Do you like it?"

"I'm not sure. I think so. It's just that it has an unusual aftertaste to it."

"It's a locally made retsina, which is white wine fermented with pine resin. It is also very potent so be warned because it, how you say? Grows on people." Kassia winked before she added, "Anyway, we have talked enough about me. I want to hear all about you, starting with how you are feeling these days as a single woman?" She reached forward and popped a piece of marinated eggplant in her mouth before she looked at her friend expectantly.

Annie had to think about her answer for a moment because her feelings were still in a jumble. "Well, I know that breaking up with Tony was the right thing to do, but that's not to say that I don't miss him or at least the idea of him. I'm not sure I miss the reality of our relationship, though, if that makes sense?"

"I think you mean you are remembering the good times now, not the bad times, which is natural."

"Yes, I suppose I am and we did have some good times." Annie sighed and toyed with her glass. "I still can't quite believe that less than two months ago I was trying on a wedding dress and now here I am suddenly single, sitting amid the olive trees with you in Crete."

Kassia laughed. "Well, I am glad you are! And yes, life can take many strange turns." Her expression sobered as she added, "I never thought I would wind up living here with my mother-in-law." She shook her head. "Don't you worry—you will get to wear your beautiful dress one day but it will be for the right man, I think."

"Actually, for now I don't really want to think about men and as for that dress—as gorgeous as it was, it wasn't me, not really."

"But you said it was your dream dress. Was it very expensive, yes?"

"Yes very, very but that's not why I changed my mind about it." Annie popped an olive in her mouth and enjoyed the salty burst as she bit into it.

"Oh?"

"No. Don't tell Carl but it was too bloody tight!"

They broke into laughter and made light work of the platter until Kassia urged Annie to tell her all about her and Carl's adventures since they'd left New Zealand.

"You'd better fill up our glasses then." Annie held her empty glass out.

"REMIND ME TO NEVER fly anywhere with him! It sounds terrible." Kassia laughed and by the time Annie had finished telling her about Carl's misadventures in Athens thanks to his dodgy stomach, she was bent double.

"Stop!" She held up her hand. "My stomach, it is hurting."

"It's funny now but believe you me, it wasn't at the time."

"I can imagine it would have been quite desperate at the time." They looked at each other and erupted into peals of laughter.

"What's so funny, you two?" A red-faced, sweaty Carl flopped down onto the ground next to the table. He took off his hat and fanned himself. "And where's the worker's glass of vino, you two lushes?"

"You're what is so funny, Carl. I have been hearing all about your little problem in Athens." Kassia wiped the corner of her eyes before she reached for one of the water tumblers. "Will this do? I am too exhausted from laughing to go up to the house to fetch you a proper wine glass."

"Hmm, hostess with the mostess—I'm kidding, sit back down! It will do just fine and you may well laugh now but it was not funny at the time. I lost nearly half a stone in weight!"

"Perhaps I should visit Athens." Kassia looked down at her midriff. "Believe me, Mama's cooking will soon put the meat back on your bones; it has mine and some. Here..."

Carl took the glass and drank deeply. "Ah, 'tis nectar from the gods. Retsina, am I right?

Kassia nodded and looked pleased as he added, "And you have what we in the biz call womanly curves, my dear girl."

Annie smiled fondly at him and loved the way they had only been here a couple of hours and already they had slotted in and been made to feel right at home.

"Is Spiros still working in the garden?" Kassia asked.

"Yes. He said he would square off the patch he was working on and then call it a day. You've done well there; he is a lovely man."

"Yes, I think so."

"That's an impressive veggie patch he has got going on, too, considering the soil is like rock—once you get past the top layer of sand, that is."

"You sound like a professional gardener," Annie said, impressed.

"Too much bloody hard work for me, thanks very much. Spiros said I looked like I was about to keel over, so I should come and sit in the shade with you girls for a while. If I'd known there was wine on offer, I would have been over earlier."

"Yes, Spiros is in his element, growing things and catching things. I think it is his caveman instincts coming to the fore."

"He was telling me about his novel, too. It sounds a rather intriguing mystery."

"I haven't read any of it yet because he won't let me see it until it is finished but he is a talented writer."

"When does he find the time to sit down and actually write, Kas?" Annie asked.

"He goes to the office at three o'clock and writes until five o'clock most days because he says if he doesn't set aside this time he will never get his book finished." Kassia shrugged. "He is right, I suppose."

"Good for him." Carl took another drink. "He's really living his dream."

"Yes, *he* is." The inflection in her voice didn't escape him and he raised a quizzical eyebrow in Annie's direction. She shook her head slightly, in warning not to go there.

Kassia ran a finger round the rim of her wine glass before she seemed to pull herself up as she visibly brightened. "Well, now that I have you both here, tell me—what has been your favourite of the Greek islands so far?"

"Not counting here?" Carl asked. Annie noticed his normal colour had returned.

"Not counting here." Kassia smiled.

"Okay, well, every island has been beautiful, of course, and each island had something special about it. But I think my favourite in the Cyclades would have to be Naxos."

Annie nodded her agreement. "We stayed in the old town of Hora."

"Ah, Naxos! Yes, it is beautiful—the most verdant of the Cyclades, I think?"

"That's a big word, verdant." Annie rolled it off her tongue. "I like it and yes, it was the greenest of the islands once you got inland, which we did when we visited this gorgeous little village. It had the most stunning Venetian architecture and every corner we turned was a photograph waiting to be taken. What was it called again, Carl?"

"Halki, we had the best spinach and cheese pie from that bakery while we waited for the bus to take us back to Hora."

"Oh yeah, it was good. I could have gone two if the bus hadn't shown up when it did. Remember the teacher chap I told you I met at the Acropolis, Kas? His name's Kristofr and he was the one who insisted that we must go to Naxos. It's where he came from originally."

"Ah, I see! It is Kristofr now. And did you get this Kristofr's phone number or he yours?"

"No! It wasn't like that. He felt sorry for me, that was all, and was being helpful."

Kassia and Carl exchanged glances as Kassia replied, "Yes, in the way that men are always helpful to a beautiful woman when she is sad."

"You should have seen her mooning after him," Carl said.

"I was not."

"Yes, you were."

"Now, now children!" Kassia intervened.

"Alright, I'll admit he was rather nice."

"Bloody gorgeous more like," Carl interrupted, and Annie glared at him.

"But we didn't swap numbers and like I keep saying, I don't want to meet anybody anyway. Besides, I probably came across as a bit of a loon, offloading to him the way I did about Roz."

"Take it from me that life has a funny way of not going to plan and in my experience, when you really want to meet someone, you stay single and lonely but when you decide that no, you want to be on your own that is when the right person comes along."

"Well said, Kas, my dear." The flicker of sadness that crossed Carl's face didn't escape Annie. He really missed David, she realised and softened her tone.

"Like I said, we didn't exchange numbers and I'll never see him again, so I don't think it was the start of something beautiful."

"Ah, it's a pity." Kassia shook her dark head as Annie sighed exasperatedly.

"Can we please move on?"

"If we have to," she said.

"You have to."

"Okay, so you loved Naxos."

This was a theme Annie was far more comfortable discussing and she began to wax lyrical. "Oh, I did! It was everything I hoped a Greek island would be. The old town was so beautiful with the bright reds, purples, and pinks of the bougainvillea climbing everywhere. I always feel like I am on holiday when I see bougainvillea. Remember that cute little black cat that kept showing up everywhere we went, Carl?"

He nodded. "Worm-riddled old fleabag, more like."

Annie recalled how it had seemed like the little cat's green eyes had followed them wherever they went. She shook the idea away as being silly. "The sunset through the Temple of Apollo and all those gorgeous little tavernas tucked away down cobbled alleys covered in grapevines and lit up by fairy lights at night. It was magical, wasn't it, Carl?"

"It was."

"I mean it was definitely geared up for the tourists but it just felt more authentic than Santorini did, which surprised me because whenever I thought of Roz, Santorini was her Greece, and I thought it would be mine too. Before we went there, I thought it would be a place I'd never want to leave but actually it was a relief to get on the ferry."

"Yes, I know what you mean. Santorini is the crowned beauty queen; she is glitzy and breathtaking but it is the islands like Naxos that are the true gems."

"Yes, that's it exactly," Carl said. "Santorini lived up to all the paintings and photographs I have seen of it but it was, well, it was a bit—"

"Touristy, hot, and overcrowded," Kassia finished for him with a smile.

"Yes!" Annie exclaimed. "I couldn't believe the hordes of people we had to fight our way through, especially in Oia. Everybody wanted their windmill photo! We're not used to crowds like that in New Zealand, and I tell you, something horrible came over me. I wanted to walk up and down the little paths with my arms sticking out like rotary blades so that I could smack anybody who dared step into my personal space." Annie demonstrated what she meant and Carl and Kassia laughed.

"Don't get me wrong, though, I did love it. The views of the caldera took my breath away—they are truly mind-blowing. It was amazing but there was such a hectic pace of people all the time vying for photographs—gosh, the Europeans are posers, by the way. The women are all the next Jennifer Aniston and the men are all sumos in Speedos. I felt like I couldn't breathe and enjoy it all like, well, like we are doing here right now."

"Well said, Annie, my love."

"To here right now, I say." Kassia raised her glass, which was nearly empty, and looked sorrowfully at the empty carafe.

The other two grinned and reiterated her sentiment as they drained their own glasses.

A companionable silence settled over the threesome as Carl and Annie enjoyed the vista while Kassia popped another olive in her mouth and contemplated going up to the house to refill the carafe. She was about to get to her feet when Annie spoke.

"Oh, and I nearly forgot—we didn't just get legless on Mykonos, we went to see the *Shirley Valentine* beach too. It was every bit as gorgeous as it looked in the film so I can see why Shirley never went home."

"Who is this Shirley Valentine?" Kassia frowned.

Annie relayed the story of the downtrodden Liverpudlian housewife who has lost her lust for life only to find it again on holiday in Greece, while Kassia listened, head tilted to one side. When she got to the part where the taverna owner, with his well-practiced lines, takes Shirley out for a 'ride' on his boat, she interrupted to exclaim, "Ha! This man, he sounds like an older version of Alexandros. He is always taking the women out on his boat and now I know why!"

Kassia got to her feet as Annie and Carl laughed. She took hold of the carafe and waved it at them. "I should check on the boys and I think perhaps it might be time for some more. I'll be back in a moment."

As she walked off, Annie looked over at Carl, whose expression had sobered. She reached over and rested her hand on his shoulder. "You okay?"

"Yeah, just a bit tired. It's been a big day and I am not used to handling a spade."

"That's not why you look sad, though. You're missing David, aren't you?" Annie took his silence to mean yes. There had been times over the last few weeks that she'd sensed the dip in his mood and she knew that for all his bluster and bravado, he was indeed missing his boyfriend of the past two years. "Did you reply to that happy birthday text message he sent you?" Again there was no reply. "Carl! He held out an olive branch." She glanced at the branches over her head. "Er, so to speak. You should have taken it."

"He walked out on me." His bottom lip drooped.

"You had a fight! Couples fight—that is how they clear the air before moving on. David needed some breathing space and now he is obviously ready to talk but if you don't let him know that you are ready to listen, then the pair of you will remain in this stupid stand-off." It was so glaringly obvious, Annie thought with frustration. "Come on, what are you waiting for? Text him now."

"Do you think I should?" Carl pushed his fringe out of his eyes and Annie detected the flicker of hope in them as he looked up at her. "What if he doesn't want to know?"

"Well, at least it will be better than being in limbo like you are now, won't it? Besides, he wouldn't have bothered to wish you a happy birthday if he wasn't keen to patch things up."

"I guess." He stood and brushed the dust from the back of his shorts with his phone in hand. "I am going to wander down to the beach for a bit to think about what I want to say."

"Good for you." Annie got up and gave him a hug. "It will be fine. You'll see." As he padded across the burnt blades of grass, she hoped for his sake she was right.

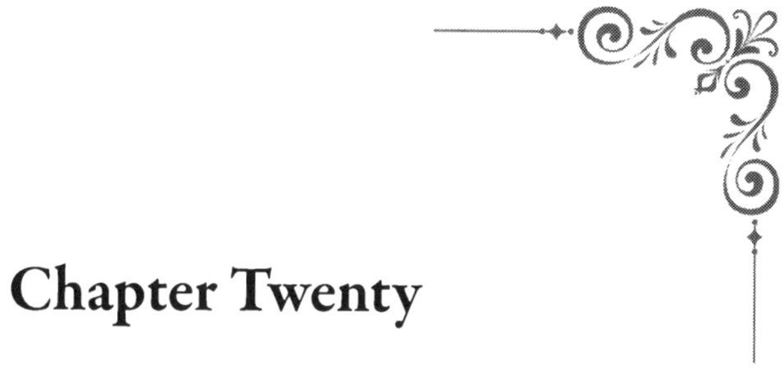

Chapter Twenty

ANNIE'S FACE WAS BURIED in the pillow as she lay on her stomach in the single bed, dimly aware of a spring in the mattress that dug into her hip bone. Her eyes were shut and she wished that the little hammer that tip-tapped away inside her brain would give it a rest. It was confirmation that she had indeed consumed far too much retsina when she dined with Carl, Kassia, and the rest of the Bikakis family yesterday evening. Perhaps that third carafe of wine had been a bit over the top and she should have accepted a second helping of Mama's delicious moussaka when it was offered to her. But she hadn't wanted to seem greedy. Besides, she had been so busy enjoying the banter around the table that she'd barely noticed just how much of the potent wine she had managed to tip down her throat.

Okay, so spontaneously hugging a startled Spiros before she told him that she was so happy he and Kassia had met and married because otherwise Mateo and Nikolos wouldn't exist should have been a clue that it might be time to bid the alcoholic beverages goodnight. She hadn't left it there, though. Annie groaned aloud as she recalled how she had gone on to state that as they were the most gorgeous children to ever walk the earth, it would have been a tragedy had they never been born. Yes, she decided, still refusing to open her eyes and greet the cold light of day, that should have been the giveaway that it was time for a glass of water because, even by Greek standards, she had been a bit over the top.

Carl, however, had had the good sense to take himself off to bed at a reasonable time and now she wished she'd followed his lead instead of agreeing that an after-dinner aperitif of raki was a splendid idea. Now that she thought about it, Carl had been subdued by his normal standards, especially given the party atmosphere last night. She hoped he hadn't received a short-shrift reply from David. She hadn't had a chance to talk to him before he went to bed. Oh well, she thought as she rolled over onto her back and then wished she hadn't as it took a moment for her brain to catch up with her body; she'd find out if he had heard back from him today.

She massaged her temples. She hoped Kas's head wasn't in the process of doing a Morris dance, too, because she could only imagine what it would be like to feel the way she did right at this moment and have to sort out the demands of two little boys as well. Life did not stand still when you were a mother—hangover or no hangover. This would probably be one morning when she'd be more than happy to let Mama take over where Mateo and Nikolos were concerned. She became aware that she was being watched. She noticed her bedroom door had opened a crack and as she looked over the side of her bed, her eyes met a pair of yellowy, green ones. "Oh hello, Adonis," she croaked, reaching to give him a pat. It was all the invitation he needed and with a mewl, he leaped up on the bed, rotated a couple of times and settled himself down in the crook of her knees. She remembered Jazz doing the same and the warmth of the bundle curled up against her was comforting. She was just dozing off, lulled by his purring, when a herd of stampeding wildebeests sounded from somewhere above her head. Annie's eyes flew open; she looked up at the sloped ceiling and remembered the locale of her room under the stairs. Guests heading down for breakfast, she surmised and reminded herself not to smack her head on the ceiling when she sat up. Kassia had been concerned that she would find the room too noisy but Annie had assured her that it was just perfect.

"You should be in that kitchen, helping to get breakfast ready for the guests and earning your keep, not lying here like a giant sloth, Annie Rivers." She scratched behind the cat's ears. "Sorry, Adonis. I am going to have to love you and leave you." She willed herself to get moving and tossed back the covers. As she sat up, she promptly smacked her head on the ceiling.

"HOW ARE YOU FEELING this morning?" Spiros winked across the table at Annie as she pulled a chair out and sat down opposite him. She tried to summon up a smile and hoped it wasn't a grimace. Nikolos was perched in his highchair next to his father flicking yoghurt about while Mateo on the other side chomped his way through a thick slice of jammy brown bread. The homely scene was comforting.

"I have been better, thank you, Spiros," Annie croaked as a glass of water and a packet of pills were slapped down in front of her. She turned her head to find Carl stood behind her smirking knowingly.

"That will teach you to be a lush. I thought you might need a couple of those."

"And a coffee would be wonderful." Annie looked at him hopefully. Her nose twitched at the smell of thick and heavy liquid gold wafting around what was obviously the heart of this home.

"Seeing as it's you, sweetheart."

She popped a couple of painkillers before she glanced round the kitchen. Mama, an array of pots and pans dangling above her head from a rack, wielded an egg whisk. She'd already greeted Annie with a cheery—and in her fragile condition, far too loud—good morning. Carl poured her a coffee from the pot that warmed on the stove and at that moment the door to the dining room swung open as Kassia, having used her rear to push it open, backed into the kitchen. Annie caught a glimpse through to the dining room of a middle-aged couple buttering their toast. They were seated at the table by the window. You'd pay an absolute fortune to eat your toast in front of a vista like that at home, Annie thought as the door closed. She watched as Kassia deftly deposited the assortment of dirty dishes she balanced onto the worktop alongside a pile of washing up. She wiped her hands on her apron and then turned to Annie. Her face broke into a wide smile.

"Ah, you are up and about! I hope you are feeling alright?" Kas obviously was, Annie thought and wondered whether her friend's cheeriness could be due to her having hollow legs.

"I will be in a minute when these kick in, thanks." She waved the packet of pills.

"I see you have showered—you found the towels I left outside your room for you last night then?"

"Yes, thanks." Annie was aware that her freshly shampooed hair was probably drying into tight corkscrews and she ran her fingers through them in an attempt to straighten the inevitable frizz. Mateo watched with fascination and his little hand snaked out to give them another good tug. His father swiped his hand away and barked at him. Annie didn't need to speak Greek to know that it was along the lines of, "Don't even think about it." She wouldn't have minded if the little boy had.

"The horrible Mr Palmer and his wife were last up and they are eating now, so I think maybe some toast and scrambled eggs will fix us both, yes?" Annie nodded, not having the energy to inquire as to what made Mr Palmer horrible as Kassia asked, "Carl, are you hungry?"

"No, I've had some of that delicious yoghurt and toast. I'm fine, thanks." He patted his middle.

"Go sit down, Kassia. I am already making the eggs." Mama pushed her daughter-in-law in the small of her back towards the table. She rolled her eyes and did as she was told.

"Where's Alexandros?" Annie asked innocently. As she sat down, Kassia raised an eyebrow towards her husband. "Yes, Spiros, where's your little brother?"

He looked sheepish and busied himself wiping up Nikolos's tray. "He has taken a guest out on the boat for the morning. He promised to show her the sights."

Kassia's lips pursed. She muttered, "You see, Annie, Carl—what did I tell you? He is just like that man in your *Shirley Valentine*."

Carl snorted and everybody looked at him in alarm. "I'm fine—my coffee just went down the wrong way, that's all."

"Who is this Shirley Valentine?" Mama called over.

"Nobody, Mama."

Mama shook her head and muttered something as she stirred the eggs about the pan.

"I'm sorry I wasn't up earlier. I should have been giving you a hand." Annie took a sip of her coffee as the pills slowly worked their magic.

"Don't be silly, we managed fine. Carl did a good job at being our waiter this morning seeing as Alexandros is off playing the friendly tour guide once again. Carl here—he has a way with the guests... a... oh, what do you call it?" Kassia frowned and searched for the correct word.

"A banter? Rapport maybe?" Annie supplied.

"Yes, yes, both of these."

Carl looked pleased. “I enjoyed myself. That couple from Manchester liked a bit of a laugh. I’m no virgin either.”

This time Annie snorted.

“Don’t lower the tone.” Carl shot her a look. “I paid my way through polytechnic by waiting tables. The tips I earned on top of my wages paid for my camera equipment.”

Mama placed two heaped plates down in front of Kassia and Annie. “Eat up, girls. This one here, she is too skinny.” Annie looked up and felt a bit like Hansel’s Gretel as she squeezed her arm.

“This looks wonderful, thank you, Mama.” She didn’t need to be told to eat up twice; her poor tummy cried out for sustenance. She picked up her knife and fork to tuck in as the older woman went over to Nikolos and clucked him under the chin. She worked her way round the table to pat Mateo on the head and told him he could go and play as she picked up his crumb-filled plate.

Annie glanced over at Kassia. Her shoulders had visibly tensed as she kept her eyes fixed on her plate.

“So what are you going to do today?” Spiros asked, oblivious of his wife’s irritation. He went over to the sink and came back with a wet cloth to wipe Nikolos’s face and hands with.

Annie put her fork down and looked over at Carl, who shrugged. “We’d like to help you, so give us some jobs to do and we’ll roll up our sleeves and get stuck in.”

“No, no! You go and explore Elounda—you are our guests.”

“Well, at least let us sort the dishes out.” Annie glanced guiltily over at the pile on the bench but Mama was already busy stacking them in the dishwasher.

Kassia, who pushed the eggs around her plate but hadn’t eaten more than a few mouthfuls, said, “I have the rooms to make up and some paperwork to catch up on this morning, so why don’t you two wander into the village and have a good look around. Maybe later if the boat is back, Spiros will take you across to Spinalonga.”

“We’ll help you make up the guests’ rooms.”

“And I could clean the bathroom,” Annie added.

"There is always tomorrow to help out. Today, we want you to go and enjoy yourselves."

"SO COME ON THEN, DID you text David?" Annie and Carl meandered at a snail's pace. Their respective jandals slapped along a pavement you could fry an egg on, that would take them back up to the main road and then down to the village. Carl's arm was linked through Annie's and they both smelled like coconut thanks to the copious amounts of sunscreen they had slapped on before they left Eleni's. As she'd squeezed a generous dollop from the bottle earlier, she'd rubbed the cream into legs with a derisive sniff. She knew a decent tan was a lost cause. "I can't get over the mahogany colour of some of the tourists about the place, especially the Germans. They've obviously never heard of sun safety."

"Or the fact that the wearing of Speedos when you have a hairy stomach and look nine months gone is offensive to some viewers." Carl had held his hand out for the bottle of Le Tan.

Now as Annie looked up at him, his expression was inscrutable thanks to the hat that shaded his face and set of Ray-Bans that gave nothing away.

"I did, actually."

"And?" She tugged at his arm impatiently.

"And I am going home."

"What?" Her jaw dropped as his words pulled her up short.

He stopped and placed a hand on either side of her shoulders. "Well, now that my mission is complete and I have delivered you into the bosom of the Bikakis family safe and sound, I am going to go home. It's been wonderful. I have loved every minute of our little holiday together." He frowned. "Well, almost every minute but I've been away long enough and David wants to give things another go and..." he shrugged, "so do I. I miss him, Annie."

"But what about me? I'll miss you." Her lip quivered. This great big adventure she was on suddenly seemed daunting without her trusty, albeit sometimes annoying, travel companion at her side.

"And I you, Annie, my sweets, but you will be fine. You are where you need to be for a little while longer, I think."

"Hmm." She shook his arms off, not ready to be convinced, and they wandered along in silence for a few moments until she broke it. "Carl?"

"Yes?"

"I am really happy for you."

"I know you are, sweetheart. I know." They stopped and had a quick hug, both agreeing as they quickly untangled themselves that it was too hot to engage in that kind of carry-on for long.

"So when do you think you are going to go?"

"As soon as I can. I'll sort out my ferry ticket back to Athens today and go from there."

THE VILLAGE OF ELOUNDA was a bustling mix of smartly dressed locals touting for customers outside their tavernas and swarthy seamen in cut-off shorts who offered boat rides to the island of Spinalonga. All the while, their targeted tourists wandered in and out of the shops that abutted the busy port in various states of undress. It was a scene that was watched over by the square's prominent clock tower. Annie and Carl paused to squint at the burnished copper view of Spinalonga out in the harbour. The former leper colony was a surreal rocky mass floating a short distance out to sea. The buildings it was home to looked as though they had been carved straight from the brown rocks on which they sat. Carl fished around inside his day pack and produced their guide book. He flicked through the pages for a moment until he found what he was after. His eyes skimmed over the text. "According to this, Spinalonga has been used as a Venetian fortress, a castle colony, and as a rebel refuge before it became a leper colony in 1903. Oh, and listen to this, the last leper died there in 1953."

"Really? 1953? But that's so recent." Annie shook her head in disbelief.

"I know. It seems unbelievable." They both stared out to sea at it for a moment before Carl continued to read. "And in the peak summer months, between twelve to fifteen hundred people visit it. Spinalonga is also known as Kalydon and sometimes referred to by the locals as the island of the living dead."

Looking out at the busy water scene with boats toing and froing from the island, the statistic wasn't all that surprising. Annie shivered despite the sizzling midday sun. It was really quite stunning and she could see why it was one of Crete's main drawcards, standing guard in the harbour the way it was but it had had such a sad history too. Imagine spending your whole life ostracised as a leper out on that arid mound, knowing that a short boat ride away a whole other world was going about its day-to-day business. She shook her head, glad when Carl pulled on her arm to haul her over to one of the many souvenir shops dotted around the township. As he led her into the closest treasure trove of tack, he announced he wanted to take a Greek music CD home with him. "So I'll think of sunnier, happy climes when I'm huddled by the fire in the long winter months ahead at home with a plateful of moussaka. Do you think Mama will give me her recipe?"

"She might, if you sign a secrecy agreement. And anyway, you'll be huddled by the fire eating moussaka with David, so I won't feel too sorry for you." Annie picked up a paperweight.

"Has this one got that song from *Zorba the Greek* that gets played at Zumba sometimes?" Carl waved a CD at the bored shopkeeper, who held his hands out to demonstrate his lack of understanding. Carl clicked his fingers and lifted his leg in what he obviously thought was a demonstration of Greek dancing. The shopkeeper nodded and looked at Carl as though he was considering putting one hand on his non-existent under-the-counter panic button. While he rang the CD up and popped it in a brown bag, Annie held the paperweight up for inspection. It had a teeny replica Greek monastery inside it; she shook the globe and watched as little gold flecks swirled around inside, the relevance of which she wasn't sure other than it was pretty. With a wish that it was a fortune teller's ball, she placed it back on the shelf and headed over to their next port of call, the travel agent's.

It didn't take long to sort Carl's return sailing out and, with his tickets purchased for a boat leaving in two days' time, they decided it was time to have a drink and maybe a bite to eat too.

"It looks nice over there." Annie pointed over at the edge of the wharf to where the sea wall was lined with seats and tables. "Hey, look—isn't that

Alexandros?" She held her hand up to her brow as though saluting and squinted into the sun towards the table the man and his female companion had just gotten up from. "My God, she could be arrested for indecent exposure!" she screeched, as the woman he was with wiggled her way over to the restaurant kiosk to pay. "It's definitely him." Alexandros leaned up against the wall with that unmistakable languor of his to wait while their bill was paid.

"Gigolo!" Carl exclaimed. "He gets a free lunch and goodness knows what else when he entertains Eleni's female guests."

"How do you know she is from Eleni's?"

"I saw her this morning at breakfast—a bleached blonde floozy if ever I saw one, with a chest you could stand a pint of beer on. Hard to miss her."

As the woman tucked her purse back into her shoulder bag, they watched the scene like a fascinated pair of voyeurs. Alexandros draped a casual arm around her shoulder and as they turned to stroll off into the horizon, both their eyes widened. "Really, what is she thinking? A G-string? They're so nineties!" Carl exclaimed.

Once they had gotten over their shock, they took themselves over to the same café and flopped gratefully down onto the twin two-seater couches. A coffee table separated them and they enjoyed the respite from the sun that the wide umbrella offered while they waited for the young girl, ponytail swinging as she rushed about with menus, to head their way.

"I wonder if they have a loo over there." Carl gesticulated to where the actual restaurant area whose seating they were ensconced in was.

"Bound to—why, do you need to go?"

"No. I just like to know there's one handy. That's all. I find it comforting since Athens."

Annie looked across at him fondly. She really was going to miss him.

Their menus arrived with a flourish and as she glanced over the list of alcoholic beverages, her stomach rolled. She'd just have to toast Carl's departure with a glass of lemonade, she decided and took him up on his offer to share a plate of club sandwiches. The drinks didn't take long to arrive and after they raised their glasses to both safe travels and a bright, romantic future for Carl and David, she took a grateful slurp of the cold, sweet fizz. The water lapped at the sea wall next to them and looked so tempting that she put her glass down and slid off the couch to sit on the damp stone. She dipped her toes in the clear water and noticed the swarms of tiny fish hoping a stray breadcrumb or two would float their way.

"Watch they don't nibble them," Carl admonished as he looked at her feet.

"People pay good money for a fish foot massage. They eat all the dead bits of skin and mine are a bit dry from all the walking around in jandals we've done lately. Here fishy, fish, fish." Annie made a kissy noise and Carl shuddered in disgust.

By the time lunch was produced, Annie decided the fish were probably full and that it was her turn to eat. She hauled herself back up onto her seat and eyed the platter. "Whoa, it's huge!"

"Heard that before, sweetheart."

"Carl!"

He winked and tucked in. Despite the amount of food, they still managed to plough their way through most of the triangle-filled pieces of bread and admired the stunning outlook as they ate.

"It's a slice of paradise, isn't it?" Annie mumbled.

"Don't talk with your mouth full, and yes it is."

She finished chewing and swallowed this time before she announced, "That was yum but I'm stuffed."

"Me too." Carl dropped a crust onto the plate and leaned back in his seat. He was a Buddha-like mirror image of Annie, whose own arms were wrapped round her stomach as she moaned that she really shouldn't have had that last sandwich.

"Look over there." He sat up, suddenly animated, and Annie swivelled round in her seat to watch as a little choo-choo train pulled up at the beach opposite where they sat.

His eyes sparkled like a child who had just been handed a lollypop. "Shall we?"

"Yes, let's."

"WE SHOULDN'T HAVE BOTHERED. It was a bloody rip-off," Carl muttered as they disembarked the train. Nevertheless, he gave their hostess, an overtly friendly Greek woman, whose monologue they could barely decipher as they'd chugged along the coastline, a smile that said we had lots of fun. The train had only gone a short distance up the road and the highlight had been waving at the odd child and over-enthusiastic holidaymaker on the pebbly beaches as it toot-tooted at them. "No wonder she's so bloody happy, she's coining it," he whispered out the side of his mouth as they walked away in an unspoken agreement to follow the path that looped around the waterfront.

"I did pick up that sheikh something or other likes to stay in that luxury villa up there when he comes to Elounda." Annie pointed up at the sprawling hillside complex. "Oh and Leonardo DiCaprio likes to water ski but then Kas already told us that."

"Bully for Leo. I don't know about you but I'm about ready to head back to Eleni's to put my feet up for a while."

"We might get that trip out to Spinalonga with Spiros, seeing as Alexandros is obviously back on dry land."

Carl frowned. "Don't mention we saw him when we get back. I get the feeling that it might stir the pot."

"No, I won't. You're right. Besides, I think Kas has enough on her mind with Mama at the moment. She doesn't need to be worrying about what the Cretan Stud gets up to when he is supposed to be working as well. Let's just pop into that gorgeous bakery we saw earlier and pick up something nice to take back for dessert tonight."

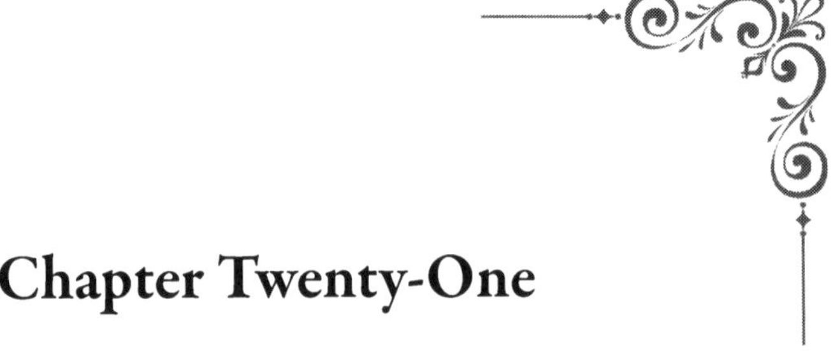

Chapter Twenty-One

THE SEA BREEZE COOLED the hot air and left a tang of salt on Annie's lips as the Bikakis family's little runabout boat, that Spiros had taken her and Carl over to Spinalonga in, made its return trip. She was glad she'd worn her cap or her hair would have been tangled beyond redemption by the time she got back to Eleni's. As the island retreated into the distance, she gripped the wooden seat and wished for the first time in her life that she had a bit more padding on her bottom as they bounced over the waves. Spiros shouted at Carl over the noise of the engine and pointed out different points of interest along the peninsula as Spinalonga got farther away and the shoreline closer. Annie's mind was still on the island, though.

The crowds had dispersed a little by the time they had dragged the boat ashore on the island, thanks to the lateness of the afternoon. Spiros, after arguing over the entry fee with the gatekeeper, who would not budge in his insistence that local or no local, he should pay, opted to sit on a rock in the shade of a tree near the water's edge. He was content to read his book and leave them to explore the broken cobbled streets on their own. The very emptiness—apart from a straggler tourist or two and the odd lizard skittering past—of the crumbling buildings that had once housed a functioning, albeit ostracised, community hinted at the isolation the people who had dwelled here had lived with.

They picked their way under stone archways and through stone walled gardens, now filled with nothing but scrub, leading them into decrepit creeper-clad houses made of pile upon pile of rocks. It was difficult to reconcile the buildings they explored now with the busy community the plaques and photographs, inside the rooms they wandered freely, depicted them as having been. The human spirit was indeed indomitable. Annie noted the smiles on the faces of those captured on film, despite their hardship.

There was a strange beauty to it all, she decided, as they followed the main path round the island. They paused when they reached a viewpoint to marvel at the three-sixty-degree vistas it offered up. It really was breathtaking, they agreed, and Carl had mumbled something about being able to think of worse places to see out your days. Annie had thumped him, pointed across to the mainland and told him that some of the people living here had left their families behind and had to live with them forever in their sights but out of their grasp.

As they stumbled across the open cemetery with its rows of unnamed rectangular graves covered in stones, even he was chastened. They were both quiet by the time they arrived back to where Spiros was engrossed in his book. On their approach, he bent the page to save his place and shut his book. He took note of their sober expressions. "Yes, this place, it sometimes has this effect on people."

Now as they reached the shallow waters of the mainland, Annie hopped out of the boat. Her feet sank into the pebbles beneath as she trudged up the beach. She watched as Carl and Spiros dragged the boat up on the bank and heard the tinkle of goat bells in the hills beyond. The charming sound, along with the buttery hues of the gentle slopes the goats roamed, as they searched out blades of grass amid the rocks and soil, cleared the last of the fug left behind by Spinalonga's tarnished history.

The blonde guest they'd spied with Alexandros earlier in the day headed down the path towards their little group as they veered off the pavement to cut across the frontage to Eleni's. Thankfully, Annie noted, she was dressed. Her hire car keys dangled from her fingers as she waved at Spiros with her other hand. It caused her bosoms to jiggle and drew one's eyes to an impressive cleavage that was impossible to miss, anyway, encased as it was in a tight, white number. The white showed off the mahogany tan she had acquired by lying prone in the sun over the last week.

Obviously fond of lying on her back then, and not a natural blonde, even if her boobs were real, because there were telltale dark roots that showed along her part line. Stop being so bitchy, Annie told herself; she's probably a really nice girl. The little voice continued to snipe in her head: a really nice girl who got around in G-strings when she had a bum like Kim Kardashian. *Meow—Annie!* She mentally slapped herself on the hand while she noticed that Blondie had a somewhat mousey friend with her. They were dressed for a night on the town and she felt sorry for the mousey girl; she would definitely spend her evening in Blondie's blousy shadow. She wondered idly whether Alexandros had plans to meet up with them later.

As they walked in through the side door to the kitchen, they were assailed by a full-blown row. Kassia's hands were on her hips and her normally wide brown eyes were narrowed as she spoke in rapid-fire Greek. The source of her annoyance was clearly her brother-in-law, who had his hands in the air as though trying to ward off her words. Mama muttered over by the stove and stirred something, that despite the tense atmosphere in the kitchen, smelled mouth-wateringly divine. Annie's tummy grumbled involuntarily and she wrapped her hands around her middle to silence it. She hoped that Mama would stop stirring whatever was in the pot quite so forcibly because she was losing half the sauce over the side. Spiros pushed past her. He joined in the mix, his tone placatory as he scooped a wide-eyed Nikolos out of the highchair and sidestepped Mateo, who was busy ramming a truck into the table leg. Annie grabbed Carl's arm and pulled him back the way they had come, deciding it might be best if they left the family to sort things out on their own.

"I'm guessing that's over his no-show at breakfast this morning," Annie whispered as they walked down the hall. Carl stopped at the bottom of the stairs.

"Yeah, you're probably right. He was too busy skipping the light fandango with Ms G-String. Now, that's a sight I won't forget in a hurry." He yawned, his hand on the rail as he took the first step. "I am knackered. I might go and lie down for half an hour, or at least until the dust settles."

"It's all that sunshine and sea air." Annie stifled a yawn of her own but knew if she lay down, she'd probably fall asleep and feel like rubbish by the time she got up again to join the others. "I might go and explore the back garden. I didn't have a look round there yesterday."

Carl gave her a wave and headed up the steps. "See you soon."

Pleased to escape the tension that seeped out from under the kitchen door, Annie headed around the back of the house to where Spiros and Carl had toiled yesterday. She stood for a moment and admired the unexpected oasis Spiros had created. The air, she noticed as she inhaled deeply, was thick with the mingling scents of oregano and rosemary. A lemon tree stood sentry in the far corner of the square garden and the raised beds overflowed with a summer's bounty of heavy, ripe tomatoes clinging on to their vines and vying for space alongside the high gloss aubergines. Across the bricked back wall, a grapevine snaked its way upwards, laden with fruit that was only just beginning to ripen. Annie snapped off a piece of rosemary and jumped back in shock as a little lizard skittered out from under the shade of a nearby leafy courgette plant.

The raised bed Carl had been helping Spiros fill yesterday had a fresh planting of lettuce seedlings that drooped in the heat. She spied a tap with a watering can next to it by the side of the house, so she walked over and filled it. She started at the sight of Alexandros as he leaned against the wall by the back door and watched her curiously.

Her face flamed and she knew it was probably the same colour as her hair. She was glad her face was shaded by the cap her hair was tucked under; otherwise, she would resemble one of the giant tomatoes she had just admired. Knowing that he must be well used to having this kind of effect on women, Annie turned the tap off and wished he would go away.

"I am sorry you had to hear all that earlier." His English, while good, was not as precise as Kassia's and his accent had a melodic twang to it that would most certainly woo the ladies.

Annie shrugged, not meeting his gaze on purpose, as she tilted the can and sprinkled water over the thirsty lettuces. "It's not as though we could understand any of it, anyway, and all families fight from time to time. It's part of the dynamic of being in a family." It wasn't her place to add that of course his family might not fight quite so often if he weren't such a lazy swine. If he helped out more instead of swanning off with a busty blonde who, if she insisted on the wearing of skimpy swimwear, really should spend a bit more time doing her glute exercises, then family life might be more congenial.

"Yes, there are too many—how you would say? Chiefs in our house."

Annie assumed he referred to his mother and sister-in-law, and out of the corner of her eye, she saw him kick at the soil his brother had worked so hard to turn into a garden, before he sighed heavily. Then he was gone. Feeling unsettled and thoroughly annoyed with herself for letting him have any kind of effect on her whatsoever, Annie emptied the can. She watched the water soak its way into the soil for a moment before she decided to head back inside. As she caught sight of herself in the window, she realised she would need to smarten her act up before dinner, but first she would brave sticking her head back into the kitchen to see whether she could help Mama with the prep work.

KASSIA TAPPED ON ANNIE'S door before she pushed it open to find her friend trying to work a comb through her hair.

"I offered to help Mama with dinner but she wouldn't hear of it. So now I am trying to tidy myself up a bit before we eat though with my mop it's a bit of a lost cause. Ow!"

Kassia smiled. "Your hair is beautiful—leave it." She flopped down on the edge of the bed and apologised for the fight they had borne witness to earlier.

It was the second apology regarding the Bikakis family set-to in under half an hour, Annie realised as she waved it away. "It's no big deal. Families fight, so what?"

"But mine is fighting all of the time lately. I was telling Alexandros he is lazy and that he needs to do his fair share about the place."

"I thought you might be and quite right, too. Ouch! Bloody knots."

"Your nose is very pink too, like that cute little reindeer—you know."

"Rudolph. Cheers for that." Annie peered into the mirror to find she indeed glowed; it was probably a touch of windburn from the boat ride earlier. Still, she'd have to be more careful with reapplying the sunscreen from now on. "Do you think he listened?"

"Pah! I doubt it. Mama, well, she never backs me up, even though she knows I am right, because she is terrified he will pack his bags and leave again." Kassia shrugged. "What she doesn't see is that he'll do that anyway just as soon as he gets a better offer. So she continues to tiptoe around him. She is blind when it comes to her son."

"A mother's prerogative perhaps?" Annie smiled at her as she put the comb down. It was a lost cause and twisting it into a topknot, she decided that would have to do.

"No! When Mateo does something horrendous like the time he is peeing in the geranium pot, I tell him so and he gets a smack on the bottom." She clapped her hands to emphasise her point but her grin gave away the fact that she knew Alexandros was a tad too big for smacks on his bottom from his mama.

"Did Spiros back you up?"

"Yes, in his usual way. He told his brother he shouldn't leave it all up to me and Mama but Alexandros, he never listens because he doesn't really care. It is all about him, and his attention at the moment is on a certain blonde guest we have staying."

"Yes, the girl with enormous bosoms. Carl said you could rest a pint of beer on them."

Kassia snorted. "And have you seen that piece of elastic she calls a bikini?"

Annie nodded. They looked at each other and giggled. Carl tapped on the door, pushed it open, walked into the room and looked at the girls with amusement.

"What's so funny?"

Kassia managed to gasp out between her giggles what they were laughing about and Carl joined in. He swore that next time he saw Blondie mincing past in her G-string, he'd give her a wedgie. "That will make her think twice about inappropriate swimwear!"

As she laughed, Annie was once again struck by a pang. She was so going to miss him when he'd gone. Lately it seemed that her life had been filled with goodbyes.

"Come on, you two." He held his hands out to them in order to haul them both off the bed. "Mama sent me to tell you that dinner is nearly ready."

A COLOURFUL SALAD STRAIGHT from the garden she had been admiring a short while ago took centre stage at the old wooden table, which had been smartly dressed for dinner. Annie gestured towards it. "That looks wonderful."

"So do you. I like your hair up like that—it suits you." Alexandros poured retsina into her wine glass.

Annie's hand involuntarily flew up to pat her loose up-do. "Oh, um, thanks."

"Mateo picked the tomatoes, didn't you?" His mother spoke to him in English as she pulled a chair out next to her son and sat down too. He nodded shyly over at Annie as Kassia grabbed hold of one of his hands. "Have you washed them?" She suspiciously inspected his fingernails. He nodded with such an emphatic yes that she decided he hadn't and promptly took him off to do the job properly this time round.

A few minutes later, with the smell of soap wafting across the table, Mama, with her hands stuffed into oven gloves and satisfied her audience was in full attendance, picked up a steaming casserole dish and waddled over to the table. Annie inhaled the rich aroma of the stew inside the dish as she placed it in pride of place on a waiting pot stand before she whipped the lid off with a magician-like flourish.

"Opa! A traditional Greek dinner for our guests! Lamb kleftico," she declared in her well-practised English. She seemed to stand a little taller as around the table they clapped and oohed and aahed over the meal she had produced for them. The tense atmosphere of earlier had dispersed as the heated words Kassia and Alexandros had exchanged were seemingly forgotten. Good food had the power to do that, Annie surmised. She wondered idly whether, if warring factions around the world were to simply sit down over a hearty meal like this, they could work their problems out with so much more ease than by shedding blood on a battlefield. With that thought in mind, she eyed up the loaf of thickly sliced crusty bread just waiting for them to mop up the juices left behind by the stew. Nikolos banged his spoon on his highchair in anticipation of being fed and Mateo kneeled up on his chair, about to lean over the table to see for himself what was in the pot. It was a futile attempt as his mother grabbed the back of his T-shirt and hauled him back down to a sitting position.

"So, Alexandros, how is your new friend? Perhaps instead of taking her out on the boat tomorrow, you could take her into town to buy some new swimwear. Her bikini bottoms seem to have disintegrated!" Spiros tossed over the table at his brother with a smirk on his face.

"Sharon is fine, as is her bikini, but thank you for your concern, Spiros," Alexandros shot back. Mama ladled the stew into her oldest son's bowl, placed the spoon back in the casserole dish and swiped him across the back of his head.

She fired something off in Greek, which Annie decided was probably along the lines of "Don't wind your brother up."

"And just what were you doing looking at *Sharon's* non-existent bikini bottoms, Spiros?" Kassia bantered to her husband.

"I was concerned she might catch a cold, or worse, suffer from sunburn of the bottom. You know, it is a terrible thing not being able to sit down." There were snorts of stifled laughter around the table and Spiros, a smile playing at the corner of his mouth, carried on. "It was nothing more than that, Kassia, my love, I can assure you. You know I only have eyes for you, my wife." The tender look in his eyes, despite the playfulness of his words, spoke volumes. Annie suddenly found herself hoping that one day someone would feel that way about her. Tony had never looked at her the way in which Spiros just had at his wife. It was a realisation that filled her with sadness but she steeled herself against it and told herself once more that she had indeed made the right decision in breaking things off with him. They both deserved better than what they had been able to give each other.

Mama sat down and urged them all to start. Calls of *pass the salad* and *pass the bread* went up. Annie's gaze swept round the table and her heart swelled. It was true that she had been saying an awful lot of goodbyes over the last few months but she'd also said hello too, and now here she was in the midst of this crazy, lovely Greek family. She watched Carl break off a piece of bread and place it down on Nikolos's highchair tray. She knew that she'd miss him like crazy but she also knew she would be okay without him. He was right in what he had said to her earlier in the day. She was exactly where she needed to be at the moment.

Carl announced his plans to leave in two days to begin his return trip to New Zealand after the last scraping from the pot of tender lamb, feta cheese, and onions had been consumed and the last drop of the delicious gravy mopped from each of their plates. The children had gotten down from the table and the first thing Mateo had done was race over to the kitchen worktop to swipe a piece of baklava. Annie and Carl had bought the box of sticky honeyed pastry back from Elounda with them. He'd shovelled it into his mouth before his mother could stop him and the sight of him trying to chew with chipmunk cheeks sent them all into fits of laughter.

The knowledge that Carl's visit was to be fleeting was all the excuse needed. And so as they sat back in their chairs, satiated, hands sticky from the baklava they'd just polished off for dessert, the raki had been produced again. Despite her protestations that the aniseed liqueur was responsible for her hangover that morning, Annie still found herself raising her shot glass to toast her friend.

She shuddered as the potent liquid went down and a rush of heat went to her cheeks.

"What about you, Annie? What are your plans?" Kassia asked.

"Yes, Annie, what are your plans?" Alexandros looked at her with open interest on his handsome features and received a kick under the table from Kassia. "Ouch!"

"Don't you have some place to be Alexandros?" Spiros said pointedly.

"Sharon and Tracey have gone to Malia to have dinner with some friends staying at a resort there and I'm not meeting them in town until ten o'clock."

"Well, just make sure you don't go drinking and dancing the night away. Not when you have the breakfast orders to help me with in the morning. And don't forget that it's your turn to make the rooms up tomorrow. Annie?"

Annie's eyes stopped swivelling from one to the other; she was only just getting used to these three-way table conversations.

"Oh, I'm definitely staying for a while yet. If that is okay with you all?"

Kassia's grin as Spiros got up to fill the glasses for another toast said it all.

"Opa!" Mama raised her glass.

Chapter Twenty-Two

ANNIE'S PHONE BLEEPED. The sound intruded on the peaceful murmurings of distant conversations and slushing waves of the incoming tide. It was a reminder of the real world and one she couldn't ignore, just in case. That was the thing with text messages, she thought as she sighed; it might be something really important or it might not. Unless she checked her phone, though, it would niggle at her because of that all-important 'just in case'. She held her book in her right hand and reached over the side of the sun lounger with her left to pat the warm sand in a lazy attempt to locate her bag. At last her hand settled on the scratchy cane of her tote. She found her phone inside it, held it aloft to read the message, and squinted into the mid-morning glare, despite her sunglasses. It was no good; she'd have to move if she wanted to see who it was from. Reluctantly, she pulled herself up into a sitting position and shaded the screen of the phone by holding up a corner of her towel. Annie smiled as she saw the message was from Carl. He'd made it from Athens to Heathrow and was at present devouring a Mars bar while he waited to board his flight to LA. Okay, so this earth-shattering news could have waited but it made her smile anyway.

She pitied the poor sod who wound up seated next to him for the next leg of his trip home. Despite his best efforts to secure a business class seat, the plane had been full and there had been no last-minute cancellations, so once more he was forced to join the heaving masses in economy. She tapped out a reply to ask him whether he had invested in compression socks this time round and pushed Send. A couple playing catch in the shallows caught her eye. They must have been in their late thirties but the holiday spirit had them cavorting in the water like a couple of kids.

It was nice to see. Sea, sand, and sunshine were definitely good for the soul, Annie mused as she waited for Carl's reply. She didn't have to wait long and she laughed out loud as she skimmed over the shorthand that said she had better not be mocking him because swollen ankles were a serious business. Never one to cut a long story short, he went on to say that he was at risk of becoming a forty-year-old sufferer of the dreaded cankle but he'd decided it was a risk he was going to have to take. No way was he forking out a small fortune to wear what equated to knee-high pantyhose. Look at Mama—the knee-high tights she insisted on wearing hadn't done anything for her, he finished. With a grin at the mental image of him holding up a packet of the ugly socks in the airport's pharmacy, Annie quickly replied and signed off by wishing him safe travels.

She put the phone away in anticipation of settling herself back down on the lounger. It was costing her good money, five euro, for the privilege of reclining on it. As she'd reluctantly handed the note over to the girl who manned the beds, she'd reminded herself that everybody had a living to make. The locals had to make hay while the sun was shining—fair enough—so she was going to bloody well make sure she enjoyed it. Besides, an hour or two's R&R after the morning she'd had was just what the doctor ordered.

She tried to submerge herself into the pages of her book once more, but Annie found her mind wandering. Carl had been gone for three whole days now. They'd filled the last of his time in Crete from sunset to sundown, exploring their surrounds and spending time with Kassia and the family. Borrowing the courtesy wagon, a morning had whizzed by in Heraklion as they mooched around a market together before a visit to the ruins of Knossos. They'd both been in awe of the fact that the rubble remains they walked amid had been home to the Minoans, the earliest known civilisation in Europe. Carl had announced with loud passion that it had inspired him, and he was seriously thinking about redecorating in the style of Modern Greek Revival when he got home. Annie had told him not to be such a tosser.

The next day, Kassia had taken them with her to pick up supplies in Agios Nikolaos and used the trip as an excuse to while away the hours over lunch. She'd taken them to a tucked away tavern that overlooked an inlet bustling with boats and afterwards they'd worked the meal off with a walk along the waterfront to watch the never-ending stream of bad drivers. When they'd arrived back in Elounda later that afternoon, Annie had asked whether they might be able to take Mateo down to the beach for an hour. It was a request that saw the little boy plonked in front of them, swim togs on, towel in hand, before either of them had a chance to change their minds!

The first ten minutes on the beach, he had sporadically pulled Annie's hair as though he still wasn't convinced it was real. This was a game he seemed never to tire of, not even when there was a bucket and spade he could make use of. Annie's scalp, however, had tired of the game and so to distract him, she had suggested they have a game of jump the waves. With Carl holding one of Mateo's little hands and Annie the other, the threesome had paddled into the water and they hauled him up into the air whenever a wave rolled in. His giggles were infectious and as people paused to smile at the happy scene, they'd smiled proudly at each other over the top of his head. It had been fun. Mind you, Carl had commented sagely, as the tired trio walked the few metres back from the beach to the house, parenting always was fun so long as you could give the child back at the end of the day.

On Carl's last night, revved up by too many glasses of raki, they had decided to check out the local nightlife. Kassia and Spiros had joined them at a club, whose music pumped out onto the street and promised a lively time to all who ventured in. They had stayed for an hour before declaring themselves to be past it. Kassia had whispered in Annie's ear that although it had been nice to put on a dress and some make-up, the thought of being woken at the crack of dawn by the boys was enough to make anyone want to crawl into bed! Sadly for them, they'd missed the highlight of the evening when a short while after they'd headed off, Carl had spotted Alexandros and Blondie. The dynamic duo cut a few moves on the crowded dance floor.

The pair had been a great source of entertainment for Carl and Annie so far, and now, as she thought back on his comments about when a jazzed-up version of Van Morrison's *Gloria* had blared out and Blondie had thrown herself about the dance floor—"God help us all if she ever takes up Irish dancing," followed swiftly by "If Alexandros's nose dives any further down her top he will most likely lose consciousness"—she felt a pang. She missed him already, although with Carl winging his way home, she had quickly settled into her own routine. As her attempts at paying for her lodgings had been thwarted by both Mama and Kassia, she had decided that rather than fall into the freeloading bracket of Alexandros, who had far more right to do so than she did, she would make herself useful.

It wasn't difficult to do at this time of year. Kassia, Mama, and Spiros were run off their feet with a full house and two young boys to look after. There were the breakfasts to prepare and clear away, the beds to be made, a never-ending pile of towels to wash, as well as the guests' laundry, and bathrooms to scrub. There were booking requests to be responded to, tours to be organised, accounts to be maintained, a garden to upkeep, fishing excursions and day trips to Spinalonga. The list went on and on. It was all hands to the deck, so to speak—apart from Alexandros, who was hit-and-miss most days. It was as though he sensed just how far he could go with his mama and when he had stretched the cord far enough, he rallied round and became indispensable, if only for a few hours. Those few hours, though, were enough to have her beaming with delight as she elbowed Kassia. "You see, my Alexandrosaki mou, he does work hard. You need to stop being so hard on the boy."

"What does it mean when she adds 'aki' to the end of his name?" Annie had asked.

"It means my little Alexandros. He's hardly little or a boy, and I don't think it is a good thing to always be the reliable ones in this family," Kassia muttered, "The more you do, the more is expected."

Annie would be happy for them to take her for granted, she thought as she stretched out on the lounger with the languor of someone who, right at that moment in time, didn't have to be anywhere else in the world. It was a lovely feeling and she did feel a little sleepy. This morning, she had woken just as the sun tried to sneak in through the worn patches of her calico curtains. Adonis was curled up in the crook of her knees once more and she'd lain in bed for a moment to watch the shards of light penetrate the faded spots of fabric and grow ever brighter before she roused herself.

The family's bathroom, as she'd tiptoed down the silent, still darkened hallway, was empty, which gave her the chance to wake herself properly under a hot shower. Afterwards, she had padded back to her room to make herself presentable. If she was to be serving breakfast, she'd have to make sure she tied her hair up. There could be no random hairs in the eggs of paying guests, she thought with a rueful flashback to the night of the Playboy Bunny outfit incident. As she pulled her damp hair back into a ponytail, she was pleased to find the sting had gone out of that episode now. She wondered fleetingly, as she rummaged in her make-up bag, how Tony was getting on. She had made a point of steering clear of all social networking sites for the simple reason that, although she wanted to know he was okay, she had no need to know how or maybe even with whom he spent his weekends these days. She swept her mascara under her lashes before she finished off with a swipe of lip gloss. She stepped back from the mirror and decided she was ready to face the day. As for her black skirt and white T-shirt—well, that was the closest thing to waitressing attire she'd brought with her. It would have to do.

Nobody had surfaced by the time she pushed the door to the kitchen open, though she had noticed a light peeping out from under the crack of Mama's door. She wouldn't be too far away, Annie thought as she switched on the light, but in the meantime she'd pop the pot on and grab a much-needed cup of coffee.

Mama appeared just as Annie drained the dregs from her cup. She helped herself to a cup of the steaming brew in the pot before she sat down heavily at the table opposite Annie. "You are up early, Annieaki." She took a sip from her cup. "I hope you are sleeping okay?"

"Like a log, Mama."

She looked at her blankly. Her English was good but like Kassia's, it didn't always stretch to idioms, Annie realised. "I have been sleeping very well, thank you."

The old woman beamed. "Good, good." Then she yawned and held her plump hand to her mouth, her thick gold wedding band still firmly embedded in the folds of flesh. "I am sorry; it is Nikolos. He is still waking in the night. I hear him sometimes."

She did look tired. Annie noticed the paunches under her eyes and the pinched look around her mouth. As much as she obviously loved being surrounded by her family, having little children in the house again at her age must take its toll. Though now that she thought about it, she didn't actually know what age Mama was. She could be anywhere between sixty and eighty—she just had one of those faces. The living arrangement probably wasn't easy for any of them at times, something that was becoming evident from her vantage point as an outsider looking in. Still, now that she was here, perhaps she could help ease the load a bit for them all. "Um, Mama, the reason I am up so early is that I'd like you to put me to work this morning. I want to earn my keep." Annie smiled at the older woman, who smiled beatifically back at her before doing just that.

By the time Annie had finished setting the tables for breakfast in the dining room the way Mama had shown her how to, Kassia, Spiros, and the children had trooped into the kitchen. An air of chaos circulated as Nikolos loudly let it be known he was hungry. Mateo, not to be beaten, grabbed his spoon and banged it down on the table in anticipation of food. His weary-looking father rubbed his hand over his layer of stubble as he told him to stop it. Kassia, looking marginally more awake than her husband, sidestepped Mama in order to sort the boys' breakfasts before she tended to her and Spiros's own desperate need for coffee. Mama was busy cracking eggs into a bowl and asked Annie whether she could go find the bacon in the fridge because she couldn't see it.

"Mama, it might help if you wore your glasses." Spiros snatched the spoon from Mateo's hand, which caused his oldest son to wail.

She threw her hands in the air. "Pah, I don't need them. My eyes are fine." She blew kisses over to Mateo. "Agoraki mou." He stopped crying and smiled at his yaya as though butter would not melt.

"It means my little boy." Kassia rolled her eyes at Annie before she carried the two bowls over to the table and banged them down in front of her sons.

Eleni's served breakfast between eight am and ten am. With the twelve guests currently accommodated and trickling through at different times, Annie knew it was going to make for a busy morning. There was a moment's blissful silence as the boys tucked into their food, broken by the bell ringing in the room next door, which signified the first guests' arrival to the dining room. Right, Annie, she told herself as she smoothed her hair back and picked up the notepad and pen from the bench. It's showtime!

Kassia gave her the thumbs-up as Mama placed toast in front of her grandsons and fussed over them. Annie pushed open the door and spied a dourly elegant, elderly couple sitting at the prime table by the window. She paused for a split second to admire the view they were being treated to. *It was bound to lift anyone's spirits, even this pair who looked completely miserable in each other's company*. She walked towards them, her brightest smile firmly in place.

"Er, good morning, sir, madam. I'm Annie. Are you ready to order?" She hoped her bright breeziness might be infectious. It wasn't and neither he nor she raised a smile as they stared blankly at her before he put in a request for two full English breakfasts and a pot of Earl Grey. His British accent was clipped and his posture ramrod. Annie imagined he had either been a colonel in the army or a headmaster at a boys' public school in his former life. She couldn't help but think, as she jotted down their order, that a full English with a pot of tea was a bit of a sad thing to breakfast on when in Greece. Assuring them they wouldn't have to wait long, she turned her back to walk away and felt a sharp pinch on her bottom as she did so. She swung round instantly to object but found the couple both gazing woefully out to sea and wondered whether she had imagined it. *Perhaps she had just experienced some sort of weird bottom spasm in her right cheek.* She marched back into the kitchen, tore off the piece of notepaper and handed it to Mama, who launched into action with the fry pan.

Still seated at the table with a teaspoon in her hand and trying to coax Nikolos into tasting what was on it, Kassia glanced up from her task. At Annie's disgruntled face, she burst out laughing. "Let me guess—you have had your bottom pinched, yes?"

Annie stared at her. *So she hadn't imagined it after all.* "He's done it to you? You could have warned me, Kas."

"Ah, but then I wouldn't have had the enjoyment of seeing the look on your face right now. You will learn as I did to take his order and then back away a safe distance before you turn around."

Annie poked her tongue out at her friend. "Humph! Dirty old sod! I don't know how he manages to stay so poker faced."

"He is, how you say, well-practiced? His poor wife, I think she knows nothing. This is the only reason I did not slap him."

"Yes, you're right. She looked miserable enough without adding to her woes. He shouldn't be allowed to get away with it, though."

"No, I agree but what do you suggest?"

"I don't know yet. I'll think of something, though."

Alexandros wandered in, freshly shaved and showered so his bleary eyes could be forgiven.

"How lovely you could join us this morning," Kassia greeted him, with more than a tinge of sarcasm before she nibbled at her toast.

He ignored her. He pulled out a chair at the table and sat down next to his oldest nephew, who after receiving a hair tousle, gazed up at his uncle with adoration. Annie flushed as he smiled at her, his eyes lingering a moment too long. Unnerved, she dropped the box of Earl Grey she'd been holding and bent down to pick it up, feeling foolish for her reaction to him. As she set about making the pot of tea, she overheard him inform his brother he was taking the Austrian couple from room four over to Spinalonga for the day. They were leaving in fifteen minutes.

"They haven't requested packed lunches, have they?" Kassia's eyes narrowed.

"Yes, yes but it is simple—just a couple of rolls and some fruit. It won't take long to put together."

Kassia let rip with what could only be a Greek expletive as Mama's hand flew to her mouth in feigned shock before she told Spiros to cover the children's ears. She pushed back her chair and got to her feet. "Why didn't you tell me this last night?"

Alexandros shrugged, indifferent to the panic he had just caused his sister-in-law, who had left her toast half eaten and now frantically rifled through the freezer for a packet of rolls. As his mama placed a cup of coffee down in front of him, she gave him an affectionate pat on his shoulder. "Not to worry, Alexandrosaki mou." He smiled up at her, not worried in the slightest and said, "Thank you, Mama mou."

Mama beamed before she frowned at her daughter-in-law's back, which was stiff with indignation as she slammed the microwave door shut. Annie marvelled at Alexandros's ability to wrap his mama around his little finger and felt a frisson of sympathy for Kassia. She was up against it with that brother-in-law of hers, she thought as she carried the tea through to the dining room, both cheeks clenched defensively.

Thankfully, there was no more bottom pinching or further upset behind the scenes in the kitchen that morning. Although Blondie and her mousey-haired friend's arrival in the dining room at three minutes to ten o'clock did cause some mutterings and a lot of pot banging from Mama. The two women were looking worse for wear, Annie noted as she took in Blondie's puffy, pig-like eyes. She couldn't see what Alexandros saw in her. Well, that was a lie; she could see exactly what Alexandros saw in her. It was impossible to miss them resting on the table top as she gazed at the menu. As she scribbled down their requests for scrambled eggs on toast and a bacon sarnie, she overheard Blondie mention that they should finish their packing after breakfast before squeezing an hour in down at the beach. So they were off, then, she thought, not knowing why she felt so pleased.

ANNIE DIDN'T KNOW HOW long she had been asleep on the sun lounger nor did she enjoy the bizarre dream she was in the middle of. For some reason, she was herding goats in a G-string and as she roamed the hillsides, it had become clear that things were moving that had no business doing so. Despite the hard ground, she had gotten down on her hands and knees to kick her leg back, an exercise sure to tone those stubborn glutes, when she was woken by rain. Startled, her eyes flew open and her mouth simultaneously snapped shut. She blinked and expected to find the beach deserted and herself under siege by black clouds. Instead, she saw Alexandros shaking the remnants of water from his hands.

"Did you just tip water over me?" she asked indignantly as she wiped the sticky line of drool from her mouth and tried to ignore his cheeky grin.

"I couldn't resist it. You were so sound asleep. But if you don't move your umbrella around, you will turn into a lobster in a short while."

Annie could feel a telltale stinging on her shins. He was right. Groggily, she got to her feet and shifted the umbrella, which, if he was so concerned about her burning, he could quite easily have moved for her. There had been no need to douse her in water. It was an excuse to check her out, she realised. She sat back down in a hurry and spread her towel out over her legs. Still, she was secretly pleased that her post-flight bruises had all cleared up and that she was no longer as lily white as she had been the first time she'd aired her togs on a Greek beach. Carl had shielded his eyes and made out he'd been blinded by the glare.

"How was Spinalonga?" She wished he would go away but saw he had no intention of doing so just yet.

He shrugged. "It was okay. Me—I don't like the place. Too much sadness there, but the guests, you know, they all want to go there to see what it's like for themselves."

She was surprised to hear him say this, not really having him down as the sensitive type. "I think it's a good thing people want to go and see it for themselves. It's like the concentration camps in Germany and Poland. They are a visual reminder that such things should never happen again. Not that the leprosy sufferers were sent to Spinalonga with any evil intent, but still..." She knew she sounded self-righteous, but then rightly so.

"Yes, these days it seems an inhumane way to treat people."

"Yes." Annie shaded her eyes and looked up at him. *His eyes really were the colour of maple syrup.*

"I could take you out for a ride on the boat. I have a couple of hours before I have to drive Sharon and Tracey to the airport. Maybe we could go to another bay I know around the peninsula? One where the water is even clearer than here."

That culled her sweet thoughts because she was not silly: oh no, she had seen *Shirley Valentine* too many times not to know that *taking her for a ride on his boat* literally meant taking her for a ride. Give the girl a few smooth, sensitive lines and she'd be putty in hands; that was his modus operandi. He was lining her up now that his little—well, not so little—blonde friend was headed back to the UK. "Um, well, I am pretty busy at the moment," she muttered.

"Yes, it looks like it." He smirked down at her. "We do it another time then." This he stated with such certainty, before he turned and walked up the beach, that Annie was left with her mouth hanging open at his audacity.

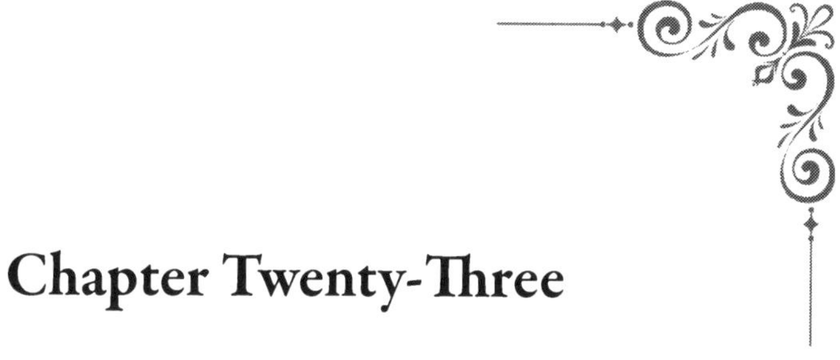

Chapter Twenty-Three

ANNIE WANDERED ACROSS the car park, careful to look left and right then left again—or was it the other way round? She tried to remember the words her mother had drummed into her as a little girl. She was learning to mistrust the holidaymakers on the roads nearly as much as the Greeks. Something about the carefree vibe of being on holiday spilled over into the way they whizzed, helmetless, around the streets on scooters, that seemed to make it okay to employ no road sense whatsoever. Over to her left was an inlet filled with boats of all shapes and sizes and monetary value. She wondered idly whether one of them might belong to Leonardo. Perhaps he was even on one of the luxury yachts moored there right now, with his latest supermodel girlfriend, sipping champers or whatever it was movie stars and their gal pals drank. To her right, she could see Elounda's beach with its cluster of umbrellas and sun loungers filled with tourists lapping up the vitamin D.

The taverna Annie headed towards was called Georgios', according to the sign out on the street, and it was to be her fourth port of call in her morning's quest to find work. She spied a group of people who lounged around one of its outside tables, sipped beers and ate pizza as she drew closer. An early lunch, she thought. Her stomach grumbled at the sight of all that food. Oh well, there would be plenty of time to eat when she'd found herself a job. She smiled over at the merry group and received a leer from a paunchy chap with no hair and a thick gold chain round his neck for her trouble. That would teach her to be friendly. She ducked her head under the grapevine that entwined its way over the entrance, stepped inside, and was instantly grateful for the cool respite from the relentless sunshine outside.

A handful of couples sat scattered about, tucking in to their brunches. Annie paused for a moment to soak in the atmosphere afforded by the dim interior. From the low wooden beams of the ceiling, various seafaring paraphernalia dangled. There was a lifebuoy, lanterns, and thick, gnarly ropes coiled and draped. In one corner a fishing net was slung low, sagging in its middle. In the other corner by the door to the restrooms, a barnacled anchor made its presence known. Annie made her way up to the counter at the far end of the restaurant and stood in front of the till for a moment. She toyed with the idea of stealing a mint from the jar while she waited for someone to appear. Feeling a bit foolish when no one did, she called out a tentative, "Hello!"

From behind the hanging beads, a relic from the seventies, an almighty clattering sounded. Several diners glanced over at her accusingly, as though it were she who had just dropped what sounded like a dozen pots and pans. She avoided their gaze and shifted from foot to foot. Maybe she should just make a run for it because she didn't fancy her chances of being given paid employment now. Before she could put her plan into action, a wiry little man burst through the beads and sent up a clacking symphony. He wiped his hands on a tea towel and looked at her with the harried expression of someone who had far too much to do and not enough hands to do it with. Right, Annie thought as he arranged his features into one of greeting and picked up a menu from the stack by the till; best foot forward and all that. "Um, I'm not actually wanting to eat. What it is, you see, is... well..." Oh, get on with it girl, she told herself. She licked her lips. "Er, my name's Annie, and I was wondering if you might need a waitress."

Oh dear, she hoped that hadn't sounded too much like the opening line to an AA meeting. From under his impressive thatch of silver hair, the man looked at her with disbelief. The next thing she knew, he clapped his hands delightedly and then reached forward to grab her face and plant a big kiss on both cheeks. She could take that as a yes then, Annie thought as she took a startled step backwards.

"Paidi mou, you are an angel. An angel has been sent to me on this day." He beamed and displayed a gleaming gold tooth. It was like Mama's. Gold teeth must have been all the fashion at some point, or perhaps they were a form of compulsory saving, Annie thought. She found herself propelled through the beads into the kitchen.

"I am Georgios and this is my daughter Koula," he announced, introducing the flushed woman in the apron who frantically stacked dishes. She looked to be in her late thirties and her hair had escaped from her ponytail in wispy bits. It was a look Annie could relate to and she knew instantly that she would get along with this woman. "Koula, meet Annie. She has been sent from the heavens to help us."

Koula's pretty face lit up and she stepped forward with her hand outstretched in greeting.

"YES, IT WAS PERFECT timing, Kas." Annie had found her sitting down on the grass verge by the beach as she had headed back to Eleni's that afternoon. The sun sat a little lower in the sky and the bite had gone out of it for the day by the time she flopped wearily down next to her friend. Nikolos wore nothing but a nappy as he waved a spade around and Mateo collected pebbles and interrupted his mama every now and then to show her a treasure he had found. "Because it turned out his waitress had telephoned him last night to say her uncle had offered her work on his boat. She'd only wanted work while she was on her university holidays anyway, and she reckoned she could earn more helping this uncle of hers. So, that was that; she didn't give poor Georgios any warning, which given how lovely he is, seems really unfair to me." She shrugged. "Anyway, Koula—that's his daughter; she's about your age and gorgeous too—said the girl was hopeless and that she wouldn't have known what fresh squid was if it inked in her the eye, so good luck to her uncle. Her surly manner didn't do much for their trade, either, so she was no great loss." Annie paused and drew breath. "Koula helps run the restaurant, and she and Georgios muddled through last night but they'd have been up all night if they'd sorted all the dishes out. Her husband is a fisherman, so he keeps the taverna supplied with fresh fish and they have three children who are all at school." Annie knew she was gushing but it had been an exciting afternoon. "Honestly, I don't think I have ever washed and dried so many dishes in my life! Talk about getting thrown in at the deep end! And I have got to be back there in a few hours."

"You say the taverna is called Georgios', yes?" Kassia frowned as she tried to place it.

"Yes, that's his name too. It's down by the port, not far from the clock tower." Annie paused for a moment and laughed. "Actually, that's not very helpful, is it? Because everywhere in Elounda is near the clock tower." Her brain was mush, she realised as she rotated her ankles, and her poor feet were killing her. How she was going to get through another shift, she did not know! "It's got a gorgeous grapevine growing over the entrance and Georgios said his taverna is famous locally for the fresh fish dishes he cooks up."

Kassia nodded. "Ah yes, now I know where you mean! Spiros and I went there once. The food, it was very good. Mama knows Georgios from way back but then she knows everybody in Elounda. He runs the taverna with his wife too. She was working when we were there. I remember her because she reminded me a little of my own mama."

"His wife died a year and a half ago, which has taken its toll on him. You can tell by the way he and Koula talk about her as though she is still with them. They had four children together but only Koula still lives nearby. The others are scattered in Hania and Rethymnon for work."

"Ah, this is sad."

Annie wasn't sure whether she meant that his wife had died or that his children were scattered around different parts of Crete. She decided Kas probably meant both. The need to work away in Greece was something Kristofr had touched on when she had talked to him at the Acropolis. And look at the situation Kas and Spiros had found themselves in in Athens, she thought with a rueful glance at her toenails peeking out of her sandals. They were in need of a lick of polish; she'd do that before she headed back to work tonight.

"So you were put to work straight away?"

"Yes." Annie nodded and her red curls bobbed madly. "I helped clear away the dishes from the night before and took the lunch orders. It was so busy, the time just flew by but from now on, I'll just be doing an evening shift, which will work well with helping in the morning at Eleni's." The fiery ringlets bouncing up and down were a sight that caused Mateo's eyes to light up. It was a look Annie recognised and as she saw him make a beeline towards her, she hastily pulled a hair-bobble off her wrist and twisted her hair back into a ponytail. She was already bone-weary; she didn't need a sore scalp too. Disappointed but thankfully deterred, Mateo turned his attention back to a large pebble he had been inspecting and Annie laughed. It was then that she noticed that Kas didn't join in with her. She realised there was something about the droop in her shoulders.

"Hey, I'm sorry. I have been so busy talking about myself and my day that I haven't asked you how yours has been. Are you okay?"

Kassia sighed and picked at the grass. "It is just the usual problem. Mama and Alexandros and the way she takes over everything and the way he does nothing." She threw her hands up. "I know this problem of mine, it is silly, and I don't like to feel this way, but I wish she would stop interfering with the boys and that Alexandros would pull his weight. That is why the boys and I came down here for a little while."

Annie reached over and patted her friend's hand. "A bit of breathing space?"

She nodded. "Spiros is busy with his book, which makes him happy. He loves his life here but me..." She shrugged. "Sometimes I just don't know."

Poor Kas. Annie studied her friend's strong features for a moment. This new life they were making for themselves in Elounda hadn't been hers by choice, but if she and Mama could find a way to make it work, to rub along together in harmony, then Annie was certain she would love it as much as Spiros did. There was nothing not to love. She glanced at the boys and saw that they were lost in their games. They had been so tiny when they had come to Elounda that they didn't know any different now. The entire beach was their playground. At home, they were surrounded by people who loved them; a better life she couldn't imagine. It was idyllic.

Unsure as to whether she should offer an opinion or whether Kas was just in need of a sounding board, Annie swallowed and decided to say her piece anyway. "You know, from where I sit, I think the problem is straightforward. Mama *needs* to be needed and that's why she focuses so much of her time and energy on the boys and on Alexandros. Maybe if she had an interest or something..." She trailed off lamely then because that was as far as she had gotten with her theory.

"You think perhaps she should take up golf?"

Annie swatted at her. "You know what I mean."

"I do and you are right but it is, how you would say? Easier said than done."

Annie nodded and Kassia smiled at her.

"I do feel better, though, because you, my lovely friend, can always make me smile."

Annie felt pleased and sad at the same time because she knew she hadn't really helped at all.

"Now you have lifted my bad mood. Tell me again what you did to our friend the bottom pincher."

Annie formed pincers with her thumb and forefinger. "I pinched his bottom when he got up to leave the dining room. Really hard." She grinned evilly. "He yelped and jumped in the air, which made his wife turn round to see what all the fuss was about. But of course he couldn't say anything, so he pretended he had banged his toe on the table leg. Ha! Served him right. He scuttled off with his tail between his legs, or cheeks clenched, or however you want to word it!"

Kassia roared with laughter. "I can't believe you did that!"

"Carl taught me not to let anyone intimidate me and that the best way to deal with a bully is to play them at their own game."

"A wise man, that Carl."

"Indeed and thanks to Carl, yours, mine, and every other bottom old Silver Top has ever pinched thanks him for his advice. I have a feeling he will be keeping his hands to himself from now on."

The sun dipped a little lower. "You had better get back to the house and get yourself ready for your next shift."

Annie hesitated, not ready to leave her friend when she knew she was down despite her feigned joviality, but Kassia gave her a gentle shove. "Go! I told you I am being silly. I will enjoy the sunset and head back with the boys shortly."

With a glance at her watch, she saw that Kassia was right. She did need to get going if she was going to have a shower and get back to Georgios' in time for her evening shift.

SHE SPIED SPIROS MAKING his way towards where she had just come from as she headed up the front path of Eleni's. Annie waved out but he didn't see her. She hoped that some time alone with Kas and their boys might give them the chance to talk things through properly.

Ten minutes later, she was freshly showered and felt much revived as she slipped into jeans and a white T-shirt. It was an outfit that Koula had assured her would be perfectly fine for that evening's shift when she had inquired earlier in the day. She found Mama in the kitchen, busy as usual as she stirred something divine-smelling in the pot on the stove. To her surprise, Alexandros sat at the table with the chopping board, a knife in hand as he sliced his way through a colander of tomatoes. *Well, wonders would never cease.* She looked at him preparing the salad with approval. The thought that he really was a handsome man crossed her mind, not for the first time, and she forced her attentions back to Mama. She didn't want him to catch her gawping and so she filled the older woman in on her new job and told her regretfully, as she inhaled the herbed aroma from the pot, that she would not be in for dinner.

Mama paused in her stirring, her expression suddenly wistful. "I know this Georgios. He was friends with my Abram but I have not seen him for a long time. Life, it gets so busy, you know?" She shrugged heavily. "I was very sad to hear of his Althea's passing. I should have gone to see him but it had been so many years since I had seen them both and I was on my own here with a full house..." She shrugged again and shook her head sadly. "Pah! These are excuses... I should have gone. But then the time, it passes, and the distance, it becomes too great, I think. But you tell him tonight, Annie, that his old friend Anya Bikakis sends her sympatheia for his loss. Tell him I am sorry I have not been to see him and that it has been too long."

It was strange, Annie thought, to think of Mama being known as anything other than, well, Mama. It was rather sad, too, that Georgios and Mama had once been friends and yet despite their businesses being less than a half hour's walk apart, they hadn't seen each other in years. She had heard it said that it was hard to be a widow because the friends you had shared as a couple tended to drift away. Perhaps that was what had happened to Mama after Abram passed away.

"Spiros and Kassia have been to his taverna and they told me they had a very nice meal. You have done well finding yourself work there, Annie. I think Georgios will love you as we love our girl with the hair made of fire." She reached over and stroked Annie's hair affectionately, her currant eyes full of warmth. Annie basked in that warmth for a moment. She had done well getting herself a job. It meant she could relax where her dwindling savings were concerned. She gave herself a mental pat on the back as Adonis brushed past her legs and mewled to be picked up. She scooped him up and cuddled him to her.

"You see, even the cat, he loves you," Mama laughed.

Annie grinned and gave Adonis a kiss before she popped him back down on the ground to go on his merry way.

"But what will you eat if you don't have dinner with us? Will Georgios feed you? You will be busy, no?"

"I don't know, Mama, but I'll be fine." It wouldn't do her any harm to skip a meal, Annie thought, not with all the wonderful dinners she'd been scoffing since she'd arrived at Eleni's. It was thanks to Mama she'd had a battle with the zipper of her jeans earlier.

Mama made a peculiar tsking sort of noise with her tongue on the roof of her mouth before she abandoned her spoon to the pot to break a hunk off the loaf of bread sitting under a tea towel on the bench. She dunked it in the pot and brought it up, covered in the thick fragrant thyme and lemon sauce that bubbled away inside it and handed it to Annie. "You are too skinny! Eat this, kopela mou; it will fill your tummy for a while and I will leave you a plate in the kitchen for you to heat up when you get home."

Annie didn't need to be asked twice. As she chomped into the bread, Alexandros watched her with amusement. She raised a hand to her chin self-consciously as she felt a trickle of sauce dribble down it.

"And what time will you finish?" Mama waggled the wooden spoon and sent drops of sauce flying. It was a gesture that warranted a prompt answer, so Annie replied despite her full mouth and tried to move the bread over to her cheeks.

"Um, around eleven, I think. Koula said things have usually wound down by then."

"Koula—she is Georgios' youngest daughter, yes?"

"Yes, she's lovely."

Mama raised an un-plucked eyebrow and glanced over at Alexandros. "She was always a sweet girl and very pretty—is she married yet?"

Alexandros rolled his eyes and Annie grinned. She could see where Mama was headed with this now. "Yes, she is. She has three children."

With a disappointed look, she returned the spoon to the pot and carried on stirring while Annie munched down the rest of her bread. "Alexandros will pick you up when you finish tonight."

Annie glanced over at Alexandros in alarm, to see that he hadn't paused in his chopping of tomatoes. "No, Mama, I am fine. It is not far to walk. I don't want to be any bother." She made to go before there was any further discussion but she should have known the older woman well enough by now to know that this wouldn't wash.

"Alexandrosaki, tell her."

"I'll pick you up. You heard Mama mou." He looked up and fixed her with those maple syrup coloured eyes of his, just as she walked into the door.

HER FACE HAD FLAMED all the way back to Georgios' taverna but she was greeted with such enthusiasm by both him and Koula that she quickly shelved the embarrassing incident. The taverna had a full house by the time nine o'clock rolled around and Annie had not stopped to gather her breath from the moment she had arrived. To her surprise, she was in her element and thoroughly enjoyed the banter with the guests, who were surprised to find a New Zealander so far from home.

By the time eleven o'clock rolled around, Georgios was ringing the till off for the night, pleased with the night's takings, and Koula was in the kitchen. She loaded the dishes into the dishwasher that had seemed to run all night long and billowed steam into the small kitchen each time it was opened and emptied. Annie had wiped the tables down.

She was tired but it was a good tired, she realised. She paused to thank the last of their diners as the merry group made their way out the door and into the inky, starlit night. She wondered briefly before she carried on with her task whether they headed home or off in search of somewhere to dance their dinner off. She put her hand in the pocket of the apron Georgios had given her to wear over the top of her clothes and felt that it was heavy with loose change. She reckoned she had probably earned a small fortune in tips tonight. Georgios slammed the till shut and came over to her with a wad of notes in his hand. "Your wages for the night." He smiled, his gold tooth glinting under the lights. "You did well. Thank you, Annie. Like I said, you are an angel sent to us."

She liked the way he accented the *e* at the end of her name just like Mama did and she couldn't help but grin at the thought of Attila hearing what he had just said to her. "I enjoyed myself, Georgios—it was fun." She *had* enjoyed herself; it was true. It had been so long since she'd gleaned pleasure out of working hard. It felt good, really good. Georgios' old eyes crinkled as he flashed her another gleaming grin. He had such kind eyes, Annie thought, kind but sad eyes. She remembered what Mama had asked her to tell him. "Anya Bikakis, who runs Eleni's guesthouse where I am staying, asked me to tell you that she was very sorry to hear of your wife's passing and that it has been too long."

Georgios's bushy grey eyebrows shot up. "Anya Bikakis—my dear friend Abram's wife! I haven't heard that name for a long time. Such a lovely woman. How is she?"

Annie filled him in on the fact that the guesthouse kept her very busy but that she had both her sons home with her now, along with Kassia and the children, so that helped. His expression grew pensive for a moment upon hearing that. He missed having all his children around him, she realised. She told him about her email friendship with Kassia and finished by telling him that was how she'd come to be in Crete.

Georgios' voice was judicious as he said, "The world, it is getting a smaller place, I think. Sometimes it is a very good thing and sometimes not." A scooter roared to a halt outside and he called out, "We are closed."

Alexandros appeared in the doorway, an impossibly handsome study of casualness in his jeans and black T-shirt. Annie watched as he ran his fingers through his hair before he strode forward with his hand outstretched to greet Georgios.

"I am Alexandros Bikakis."

Georgios clasped his hand with both of his and shook it before he pulled him into a bear hug. "I know you! You don't remember me, your uncle Georgios? I knew you when you were a little boy who came up to here." He released Alexandros and stepped back. "And now look at you—so tall and grown up—a man." His expression sobered. "The time, it passes too quickly. Ten years since my good friend Abram died and over a year since my beloved Althea passed away."

"My sympatheia for your loss," Alexandros said.

"Thank you, paidi mou." Georgios looked lost in his memories for a moment before he clapped his hands as though banishing the sadness. "Tell your mama that I said she is right; it has been too long and that I would like to invite the whole Bikakis family to my taverna. Koula!" He called his daughter.

"I will, thank you," Alexandros stood a little taller as a moment later Koula's head popped out through the beads to see what her father wanted. She looked like an exotic Cleopatra, Annie thought, amused by Alexandros's instinctive reaction to her.

"Come here, I want you to meet someone."

Koula looked bemused at the sight of the vaguely familiar, good-looking man who had appeared at such a late hour in the tavern. She put the dish cloth she held in her hand down by the till and wiped her hands on her apron. She strode over and Alexandros kissed her on both cheeks while her father explained their association to her.

"Ah, it is a small world, I think—our Annie staying with the Bikakis family. I can recall playing on the beach with you and your brother when we were children." Her smile was warm. "I agree with my pateras—your family must come and eat at our taverna soon. They are most welcome." She looked at Annie then with dancing, knowing eyes.

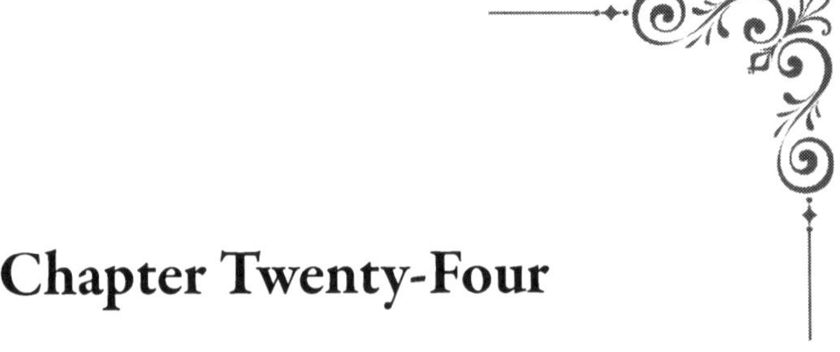

Chapter Twenty-Four

ANNIE HADN'T INTENDED to sleep with Alexandros. In fact, it had been the furthest thing from her mind as she kissed Georgios goodnight on his weathered, bristly cheek and tried to ignore Koula's all-knowing smile. No, as she'd swung a leg over the back of Alexandros's scooter, she was far more concerned with getting back to Eleni's in one piece; she'd borne witness to his reckless driving on more than one occasion. However, as he gunned the bike's engine and they took off down the darkened street at what felt like breakneck speed, something strange had happened. Instead of being frightened, she had been filled with such an intoxicating sense of freedom it had, quite literally, taken her breath away.

She squeezed her eyes shut against the wind and thought about how a few short months ago, she had been contemplating marriage and mortgages. Then, she had been so determined to squeeze herself into a wedding dress she could neither afford nor properly fit, and now here she was with the balmy Grecian night breeze whipping her hair back as she rode on the back of an insanely gorgeous Greek man's scooter. It was crazy! Her arms were wrapped tightly around Alexandros's middle, and she could feel the promise of what lay beneath his T-shirt rippling beneath her fingertips as they whizzed up the darkened road.

Annie felt alive—truly alive for the first time in—well, since she could remember. So many sorrows had been lifted from her shoulders in so many different ways since she had embarked on this journey. She walked a little lighter these days; sadly not literally, she thought, not with all the delicious food Mama kept plying her with.

So, when Alexandros turned his head slightly to yell over the noise of the engine, "Do you want to go home or do you want to look at the stars down by the beach for a while?" she knew with an absolute certainty that she did not want to go home. Not just yet. She had yelled back, "Let's go look at the stars." She would shortly be doing something a tad more strenuous than star gazing.

Alexandros had bumped off-road and braked to a stop under the arbour of a tall spruce tree and she'd let him lead her by the hand down the grassy embankment. They followed the scrubby path for a minute and as it came to an end, she heard the unmistakable sluicing of the sea directly below them. They were on some sort of cliff and he helped her to jump down on to a boulder a short distance below. It was pancake flat and still warm from the heat of the day despite the lateness of the hour. The spruce tree shielded it from the road. This was obviously a hidden spot Alexandros knew well, Annie thought as she took in the glittering invitation in his eyes as he asked her whether she wanted to swim.

"But it's dark." She'd stated the obvious and nearly added *and I don't have a swim-suit* but stopped herself just in time as she was mesmerised by the outline of his chest as he whipped his shirt off over his head and unbuckled his jeans.

Oh what the hell. She took her own T-shirt off and unclipped her bra before she pulled her jeans down, taking her knickers with them, and kicked them all to one side. *When in Rome...* Only she wasn't in Rome; she was in Greece but by the time this thought had registered she already held Alexandros's hand and was taking a leap of faith into the black night.

They surfaced from the cold waters below, laughing.

"It is good, yes?" Alexandros laughed, his teeth gleaming white against the tan of his skin.

"Yes!" Annie squealed. She splashed him with water before she swam a short distance away. He disappeared under the water and she bobbed about in the dark nervously. Her legs treaded water as she waited for him to surface nearby. Suddenly, she felt hands wrap around her ankles and before she had a chance to scream, she was pulled under. He let her go and she re-surfaced, ready for revenge, but he was already swimming away back to the rock shelf. She swam over and made to splash him again but he grabbed her arm and pulled him to her. His hands ran down the goosy flesh of the tops of her arms and caused a bolt of something she hadn't felt in a long time to ricochet through her. She'd thought that he would kiss her then—she wanted him to kiss her—but instead he asked her if she was cold.

"N-n-no," she replied through chattering teeth, unwilling to spoil the moment.

"Come." Alexandros heaved himself out of the water and found a foothold from which to hang onto the cliffside. He'd helped her up beside him before he led the way expertly upwards from jutting rock to jutting rock until they clambered back onto the ledge from which they'd jumped. As she stepped onto the ledge, Annie shook the droplets of water from her hair. If anybody had ever told her that one day she would partake in a spot of naked night-time rock climbing, she would have told them they were crazy.

Crazy times called for crazy antics, she thought, surprised at how uninhibited she felt as she stood there illuminated, milky white, with her arms wrapped round herself in an effort to keep warm. Alexandros busied himself making a bed out of their jumble of clothes. He sat down and pulled her down beside him. She wondered briefly whether he had come here with his buxom blonde friend Sharon but to her surprise she didn't really care whether he had or he hadn't because this was her moment and she was utterly lost in it. As he inclined his head to kiss her, she had let herself cast off the last of her cares just like the clothes she had discarded so casually a short while before.

Alexandros fumbled as he tried to locate the condom in his jeans pocket. He obviously never left home without one, Annie had thought, amused, as he expertly slid it on. That had been her last coherent thought as he had moved on top of her and entered her. He had launched into a fast and furious rhythm before he moved it down a notch to become tender and sweet despite the hardness of the rock on which they lay. His knees must be made of stern stuff, she'd mused, because she didn't think their makeshift bed would do much to protect them. The stars had twinkled down voyeuristically the whole time their naked bodies were entwined, occupied with the frantic business of love-making. It was a business that had been going on under those same stars since the beginning of time, Annie thought randomly, just before she climaxed. She held onto Alexandros's shoulders as tightly as she could, tipped over into that glorious abyss and took him with her.

He was a skilled lover, she thought as he collapsed on top of her panting a few moments later, but then she'd known he would be. She was under no illusions that he could probably pen the Greek version of the Karma Sutra but it didn't matter. For her, this had been closure, as much as she hated the expression. She had just officially closed the door and put the latch on her relationship with Tony forever. There would be no going back from here and that was the way it should be, Annie decided as she looked up at that carpet of stars while Alexandros's heavy breathing tickled her neck.

He'd rolled off her then and propped himself up on one elbow so he could look down at her face. He traced a finger down her nose and trailed it off the tip. She could make out the intensity of those aquiline features as he moved his hand over to stroke her sopping hair back from her face. "Annie." He crooned in that melodic voice of his, "You are wonderful, so wonderful but you must understand that I cannot give you my heart because it is not mine to give." His eyes had bored earnestly into hers and despite her best efforts not to, she burst out laughing. Alexandros's hand paused mid-stroke. "Why do you laugh at me when I am being serious? What is so funny?"

"Oh, Alexandros, how many times have you given that little speech." Annie tried to straighten her features but her mouth kept twitching of its own accord.

"I have never—"

Annie cut off his protestations by putting her fingers to his mouth. "Shush, listen to me. I don't want a relationship with you, Alexandros. I wanted to have sex with you, yes. But I don't want a relationship, so you can spare me the *you are wonderful but* speech."

Alexandros was perturbed. "Why do you not want a relationship with me? The sex, it was good, yes?"

"Yes, it was great! Tonight has been the stuff of dreams but oh, how can I explain it?" Annie looked up at that twinkling sky and thought for a moment about what she was going to say. "I think that tonight was part of me needing to cast off my past. Do you understand?"

He nodded and sent a sprinkle of water down on her.

"I needed to say goodbye to my relationship with Tony..."

"Tony? Who is this Tony?" Alexandros glanced about nervously, as though he expected a jealous boyfriend to thunder down the path towards them.

"Don't worry." Annie laughed at his concerned expression; he'd probably had to deal with more than one irate boyfriend in the past. "Tony is my ex-boyfriend and you can relax, he isn't going to track you down. We broke up before I left New Zealand but I feel as though I have finally put that relationship to bed." She realised how that sounded and giggled again as Alexandros raised an eyebrow at her choice of words.

"What I mean is—oh, I'm not making a very good job of this." She didn't want to say *I needed to get that first bonk with someone new out of the way in order to feel truly single.* So instead, she finished by saying, "It felt right what we just did but I don't want anything more from you. That's what it comes down to really."

"Ah, now I see. It is you who has used me." He feigned indignation and put his hand on his heart. "You have used my body and now I am wounded."

Annie stroked the contours of his chest while a smile played at the corner of her mouth. "I'm sorry, Alexandros, but I am sure you will find a way to forgive me."

He grinned hungrily and rolled on top of her once more. As he lowered his mouth onto hers, he murmured, "Well, maybe I will let you use me just one more time then."

THEY HAD GOTTEN DRESSED into their damp clothes and Annie tried not to think how uncomfortable her jeans felt as they squelched their way back up the path to the scooter. "What do you think you will do, Alexandros?" He peered at her curiously in the darkness.

"What do you mean?"

"I'm curious as to where you are headed because I can't see you staying at Eleni's forever." She shrugged. "You seem like a caged lion when you are there, as though you are pacing about, looking for a way out." She was thinking how eloquently she had worded that when it was his turn to laugh at her. "You women—you always, how you say? Analyse everything with your flowery words. It is the difference between us, I think—like that book, what was it called?"

"*Men are from Mars, Women Are from Venus.*"

"Yes, you are all from another planet."

Thinking back onto some of her one-sided conversations with Tony over the years, Annie knew he was right. Men were easy to read most of the time: if they said they were tired, there was no hidden meaning lurking behind their yawn, like *I don't find you attractive anymore*. They were as they had stated: tired. Poor Tony, she thought as she remembered her propensity to overanalyse everything. He had accused her of this once when he had made a passing comment that she could do with some new jeans. This he had dared utter because of the worn patch in the knee of her favourite jeans but what she had chosen to hear was *your bum's too big for them; you need new ones.* Needless to say, much to Tony's bewilderment, she had flown into a fit and accused him of saying she was fat and acted as though she were mortally wounded in her determination to overdramatise the situation. Now, with the wisdom of hindsight and a vast distance between them, she could see his being a man of few words had been a continual source of frustration to her, just as her need for more from him than he was capable of giving must have been to him. How exhausting he must have found her at times, she thought as she filed her decision not to repeat the same mistakes in the future away and Alexandros wheeled the bike back up to the road. "I'm right though, aren't I? You're not planning on sticking around."

"I was trying to tell you earlier about my plans."

Annie frowned. *How had she missed that?*

"When I told you that my heart is not mine to give."

Oh yes. She snorted and Alexandros muttered, "I still do not see what you find so funny about this."

"I'm sorry. It's just, well, who is using the flowery language now?"

"Do you want me to tell you or not?" She could see the twinkle in his eyes as they glinted in the darkness.

"Tell me. I promise, no more laughing."

"There's a woman. I met her when I was in Brazil. She is an English lady who moved to Rio with her husband. He is a big businessman." Alexandros shrugged. "He is always busy and never has time for her. She is lonely in a strange city, yes?"

"Yes." Annie gave the required response, knowing exactly how this story was going to play out.

"And so when I meet her on the famous beach..."

"Ipanema?"

"Yes. She is like the song—you know?"

"The Girl from Ipanema."

"Yes, except maybe she is not like in the song so young."

Annie bit her lip, determined to keep her promise not to laugh.

"But still, one thing, it leads to another because she is not happy and I know how to make her happy." He gave a few thrusts of his hips and Annie felt a bubbling rise up in her throat which she swallowed furiously because Alexandros was serious.

"So we have a thing for a while and it is good but you know she is married and then one day she tells me she must try one last time to make it work with her husband. I am sad but I respect her decision and so I decide the time has come for me to go home and help my mama. She is telling me all the time, 'Alexandrosaki, come home.'" His high-pitched dramatic pleading was such a good imitation of his mama's voice that Annie couldn't help but laugh this time and he grinned ruefully across at her. "This is what she is like—you have seen her for yourself—and she is getting older, you know, so I feel guilty sometimes that I am not here. There is no longer a woman to keep me in Brazil, so I do what she wants and I come home."

Annie wondered if he meant 'keep' literally as it dawned on her that he had come home under duress from his mama and not just to freeload as Kassia assumed.

"I love my family and my home but I don't want to be here. I am in the way. Spiros, Kassia, and the boys—they are making their life here but it is not for me. There is not room for me too."

"Oh, Alexandros, that's not true!" Even as she said it, she realised he was right. He was a lot more insightful than Kas gave him credit for, Annie realised, and he was in the tricky position of wanting to keep his ageing mother happy but at the same time wanting to live his own life.

"It is fine, Annie. Don't look so sad. I can visit and that is the way it should be."

"So what will you do?"

"I will be the selfish son they expect me to be and I will leave. Mama, she will be fine with Spiros, Kassia, and her grandsons. I know this now so I can leave without a heavy heart. My friend, she has written to tell me it has not worked with her husband and the marriage, it is over. She has asked me to come back to Rio to be with her, so at the end of the month I will go to her."

Kassia had read her brother-in-law well, in so much as this was exactly what she predicted he would do. On the other hand, part of the reason he was going was to make an easier life for her and her family. It was something she needed to know.

"Have you mentioned your plans to Mama?"

"Mama mou, no. I know I will make her sad." His sigh came from deep down and Annie knew it was genuine. "I will tell her soon when I feel the time is right."

Annie wondered fleetingly whether his feelings for this woman went deeper than that of just a free ride. She suspected not and that the only woman he really loved was his mama. Yes, she thought, he would move on from his woman in Brazil when another offer came along but she harboured no bad wishes towards him. Alexandros was who he was, and at least he didn't pretend to be something he wasn't. Sure, he wrapped his words in pretty packaging but if you could see past the wrapping, he didn't lie or make false promises, so good luck to him. She spontaneously kissed him on the cheek. He had revealed a hidden depth beneath the shallow surface tonight and she had a newfound respect for him.

It was a very different journey back to Eleni's from the exhilarating ride of earlier. Alexandros drove more sedately as befitted his spent mood and as they neared home, he slowed and came to a stop a few hundred metres away from the guesthouse, which was shrouded in darkness. The sea was a flat black blanket on their right and in the not so far distance, Annie could hear somebody murdering a Spice Girls song. Figures bobbed about in the brightly lit bar up the road where the karaoke was in full swing and she watched with amusement as a couple staggered out of the bar and onto the street, illuminated by a street light. They'd both be under the weather in the morning, she thought with a stirring of sympathy. She'd been there, done that. As for Mrs *Stop Right There, Thank You Very Much,* she deserved all she got after she'd inflicted that earache on people.

"I will wheel the bike from here so we don't wake anyone," Alexandros said as she got off and walked on the pavement alongside him.

"Good idea, although how anyone can sleep through that ruckus I don't know." She, however, did not want to be responsible for alerting any of the guests or members of the Bikakis family as to her and Alexandros's nocturnal shenanigans.

As he pushed the bike up the driveway, a sensor light came on and Annie waited conspicuously under it by the front door while Alexandros stowed the bike around the side of the house. He came back round the corner and fished in his pocket for the key, unlocked the door, and held a finger to his lips to signal she needed to be quiet as he crept inside. With a nod that the coast was clear, he shut the door behind her before he turned to whisper, "Goodnight, Annie." His breath tickled her ear and then he kissed her goodnight. They both knew it would be the last kiss they would ever share.

"Goodnight, Alexandros." She held her hand to his cheek for a moment and smiled at him fondly before she watched him tiptoe down the hallway with a marked effort not to stand on any squeaky boards and give the game away.

Annie ducked round the corner to her little room under the stairs but paused with her hand on the doorknob for a moment. She wasn't tired; if anything, she was wired from the night's events so perhaps she should go and make a warm milk. It might help her to wind down. She decided that was a better option than gazing at the ceiling for the next few hours, so Annie crept down to the kitchen. She pushed open the kitchen door, patted the wall to feel for the light switch and flicked it on. As the room was flooded with light, it took all her strength not to scream because sitting at the table with her head in her hands was Kassia.

Chapter Twenty-Five

"MY GOD, KAS, YOU NEARLY gave me a heart attack! What were you doing sitting here in the dark like that?" Annie's hand flew to her chest as she steadied her breathing.

"I couldn't sleep like you, although I think maybe for very different reasons, yes?" Kassia looked her friend up and down. Her demeanour was that of someone who had been disappointed. She was in her nightdress, Annie noticed, a chaste white cotton number, as she skulked over to the table like a scarlet woman to sit down opposite her friend. She had obviously heard her and Alexandros come in. "I, uh..."

Kas waved her hand. "It's none of my business but I don't want you to be hurt, Annie. I am just surprised that you too have succumbed to Alexandros's charms when you know what he is like. You have seen it for yourself. What about his friend, the big boobie one with the blonde hair?" Kassia cupped her hands a fair way out from her own ample breasts to demonstrate the scale of what she was talking about and Annie had to smile.

"Her name was Sharon, and I still can't get over the fact her breasts were actually real. They defied gravity." Annie shook her head. "As for what happened between Alexandros and I tonight being none of your business, Kas, well, as my friend *it is* your business. I haven't succumbed to his charms either. Well, not exactly."

Kassia tucked her hair behind her ears and Annie noticed her eyes were puffy and red. Surely she wasn't *that* upset by what had happened between her and Alexandros. They were both consenting adults, after all.

"It's just that I don't want you to leave because of him. He will leave, anyway—I know this—but you, if you feel you have made a mistake or..." She sniffed and wiped her nose with the back of her hand. "Maybe you will want more than a man like him will give you and then you decide to go home. I don't want you to go. I need you here." She looked very young sitting there in her nightdress with her trembling bottom lip. Annie reached across the table and rested her hand on top of her friend's.

"I'm not going anywhere, Kas, not for a good while yet. I love it here, I love you and Spiros and the boys and Mama and..." She didn't think adding Alexandros to her list would go down well. "Well, you get the idea and just so you know, I have no plans of heading off anywhere, at least not until you all get really sick of me and then maybe I will think about packing my bags."

Kas raised a weak smile and Annie decided she needed to clarify what had happened between her and Alexandros before she got to the bottom of what had upset her so much that she was sitting up at this late hour crying.

"You know, Alexandros and I, we pretty much used each other tonight, which was fine by me because I needed to move on from Tony. As for him, well, he just wanted to throw a leg over. It was nice, too—better than nice actually..." A dreamy look came over her and Kassia pulled a face.

"Don't worry—it didn't mean anything and it won't happen again. There won't be any weird atmosphere tomorrow, either. I promise you, we are both cool about it." Now was not the time to confirm that Kas was right, Alexandros would soon be leaving. Besides, that was his news to tell, not hers. She did want Kas to know that he wasn't quite the man she had painted him to be, though. "There's more to him than you think, though, you know."

Kas raised a dark sceptical eyebrow. "So you *have* fallen for his charms then."

"No—well, not like that. What I mean is that if you scratch a little deeper and get past all that smooth Romeo stuff, there is actually quite a nice man lurking there. A man, who despite his shortcomings, really loves his family. He's only here because of Mama pleading with him to come home. Did you know that?"

"Pah, this is what he has told you so he can, as you say, throw the leg over. I know there was a woman involved in his decision to come back here, though—there always is. As for Mama, I do not want to talk about her." Her face closed.

Annie could see this was a discussion she was not going to get very far with and she had just been given her first clue as to why Kas was upset. "Okay, so forget Alexandros for a moment and tell me what has had you so upset tonight?"

Her expression crumpled and she ducked her head so her dark hair tumbled over her face. Annie stared at her friend in alarm. This was not the strong, feisty Kas she knew. She walked around the table to put a comforting arm around her and gave her shoulder a firm squeeze. "Come on, tell me—what is it? What's wrong?"

Kas didn't answer at first but sniffed loudly before she straightened herself and swiped angrily at her nose once again.

"Hang on a sec. I'll get you a tissue." Annie released her grip and headed over to grab the box that sat on top of the fridge. She pulled a handful of tissues out and thrust them at her. "Here, you give your nose a good old blow." The words echoed her own mother's cure for tears.

Kassia noisily did as she was told and then crumpled the sodden wad into a ball. "I'm sorry, Annie. All I have done since you have been here is moan to you that I am unhappy. It is not what you came here for, I know that."

"It's not moaning, it's expressing your feelings." Annie's reply caused Kassia's mouth to twitch. "Anyway, friends listen." She angled her chair so that she could see her friend's face from beneath all that dark hair. "That's what friends do. How many times over the years have I poured mine out to you? Now it is my turn to listen."

"That is different because I think you had every right to, how you are saying—pour your feelings out. Losing Roz, your sister, that was big and I never did anything—not really, except keep in touch."

"Exactly. You kept in touch; you never drifted away once I found you. You were there, never judging, and knowing you were only ever an email away meant so much. I could tell you anything. You were like my own online counsellor because you always listened and never once told me to pull my socks up and get on with things. You and Carl were the only people I could be entirely honest with. I don't know how I would have made it through without you both."

"So tell me now, do you think you have made it through?"

"I think that for the first time since Roz died, I feel at peace with what happened. The anger I held on to for all those years has finally gone. You know, for so long I wondered what I could have done to make things turn out differently. Sometimes I'd play these dumb mind games where I'd tell myself that maybe if I hadn't pinched her make-up or tried on her clothes when she was out, if I hadn't been so annoying, then maybe she would still be here—no, Kas, sit down. I'm okay because I finally get it. She made her own choices and I have to be strong enough to make mine. I think she brought me to Greece for that reason. To prove to me that I could take a different path than the one I was on, like she should have done."

"You have found your Yanni, yes?"

Annie smiled. "Well said."

"I, too, would not mind finding Yanni. I like it when he wears those white trousers of his."

"Ugh, Kas!"

"Sorry, but I was always with Roz on that one."

Annie shook the spectre of the musician's white pants away. "That's enough about me and Yanni. If you are upset like this, then whatever the problem is, it can't be trivial. I shared with you, now it's your turn to spill."

"Ah, but you see that is the problem, Annie—it is trivial. It is all of these trivial little things that have got bigger and bigger and then tonight KABOOM! Spiros and I had a fight."

At last they had gotten to the crux of what had her in a state. "What about?"

"It was stupid."

"Well, talking about it might help and then I can tell you just how stupid the fight was and that all couples do it from time to time in order to make up because we all know that's the fun part." She smiled encouragingly at her friend, who graced her with a watery one in return.

"See, I told you I need you. You always make me smile and not just because you have a big red rash all over your chin."

Annie's hand flew up to her chin; it felt tender. Oh dear, the dreaded pash-rash. That would be a tricky one to explain away tomorrow.

Kassia's smile was more defined this time. "Don't worry, we will say you were doing the waxing and then you have an allergic reaction."

"No! I am not having everyone thinking I have a beard."

Kassia began to giggle. "Redbeard."

"It was Bluebeard, actually, and that was a horrible story. He murdered all his wives." She fished around for a suitable cover story but nothing sprang to mind.

"Alright then, we will say you have had an allergic reaction to your sun cream—yes?"

"Excellent—an allergy! That's a good one, thanks, Kas. Now, are you going to tell me about your fight or would you like me to make us a hot drink before we head off to bed?"

"Both please."

"Okay, you talk and I'll heat some milk."

Annie set about pouring milk into a pan to warm while Kassia talked. "Spiros came down to the beach after you left."

"Yes, I saw him." Annie decided to add a sprinkle of cinnamon from the little packet she had just spied on the shelf to her sweetened brew.

"Well, I told him that I feel I cannot be my own woman here. I told him that it is not working."

Annie turned away from the stove to look at her friend, startled. She could well imagine how that had gone.

"He told me this problem with his family, it is mine and that I have to stop blaming him for us being here. He blames himself enough for both of us. He said I need to learn to compromise with Mama, and I said in other words he wasn't man enough to tell his mama to leave us to raise the boys our way." At Annie's expression, she added, "The words, they came out of my mouth before I could stop them. Spiros, he said I was a selfish woman who didn't know how lucky she was to have gotten the second chance we have had here at Eleni's with his mama when there are families that are really struggling in Athens." Her voice trailed off and she chewed her thumbnail in agitation before she pulled what was left of the ragged nail off. "I know this and I hate that we had no choice. It was taken away from us when he lost his job. I have been so angry at him but at the same time I know this is wrong because it wasn't his fault."

Annie poured the milk into two mugs. "I can understand you feeling like that, powerless, but I don't think it is Spiros you are angry with. I think it is just the situation you found yourselves in."

"I know you are right. It is a frightening thing to have your life as you know it taken away from you, and Spiros, he did not cope well at the time. That was horrible for me because he has always been my, my..." She looked frustrated.

"Rock."

"My rock, yes, and then one day," she clicked her fingers, "just like that, it all changes."

"It must have been so hard for him to come home and tell you he had lost his job." Annie recalled the email she'd had from Kas telling her what had happened. She'd thought at the time that it must have been tough, what with her at home with a young child and a baby on the way. How unfair the situation they'd found themselves in, along with thousands of others judging by what the news reports at home had stated. She hadn't thought about the emotional impact that she could see etched clearly on Kas's face now, though, not once.

"I'm sorry I wasn't there for you more. I just didn't understand."

"It is not your fault, Annie. It is our life here in Greece at the moment. It is the times we live in and we were luckier than most—Spiros, the boys, and I—to have Eleni's to come to. I just have to find a way to make it work."

"You need to tell Spiros you love him."

"I know. I wanted to earlier but he walked off. He did not want to hear it."

Annie sat down and pushed Kassia's drink across the table to her. "And you haven't talked since?"

"No but we are being polite to each other, you know?"

Annie did know—that horrible, stiff politeness that meant neither of you was going to back down and that words had been said that couldn't be retracted without the distance of a night's sleep.

She took a sip of her warm, sweet drink. "It will be different in the morning after a good night's sleep, you'll see."

Kassia frowned into her drink. "That's another thing. I won't sleep. I never do when things aren't right between us but he will be snoring like a, a..."

"Log," Annie supplied just as she had for Mama. It felt like a lifetime ago now when she had asked her how she had slept that first morning she had been put to work helping with the guests' breakfasts.

"Yes, like a log."

"Typical man." Annie recalled the very same situation with Tony. It had always irked her how he could shelve the fight, put it aside until the morning, while she would brood on it all night long And play out imaginary comebacks in her head over and over so that she'd wake tired and frazzled. She sipped on her drink and closed her eyes for a moment.

"You are tired."

"A little." Annie opened her eyes.

"It is all that sex."

"You are probably right." Annie smiled over the rim of her mug. "And you look worn–out, Kas."

"It is not from all the sex I am having. I have not been sleeping well lately. Perhaps this will help." She lifted her own mug to her lips.

"You have so much on your mind, it is no wonder you are not sleeping. First thing tomorrow, I want you to make things up with Spiros, and you need to find a way to tell Mama that you have to be allowed to make your own mistakes with the boys because otherwise how will you know when you are getting it right?"

"You mean tell her that I feel I am being pushed aside where my own children are concerned. You can imagine how she would take that, can't you? There would be noisy crying and much wringing of the hands. She is good at the theatrics when it suits and Spiros would never forgive me for upsetting his mama so."

"Well, you could word it a bit more diplomatically than that," Annie chastised gently. "Her intentions are good. You know she loves the children and wants the best for them. She thinks she is helping you and has no idea how you feel. So unless you can find a way to tell her, things won't change."

Kassia stared into her mug as though the answer lay there. "You are right. I have to do something. I will talk to her tomorrow." She looked up, her brown eyes exhausted as she drained her milk. She wandered over to the worktop. "Come on, Annie. We will have to be up early for the breakfast in the morning. We should try to get some sleep."

Annie pushed her chair back and followed her over to the sink. The two women hugged tightly. "You are my sister. My Kiwi bird sister and I am so glad you are here with us," Kassia whispered.

"And you are mine and Roz's Greek sister. She would have loved you if she had gotten to meet you, just as much as I do," Annie whispered back. They released each other then, switched the kitchen light off and tiptoed off to their respective rooms. Both women tried not to think about the fact that they would be back in the kitchen in a few short hours' time.

Chapter Twenty-Six

ANNIE STUMBLED INTO the kitchen, bleary-eyed. She felt like her head had hardly touched the pillow and when she'd rubbed the steam from the bathroom mirror, she'd had been horrified at her resemblance to the Raggedy Anne doll she'd played with as a child.

Now, as she cut a zombie-like path towards the coffee pot, she caught sight of Alexandros's amused glance and her hand inadvertently flew up to her chin. She gave it a rub and hoped that the foundation she had smeared over it in an attempt to hide the rough patch of red skin beneath wasn't too much of an obvious cover-up job. She decided the best course to take until she was wide awake was to ignore him, so she filled her mug with the thick brew and turned her attention to Spiros instead. He was seated next to his brother and, in what had become a familiar sight in the mornings, tried to coax Nikolos into finishing the last few mouthfuls of his breakfast. His hooded brow as he waved the spoon in front of his son's firmly shut mouth gave nothing away. Feeling her gaze upon him, he glanced up and greeted her with a good morning and at the same time held out a restraining arm to prevent Mateo from carrying out his mission. At the sight of her freshly washed hair springing into curls, his eyes had lit up, the toast on his plate a distant memory.

"Good morning, Spiros." She managed to muster up a smile. "Who ever said men can't multitask?" Her comment went over the top of his head, as he was too intent on holding Mateo back and not sending the spoonful of yoghurt in his other hand flying across the kitchen. She watched in amusement as the little boy's plump fingers twitched in eagerness at the sight of her ringlets and she contemplated just letting him give her hair a few good tugs. It might get the urge out of his system once and for all. Then again, it might not and anyway, today was not the day. Her eyes were dry and scratchy, and she felt far too fragile from a lack of sleep for that sort of carry-on. Instead, she carried her coffee over to the table, placed it down well out of little hands' reach and held her hair back in a ponytail as she bent to kiss the tops of the boys' silky, dark heads and inhaled the lingering scent of baby shampoo.

Not bothering to pull out a chair, she stood by the table and sipped greedily at her drink. The familiar tingly sensation of the caffeine coursed its way through her veins. Mama pushed her way in through the dining room, having obviously finished setting the tables, and Annie felt a guilty jolt. That was her job. Still, she thought as she shot a dirty look over at Alexandros, who graced her with a knowing wink, there was no reason he couldn't have done it, just this once.

"Good morning, Annie." Mama, unbothered by her apprentice's tardiness, called cheerily and took up arms, or rather the whisk, at the bench. "I cook you some eggs, yes."

"I can do it, Mama." Annie moved to the stove and tried to take the whisk from her. It was like trying to snatch a bottle from a hungry baby as she attempted to wrest it from the older woman, who was having none of it. Flicking the whisk at her, she shooed Annie back to the table. "You go sit down. You do not look well this morning, paidi mou. Have you had a rough night?"

Alexandros snorted at his mama's unwittingly appropriate choice of words and she swung round to look at her last born. "Alexandrosaki mou, are you alright?"

"I am fine, Mama mou, don't worry. It is my coffee, that is all. It went down the wrong way."

He smirked knowingly as Annie shot him a look and Spiros's gaze flicked curiously between the two of them before he shook his head and pushed his chair back. He stood and hauled Nikolos up, who was intent now on licking his spoon and squealed ear-piercingly when his father took him out of his highchair. He swung him up onto his hip and beckoned to Mateo. "Come on, you are obviously not going to finish that so we might as well get you washed and dressed." His older son's piece of toast had now had all the Nutella licked from it and Mateo had managed to smear the chocolate spread all over his face in the process. He reminded her of a Dickensian chimney sweep boy as he hopped down from his chair, grateful for release, and cast one last lingering look at Annie's hair before he trailed after his father.

"Is Kassia still in bed, Spiros?" Annie called after him.

"Yes, she was tired so I decided not to wake her." His expression was as inscrutable as ever as he led the boys out of the kitchen.

"They have a fight, I think," Alexandros stated matter-of-factly as the door shut behind Mateo.

"If they did, it is none of your business, Alexandrosaki mou," Mama admonished with a wave of the wooden spoon. "It is between them, and they will sort it out."

Annie's gaze swung between the two of them. They were completely unaware that it was the pair of them who were behind the couple's fight in the first place, she realised. Mama was right, though; it was up to them to sort things out now. She had said her bit last night. Her toast popped, so she drained her cup and placed it on a plate before she poured herself another cup. She tried not to look horrified as a moment later Mama had whipped the plate away and with that heavy hand of hers, slathered the two slices in butter.

"Our guests, they are sleeping in today, I think." She scraped the mound of creamy eggs from the pan and onto the toast. "There was a karaoke party at Wendy's place." She tapped the side of her head. "They are probably all, how you say?"

"Worse for wear."

"Yes, worse for wear. Serves them right." Her face creased into a smile as she held the laden plate out to Annie. "You eat it all, Annie, kopela mou. You are too skinny." She gave her the once-over as she muttered again with a shake of her head, "Too skinny."

Annie took the plate and thanked her. It would be a waste of her time to add that unless Mama stopped loading up her plate this way, she would soon be saying *too fat, Annie, my girl, too fat*. As it was, she was going to have to buy herself some new jeans if she didn't want to keep feeling like an overstuffed tube of cannelloni each time she squeezed herself into them. Mama thrust the pan in the sink and rolled her sleeves up; Annie felt a pang of sympathy for her bustling about, happy in her work. Little did she know that Alexandros was going to drop a bombshell on her in the next few days by announcing he was returning to Brazil. Not only that, her daughter-in-law planned to have a word in her ear too.

She sat back down and made light work of her breakfast as Alexandros winked at her and got to his feet. He carried his cup and plate over to the sink. "I have a few things to do in Elounda, Mama mou. Can you spare me this morning?"

Mama's eyes glowed with warmth as they settled on her youngest son. "Of course, agoraki mou—you go. We will manage, no problem."

Annie scooped the last of her eggs on to the remaining triangle of toast and stuffed it in her mouth. She marvelled once more at his ability to wrap Mama around his little finger, just as Kassia pushed the door open. She looked as dishevelled as Annie felt and as she spied Alexandros taking his leave, she scowled before she called out, "Hey, where are you going? It's your turn to clear up this morning!" It fell on deaf ears as he shut the door behind him. Annie lined her knife and fork up on the plate and told her friend to sit down. "I'll make you a coffee." Kassia sat down gratefully and Annie carried her dirty dishes over to the sink. Alexandros hadn't even bothered to load his in the dishwasher, she noticed, as she fixed her friend a strong brew.

Annie placed it in front of her. She heard the bell as the first guests pushed the dining room door open. They were up and about, and ready to start their day. It was time hers started properly, too, she thought and ordered Kassia, who had pushed her chair back at the sound, to stay put, just as Mama had done her. "I can manage. You sit and have your breakfast." Then, pen and notepad in hand, she pushed the door to the dining room open with her hip, in the manner she had become so well-practised at.

ANNIE WAS FEELING DECIDEDLY washed-out by the time the breakfast service was over and as she loaded the last cup and saucer into the dishwasher, she mentally cursed Alexandros. She frowned. Knowing him, he probably had nothing to do in Elounda other than lie on the beach and watch the world go by. Actually, lying on the beach sounded like a wonderful idea, she thought as she sprinkled in the powder and set the machine to run. She could do with grabbing half an hour or so of shut-eye if she were going to make it through tonight's shift at Georgios' with her happy face firmly in place.

With that thought in mind, she headed to her room and fished her bikini out of her drawers. She wriggled into her bikini bottoms before she hooked their matching top at the back with a disparaging glance down at her burgeoning middle. Thank goodness for sarongs, she thought as she flapped hers open and wrapped it around her waist before she unhooked her tote bag from the back of the door. Her gaze rested on the cover of the book from the bedside table for a moment. One of the guests had left it behind and so far it was a good read. She stuffed it, along with her sunblock and a towel, into the bag. She'd fill up her water bottle on the way out. First things first, though, she thought as she slid her feet into her jandals and swung the bag over her shoulder. She'd pop her head in to say cheerio to Kas.

She tapped on the door to the office and waited a moment before she stuck her head round it. Kassia's dark head was bent over a stack of accounts she had announced she had to see to once the breakfast rush was over. "Hey, how are you feeling today? Did you manage to get some sleep?" She still looked pale.

Kassia looked over the top of her glasses at her and smiled. "Sort of."

"Will you talk to Mama today?" Annie perched on the edge of the desk.

"Yes." She took her glasses off and rubbed her eyes. "I have thought about what I want to say, and I think I can tell her things have to change without upsetting her."

"Good. And what about Spiros—have you cleared the air with him?"

"Not yet." She reached over and patted Annie's arm. "Go enjoy the sunshine. It will all be fine. I promise."

Annie smiled back at her. Yes, it would be fine, she thought as she hopped off the desk. With a final wave, she wandered through to the kitchen to fill up her bottle. As she walked across the expanse of grass down to the pavement a moment later, she glanced over to where Mama sat at the picnic table. Nikolos dandled on her knee and chewed furiously on a toy. His tooth still wasn't through then, she mused and watched for a moment as Mama cheered Mateo. He kicked a soccer ball to his father. She waved over and called out that she was going to the beach for a while. They waved back and she set off again with a spring in her step. It was going to be a good day because as her mother used to say, "She could feel it in her water."

ANNIE'S EYES FLEW OPEN and she blinked against the sun's mid-afternoon glare as she tried to remember where she was. Her book lay open on her chest. She must have dozed off. Something about lying around in the sun knocked her out cold every time. She remembered how she had put the book down and closed her eyes; she'd told herself she'd just rest them for half an hour. Now, as she reached over and rummaged in her bag, she produced her phone and saw that two whole hours had slipped by. Carl had texted her, too. As she scrolled through the typically long-winded message, she had to smile. Carl and David had flown up to Auckland last weekend to see Bruno Mars play. Now that gay marriage was legal in New Zealand, David had decided that should they eventually tie the knot, he wanted Bruno's song *Just the Way You Are* played at their wedding. Carl had pushed for John Legend's *All of Me* and apparently they weren't talking at the moment, both in stand-off mode, although they had both agreed on the fact that she should be their best woman. She could just picture Carl, hand on hip, telling David that his choice was the number one wedding song of 2013 as she pondered what she as a best woman would wear to their hypothetical wedding. She tapped out a quick reply and sent it then she sat up to have a swig on her water bottle. She was really dry, which meant she had probably been doing her usual mouth-wide-open dribbling routine. She glanced round, pleased to see there was nobody nearby.

Her mind flicked back to the adventures of the night before and she felt a warm glow. That was all, though, she realised. It was true what she had told Kassia. Her and Alexandros had both in their own ways used each other, and she wished him well. He was one of life's characters that you couldn't help but be fond of—unless he was your brother-in-law. Her feelings for him went no further than that, though, she thought as she turned her attention to the sea.

It was like glass today and there were only a handful of bathers in the water. She'd have a quick dip to cool off and wake herself up properly before she headed back to Eleni's for a nice strong cup of coffee and a bite of something to eat. By then, it would be time to get herself ready for her evening shift at Georgios'. "Sounds like a plan, Annie," she said aloud. She stood up and stretched before she padded over the pebbles. Enjoying the feel of the cool water as it covered her ankles, she stood for a moment at the point where the pebbles dipped and gave way to waist deep water before she plunged in. Swimming a few strokes, she flipped over onto her back and gazed up at the cloudless sky. Life was glorious, she thought, feeling as if she really didn't have a care in the world.

ANNIE WRAPPED HERSELF in her towel and packed up her bag. With her feet in her jandals, she ambled back up the path to the road in order to walk the short distance back to Eleni's. A handful of tourists meandered ahead of her at a pace set by the afternoon heat. It was funny how she no longer classed herself as a tourist, she mused. She saw a figure dawdle along in the distance. It looked like Alexandros and, with her hand up to shade her eyes, she squinted in his direction. The man had paused to speak to a group of girls heading out of one of the serviced apartments. Definitely Alexandros then, she thought and veered off the pavement and onto the slope of the front garden. It was then that she spied Mama and Kassia among the olive trees. She could tell by their rigid stances that neither woman was happy. Mama, as predicted, wrung her hands and Kassia, her own hands palms up towards her, looked to be pleading. Mateo ran past them, too caught up in his game to be aware of anything being wrong. He played with a homemade kite, a plastic bag tied with a string that caught the wind that in the last few days had begun to blow up at the same time each afternoon. Nikolos was in the baby swing under the tree and kicked his chubby little legs but didn't really go anywhere.

Annie hesitated for a moment, unsure what she should do. Their argument wasn't to do with her but it was obvious that Kassia had not managed to convey her feelings in a diplomatic way. She would hate for things to be said between these two women, about whom she cared so much, that couldn't be taken back. Her mouth set in a line of resolve. She owed it to them both to try to smooth things over.

It all happened very quickly after that because as Annie marched over, clear in her role of peacemaker, Mateo shot past her, racing after his kite. His legs pumped as he ran down the grass verge that disappeared through the gap between the parked row of hire cars. "Mateo! Stop!" Annie screamed. Mama and Kassia's eyes swung towards the road just as a woman's scream mingled with a screech of brakes. It was followed by a dull thwack.

Chapter Twenty-Seven

ANNIE WAS THE FIRST to reach the road. A cold fog descended as she ran on automatic pilot and pushed past the woman who stood by the kerb, frozen in shock, murmuring, "We were talking and then the little boy—he just ran out."

As she crouched down next to the body splayed in the middle of the road, she dimly registered a car door slamming behind her. "Alexandros, can you hear me?" She leaned over him and sent up a silent prayer that he was still with them. Her eyes locked on his and pleaded with him to be okay but his stare was flat and uncomprehending. "Please, God." This time she begged out loud, "Alexandros, come on, talk to me!" As the light drifted back into his irises, she took hold of his hand with both of hers. "Oh thank you, thank you, God."

He licked his lips and rasped, "Mateo? Is Mateo alright?" Annie hadn't realised she held her breath until that moment and as she exhaled, she glanced up and saw that Kassia had scooped her oldest son up into her arms. She held him to her so tightly that he squirmed, not comprehending what had just happened and how close he had come to breaking his mama's heart. "It's okay. He's fine—Kas's got him," she soothed as he groaned.

"My arm, it hurts."

"Stop moving. You need to lie still until we can get you some help." She cast her eyes around, frantic for a phone.

"He came out of nowhere. My God. I braked but there was nothing I could do. I am so sorry, so sorry." A man's quavering Germanic accent sounded behind her but Annie ignored him and yelled for someone to ring an ambulance.

"I'll do it." The woman Annie had pushed past swung into action. "What's the number?"

Kassia held her hand out for the phone, still holding tightly onto Mateo with her other arm. "Let me do it. I'll be quicker."

"I'll go and fetch the doctor." Annie recognised the voice as belonging to Wendy, the English woman who managed the apartments up the road. She watched as she took off up the road and willed her to run her fastest.

"My arm, it hurts." Alexandros groaned again just as his mama joined the little huddle. At the sight of her youngest son lying crumpled on the road, she set up a keening that would have put the worshippers gathered at Jerusalem's Wailing Wall to shame. She only stopped when, despite Annie and Kassia's protestations that he should stay where he was, he sat up, clutched his bad arm with his good and assured her he would be okay. Annie remembered the car's driver and turned to give him a reassuring smile. The relief was etched into his ruddy features.

Spiros appeared at the edge of the fray with Nikolos, whose cries at having been abandoned in the swing had alerted him to something not being right. He saw his brother and pushed through the little crowd that had begun to gather, and kneeled down beside him. Annie watched the panic, plastered all over his normally unreadable features, clear as he established that apart from his arm, Alexandros appeared to be fine.

"Has anyone called for an ambulance?" His head swivelled round the throng.

Annie crouched down beside him and rested her hand on his shoulder. "It's on its way. Wendy from Sunrise Apartments has gone to get the doctor." She filled him in on how Alexandros had pushed Mateo out of the way of the car. "He's a bit of a hero, your brother."

Alexandros waved the comment away with his good arm, and winced as he did so.

"Don't move." Spiros reiterated Annie's earlier sentiments before he kissed his brother on the top of his head. He then turned his attention to his sobbing mama. "Calm down, Mama mou. Alexandros will be okay." He carried on in Greek, his words settling her.

"It's the shock that has upset her so much," Annie said to no one in particular. "We saw Mateo run out and we thought, well, we thought..." Her voice trailed off. It didn't bear thinking about. She glanced over at Mateo, who was still trying to disentangle himself from his mama's arms, too young to understand her need to hold him close.

The woman Alexandros had stopped to chat up just as his nephew ran past him had gathered herself and leaned over him. A pretty brunette, who was oblivious to the magical healing power the eyeful of cleavage stuffed inside her blue tank top, had on him.

"I will be alright, I think." His voice dripped with brave stoicism as he added that she could come by and visit him at Eleni's tomorrow if she liked.

Annie rolled her eyes. *Only he could think about that kind of bedside care in his current condition.* Still, it was a good sign. She felt a stab of pity for his lady friend in Brazil. She would have her work cut out for her trying to keep him on the straight and narrow, especially with all those young Rio de Janeiro sun worshippers strutting their stuff up and down the beach.

Spiros, who had his arm around his mama's rounded shoulders, had handed Nikolos to her as a distraction. He held his free arm out to Kassia and Mateo. She walked towards him and rested her head on his shoulder as he pulled them in close.

The sun sat low in the sky and she shivered. Wanting to be useful, Annie decided Alexandros could probably do with a blanket wrapped around him and that a cup of hot sugary tea for them all would go down well. She headed up to the house and fetched a blanket from the hallway cupboard before she made the one-size-fits-all mugs of tea and placed them on a tray. With the blanket draped over her shoulder, she carried the tray carefully back down to the road.

The local doctor had arrived in her absence and was busy examining Alexandros when she passed the steaming brews round. She had made a cup for the car's driver too because it was obvious the poor man was in a state as he stood to one side of the huddle around Alexandros. The doctor brushed the dust from his pants before he pronounced that Alexandros's arm was almost certainly broken in two places but an X-ray would be needed to confirm this. Apart from that and a badly bruised ankle, he would live. The crowd, satisfied that there was no more drama to be wrung out of the accident scene, dispersed, and his brunette friend crouched down and kissed him on his cheek. "You're so brave." She promised to pop by the following day to check on his progress. The familiar twinkle sparked in Alexandros's eyes as he watched her sashay away, her tight shorts a welcome distraction from the throbbing of his arm.

Annie turned her attention to the German driver, whose face beneath his mahogany tan was white. The accident had been unavoidable and could have been so much worse but despite this, he still looked as though he had been given a death-row reprieve as he drained his tea and handed it back to her with a grateful nod. He went back to his car but returned a few moments later with a piece of paper, upon which he had scribbled his details, and handed it to Spiros. He took it and gave the man a reassuring pat on his shoulder. "He is going to be okay. This was not your fault."

They then heard the unmistakable wail of a siren. Annie expected to see an ambulance careen round the bend at the end of the street; instead, the flashing blue light that appeared came from a motorbike.

Spiros, sounding not unlike his brother, groaned. "It would have to be Dimitris." They all held their hands over their ears as he roared up alongside them, only then turning his siren off. As he got off his bike and put the stand on, Annie couldn't help but think all that noise had been overkill. Then, as she watched him take his helmet off and saw that he left his dark aviator glasses on, she'd have taken money on his being a fan of American cop shows—if it had been appropriate. Helmet in hand, Dimitris raked his fingers through his hair before he swaggered over to the scene with notebook in hand and pen at the ready. He fired off a sentence in Greek to Spiros and his reply was equally rapid-fire. There was much hand gesticulating and glances over at the poor German, who looked like he would rather be anywhere but standing where he was at that precise moment in time.

The officer took off his glasses and fixed him with an eagle's stare before he told him in stilted English that he would need to follow him down to the station once the ambulance had arrived and the road was clear.

Annie overheard Spiros tell the poor man, who now looked as though he thought he was going to be starring in the next episode of *Banged Up Abroad*, that it was just a formality for insurance purposes and that once he had filled out the necessary forms, he would be free to go on his way.

A moment later, they heard another siren and this time it was the ambulance that hurtled down the hill with its siren blazing. The Greeks were nothing if not dramatic, Annie thought as it screeched to a halt and two paramedics leaped out and charged over. The doctor spoke to one of them as the other crouched down next to Alexandros and checked him over. Satisfied it wasn't life and death, he stood back up for a bit of a confab with his fellow medics. The little group watched as the taller of the two medics opened the back of the ambulance and pushed a stretcher out to his partner, who grabbed the end and lowered it to the ground. Alexandros refused to be rolled onto it, so he did a bit of a shuffle and then lying down, was lifted into the back of the ambulance.

"I will go with my Alexandrosaki mou, my agoraki mou." Mama hitched her skirts up in anticipation of climbing into the back of the ambulance. At the sight of her dimpled knees, Mateo laughed and pointed.

Obviously not traumatised then, Annie thought with a smile.

"No, Mama. I will go with my brother." Spiros's tone brooked no argument. Mama opened her mouth to argue but then, at her son's expression, decided not to.

"We can follow behind in the car." Kassia turned to Annie. "Do you think—"

Annie cut her off. "You don't have to ask. You two go—the boys will be fine with me." Kassia flashed her a grateful look as Annie held her arms out for Nikolos, and swung him round onto her hip. Then, with Mateo firmly in hand, she shooed the two women up to the house. She stood with the boys and watched as one of the paramedics closed the back of the ambulance and headed round to the driver's side. Their departure was just as noisy as their arrival, and Annie whispered to Nikolas that they probably wanted to get his uncle dropped off at hospital quick smart so they'd be home in time for their dinner. Dimitris also opted for siren on, although this time he set a slightly more sedate pace in order to let his German prisoner follow.

With the street now empty, Annie saw that the sun was getting ready to set. She had better phone Georgios and tell him she wouldn't be in to work. "Come on, boys. Let's go and see what we can find for your dinner, shall we?" Nikolos wrapped his pudgy little hand around one of her curls and pulled with a gleeful giggle as Annie yelped and tried to disentangle his fingers to no avail. Mateo looked on enviously and then with the homemade kite that had caused all the bother in the first place, he ran up the path.

Mama and Kassia were just coming out as they reached the front door. Kassia had changed from her shorts into jeans and a light sweater and Mama was swaddled inside a cardigan.

"Are you sure you will be alright here on your own? I can take the boys with me." Kassia unlocked the van doors.

"Don't be silly. You don't want to cart them all the way to Heraklion. Besides, you could be hours. You don't know how long it will take them to see to Alexandros. I am perfectly capable of giving them dinner, and getting them sorted for bed. Please don't worry."

Kassia gave her a wan smile. "Thank you." She went to the passenger side, helped Mama up into her seat, and pulled the seatbelt out for her. "I'll phone you from the hospital when I have an idea as to how long we will be." She gave Mateo a quick hug and a kiss before she stroked Nikolos's soft cheek and gave him a kiss.

"Drive carefully, Kas."

"I will." She climbed into her seat and backed slowly down the driveway to the road and then with a toot they were gone. The journey to the hospital would be a chance for the two women to sort their differences out, Annie hoped, because surely the events of the afternoon would have put things into perspective for them and shown them what really mattered. Annie reached down and ruffled Mateo's hair before she gave him a gentle push in the door. She'd ring Georgios and then see what she could sort out for their dinner. But first things first, she thought with a frown at Nikolos's fist—she would find a way to release his stranglehold.

Chapter Twenty-Eight

"AND THE TRAIN WENT choo-choo-choo." Annie waved the spoon in mid-air as she waited for Nikolos to oblige and open his mouth so she could complete her rhyme. He didn't. Instead, he continued to stare at her with his lips clamped shut tighter than a clam's shell. She rubbed at the sore spot on her head with her other hand and winced. Still, at least it wasn't a bald spot. It could have been if she hadn't come up with the magpie technique to divert him. A bright and shiny object in the form of her gold watch dangled in front of his nose had been the incentive needed for him to release his grip from her hair in the end.

With a sigh, she eyed the bowl of tomato pasta she'd hastily thrown together for the boys. So far she had only managed to get four spoonfuls into Nikolos and it was clear by the way Mateo swung a noodle back and forth that while he was having lots of fun, he wasn't actually eating. She didn't need to be Einstein to figure out that both boys preferred their yaya's cooking.

She put the spoon back in the bowl, deciding that desperate times called for desperate measures. Besides, there was nobody here at the moment other than the Austrian couple upstairs to witness her poor parenting skills. She opened the freezer door and pulled out the tub of Mama's homemade ice cream and filled two bowls. Then, feeling a stab of guilt at the quality of her nutritional choices, she grabbed a pear from the fruit dish and sliced it into quarters before she placed them in the ice cream. Mateo clapped excitedly at the unusually large dessert headed his way and Nikolos followed suit and giggled as she put his dish down on his highchair tray. The pears stood like sentry soldiers and he frowned, bottom lip pouting before he plucked them out of the frozen dessert and flung them onto the ground.

"Don't say I didn't try to give you your five plus serving of fruit and veg a day." Annie sat down again and watched as Mateo shovelled his down as if he hadn't seen food in months.

Oh yes, it was true, she thought as he looked up from his feeding frenzy to fix her with a smile of glazed delight; the way to a man's heart really was through his stomach.

An impatient grunting sound came from the highchair and Nikolos banged his hands down on his tray to get her attention. As she scooped up a spoonful of ice cream for him, he lunged for it but she held it out of reach. "No way. I don't think so, buddy." This time she'd get to say her piece. She started her choo-choo-chooing all over again and steered the spoon in the direction of his open mouth. "Down the little red lane," she finished with satisfaction.

The boys played under the table while she cleared the dishes away. Mateo pushed a toy car around and Nikolos watched him with a pillow behind his back as he stuffed his plastic keyring set in his mouth. Annie kept a watchful eye on her phone as she scraped the remnants of the barely touched pasta into the bin. There was no word from Kas yet but then, doing a quick mental calculation, she figured they'd probably only just arrived at the hospital.

She stacked the dishes into the dishwasher and set it to run. Annie smiled to herself as she thought back on how sweet Georgios had been when she'd rung him to tell him what had happened. He had told her that the family must come first and that she wasn't to come in to work tomorrow either if they needed her. She'd assured him that she was certain they would manage just fine without her and that there would more than likely be a queue outside the guesthouse in the morning of shapely volunteer nursemaids. She picked up the cloth to wipe the worktop down and recalled his concern for the shock Mama had suffered. It had been touching. The cloth hovered mid-wipe as an idea began to take shape but it wasn't given the chance to form because a war cry went up from under the table. At a quick glance, it appeared Nikolos had tried to do a snatch and grab of Mateo's car, for which he had received a thump. Oh dear, she thought. She dropped the sponge and got down on her hands and knees to crawl under the table before Mateo could go round two.

BY SEVEN FORTY-FIVE that evening, Annie had tucked Mateo into bed after a fifteen-minute search for the elusive teddy that he had informed her he could not sleep without. She had found Teddy tucked down the side of his bed and with a sense of victory, placed him in the little boy's arms before she planted a kiss on his forehead. Nikolos lay on his back in his cot and gurgled at the mobile above his bed, sporadically reaching up to pat at it. Butter wouldn't melt, she thought as she kissed her fingers and touched them to his satiny cheek. Seeing them both lying in their beds, sweet smelling and rosy cheeked, was like receiving an award for a job well done. She turned the light out and told them to sleep tight, tacking on another of her remembered childhood adages, "And don't let the bedbugs bite," before she tiptoed out of the room. She left their door slightly ajar and wandered back to the kitchen. Deciding she could do with a drink now that she was off duty, she headed for the fridge. Spotting a half empty bottle of wine next to the milk, she helped herself to a glass.

She savoured her first sip and enjoyed the tingling on her tongue for a moment. It had been a busy evening and Annie was relieved she'd gotten through it. In the last few hours, she had been a cook, a cleaner, a UN peacekeeper, a hostage negotiator, a nurse (after an unfortunate incident involving Nikolos and Adonis's tail), and a caregiver. She had been on a search-and-rescue mission for Teddy and she had, upon removing Nikolos's nappy before she popped him in the bath, been piddled on. Yes, indeed, there was a first time for everything and all this in the space of three hours! Annie let out a long, slow exhalation. She took her hat off to Kas being a mum on a daily basis—she really did—and quite honestly, an extra set of hands could only be a good thing. Surely she and Mama could find a way to work together without stepping on each other's toes? She racked her brains for the saying that tickled its periphery. *It takes a village to raise a child* sprang to mind and she thought how true it was. "Hats off to all you single mothers." She raised her glass to the empty kitchen.

Kas had telephoned her half an hour ago and Annie had held her wet T-shirt away from her chest as she kept one eye on Nikolos happily splashing in the bath with his brother as she listened. They would be on their way home from hospital shortly with Alexandros. He'd had a cast put on and his ankle strapped as well, having been thoroughly checked over and given the all-clear to go home. It was good news. He really was going to be okay. She rang off after she'd assured Kas that the boys were fine. "They've been fed." She added that after their bath, they'd be off to bed. She decided not to mention that there was an ominous brown pebble currently floating past Mateo, merely saying that she'd better go because it was time for them to get out before the water got too cold.

ANNIE WAS TIPPLING on her second glass of wine by the time she heard the van pull up the drive. Between sips, she had whipped up a plate of cold meat sandwiches and filled the kettle in anticipation of them all having had no dinner. As a succession of slamming doors followed, she got up and moved down the hallway to hold the front door open for them. Spiros glanced in her direction briefly to greet her but quickly returned his attention to helping Alexandros, who managed to toss her his customary cheeky grin as he brushed past. He was still awfully pale, though, she noticed. With his good arm draped round his brother's shoulder, he hobbled down the hallway to the kitchen. Mama waddled after them and paused to pat Annie's cheek and tell her she was a good girl before she followed her sons.

Kassia locked the van and, as she stepped into the light, Annie saw how washed-out she looked. "You okay?"

"Yes, I am now." Her smile was reassuring but Annie wasn't fooled, taking in her over-bright eyes that said otherwise. She hugged her friend and they clung to each other for a moment. All the unspoken sentiments of what could have happened—of what might have been if Alexandros hadn't happened to be standing on the sidewalk at that particular moment in time—passed between them until, with a final squeeze, Kassia released her. "Thank you for watching Mateo and Nikolos."

"I loved it and they're both sound asleep now," Annie said proudly. She'd spare her friends the finer details of her evening. "Come on, let's get you inside. I made some sandwiches if you're hungry."

"Actually, I'm starving." Kassia sounded surprised as she locked the door behind her. "I will just check on the boys and then I will come through. You go ahead." She gave Annie a gentle push in the direction of the kitchen.

Annie found Mama seated next to Alexandros waving a sandwich under his nose, not unlike she had done a few short hours ago with the spoon under Nikolos's nose.

"You need food if you want your body to heal, Alexandrosaki mou," she bossed. Now that she was over her fright, she was back to being the Mama they all knew and loved. Annie sat down opposite her with a fond smile.

He would not get any peace from her until he did as he was told, so Alexandros frowned and took a small bite of the sandwich. As he chewed mutinously, Annie caught a flash of what he would have looked like as a small boy. She could see Mateo in him and she wondered whether he would take after his uncle in personality as he grew, too.

"The same goes for you, Mama mou." Spiros passed the plate over to his mama as Kassia joined them at the table.

"Mateo is snoring again and Nikolos has his thumb in his mouth, sound asleep." She smiled and sat down, pushing her hair away from her face as she did so.

"Kas, do you want a glass?' Annie lifted her wine glass. "Anybody else?"

Spiros nodded before frowning at his brother. "No, Alexandros. The doctor said alcohol doesn't mix with the pain medication he has given you. A water will have to do."

"Mama?"

"Tea, Annie, please." The old woman leaned over to stroke her son's cheek. "You must listen to what the doctor has told you, Alexandrosaki mou, and be a good boy, yes?"

Annie smiled as she heard him answer, "Yes, Mama."

It didn't matter how old you got; your parents were always your parents, she thought as she flicked the switch to re-boil the kettle. She let Mama's tea steep as she fetched Alexandros a glass of water and opened another bottle of wine. "Mama, Georgios sends his best wishes. He wants us all to come to lunch once Alexandros is up to it."

Annie didn't miss the sudden spark of interest in Mama's eyes as she nodded and told her to tell him that the Bikakis family would love to come to his taverna for lunch. She remembered the idea that had begun to germinate earlier. Once things had settled down, it could be time for a spot of matchmaking—oh yes, Georgios could be just the distraction Mama needed.

As she poured the wine, she listened to Kassia as she spoke to Alexandros.

"Thank you for what you did today—from the bottom of my heart, thank you."

Annie watched him wave his good hand dismissively.

"I didn't do anything that anybody else wouldn't have done."

"Yes, you did. You saved our son's life, and Spiros and I will never forget that." Her voice thickened. "I know we haven't always got on well and that at times I have not been kind. I am truly sorry for that but today has shown me how fragile life is and how easy it is to forget that. I have spent too much time worrying over things that don't matter so long as we all have each other." Her gaze met Mama's across the table and the older woman smiled at her encouragingly as she reached across the table and patted her hand. Kassia blinked rapidly, determined to finish. "I want us to start fresh, Alexandros. A new beginning—do you think we can?" She looked at him hopefully. His cheeks had flushed, unaccustomed to such an outpouring from his acerbic sister-in-law.

Annie felt her own throat tighten as she waited for Alexandros to take the olive branch that was held out, pleased to see that Mama and Kassia had obviously mended their own bridges too. Spiros concentrated on the salt and pepper shakers in the middle of the table as though they were objects of intense fascination.

"Of course," Alexandros said. "But there is something I need to tell you all."

Chapter Twenty-Nine

ANNIE LAY ON HER BACK in bed with her eyes open, woozy from all the wine she had knocked back on an empty stomach. It wasn't often she forgot to eat but tonight with sorting the children, she'd foregone dinner herself and by the time the others came back, the wine was going down rather too well to contemplate a sandwich. Well, she was paying for it now. She concentrated on the stars she could see from her window that decorated the black velvet sky. She hadn't drawn the curtains; fully dressed and all set for sleep, she'd fallen into bed only to find that when she shut her eyes, the room spun. Wishing she could stop the merry-go-round and get off, she found herself turning the events of the evening over in her mind.

Instead of the expected histrionics from Mama at Alexandros's announcement, she had merely looked resigned. She'd listened stoically as he told them that as soon as his plaster cast was off and the doctor had told him he was good to go, he was heading back to Brazil. He would stay, he'd told them, with an, eh-hem, 'friend'. She'd shaken her head sadly as he finished. It was clear Mama was simply too exhausted from the emotions of the day to summon up her usual response to her youngest son's shenanigans.

"I am only a phone call away, Mama," Alexandros added, not liking her quiet response. He was equipped to deal with his crying, hand-wringing Mama. Not this calm version who suddenly looked shrunken and old as she announced she was tired and going to bed. They all watched in silence as she shuffled from the room.

"You could have waited. When are you going to grow up?" Kassia shot him a look, at which Alexandros scowled.

Annie watched Spiros roll his eyes. He loved his wife and he loved his brother—he really did—but sometimes he could bang their heads together. So much for their fresh start, she thought, reading his mind.

To head off the argument before it could start, Spiros got to his feet and told his brother he would see him to his bed. He kissed Kassia on the top of her head before he helped Alexandros to his feet and told her he would turn in too. "It's been a long day. Goodnight, Annie. Thank you for looking after the children."

She waved his thanks away before she got up too. "You don't need to thank me, Spiros, you know that." She held the door open for them once more. As Alexandros limped past, leaning heavily on his brother, she added, "I hope you both sleep well." She doubted Alexandros would. He wouldn't be very comfortable with that arm of his but then perhaps everything that had happened combined with the pain relief the doctor had given him would knock him out.

"What a day." Kassia sighed wearily when the two men had gone and Annie had sat back down. She topped up their glasses.

"I'll say." Annie smiled her thanks before she took a sip. She looked over at her friend, who leaned back in her chair with her eyes shut. "You patched things up with Mama then?"

Kassia opened her eyes and rubbed at them, leaving red marks underneath them. "You saw our fight?"

"Yes. I was coming back from the beach and I saw the two of you having an argument and that's when Mateo ran past after his kite."

Kassia shook her head. "It was my fault. If that car had hit him, I couldn't have lived with myself."

"No, it—"

"Yes, Annie. I should have been watching him. Instead, I was telling my mother-in-law that she needed to let me raise the boys my way."

Annie went round the table to comfort her and Kassia leaned her head onto her shoulder. Her weariness was palpable.

"We talked on the way to the hospital, Mama and I."

"I thought you might."

"I was honest with her, like I should have been with myself. It was never her problem; it was mine."

"What do you mean?"

"I told you how I felt after Spiros lost his job. The choices other people take for granted as their right were gone and the life we had, it changed so fast. I was so angry and I directed some of that onto Mama. I tried to apologise for what I'd said to her this afternoon but she told me I was right and that Eleni's was our home now too. All she wants is for us to be happy here and not grateful. She said she would learn to stop interfering and let us find our own way."

"She said all that?"

"Yes, she is a very wise woman. I probably should listen to her more often." Kassia raised a weak smile as Annie sat back down. They'd drunk their wine in silence after that. Her friend needed the quiet to process the day.

Now, as she blinked in the darkness of her bedroom, her stomach rolled. *Uh-oh, she knew what was coming next.* Annie flung the covers back and charged for the bathroom. She made it just in time and with nothing left to heave, flushed the loo before she splashed cold water on her face. Good grief, she looked like a Chucky doll, she thought as she caught sight of herself. She wiped her mouth before she headed back to bed. Not surprisingly, she slept well.

THE NEXT MORNING, AN air of shell-shock still hung in the air and with the strong painkillers the doctor had prescribed beginning to wear off, Alexandros proved to be a crotchety patient. He only brightened when his brunette friend came calling, managing to don his brave face for the hour she stayed to fuss over him. Annie, too, felt a bit worse for wear but she'd gotten through the day and made it into Georgios'. To her relief, the taverna had been quiet and Georgios had sent her home early.

The following morning had dawned brighter. Annie woke clearheaded and ready for whatever the day may bring her way. What she hadn't expected it to bring was Georgios. He had appeared at the back door and clutched such a large bouquet of flowers she could barely make out who was behind the beautiful red blooms. Mama, who had been sitting with a cup of coffee having finished serving the breakfasts, had turned into a coy teenager at the sight of him. She leaped up from her seat with surprising sprightliness to take the bunch from him, before she exclaimed over their beauty and buried her nose in their soft petals to peer shyly up at him. Annie had to bite her lip at the way she fluttered her eyelashes and giggled. She'd made Georgios a drink and left them to talk at the kitchen table, desperate to find Kas to tell her what was going on in the kitchen. She had a sneaking suspicion that the distraction she had said Mama needed had just shown up at their back door without any prompting on her part.

Two Months Later

Annie had turned thirty-two today. Thirty-two! When did that happen! She shook her head and gazed out to the flat expanse of water. She sat at a table borrowed from Eleni's dining room and carried by Spiros and Alexandros down to the pebbly beach. A glass of bubbles rested on it. Those undulating arid hills turning golden in the early evening light and the intense aquamarine water were a panorama she had fallen head over heels in love with these last six months and this was her very own *Shirley Valentine* moment.

She'd told Kas that all she wanted for her birthday was to sit at a table by the sea on her own with a glass of champers as the sun began to set low in the Cretan sky. This was her version of her favourite scene in the movie, and although she'd felt a bit of a plonker sitting there alone at first, it had given her a chance to ponder everything that had happened over the last year. So what if it wasn't the Shirley Valentine beach on Mykonos and she hadn't left her husband—nor was she middle-aged, for that matter—but she'd still been on her own journey and what a journey it had been. She saw a young couple, arms linked, as they strolled the path that traced the shoreline. Annie raised her fluted glass to them. They smiled nervously down at her and walked just a little faster as she called out, "It's my birthday—cheers!"

She would meet the others for dinner at Georgios' later, once the sun had officially set. Her lovely extended Greek family. It was to be both a birthday dinner for her and a leaving dinner for Alexandros. Georgios and Mama's 'friendship' had definitely softened the blow he had delivered by announcing he was leaving, although Alexandros did seem a little bit put out that his mama was no longer devastated by his impending departure. He was a big baby, really. She knew he would enjoy being looked after by his English lady friend in Brazil.

Mama and Georgios' burgeoning romance was lovely to watch, they all agreed, and the thought of them made Annie smile as she took a sip of her drink. The bubbles tickled the tip of her nose. They had been so shy around each other at first but now that they had their families' approval, they were being so risqué as to actually hold hands in public. Proof that you were never too old for a new romance—there was hope for her yet!

She'd been right, too, in a romance being just the distraction Mama needed. She gave herself a mental pat on the back and let the soothing shush of the water swishing over the pebbles wash over her. It was the sound of profound peace, she decided, glad that Kas had found it so at last too.

The boys were still the apple of their yaya's eye, of course, but these days she was too busy with Georgios to be worrying about what they were eating and when they were sleeping. Mama had been true to her word and left her daughter-in-law to it in that department. So much so that Kas had confided the other day she sometimes wished Mama were around a bit more often because she was actually missing the extra help! Be careful what you wish for and all that. Her friend was happier in herself, though, enjoying her life here in Elounda at last, and felt settled—much to Spiros's relief.

The sun sank a little lower and shards of burnt umber shot across the darkening sky. Annie sighed contentedly. It was so beautiful, this pocket of paradise she had found. She took another contemplative sip of her drink. Carl had telephoned to wish her happy birthday that morning, full of the joys of his re-kindled romance with David. Although, he had gone on to inform her, they had agreed there was no rush to get to the altar. That meant she didn't have to worry about flying home for a big do in the near future; he'd quickly added, not that he didn't miss her. His big goss was that he'd bumped into Tony with his new girlfriend at the mall and it had been awkward. Annie had been unable to resist asking what she was like and Carl had told her with relish that she was a frowsy brunette whose fashion sense was stuck in the nineties. They were a good match, he'd sniped, and she'd laughed. "I do miss you, you know, Carl."

"I miss you, too, sweetheart," he'd told her before ringing off.

She had spoken to her parents that morning too. They were setting sail on their second cruise in a week's time, having thoroughly enjoyed their first taste of sailing the Seven Seas. Their jet setting was helping soften the blow of her being away and Annie was pleased at how happy and animated they'd sounded about their trip. It seemed her mother's diet was a distant memory these days now that she'd fallen in love with the cruise ship's daily buffet. "You want to see all the food, Annie," she'd gushed, making Annie smile. "Who knows..." she'd continued excitedly, "perhaps they'd cruise the Greek islands next."

"I hope you do, Mum," Annie had replied realising she meant it before she rang off.

Her glass was nearly empty, she realised. "Cheers, Roz." She raised it and drained what was left before she sat back in her chair, filled with wonder at how this time here had seen her move on with her life properly. No longer was there sadness lurking at the peripheral edges. The sun was seconds off dipping behind the hills and it was time she went. She glanced towards the road. A figure watched her from the path. She frowned. The dark outline of a man moved towards her and as he drew closer, Annie gasped. It was Kristofr, the man she had met at the Acropolis!

"Hello, Annie. I am on my holidays and so I have come to see if you have found your Yanni." He joined her at the table as the sun set.

The End

Also by Michelle Vernal

A standalone new novel featuring Annie, Kristofr and Carl ...

'A lovely read, it's like catching up with old friends.' Amazon Reviewer

Sweet Home Summer

SOMETIMES, HOME REALLY is where the heart is...

Leaving behind her hi-flying career in London, Isla Brookes has had enough. Burnt out and tired of an unfulfilling profession and lousy boyfriends, it's time for her to go home.

Arriving back in cosy Bibury to stay with her grandmother, Bridget, everything is charmingly familiar. Even her childhood sweetheart, Ben, is as handsome as she remembered...

And when she discovers a stack of long-forgotten Valentine's Day cards, Isla, with the help of Ben, begins to realise exactly what is most important in life.

Available to read on your favourite ebook platform or in paperback format.

https://books2read.com/u/meBvel

If you enjoyed Staying at Eleni's then taking the time to say so by leaving a review would be wonderful. A book review is the best present you can give an author. If you'd like to hear about Michelle's new releases, you can subscribe to her Newsletter here:

http://tiny.cc/0r27az

To say thank you, you'll receive an exclusive O'Mara women character profile!

https://www.michellevernalbooks.com/

https://www.facebook.com/michellevernalnovelist/

https://www.bookbub.com/authors/michelle-vernal

Come and Stay at O'Mara's

O'Mara's–The Guesthouse on the Green, Book 1

A jilted bride to be, a woman with a secret past and a pesky red fox...

Take a break you'll never forget at O'Mara's Manor House—the Georgian Guesthouse in the heart of Dublin's Fair City. Its cozy and elegant setting is where you'll fall in love with a cast of characters who'll stay with you long after you finish the book. Oh, and a full Irish breakfast is included.

If Aisling O'Mara hadn't winged her way home to the Emerald Isle to take over the running of the family guesthouse, she'd never have met Finn, and her heart wouldn't have been broken. She's been trying to put her life back together since he left, but now he's back and says he's sorry. Can she trust him again?

Una Brennan's booked into the guesthouse she used to walk past each morning when she was a girl full of hopes and dreams for her happy ever after. She left Dublin more than fifty years ago vowing she'd never set foot in the city again. Why did she leave and what's brought her back?

Meanwhile, the little red fox who raids the bins outside O'Mara's basement kitchen door at night would like to know why the woman in Room 1, cries herself to sleep each night.

Witty, sad, and insightful with a touch of romance. Come and stay at O'Mara's.

https://books2read.com/u/bwq7ny

Printed in Great Britain
by Amazon

59933933R00158